3 9048 09686873 6

APR 15

100 DAYS

100 DAYS

Mimsy Hale

interlude press

BOOK DESIGN by Lex Huffman
COVER DESIGN by Buckeyegrrl Designs
FRONT COVER CONCEPT by Abbi Lawson

PHOTO CREDITS:
The following photos were used under a Creative Commons Attribution 2.0 Generic License (CC by 2.0), and were accessed September 30, 2014.
Desert Road II by picturesofyou, http://bit.ly/1pJCcK5
Times Square Crossing by mssarakelly, http://bit.ly/1mWHcQH
Laser Hands In The Air by Gadgee Fadgee, http://bit.ly/1CHRbNL
Grand Canyon, South rim (Yaki point) by Deepti Hari, http://bit.ly/1xHNCao
Welcome to Fabulous Las Vegas by djfpaagman, http://bit.ly/1xHNW8Q
Welcome to Florida - The Sunshine State by Tournament Committee, http://bit.ly/1BCBNj8
Elvis Has Left the Building by Jamie/jbcurio, http://bit.ly/1E6pgJ5
Lantern Floating Festival 2013 by Kyle Nishioka/ madmarv00, http://bit.ly/1vBJXIE
Françoise et Richard à la plage by diogo86/ Yuri, http://bit.ly/1rBt8gZ

ADDITIONAL COVER PHOTO CREDITS: ©Depositphoto.com/ svyatoslavlipi/ Rangizzz/
CHAPTER HEADER PHOTO CREDIT: ©Depositphoto.com/ jentara

View full art listing at: https://drive.google.com/file/d/0B422KYO8oC15VUEwWmtLS2RFX28/view?usp=sharing

For Danielle.
You may be my best friend,
but you put up with way more than you
should.

"The road must eventually lead
to the whole world."

&❧ Jack Kerouac, *On the Road*

OPENING CREDITS

SATURDAY, SEPTEMBER 15, 2012

"Well, if I didn't know how much you hated Maine before..." Jake Valentine trails off and glances up at Aiden, who drinks deeply from a bottle of water and wipes his mouth with the back of his hand.

"I don't hate it," he says, setting the bottle down next to Jake's and leaning back against the table. The sticky, weathered wood is entirely characteristic of The Cannery, their local bar; everything in it is worn and in dire need of replacement. "I'm just done here."

"I know you are. It's time we both got out." Jake runs a hand through his mop of thick blond hair; the product is long gone in the mid-September humidity. "For good this time, not just for a year across the pond."

"I still wish you could have come with me," Aiden says, a wistful smile tugging at the corners of his mouth. He shakes his head and adds, "That's exactly why I'm happy we're doing this, though. But first, I have a gig to finish. Two more songs, I promise."

"Okay. But Aiden—"

Jake stops abruptly when Aiden places a finger across his lips and fights the childish impulse to stick out his tongue and lick.

"They're good ones, I swear," Aiden tells him with a wink that Jake would consider flirtatious had it come from anyone else. But this is Aiden, his best friend of sixteen years; and despite the crush on Aiden that Jake tends to harbor whenever he finds himself single, he would never think of acting on it. They have so much shared history and so many unspoken boundaries in place that help keep them exactly what they are to one another. It is nothing more than an occasional, harmless crush, perhaps even some bastardized version of hero worship. Jake never spends too long thinking about it.

He watches Aiden walk back to the stage under the low lights and takes in the sight of his broader shoulders, darker brown, taller hair and the new confidence in his walk and thinks, *He looks different.* Jake has lost count of how many times he has made this observation since Aiden's return from London.

Aiden takes his place amongst the other members of his old college band—The Spinning Cogs, reunited for one night only—and shoots Jake a grin. For the past hour or so, the band has been performing songs about getting out, taking off, breaking free. Some of them Jake remembers Aiden writing between classes and others he's never heard before, but either way the message is difficult to miss.

"You've got it bad."

Jake almost jumps out of his skin; his knuckles are white on the edge of the table and his breathing is ragged as he glares at the girl folding her willowy frame into a seat across the booth. April Matheson, Jake's other best friend, looks innocently from beneath thick, red sideswept bangs and smiles.

"April, I swear to god, if you keep on about that..."

"Aw, Jakey, come on," April cajoles, nudging his foot underneath the table. "You know they say you tell the truth when you're drunk."

"Okay, one: I wasn't drunk," Jake says, entirely sick of this conversation. It's been playing on a loop for the past three weeks. "Two: I was speaking *objectively*. Of course Aiden's hot, have you seen him? I mean, you'd have to be blind. But I don't think of him that way. It's *weird.*"

"Denial is not just a river in Egypt," April quips, giving him one of her patented mind-reader stares. His grip tightens on the edge of the table and he fights not to clench his teeth.

"And old clichés are not going to make me start spilling my guts to you about my feelings for Aiden," Jake retorts, appending, "or lack thereof."

They stare each other down for a long moment before finally cracking up and dissolving into a fit of laughter.

"I can't believe you're leaving *tomorrow*. You know I'll miss you, right?" April says, taking his hand across the table.

"Of course I do. But it's only three months," Jake reminds her. "And anyway, you'll be leaving soon, too. You're taking your own band on tour, remember? It's not like you'll be stuck in Brunswick with nothing to do. We'll see you in Michigan and Texas and Alaska, and then we'll all be back here after New Year's."

"You'd better be coming back. It's bad enough that you're skipping town on your birthday. And 'only three months?' You're my best friend, what's gonna become of me without you?" April asks, sighing dramatically with the back of her hand to her forehead. "I swear, the next time you see me I'll be sporting only the very best Happy-Mart couture."

"Ugh, please don't talk about Happy-Mart," Jake groans. "We'll be parking the RV at one too many for my liking. Can you catch bad taste through proximity?"

April snorts, and they lapse into a comfortable silence to enjoy the end of the band's set. It's the last song of the last performance that The Spinning Cogs will ever give, and Jake catches himself thinking, *It's almost comforting, the way one thing can end and something new immediately take its place.* It doesn't always happen—and sometimes when it does it is far from comforting—but even as Aiden belts the last note, he and Jake stand at the beginning of a road, about to embark upon a journey that will take them to every state in the country.

The band winds up the song with a huge crescendo that rings in Jake's ears, and as the bar erupts in applause and cheers he watches Aiden hug Jeff, Stuart and Phil in turn. Then they begin to pack up their things, and a sense of closure seems to settle upon their slumped shoulders.

Soon, Aiden bounces over to Jake and April with his guitar case in tow, still running on his performance high. He bends down, wraps an arm around April's shoulders and presses a lingering kiss to her cheek before straightening and turning to Jake.

"Ready to go?" he asks.

Jake nods, gestures to the guitar case and asks, "That's coming with us, right?"

Aiden glances down as if only just realizing what he's carrying. Brow furrowing over his chocolate brown eyes, he says, "I didn't think we'd have room."

"We'll make room," Jake tells him. The sunny smile that breaks over Aiden's face is worth sacrificing a little closet space. He turns to April, squeezes her hand and says, "Thank you so much for throwing us this party. I'll miss you too, you know."

"You'd better, or else what have you got to come back for?" she teases, but her hazel eyes swim. She purses her lips and then all but bursts out of her seat to pull both Jake and Aiden into a tight hug.

"You're always my favorite girl in all the world," Jake says, and squeezes her so tightly that even *he* is a little short of breath.

"Okay. Go, before I take you hostage," April says, stepping back and waving a hand between them. "Be careful, be safe, and look out for each other. Get back here in one piece."

"Promise," Aiden says, and gives her another brief hug. "Later, Flower."

They remain quiet on the short drive back to sleepy Merrymeeting Road. Aiden lets Jake out and parks his beloved green Honda in his mom's garage, where it will remain until they come back.

Jake takes his brief window of alone time inside the house to run his fingers over the corners of uneven walls and the wavering mantel over the open fireplace that he's always hated for all of its ugly imperfection; now he feels inexplicably fond of it. He wanders almost aimlessly through the living room, past his parents' empty chairs and the sagging couch and into the den.

"You're going to miss this place. Admit it, Valentine," Aiden says. When he turns around, Jake's breath catches for a tiny measure at the sight of him as he leans casually against the doorframe, dressed in a white T-shirt, tight, dark-wash jeans and a leather jacket. He has the looks to give any classic greaser a run for his money—he's only missing the 1950s' hairstyle, turned-up cuffs and a pair of combat boots. The spare key from beneath the mat catches the light as Aiden turns it between his fingers.

"Don't know what you're talking about," Jake replies, coming back to himself, and reminds him, "it's not like we haven't left home before."

"But we came home most weekends. It's different this time," Aiden says, pushing off the frame and placing the key on the mantel before settling onto the arm of the couch. He looks entirely at ease in his own skin, a quality that Jake has envied as long as he can remember. "What time's Charlie back?"

"Late, I think. She mentioned something about Martin taking her to a Hitchcock retrospective at the Frontier," Jake says offhandedly, beckoning for Aiden to follow him into the kitchen, where he starts pulling ingredients from the pantry and setting them down by the stove.

"She'd never sit through Hitchcock for someone she wasn't crazy about, would she?" Aiden asks carefully.

Jake exhales sharply and opens his mouth, but says nothing.

"Are you really going to leave without at least trying to make things right? She's your sister, Jake."

"She's dating a professor who made it his mission to make my last semester of college look like hell would be a vacation."

"She has self-worth issues," Aiden says, shrugging.

"You took *one* psych class. And anyway, why am *I* the one who has to make things right?"

"Because she's your *sister,* and she's all—"

"All I have left now that Mom and Dad are gone?" Jake interrupts, rounding on Aiden, who holds up his hands in surrender.

"Okay, sorry. I'm leaving it alone."

Jake sighs. "It's fine."

"So... it's our last night," Aiden says brightly, parting the tension like Moses facing down the Red Sea. Bumping their hips together, he sidles close, rests his head on Jake's shoulder with an adoring look and asks, "What's for dinner, honey?"

Jake elbows him away and conceals the grin he isn't yet ready to give in to. "*You* are making my favorite, because it's my birthday tomorrow and it'll be a consolation for whatever awful shirt you got me this year. And I'm making *your* favorite because you were great today and I was proud of you."

"Good," Aiden says, grabbing a mixing bowl from beneath the sink and setting to work on his famous Aztec couscous. They move around one another in the kitchen with a near-silent, practiced ease that comes from years of learning one another by heart.

When everything is ready, they take their bowls of couscous and the large pan of cornbread out to the backyard, set themselves up in the Adirondack chairs on the deck and count fireflies between bites.

Jake knows that neither of them has quite learned who he is, yet. They didn't find themselves amongst the term papers and library stacks, nor in the space between their dorm beds where they held hands every night for the first week of freshman year to anchor each other in a sea of homesickness. They are both—especially Aiden—chasing elusive threads of a life that seems to be hiding around every corner, ten steps ahead and always just vanishing out of sight.

"This is going to be awesome, right?" Aiden asks, setting his plate aside and wiping his mouth with a cloth napkin. Jake takes a sip of water and nods. "It's the start of something really, really great?"

"It's going to be incredible," Jake replies, putting his hand over Aiden's and curling his fingers into the space above Aiden's thumb.

DAY ZERO: MAINE

Aiden Calloway stands outside the RV, a black and gold 2008 Dynamax Grand Sport Ultra the size of a bus, swinging the keys back and forth in his right hand. The sky is turning from periwinkle to cobalt, and the stars haven't yet made their appearance; Aiden doubts that they'll be visible through the thin layer of cirrostratus that has contained the humidity since midmorning.

The entire summer has led to this point. All the hours logged on Google Maps and Wikipedia; all the grease lodged beneath his stubby fingernails as they fixed up the RV outside his cousin's auto shop. All of it done in the name of a bond that they can trace back sixteen years, to a day not dissimilar to this one.

Aiden's bright green bike draws level with the boy's blue one, and they ride to the end of the street with shy smiles before coming to a stop near the bright yellow fire hydrant.

"I'm Aiden," he says, stuttering and holding out his hand as he's seen the grown-ups do.

The boy looks down at his hand and back up, giggling. "Your name is 'Hey, Dan?'"

Aiden shakes his head and enunciates, "Ay-den. But I guess you can call me Dan if you want to."

"Cool! I'm Jake," the boy replies, and grabs Aiden's hand to shake it firmly. "Let's be friends! Race you to my house!"

Everything is mostly the same in Brunswick. A little rougher, a little faded and fuzzy around the edges, but the same. It's the reason Aiden has reached this itchy plateau of completion: He has done all he can here. He had hoped, in the cold hours of winter nights in London, that he would be able to stick it out upon his return, but even a week after getting back and spending every waking minute with Jake he knew that it wasn't enough. There are places he needs to be, though he's not sure where. All he knows for sure is that he needs to get the hell out of Maine.

"Yes, Charlotte, I'm sure we have everything!"

Aiden grins at the irritation in Jake's voice, and turns to see him walking out of his cozy little house, the house Aiden has always felt more at home in than his own. Jake's stride is still long and his shoulders are still square, but although Aiden has been back in Brunswick all summer, he still isn't quite used to seeing his best friend in person again. He always knew that Jake was tall, with sandy blond hair, fair skin and deep, expressive green eyes, but it never seemed to mean anything.

Jake's sister Charlie is right behind him, wearing her standard uniform: plain block color T-shirt and ripped jeans, long blonde hair tied up in a messy ponytail with strands escaping from beneath her Portland Sea Dogs cap. Her expression is pinched, and seeing her like this never fails to make Aiden feel sorry for her. She and Jake lost their mother, Daisy, only a few years after Aiden's family moved to Brunswick, so he doesn't remember much of that time. He does, however, remember Charlie—and Jake, for that matter—as so much happier before the freak storm that claimed the life of their fisherman father, William, seven years ago.

He remembers seeing the same expression the day that he and Jake left for Bowdoin. Her own college years had been cut short, leaving her to get a job at Living Ink, the local tattoo parlor. She's worked her way up since, becoming a partner in the business, but she always looks laden with what might have been.

Jake catches sight of Aiden and beckons him over, and Charlie offers him a thin smile.

"Watch out for each other, okay?" she says quietly, with a halfhearted punch to his shoulder. "I want you both home in one piece."

"Yes ma'am," Aiden replies.

"Kid, how many times? I'm twenty-nine, for fuck's sake."

"Old habits die hard," Aiden says, and the ease of the familiar words rolling from his tongue brings the point into startling focus: He's truly doing this. Getting out. And he's going to *miss* this woman, this house, this dysfunctional little family he's been an extended part of for so long.

"Okay," Charlie says, sharp inhale and all business. "Get lost."

Jake crooks his fingers and salutes as Aiden hasn't seen him do since the Unmentionable Flannel Phase, and Charlie lets out an uncharacteristic chuckle, stands on tiptoe and winds her arms around Jake's neck. Aiden can hear her whisper something to him but can't discern the words, and when Jake steps back, his face is noticeably flushed. Aiden has to bite the inside of his cheek to keep from smirking, and his thoughts meander back to a sixteen-year-old version of Jake practically battering down his front door, red-faced and clutching a book about the intricacies of gay sex that Charlie got for him.

"Let's go," Jake mutters and turns on his heel with an awkward wave.

"Will you be okay?" Aiden asks Charlie, squeezing her arm.

"Always am," she answers shortly, looking past Aiden. "Do you think *he'll* be okay?"

Aiden turns and watches Jake climb up into the passenger side of the RV and slump into his seat. "He's been different since I got back," he says, and shakes his head. "You think you know someone, right?"

"You'll figure it out," Charlie says, and gets up on tiptoe again to press a dry kiss to his cheek. "Just *see* him, okay?"

"What do you mean?" Aiden asks, but Charlie simply shakes her head and gives him a push in the direction of the RV.

"Time to go," she says gently, and Aiden takes a step back. One last look at Jake's house, one last nervous smile at Charlie, one last closing of the front gate behind him and his overwhelming excitement threatens to burst out of his skin. He pulls open the door to the cab of the RV, steps up and swings himself into the driver's seat. After taking a moment to run his hands over the textured leather steering wheel cover, he pulls the door shut with a satisfying thud and fastens his seat belt.

"Stoke the fires," Jake says wryly, rolling down his window and pulling out a brand new pack of American Spirits.

"Start the engines," Aiden finishes, and turns the key in the ignition. As he pulls away from the curb and starts toward the end of the street, he says, "She should really have a name."

"Let's not think about it too hard," Jake says, flicking his lighter and taking a long drag from his cigarette. He holds it for a few seconds and exhales around the words, "I'm sure something suitably fabulous will present itself."

"Hey, do you maybe want to stop by the cemetery?" Aiden asks quietly, the goodbyes ringing in his ears prompting him to wonder about two more. Jake shakes his head vehemently as Aiden pulls the RV into a wide U-turn at the corner, and as they pass the house again they both wave to Charlie where she still stands beneath the porch light, arms wrapped around her middle against the slight chill that hangs in the air. *Will she start turning the porch light off at night, now that Jake's gone?*

"Okay, last time. Clothes, shoes, toothbrush, hair products, skin stuff," Aiden lists, trying to shake off the lingering tension between them as he turns onto Minat Avenue.

"Check. Guitar, laptop, video camera, gas card and credit card even though I *still* don't agree with accepting your dad's guilt money. I mean, I still can't believe how much this trip is costing him."

"Check," Aiden replies, jaw clenching as he pushes all thoughts of his father far into the dusty, forgotten corners of his mind. He doesn't want his anger with his father to taint their first night on the road—Baltimore is going to be bad enough. "Halloween costumes."

Jake laughs as he picks up Aiden's phone and starts scrolling through his playlists. "Check and *check*," he says in a low voice. His tone makes Aiden swivel his eyes just in time to catch Jake's gaze raking over him, and he reaches over to bat at Jake's shoulder until they're both laughing.

"All right, Valentine. This is it. Last chance to turn back."

"Are you kidding me? Do you realize how long it took me to teach Charlie how to track the GPS on my phone?"

"Just checking."

When they merge onto I-205, joining the huge trucks that will take the catch of the day all over the country, Aiden resets the odometer and Jake, having waited until now in honor of their unspoken agreement, hits play.

"Yes!" Aiden exclaims as the scratchy guitar and pounding beat of U2's "Vertigo" fill the cab. "Yes. Perfect choice."

"I know," Jake replies, with no hint of self-satisfaction. He's just good with music. The fact that he never sings anymore, hasn't since his mom died—which is, occasionally, still a bone of contention between them—has refined his talent for listening, and he supplies Aiden with a new playlist every month or so. Indie, New Age, show tunes, Top 40... there is a seeming endlessness to Jake's hunger for music, and Aiden loves that about him. Aiden bounces in his seat, singing at the top of his voice, unable to keep a grin from lighting him up inside and out. *Is this what true freedom feels like? All asphalt, open sky and your favorite person by your side? Because,* he thinks, *it can't get better than this.*

When they are about twenty miles from the campground and exiting onto Route 1, Aiden takes one hand off the steering wheel and reaches under his seat. Jake watches him with curiosity, stubs out his third cigarette in the ashtray and appears torn between dismay and anticipation when Aiden hands him two brightly wrapped packages. One is thin and soft, the other small and box-shaped.

"Happy birthday," Aiden tells him sincerely, eyes flicking between Jake and the road ahead. "Open the big one first; you know what it is anyway."

Carefully, Jake pushes his fingers beneath the edge of the paper and tears it open to reveal a bright red T-shirt emblazoned with stylized text that reads, *pale is the new tan.* Jake stares at it for a full ten seconds, muscles working in his jaw, before he bursts out laughing.

Aiden's Awesome T-Shirt Tradition—or Aiden's Terrible T-Shirt Tradition, as Jake refers to it, insisting that the alliteration is both more mellifluous and more accurate—began six years ago, on Jake's seventeenth birthday. Aiden had just gotten his first paycheck from Little Caesars, and he agonized for weeks over what to buy. Both music and movies were out since Jake just downloaded everything. He thought about clothes, but Jake's taste was infuriatingly unpredictable. And then one day, during his fourth fruitless trip to the Plaza, he came across a street vendor selling some truly awful slogan shirts. As soon as he saw the black shirt hanging proudly on display, sporting a green loading bar beneath the legend, *sarcastic comment loading,* he pulled out his wallet.

It was perfect, and despite the look of utter disdain that contorted Jake's face upon opening it, he wore it to sleep that night when Aiden stayed over.

"One day, I'm going to make a quilt from all of these terrible shirts," Jake says, refolding the shirt in his lap with the slogan facing up. "I'll give it to my kids as proof of what a dork their Uncle Aiden is."

"You've kept them all?"

"Of course I have, silly."

Aiden smiles, eyes back on the road as he nods toward the other gift. "Difference is that I got you something good this year, too."

As slow and careful as before, Jake unwraps the box. Aiden chews his lip and actively works to keep his gaze trained ahead. He's never been so nervous about a gift before, not even when he presented his mom with the portrait of her that he painted in high school for a project on Cubism. She loved it; it still hangs on her bedroom wall.

In his peripheral vision, he sees Jake open the slim, square box and remove the tissue paper, letting out a small gasp. "Aiden..."

"You don't have to wear it," Aiden rushes, his words tripping over themselves. "It's just that, you know, he's the patron saint of travelers. And I know you're not religious or anything, it wasn't about that, I just—"

"Shut up," Jake cuts in and reaches over to squeeze his knee. The silver Saint Christopher pendant catches the headlights of passing semis where its chain is already tangled between Jake's fingers. "Thank you."

"You really like it?"

"I really like it," Jake says, letting the pendant drop and swing for a moment before putting it on, settling the small disc beneath his shirt and palming it through the fabric. "It's perfect. Thank you so much."

"You're welcome."

Before long, they pull into the visitor parking lot at Hemlock Grove Campground in Arundel. Already Aiden is starting to feel like Sam in *The Lord of the Rings,* standing in the Shire and telling Frodo that if he takes one more step, it will be the farthest from home he's ever been. It isn't exactly accurate, of course—Aiden routinely visits his brother in Los Angeles, and spent his entire last year of college interning in London—but he can recognize the sentiment. This is it—this is what he's been hungering for since he was fifteen, and while he can return to Maine one day if he wants to, it will never be the same.

"I think you were right," Aiden says as they make their way toward the site office at a comfortable, ambling pace. He revels in the cool, beautifully fresh woodsy air of the grounds. "This is much better than just camping out in the backyard for our first night. I know driving an hour just to get here was kind of dumb, but... this feels more like a real *start*, doesn't it?"

Jake doesn't respond, and it isn't until Aiden pauses at the top of the steps up to the office porch that he realizes Jake isn't by his side. He looks down to see Jake standing at the bottom of the steps, his hand resting just below his collar and toying absently with his Saint Christopher.

"Would you still have taken this trip if I hadn't come, too? Would you still have left?" Jake asks quietly, taking Aiden completely aback. Vulnerability pulls at the corners of Jake's mouth, and the lights from inside the office spill out through half-closed horizontal blinds, casting a swath of shadow over his eyes.

The truth is that Aiden has been waiting for this for years, since the day the bottom dropped out of his world, mere weeks after he came out to his parents and Jake came out to Charlie. Maine represents a lot of things for him, not all of them good. He needs to see so much more of the world, leave a mark behind. He wants to be something good, something great, to reach out and affect someone—even if it's just one person.

"I..." he trails off, not knowing where to take the rest of the sentence. Would he really have been able to leave Jake behind again? Would he have found the strength to go another three and a half months—probably much longer, given his lack of desire to ever set foot in Maine again—without his hurricane of a best friend, this immutable kindred spirit who tears him apart and puts him back together in a better combination? He's never even had to think about it before; when he first brought up the idea of the road trip, there was no doubt in his mind that Jake would be with him.

"You don't get rid of me that easily, Valentine," he finally says, trying for nonchalance. Jake huffs a humorless laugh and crosses his arms over his chest.

"Aiden, be serious. What if I'd said no? Would I have lost you for good this time?"

"Is that why you said yes?"

"You know it's not," Jake says evenly. He lets out a heavy sigh and drops his arms. "I'm sorry. It's just... it's been a really long day, and I'm terrible with goodbyes. It got me thinking."

"Never a good idea," Aiden jokes, and holds out his hand. "Come on. We've got a fire pit and s'mores waiting."

"Always with the damn s'mores," Jake mutters, climbing the steps and taking Aiden's hand in a fleeting squeeze.

When the yawning young clerk has signed them in and assigned them Site Sixty-nine—much to Jake's amusement—they make the short drive around the winding track that runs through the park and pull into their space with a renewed buzz of energy. Aiden leaves Jake pulling supplies from the refrigerator to go out to the fire pit, though it becomes abundantly clear when he gets outside that a campfire is not in the cards. Everything is still too damp from the rain that drove them off the back deck last night.

He's still standing forlornly by the pit when Jake steps out of the RV, arms laden with a cooler and plates.

"You're quite the Boy Scout, I see," he quips, bending down and making a show of warming his hands over the nonexistent flames.

"Should've gotten you another sarcasm shirt," Aiden grumbles. "It's too damp; I don't think this is gonna happen tonight. Next stop?"

"Next stop. I'm tired anyway, and we have a movie to watch."

With a passing, dejected glance at the fire pit, Aiden follows him back inside. Fifteen minutes later they are both sitting on the bed in T-shirts and shorts, sucking the color from slices of honeydew melon.

"It's no campfire, but it's pretty damn perfect," Jake murmurs, chasing a trail of juice down his wrist with his tongue. Aiden swallows, averts his eyes and hits the space bar on his laptop to play the movie.

They watch in silence as the feather curls its way down to where Forrest Gump sits on the bus bench.

"I wouldn't have," Aiden says quietly, just as Forrest finishes delivering the classic line about life being like a box of chocolates. Jake questions him with a single look. "I wouldn't have left without you."

Jake smiles and curls his fingers around Aiden's in that way that only ever feels right when he does it. Aiden leans sideways to rest his head on Jake's shoulder, and settles in for the duration.

50.5 MILES

DAY ONE: NEW HAMPSHIRE

The next morning, after waking up to Aiden moving quietly around the bedroom, getting dressed for a run, Jake retrieves his yoga mat from the narrow closet and unrolls it in front of the couch in the living area. With his favorite feel-good playlist floating from the speakers, he warms up gradually, easing into the familiar stretches of his usual routine. He tries to clear his mind and sink into the peace of repetitive extended breathing, but Aiden's affirmation from last night is still weighing heavily on him, calling up memories that he's been examining for the better part of the last three months: Aiden bowing to his grandfather's coffin; Jake's fingers rubbing the crook of Aiden's elbow as they left the church; the words Aiden said as they sat with their backs to the trunk of the cherry tree in Aiden's backyard, ties loosened and shirt sleeves rolled up in the midafternoon June heat.

"*Let's go somewhere. No, wait, let's go everywhere. He left me the RV, so let's use it. Take a road trip with me. It'll be great; when we get to each state we can watch a movie that was filmed there, we can film our own stuff along the way, maybe even make a documentary… what do you think? Will you come with me?*"

Jake was systematically shredding a still-damp tissue in his lap when Aiden suggested it, and he wasn't surprised. Aiden was always looking for some place to call home—he had spent their last year of college across the Atlantic interning under Oscar-winning director Dmitri Serafino—but the fact that he came up with the idea a mere six days after returning to Maine threw Jake for a loop, so much so that he found himself agreeing with barely a thought.

And now here he is on his last morning in Maine, waiting for Aiden to return and act as arrow to his compass. As he transitions from Standing Half Forward Bend into Firefly Pose, the exertion causing sweat to bead at his temples, Jake wonders if it's a smart decision to put so much in Aiden's nomadic hands. Maybe some part of him still needs convincing after all, never mind that they're already almost past the point of no return.

No, he thinks, exhaling to a count of five. *I'm here, and I'm doing this.*

He moves smoothly back into Standing Half Forward before switching through to Downward-Facing Dog, relaxing into the stretch in his back and thighs. He had forgotten how much he enjoys this.

"Well, that's quite a view."

Jake twists to the side, looking back past his own legs to where Aiden stands just inside the door, thick strands of hair sticking damply to his forehead and the front of his heather gray Bowdoin tee dark with sweat. Jake hums noncommittally, but wiggles from side to side all the same. "I work hard for this ass."

"I know you do," Aiden says as he edges past. Jake sinks and pulls back into Upward-Facing Dog. "But you're really working out to Bowie?"

"I'll have you know that this song is a classic, and Bowie is one of the true artists of our time."

"Our parents' time, maybe," Aiden replies, leaning against the kitchen counter and draining the contents of his blue CamelBak. "Since when did you start doing yoga again, anyway?"

"It was a slow summer," Jake says, releasing the pose and moving to stand. He was almost finished, and the quiet is broken.

"Didn't look that slow the day I got back from London."

Jake glares through the rising heat in his cheeks, incensed at how efficiently Aiden can make him blush. He bends to pick up his mat and says, "I think you mean the day you started cramping my style again."

"Come on, Jake. You must already have been pretty hard up if you finally gave in to Pickup Line Guy," Aiden continues, stretching his arms out over his head with a satisfied smirk. Jake pauses halfway through rolling up the mat, watching the muscles shift beneath Aiden's skin, and feels it all over again: the tug, tug, tug of dull want that has lain mostly dormant somewhere in the bottom of his gut since Aiden came home. Every single day since, Jake has asked himself how one person could change so much in the space of a year.

Aiden was always cute, but he never bothered to do anything with his thick hair, his rich brown eyes were always hidden behind a pair of thick glasses, and his last growth spurt left him gangly. He went off to London still wearing band T-shirts and jeans that looked too big for him. Now his hair is artfully and messily upswept; most days he wears contacts. He has filled out with defined muscle, where before there was flesh and bone; and while the clothes are the same, for the most part, they no longer hang from him.

"What was it that finally did it for you?" Aiden continues. "Was it the library card one?"

"Sorry, what—"

"What about, 'People call me whatshisname, but you can call me tonight?'"

"Ade, we've had this conversation a million times already. Can you just drop it? And his name is Dylan," Jake says hotly, tucking his mat under his arm, all thoughts of wanting Aiden gone. Really, it was just that Dylan happened to be at the same Pride parade and the same post-parade party. Somehow, dancing morphed into staying out all night, into breakfast at Brunswick Diner, into finding themselves stretched out on Jake's bed as early morning summer sun filtered through the drapes. "It's not like I got to finish the job anyway, what with you barging in on us."

"Handjob or blowjob?"

"Do you know the difference, or should I draw you a diagram?"

"Of course I know the difference, Jake."

"You know, if I'm as 'hard up' as you say, practical demonstrations are always fun..."

Aiden finally raises his hands in surrender. "Fine, fine, you win!"

"Good," Jake says. "Now go take a shower; I can smell you from here."

Aiden salutes him with a wink, and soon enough Jake is left alone in the living area, a smile quirking the corners of his mouth as Aiden's singing carries over the shower.

It's noon before they drive into Hampton, and Jake has been watching the shadows ahead of the RV grow shorter as the sun shines ever brighter just above them. The windows are rolled down, and the fuzzy black dice hanging from the mirror swing back and forth in the cool breeze that whips through the cab. Jake reclines in the driver's seat, one hand on the steering wheel as he smokes with the other, and Aiden's seat is tipped as far back as it can go; his crossed ankles rest on the dashboard while he hums along to the radio.

Jake's lips curve into an easy, involuntary smile as he gets rid of his cigarette and runs his fingers back through his hair. Behind his sunglasses, his eyes flick toward the GPS, even though he and Aiden took enough trips to Hampton Beach as kids that he could drive this route in his sleep. It feels good to finally be out of Maine; until they crossed the state line, it seemed they were simply gone for the evening, visiting friends in the next town over. His lingering apprehension notwithstanding, he has to admit that leaving home behind for a while is probably going to be a good thing—he's twenty-two years old now, and a college graduate aspiring to work in the film industry. He would have needed to relocate no matter what.

"We're almost there," Aiden says absently, reaching into the spacious glove compartment to pull out Jake's folder. "Everything's in state order, right?"

"Are you questioning my organizational skills?"

"Never," Aiden answers with a chuckle. He flips past the first few pages of the thick blue folder that Jake stuffed full with printouts and reservations until he finds the one for their two-day spot on the waterfront at Hampton Beach State Park. "I can't believe it's been so long since we were last here. Remember? With those ridiculous sandwiches you tried to make?"

"That was a good day," Jake says, nodding as he recalls the smell of burning bread and the smoke alarm beeping for what felt like hours after his disastrous first attempt at croque-monsieur. "Seven years, though."

"I know; it's insane."

Jake pushes his sunglasses back up his nose and returns both hands to the steering wheel. "The paperwork's all there, right?"

"Looks like," Aiden replies, pulling the sheet of paper from its plastic pocket and scanning it as Jake guides the RV along Ocean Boulevard. "Meet you down there?"

"Sure."

Aiden closes the passenger side door behind him, and Jake eyes the camcorder he left on his seat before he pulls back out onto the main road. An old Stereophonics song plays on the radio, light and thrumming, what Jake calls "driving music." Jake opens his mouth to sing along, but instantly his throat constricts. He feels as if his tongue has swollen to twice its size and now lies thick and useless in his mouth, just as it does every time he tries to sing—except in his room while the house is empty. He shakes himself, stuffing memories of singing "The Dishes Song" with his mom back into a box and mentally taping it haphazardly shut. He sets his jaw, flexes his fingers around the steering wheel and drives on.

On this mid-September Monday the RV park is all but deserted, and the never-quite-silent beach is tranquil. He pulls into their reserved site, cuts the engine, sinks back into his seat and breathes in the familiar scent of Hampton Beach saltwater. The first lungful—uncoupled with the smell of his mother's perfume—always makes him ache, the hollow cut deep into his chest growing infinitesimally wider for a second that never fails to feel like falling. He finds himself absently rubbing the dip at the base of his neck, the chain of his Saint Christopher catching on his fingertips. He pulls it from where it lies beneath the collar of his fitted black T-shirt and studies it closely, resting the disc in his palm so that it catches the light. The design is simple: a smooth silver circle bordering an engraving of a man with a walking stick carrying a child on his back, nothing overtly religious or spiritual about it.

Jake feels ashamed for having been so surprised to receive such a thoughtful gift from Aiden. Over the course of their year apart, a number of the little things that Aiden had always done for him had become assimilated into Jake's own routine; by the time Aiden returned, Jake had begun to take his sorely won independence for granted. After the first three months of Skype calls and emails that went unanswered for days, Jake's sense of self-preservation kicked in and he simply learned how to be alone without being lonely.

And then Aiden came home, sadness over the reason for his return weighing on him like a boulder and the slightest London affectation in his voice. He came home, and suddenly there was Aztec couscous again, and a blanket covering Jake when he started awake at two a.m., having fallen asleep halfway through the movie they were watching, and the DVDs on his shelf were back in alphabetical order. Suddenly struck dumb with the fear that he needed Aiden much more than he'd thought before their symbiotic relationship was stripped away from him, Jake barely knew what to do with himself.

With a sigh, he tucks the pendant beneath his collar once more, unbuckles his seat belt and grabs the camcorder from the passenger seat. He takes it to the small diner-style table at the far end of the couch, sits in one of the high-backed, flock print chairs, plugs the camcorder into Aiden's laptop and starts to scroll through the footage Aiden has been shooting.

It's sparse, clips of passing cars and scenery rushing by with omnipresent music in the background and snatches of idle drive-time conversation. Jake transfers it all to Aiden's laptop and wipes the memory card. He and Aiden have plans for the footage they collect, plans for a documentary that will net them an Academy Award—even though they haven't quite figured out what the point of the documentary will be. Details.

After looking out the windshield to make sure he's alone, Jake flips the small screen around and holds the camcorder up in front of his face.

"It's day one, and we've just arrived in Hampton," he begins brightly, looking directly into the lens. "The sky's blue and the sun's high, which can only mean two things: two days on the beach, and lots of sunblock."

Jake pauses, his gaze faltering and slipping to his mirror image on the screen. *These video diaries are only for me,* he reminds himself. No one knows about them, not even April. They're his space to document his thoughts and feelings, something that he can call entirely his own. In light of the comeback his codependent tendencies have made, he needs something that's just his, and this video diary is it.

"Leaving home last night was... it was hard. Not just the goodbye part—I always knew that part would suck, since my relationship with Charlie is pretty crappy. She's probably happy that I'm gone. No, what's hard is knowing whether I'm really doing the right thing. I think when we got to Arundel and I brought it up, Aiden realized how much he was asking of me to just take off with him. Don't get me wrong, I'm... I'm thrilled that we're doing this together. I am. But this isn't just some day trip to Vermont or even a week on the West Coast. This is three and a half months of nothing but the road and each other, and I'm a little bit terrified that home won't ever feel like home again. And a little bit more terrified that it'll feel too much like home, and I'll never want to leave.

"But even with all that, I really am glad to be here. This place has so many memories for both of us—it's one of *our* places, and nowhere else would have felt right."

Jake smiles in spite of himself; he almost feels as though he should be lying on a leather couch. He doesn't lay himself bare like this for anyone—except perhaps Aiden, on occasion—and knowing that this video diary is just for himself... there's an odd sense of freedom in it.

He has to cut his monologue short, however, when he happens to glance through the windshield and see Aiden approaching. He shuts off the camcorder, makes short work of transferring his footage to a folder buried in the depths of Aiden's bizarre organizational system and hopes against hope that Aiden doesn't find it.

"Who were you talking to?" Aiden asks as he steps up into the RV. He pushes his sunglasses up on top of his head and regards Jake with curiosity.

"No one. Just thinking out loud."

"Anything interesting?"

"Always."

Aiden chuckles and drops the paperwork he's holding onto the passenger seat. "So I figure we can take the laptop to the beach with us and watch *Jumanji* there. And god, I'm *so* hungry. I passed, like, thirty restaurants on the way here and everything smelled fantastic. Are you hungry?"

"Yeah, actually," Jake says, his stomach quietly grumbling at the mention of food. He stands up, the prospect of getting out of the RV and stretching his legs a happy one. "What are you in the mood for?"

"I was thinking Ocean Wok, since it's close. The calamari..."

Jake groans aloud, his mouth already beginning to water. "Excellent choice."

"Or, you know, we could head up to the Urchin. See if they've added anything new to the menu lately," Aiden continues, his tone mischievous, and Jake doesn't miss the teasing gleam in his eyes.

"No. *Anything* but croque-monsieur."

95.0 MILES

DAY FOUR: VERMONT

The farther from Maine they drive, the more Aiden senses the dust settling around him. Granted, there's only actually one state between them and the place he has called home, but being on the road is freeing in a way that he never expected.

Yet he can't sleep.

He's been counting sheep for nearly an hour, trying not to toss and turn too much lest he wake Jake, who is stretched out next to him in the recovery position. The clock beneath the wall-mounted television at the end of the bed reads 2:37 a.m. Aiden sighs quietly, finally giving in and getting out of bed with slow, careful movements. Sliding the bedroom door shut behind him, he pads out into the living area in his T-shirt and pajama pants. His laptop is still on the couch with *Beetlejuice* open on the screen, and Aiden thinks about watching the rest, but it just doesn't feel right without Jake— particularly since Jake has never seen it before. Instead, he flicks on one of the spotlights over the couch, reaches for his battered messenger bag and pulls out a pen and the nondescript black notebook he bought from Sherman's in Freeport.

Two weeks ago, looking for something for Jake's birthday before the idea of the Saint Christopher occurred to him, he saw the small display rack of notebooks and bought one on the spur of the moment. But the night before they left Maine, he hadn't been able to get to sleep until he'd taken it out and written a long, rambling journal entry about the gig at The Cannery and everything he was excited for in the coming weeks and months. Journaling was something he hadn't done since his early teens, but now somehow it's already becoming a pattern again.

Aiden sits down with the notebook and pen and flips to the first blank page.

I'm an early adopter, always have been, he begins after writing the date at the top of the page. *It's odd to me that I'm choosing this medium to document everything when I could be making use of any number of blogging sites, but this somehow makes everything feel a little more... real, I guess?*

Anyway. Right now we're in Little River State Park in Waterbury, VT. Things so far are great, especially since Jake and I are finally getting to do a whole bunch of stuff around Vermont that we've wanted to do for years. I'm sure all those wide-eyed gasps and giggles made us look right at home with the rest of the kids on the Ben & Jerry's factory tour yesterday. Well, I guess it was yesterday, given that it's almost 3 a.m. now.

After the factory we headed over to the Shelburne Museum, and while we were looking at the folk art collection, Jake and I actually got to talking (again) about digital versus classic. I was completely geeking out over this fire engine weathervane, and I (stupidly) brought it up, because if I was shooting some of this stuff I just wouldn't be able to capture the level of detail and craftsmanship in some of these pieces if I was using film. And then there was this strange moment when he just looked at me, and I could see him drawing himself up like he always does when he's getting ready for a debate, but then... I don't know, it just looked like he had the wind taken out of his sails or something. Something about him—about us—*really has changed since I got back, and I'm not sure that I like it.*

I still can't figure out what Charlie meant when she said, "Just see him." *I'm trying. I've been* trying *since that day I walked in on him with Pickup Line Guy, because that was* not *the Jake Valentine I knew.*

I don't know where that Jake Valentine has gone, but he isn't here anymore.

Absently, Aiden taps his pen against his bottom lip and considers whether he needs to write any more. His eyelids are finally beginning to feel heavy, so he thinks better of it, slips the notebook back into his bag and sits back on the couch.

"Why are you awake right now? It's ridiculous o'clock," Jake's voice, gravelly and sleep-rough, comes through the now-open bedroom doorway.

"Old man," Aiden teases him, running a hand through his mussed hair as he takes in Jake's bleary eyes and the soft blanket wrapped around him. "Couldn't sleep."

"Why didn't you wake me up?"

"Jake, you're scary enough when you wake up in the morning, let alone in the middle of the night," Aiden says. He drops his head to the back of the couch, and Jake sleepily raises an eyebrow at him. "I'm serious! You're legitimately terrifying. You open your eyes and all I can see is fire, pitchforks and death."

"Cute," Jake huffs. He shuffles into the living area and collapses onto the couch, leaning over the center arm and dropping his head onto Aiden's shoulder. Aiden flicks his eyes toward his bag to make sure that his notebook is out of sight and shifts down so that Jake's forehead presses warmly against the skin of his neck. Jake clears his throat. "D'you wanna finish the movie? Or... I could make some cocoa."

Aiden wrinkles his nose. "Cocoa? We're not kids anymore, Jake."

"Shut up. You know it's delicious," Jake says, sitting up and arching his back, the pale, freckled expanse of his neck fully exposed as he tips his head.

Aiden swallows thickly, flashes of Jake's now daily yoga routine rushing unbidden to his mind. Since he's come back from London, the subtlest of shifts in their dynamic has somehow given everything a humming undercurrent, a feeling he can't pin down. Mostly, he chalks it up to the fact that they're simply settling back into being *them* after spending a year apart; but the longer it wears on, the more he wonders if there's more to it.

The moment passes when Jake adds, with a wicked grin, "And growing boys need their sustenance."

"I'm not—you have *one fucking inch* on me, Valentine," Aiden protests. Jake swats at his thigh and moves to the RV's narrow electric stove, then retrieves ingredients and a small pan from high shelves in the cupboard above. Aiden ignores the strip of exposed skin above the waistband of Jake's low-slung pajama pants as Jake goes to the fridge. He pauses there for a moment, shaking his head and chuckling at Aiden's—genius, in his opinion—reworked *Jumanji* quote in magnets: *In the jungle you must wait, until your turn to masturbate.*

"So *do* you want to finish the movie?" Jake asks a few minutes later, rolling his neck from side to side as he stirs the cocoa in the pan.

"Sure," Aiden answers, and pulls the laptop back toward him. "By the way, how and *when* did you manage to stock the cupboards so full? I didn't see you bringing in any of that stuff."

"I'm a stealth ninja and you'll never learn my secrets," Jake replies smoothly, and Aiden knows much better than to argue with that arched eyebrow.

He also knows much better than to deny, upon taking his first sip, that Jake's cocoa is indeed delicious. Jake quickly rinses the pan and spoon, returns to the couch, wraps himself up in his blanket and drops his head onto Aiden's shoulder once more.

A few moments later, he reaches up and quickly swipes his thumb across the skin above Aiden's top lip, pulls it back and sucks it into his mouth, all without taking his eyes off the screen. Aiden freezes, trying to reconcile being at once confused and oddly turned on.

"What was that?" he manages.

"Mustache," Jake says. "You always get them."

After this, Aiden can't quite relax. The remainder of the movie washes vaguely through his tired mind as he tries not to think too much about the warmth he can feel from Jake through the blanket separating them. He isn't about to let a little sleep deprivation make a creep out of him. Because that's all it is, after all—it's a little too early in the trip to be calling it cabin fever—and it isn't long before he's resting his head atop Jake's, focusing determinedly on the movie and *not* on the softness of Jake's thick, messy hair against his cheek.

It's just Jake, for crying out loud.

338 MILES

DAY SEVEN: MASSACHUSETTS

Jake (11:21 a.m.) – IMG_20122209_4976.jpg
April (11:23 a.m.) – Rude. Where are you guys and why do you both look so attractive right now? I'm still in my sweats.
Jake (11:24 a.m.) – That was yesterday, walking along the Charles River in Boston. Massachusetts is beautiful! And hey, you deserve a lazy day. I saw the video from last night and you guys were fantastic!
April (11:25 a.m.) – Are you kidding me? It was fucking ridiculous. Damn Hugh and his obsession with obscure British indie bands.
Jake (11:26 a.m.) – For what it's worth, you sounded great. Will you guys be in Boston at all?
April (11:26 a.m.) – Jen's trying to get us a gig at some bar in the North End. Why?
Jake (11:27 a.m.) – Make sure you go to Mike's Pastry for cannoli. But for the love of god, hide the fucking box when you're out.
April (11:30 a.m.) – ...am I just supposed to guess why?
Jake (11:30 a.m.) – We must have been stopped by at least thirteen people asking for directions. Just trust me on this.

At intervals since yesterday, by that very same river, Aiden's eyes have come fleetingly to rest on Jake; and Jake wishes more than anything, as he turns his gaze out the window for the umpteenth time, that he could narrow his field of vision to nothing but the asphalt ahead of them and simply not notice.

But he can't do that, any more than he can forget Aiden's stupid, throwaway comment. It was nothing, and Jake *feels* stupid for being so fixated on it; what he needs most is for Aiden *not* to show him a living, breathing reflection of what Jake himself sees every time he looks in the mirror: a kid playing dress-up in an old man's skin, a faintly haunted look in his eyes that speaks of too many things never dealt with, the way he regards himself with pity as he arranges his armor. And pityingly is exactly the way Aiden is looking at him.

"You sound like Alice, you know," Jake says fondly, shaking his head and trying to count how many times he has heard Aiden's mom utter the words, *"You'll catch your death of cold."*

"It's getting worse," Aiden admits sheepishly. *"I guess we really are all destined to become our mothers, after all."*

Just like that, Jake stiffens, the tension setting his spine arrow-straight quicker than the crack of a whip. His head spins: How quickly he's seven years old all over again, the light from Aiden's living room spilling out into the hallway, a yellow rectangle framing his dad as he kneels down in front of Jake and takes his shoulders. His grip on the blue and white string around his pastry box tightens until it cuts into the creases of his fingers, and he closes his eyes, inhaling slowly.

"I swear to god, I want to shoot everywhere in this state," Jake says now, pocketing his phone and settling back into his seat, his left leg crossed over his right. He picks up the camcorder from where it sits on the dashboard, the plastic casing warm from the midday sun beating almost oppressively down on the RV, and flips out the screen to go through some of Aiden's footage from yesterday. He has to do something to distract himself from the tension.

"It certainly has something," Aiden agrees.

Jake scrolls back through the footage until he finds the panoramic shot of the Charles River that Aiden took from their vantage point by Harvard Bridge. Even with such a state-of-the-art camcorder, there is no capturing the full magic of the blue-backed skyline and the sun sparkling out over the water; it is breathtaking, cinematic, a place where anything could happen—a place where Jake *wants* to make things happen. The location is a cinematographer's dream.

"Doesn't it? I feel like I've had this blank canvas put in front of me," Jake says. "I don't know why they don't use this place more. There's so much untapped potential."

"I can see you there. Back in Boston," Aiden says, absently tapping his fingers against the steering wheel.

"You can?"

"Cities suit you. Don't think I've forgotten the Philadelphia trip."

"I thought we agreed never to talk about the Philadelphia trip."

"Well, you know, *before* the whole public indecency thing... I've never really seen you like that. It was like you came alive; I don't know how else to put it. Here even more so. You're all color."

Jake chuckles and shakes his head, trying not to notice the way Aiden's lips strain to keep hold of his smile when his eyes catch Jake's and the mirth fades back into that same hesitant, considering look.

"Jake, about yesterday... I wasn't—"

"It's fine. Really," Jake says, cutting him off and reaching over to cover Aiden's hand with his own. He shoots him a tight smile, wishing and hoping and praying that Aiden will just let it go, file it under the list of things that Jake doesn't want to talk about and move on.

Aiden returns his eyes to the road, nods after a brief pause and, as he turns off the freeway, says, "Okay."

A few quiet minutes later, they're parked in the small beach lot behind Devon's on Commercial Street in Provincetown, the scent and sound of the ocean waves chasing after them as they make their way around to the front of the restaurant. Jake takes in the weathered white siding of the building next door, the paint battered from the wood by the salty sea air. A few couples are seated outside beneath the black awning, and Jake can't help but let his eyes linger a fraction too long on two boys sharing a stack of blueberry pancakes and proudly holding hands across the table. When one of them looks up over his boyfriend's shoulder with strands of red hair falling over his eyes, Jake offers him a small smile.

"Did you see the two boys holding hands out front?" he asks Aiden when enough silence has passed since placing their orders that it has begun to feel uncomfortable. It is as if Aiden is just itching to bring it all back up again so that he can try to fix it—or something equally frustrating.

"Adorable, right?" Aiden answers, sliding his hand palm-up across the table and waggling his fingers.

"I'm not holding hands with you," Jake says. Rather than give in to the urge to grab onto Aiden and hold on tight, he pulls his napkin from the table and sets it across his lap, giving his hands something to do. He takes a small sip of his iced tea, hoping that the cold will help clear his mind, because this is beginning to prove problematic—it's *Aiden,* for Christ's sake, Aiden, his best friend of sixteen years and *nothing more*. Feelings never lead anywhere good, and as Aiden himself always says, sex just complicates everything—though when Jake started putting "Aiden" and "sex" in the same train of thought, he doesn't know.

"Aw, Jakey," Aiden whines, with his most pathetic wounded puppy expression. Jake looks up and concentrates on the exposed white beams and the checked, cylindrical light fixtures suspended over the tables. "Come *on*, everyone else is doing it."

"Those are the exact words you said to me in Philly, and look how *that* turned out," Jake says archly, glancing around at the other patrons. Granted, he sees a smattering of same- and opposite-sex couples holding hands—but they don't exactly form a majority. "And besides, not *everyone* else is doing it."

"But they could if they wanted, and isn't that the point?"

"Can we just talk about how you've already started making plans to retire here, instead? Because I saw the look on your face down by the beach."

Finally withdrawing his hand with a sigh, Aiden shifts his gaze from side to side and fiddles with his fork. "Not true."

"*So* true, Aiden Calloway. Come on, you don't think about what it'll be like to be old?"

"All the time."

"I knew it."

"I think it's going to be fantastic. Who really wants to be young forever?"

"Ask a senior citizen."

Aiden snorts. "I guess. But just picture it—a little house down by the beach, plaid robe and slippers, newspapers in the morning..."

"Sounds pretty perfect," Jake says, "and just like your grandfather."

"We talked about it a few times," Aiden says, tracing circles on the tablecloth. A sad smile tugs at his mouth. "I miss talking to him on Sunday afternoons."

"I miss him, too," Jake says quietly.

"You know what I miss the most, though?"

"What?"

"His sense of humor," Aiden says. "Whenever I'd ask him what he wanted for his birthday or Christmas, he'd always say, 'Make sure whatever you get me is something *you* like, because you're getting it back when I die!'"

Jake laughs his first real laugh since yesterday and relaxes into his seat; the residual tension drains from him until he can almost feel it soaking out through the soles of his shoes.

"Eggs Benedict?"

Jake glances up at the waitress he hadn't noticed approaching and nods. The smell of hollandaise sauce intermingled with applewood-smoked bacon is heavenly, and he swallows thickly as his mouth begins to water. Suddenly he feels ravenous.

After the waitress has slipped their bill onto the table and excused herself, Aiden tears off a piece of his French toast with his fork and asks, "So what's the plan for tonight?"

"Go to the RV park, get signed in, watch our movie and then head to A-House," Jake answers.

"Ah, so *that's* the reason you brought those leather pants," Aiden teases. "The Halloween costume was just a convenient cover."

"The place has *three* bars, Aiden. And if you don't watch it, I might have to tie you up and leave you there for the bears to feast on."

"But..." Aiden trails off with an exaggerated look of faux puzzlement. "How did you know I like that?"

Jake just laughs, shakes his head, and takes another bite of his brunch.

647 MILES

DAY NINE: RHODE ISLAND

It's been a little over a week since they left Brunswick, and Aiden can already feel a shift taking place. Something he can't put a name to has burrowed beneath the layers of his skin and taken root, is spreading outward, and the farther back he tries to follow the thread, the more lost in his own history with Jake he becomes.

Aiden decides that it's just a sex thing. And that's fine. He can put the sex out of his mind, because sex only ever complicates things. He found that out for himself after those two fumbling encounters with one of his roommates back in London—not to mention what happened to his parents when his father decided that his mother wasn't enough anymore, that none of them were.

No, what he and Jake have is special, sacred, the kind of friendship that just doesn't come along every day, and both of them work hard at it.

So... why does he feel as if this thing that has begun to simmer in his gut is only the beginning?

"Aiden."

"Hmm?"

"Have you been listening to a word I've been saying?" Jake asks in an exasperated tone. He buries his hands in his pockets as they continue ambling around downtown Providence, walking through City Hall Park toward the river.

"Sorry, I was just..." Aiden trails off, not knowing how to finish the sentence. He shakes his head. "What were you saying?"

"I was *saying* that there are all these movies where Death appears as a person, an entity, like *Meet Joe Black*. But what about Life?" Jake asks. "Where are the stories where *Life* appears and coaxes someone back from the edge, or makes them see everything it has to offer?"

Aiden considers the notion for a moment. "I think that's kind of *our* job, you know? We're the ones who're living, who're supposed to seize the day, and do all of it in the face of everything else."

"Hmm. Maybe you're right."

"What was your favorite line?" Aiden asks. Some of the lines in the script had made him want to sit up and punch the air.

"His 'one candle wish,'" Jake answers after a few moments, eyes fixed straight ahead. "That he wants his friends and family to wake up one morning and say, 'I don't want anything more.' Wouldn't that be amazing?"

"Never wanting anything? I don't know. Going after the things we want... it's what drives us, what defines us."

"No, that's not what defines us. What defines us is whether or not we *do* go after the things we want, because either way, life ends up changing," Jake says thoughtfully, and Aiden has to admit that there is hardly room for argument.

"I'm not sure if I'll ever be done wanting things. Done... baking," Aiden says.

"That's a good thing. Trust me."

"How so?"

"You're done baking when you settle."

"Like... settle down, get married, have kids?"

Jake shakes his head. "When you settle for all you think you're ever going to get out of life. That's the timer going off," he says. "Anyway, what was *your* favorite line?"

"Oh, uh..." Aiden begins, reaching up to scratch the back of his neck as if he's thinking about it. Really, it's just to buy himself time to remember anything other than the line spoken just sixteen minutes in by Anthony Hopkins himself, the line about not being able to say you've lived if you can't say that you've tried to find that deep, passionate, crazy love. He can't say that's his favorite line; what would Jake think? What would he *say*? Jake would know. He would know right away what's been going through Aiden's head for the past couple of days, and then things would just become super awkward. They have over three months of this road trip left, and he has to think of something else... the only problem is that he can't. All he can remember are the words that had hooked him.

"Ade, seriously, what's up with you tonight?" Jake asks, stopping to face him with concern in his eyes. "Are you coming down with something?"

Aiden swallows. *"Don't blow smoke up my ass; you'll ruin my autopsy,"* he says, with as genuine a smile as he can muster.

Jake looks puzzled for a moment, and then the corners of his mouth turn up ever so slightly. "Of all the great lines in that movie, you pick that one?"

Aiden shrugs, and Jake shakes his head.

"I would have thought you'd pick something like..." Jake trails off and inclines his head toward the river. "Do you hear that?"

Aiden mirrors the motion, meeting Jake's eyes when he hears it, too: music, faint and uplifting. "Free gig?"

Jake lifts his head to sniff the air, and a slow grin curves the line of his lips. "Tell me you can smell smoke, too," he says, his eyes sparkling in the yellow glow of the streetlamps bordering the park, lighting their way to the water.

A quick, deep inhalation and Aiden nods—the scent of woodsmoke is barely detectable, just undercutting the smell of freshly cut grass. Jake's grin gets even wider. He tucks his fingers into the crook of Aiden's elbow and then they're running, faster and faster toward the river. Jake's grip falters but their pace doesn't, and Aiden calls out, "Jake, what's going on?"

"I heard about this but I didn't think there was going to be a show today!" Jake calls over his shoulder, and beckons Aiden on. "You'll see when we get there!"

In what seems like no time at all they come to an abrupt halt on the bridge just past Exchange Terrace and Aiden slots himself into the teeming crowd next to Jake. A band is set up behind them on Citizens Plaza; the song they play is one that Aiden recognizes from a study playlist one of his roommates in London had made. It soars over the heads of the people gathered to watch what is happening on the water: heat, and light, and fire.

Stately, torch-lit gondolas glide along the water, past floating braziers that burn and crackle brightly in the night. Leaning slightly over the bridge railing, Aiden can feel the heat on his face and see a long line of bonfires stretching off into the distance, lighting thousands of spectators lining the banks of the river.

Jostled by people wanting to get close to the edge, he moves closer to Jake and stands behind him with his hands resting on the bridge wall, one on either side of Jake's body. They're pressed closely enough together that Aiden can smell the spicy top notes of Jake's cologne over the scents of cedar and pine infusing the night air, and once again he tries not to feel like too much of a creep when he leans even closer to speak into Jake's ear. "What *is* this?"

"WaterFire," Jake tells him breathlessly, his eyes still fixed upon the events below. "It's a nonprofit arts thing they do through summer and fall, but I was sure we were gonna miss it. Isn't it beautiful?"

Aiden nods—the sense of magic and enchantment in the air is tangible and heady. For most of the song, they simply watch, and when he feels Jake beginning to straighten and turn around, Aiden quickly steps back. He catches his breath, taking in the sight of Jake, gently backlit by the fire show: He has never looked quite so alive and joyous. And then Jake is tugging on his elbow again, saying something about going to sit on the end of a stone platform that tapers out from the bridge. "So we can see the gondolas close up, come on!"

As they seat themselves at the end of the platform, their legs dangling over the edge, the band starts the next song. The crowd's attention is momentarily diverted from the water as they let out a cheer for the quieter, folksy introduction of the song, and Aiden's breath catches again as the singing begins—it's another song that he knows, this time intimately. The lyrics are about being the right person for somebody but damaged in some way, a lamenting of what could have been as opposed to what the two actually became to one another.

He's captured as he takes in the beatific smile on Jake's face, the flames reflected in his eyes and flickering across his freckled skin. The crowd joins in the chorus, hundreds and thousands of voices winding around him as they sing. The bright yet bittersweet mood of the song juxtaposed with the slow progression of the gondolas along the river somehow buoys Aiden. Everything is pure and beautiful, Jake most of all, and he wonders, *Did we miss our chance? Were we ever meant for something else, something more than what we've had to become in order to hold onto each other for as long as possible? Are we meant to be more?*

Jake reaches out to a woman clad in floating white robes as she glides past, standing up in her gondola, and she hands him a white carnation that he holds to his nose. His eyes flick to Aiden over the top of the petals. Without conscious thought, Aiden slides his arm around Jake's waist, shifting closer and never once letting his gaze waver from Jake's face. Strings layer the song's second chorus, a beat kicks in, and Aiden can feel himself lean forward, his tongue dart out to wet his lips. Jake tenses beneath his arm and lets the flower fall to his lap, his wide eyes moving down to Aiden's mouth and back up again, and *Oh, how have I never seen you before?* Is this moment, this single suspended moment, exactly what Charlie meant?

The song, the water and the sound of fire crackling become nothing but the score to their wonderful, unexpected, perfect movie-moment, and all at once it feels like something inevitable. He moves even closer, tilts his face slightly upward, his breath leaves his body in a single, shuddering exhalation as his eyes close, and—

Cheering, even louder than the singing that came before it. Aiden's eyes snap open and he rears back, realizing that the song is over without warning. Jake blinks at him owlishly, clears his throat and finally drops his gaze to the flower in his lap, the pristine white petals a shock against his dark jeans. Aiden mentally shakes himself.

What the fuck was that, Calloway? Your life isn't a goddamn movie; way to go about scaring off your best friend a week into the trip.

Applause, rousing and raucous: Aiden takes his arm from around Jake's waist and joins in just to give his hands something to do. He wants to slap himself silly. *What the hell was I thinking?* In the space of twenty bottomless seconds, he's almost ruined everything—and judging by the confused expression on Jake's face as he slowly, dazedly claps along with Aiden, he might have already succeeded.

769 MILES

CHAPTER 2

DAY TEN: CONNECTICUT

"What did I say to you this morning?"

Jake pauses with the last bite of pizza halfway to his mouth and regards Aiden through narrowed eyes. Aiden's gaze is too focused, like the beam of a zeroed-in laser, and his face is entirely too bright and open. It's the way he looks when he's trying to overcompensate, when he's intentionally playing dumb and acting as if something huge hasn't happened. He just hopes it will all be swept beneath the carpet like the family issues that plagued his home life throughout his teens.

It's maddening. Jake is the product of an open home, where issues are discussed at length—at least, they were before he and Charlie were orphaned. And he is not someone to shy away from confrontation; he's quick-witted, with a razor-sharp tongue, and when there's an argument to be had he knows how to stand his ground and—usually—come out on top.

Deciding that there is no argument to be had this time, Jake finally answers, "Something about a rooster." Slowly, he chews the last bite, savoring the rich blend of herbs, spices and tomato. Neither the movie nor the website lied—the Mystic Pizza is heavenly.

"Right. That fucking rooster," Aiden mutters, and Jake purses his lips against a smile—the crowing started at around five a.m. and didn't stop for at least an hour. Despite the undeniable pleasantness of getting an early start, he vowed that this would be the last time they parked the RV anywhere near a farm.

"I was only half-listening, to be honest," Jake says, wiping his hands on his napkin and setting it over his cleared plate.

"Well, I was only half-awake, so I can't blame you," Aiden says, and echoes Jake's movements. He crosses his arms over his chest and leans his elbows on the tabletop. "So you remember what happens today, right?"

"Can we not?" Jake pleads, and drops his head into his hands. "I'm already suffering pre-traumatic stress disorder."

"I swear to god, sometimes you're more melodramatic than a Chekhov play."

"Yes, well, Chekhov was never subjected to the horrors of Happy-Mart, and up until five seconds ago I was doing a great job of forgetting all about them. I mean, seriously, that has to be the worst thing that they could have possibly called it. It should be Misery-Mart."

"Aw, poor Jakey," Aiden teases in a wheedling voice. Jake shoots him a withering look and he finally relents, pulls out his wallet and leaves enough bills to cover their food and a generous tip. "Okay, let's talk about *Mystic Pizza*. Favorite scene?"

Jake considers the question as he shrugs into his jacket and follows Aiden down the stairs and out of the restaurant. He casts one last glance around to commit every inch of the place to memory and answers, "The pub. The one that looked like a house. Did it remind you of The Cannery, too?"

"If you're thinking about that one time I tried smoking, get out of my head."

"I totally was. What about you, what was your favorite scene?"

"I liked the story about the guy who built the house for his wife," Aiden says as they make their way around to the parking lot at the back of the building. "You know, you don't hear about people doing that anymore. Building a house for their significant other. It's all down payments and escrow and mortgages. Isn't there something kind of romantic about building a house with the person you love, getting to choose everything together, right down to the roof tiles?"

"First you have to decide where home actually is," Jake replies. As they reach the RV, he unlocks the passenger door and tosses the keys to Aiden—he isn't about to drive himself to his own demise, after all. "But yeah, I can see how that'd be romantic."

"Did I just hear you say the word 'romantic' without even a trace of irony, Jake Valentine? Could the ice finally be melting?"

"I only said that I could *see* how it would be romantic, not that I think it *is*."

Aiden says nothing—he doesn't need to; his grin says it all.

"Just shut up and drive. Let's get this over with."

THEIR ROUTE DOWN I-95 passes all too quickly, and the pit of dread in Jake's stomach only grows bigger the closer to New Haven they get. Before he's ready, the preprogrammed GPS voice is telling them, "You have reached your destination."

"We need to change the GPS voice," Jake says, making no move to unbuckle his seat belt when Aiden cuts the engine. "I'm going to have nightmares about it for months after we get back."

"She sounds kind of... Kathy Bates in *Misery,* doesn't she?"

"Oh my god, *thank you*. I've been trying to figure it out ever since we left."

With no response from Aiden aside from a brief, quiet laugh, Jake falls silent and glares through the windshield at the sprawling building ahead.

"You know, it might not be as bad as you think," Aiden says gently. He slowly unclips his seat belt, as if Jake is a flighty animal with a low startle point. Jake lets out a long-suffering sigh and follows suit.

"I've seen that 'People of Happy-Mart' website, Aiden. I know *exactly* how bad it's going to be."

When they're almost at the automatic sliding doors, Aiden fishes his phone out of his pocket. "Let's turn it into a game," he says. "The winner is whoever gets the most People of Happy-Mart-worthy pictures."

Jake smiles weakly, takes a bracing breath and follows him inside.

His first impression is that perhaps Aiden is right. It isn't entirely hideous—it's bright and open, and at least it smells clean. It seems that they've timed their visit well, for the size of the crowd milling around, mostly mothers with infants, isn't intolerable.

"Got one," Aiden murmurs, surreptitiously snapping a picture of a middle-aged, balding man in a white T-shirt and what looks suspiciously like pajama pants. His back is turned to them as he walks toward the housewares section, and Jake raises his eyebrows as he takes in the clear plastic hangers hooked over the back of the man's collar, two identical white T-shirts just hanging there as he goes about his business.

"Oh my god. Let's just get this over with," Jake mutters, and turns to grab a cart.

Thankfully—due in part to the number of times they've fallen back on lazy student ways and eaten out instead of cooking—their grocery list is short, and by the time they find the alcohol, their cart is only half-full. Jake had taken full control of the cart when it became obvious that Aiden couldn't be trusted not to loiter endlessly around the baked goods, and they've made good time. Jake might even go so far as to say that it hasn't been an entirely unpleasant pit stop.

And then they reach the end of the aisle, and Aiden's hand settles at the small of Jake's back. Jake almost jumps out of his skin at the contact; it's the first time Aiden has touched him since their almost-kiss—*Because that's exactly what it was, right?*—at WaterFire.

He does his best to shrug off the expectation that Aiden will get around to saying something about it, and they round the corner at the end of the aisle and slowly wander past shelves of party supplies. Jake picks up a pack of napkins printed with lassos and horseshoes. "Remember your cowboy-themed party?"

"You mean the best party ever? Of course I do," Aiden answers without missing a beat, and Jake shoots him a grateful look. "I should totally throw another one."

"You do know that having a cowboy party at twenty-one is a lot different than having a cowboy party at ten, right?"

"Cowboys are hot and you know it. After all, who was the one who was so gung-ho about *Brokeback Mountain* being our Wyoming movie when barely any of it was actually shot *in* Wyoming?"

"You saw the alternatives," Jake says, replacing the pack of napkins on the shelf and continuing their slow progress down the aisle.

"So, Jake Valentine," Aiden begins, in his best approximation of a Mr. Moviefone voice, "you've just survived your first trip to Happy-Mart. What are you going to do next?"

Jake just snorts derisively. "Barely survived. We still have to check out."

"Hey, seriously," Aiden says, catching him by the arm. Jake stops, turns and holds his breath. Aiden is doing that thing again, the thing where his whole body tenses in the most expectant way, as if he's about to get every single thing he's ever wanted all at once. It's the same thing that Jake felt in him when Aiden's arm was around his waist, when Aiden's lips were inches from his own, and Jake's heart stutters in his chest at the mere memory. A second later, the tension is gone, and Aiden wraps him in a hug, half-whispering, "I'm totally proud of you."

Just as Aiden steps back, Jake weakly lifts his arms and catches him by the elbows, capturing them both in a replay of that moment on the platform. Aiden's eyes, dark and warm, search his own for an answer to the question of what to do next. Then out of nowhere, just as Jake feels his tried-and-tested, sultry smile begin to tug at the corners of his mouth, two teenagers dressed in hoodies and jeans career past, their cart almost knocking Aiden and Jake over.

"Surviving," Jake mutters as he steps back, and Aiden sighs heavily, burying his hands in his pockets and looking anywhere but at Jake.

Jake hands over control of their cart, wrapping his arms around his middle as they set off the way they came, all thoughts of beer somehow forgotten in the shuffle. As they walk to the front of the store in silence, Jake steals only a brief glance at Aiden, taking in the set of his jaw and his furrowed brow. It's the look he wears when he's either fighting with himself, or lying to himself—or both.

And the lies we tell ourselves when we're young are throwaway compared to the ones we tell ourselves as we get older, Jake thinks. *There's so much less at stake.*

Which is the entire reason why they can talk about any topic under the sun except this one, why this is the one subject that makes Jake feel as if his throat is filled with glue. It isn't as though they met six weeks ago, or even six months ago; their entire shared history could vanish with a touch of lips or rushing hands. They could *wreck* each other, and then what?

"Okay, don't panic..." Aiden trails off, pulling Jake from his woolgathering. "But I just saw a rat."

Jake stops in his tracks and pinches the bridge of his nose. "Okay, I've done this now. I promised you that I'd try it, and I have. But it's Whole Foods from now on."

876 MILES

DAY THIRTEEN: NEW YORK

It's their third night in New York, and already Aiden knows that he will never get enough of this city of a million movies. His mind is filled to the rafters with moving snapshots of every moment so far, playing on a loop: the awestruck expression on Jake's face as he looked out over the Hudson while they breezed down the 9A; the entire world full of color and light as they turned on the spot at the bottom of the TKTS steps in Times Square, where Aiden inexplicably felt as if he were running late for something; craning his neck on the 6 train to try and catch a glimpse of the faded glory of the disused City Hall station; a bona fide breakfast at Tiffany's, with croissants from the Macaron Café; placing a single, memorial rose of gratitude on a bench in Christopher Park and stepping inside the Stonewall Inn a few minutes later, his throat thick with a borrowed memory.

After the very first item on their list—window-shopping all the way up and down Fifth Avenue—Jake dragged him to Grand Central, and they both stopped in the middle of the main concourse to look up at the arched windows set high into the brick walls. When Aiden asked why Jake looked a little sad, he answered, "You've seen all those black and white photographs of the way this place used to be, sunlight streaming in through those windows right there. It doesn't happen anymore because the buildings around this place are too tall."

"That's my star cinematographer," Aiden replied, nudging Jake's shoulder with his own. "Always worrying about where the light's coming from."

"Ade, I'm serious! Shooting in this city must be a logistical nightmare..."

Even so, Aiden has never seen Jake so full of life and wonder, not even in Boston. Last night, after deciding to capitalize on the campground's proximity to the Statue of Liberty, they fell into the bed they've taken to sharing most nights and Jake talked long into the dark hours about all the city's nuances, all the places he wants to come back and explore, everywhere he wants to work someday.

And now, standing on the observation deck atop Rockefeller Center with his gaze sweeping the horizon, Aiden wonders if it could ever get better than this. No, he hasn't found the one place he truly belongs, as he'd been hoping—and expecting, given the astounding mix of cultures to which New York plays host—but he's still in the greatest city in the world, sharing every second of the experience with his best friend.

"I can totally see why people pay so much money for penthouse apartments," Jake says as he feeds another quarter into the coin-operated binoculars. "If I could have even a tiny fraction of this view, I'd be happy."

Now that Jake has distracted Aiden from the view over Central Park, however, Aiden's attention drifts downward, to where the fabric of Jake's jacket stretches across the breadth of his back, the way the tight, dark denim of Jake's jeans hugs the curve of his ass so tightly it could be painted on. *He really is unfairly gorgeous,* Aiden thinks, and wishes that the number of spectators milling around the deck were much greater, if only to give Aiden an excuse to stand closer, close enough to justify fitting their bodies together just as he did at WaterFire. He wants to be back down on the streets, in the middle of the oppressive crush, where the danger of losing one another in the crowd is so great that Jake's fingers tightly grip the crook of Aiden's elbow.

The craving to touch and be close is agonizingly frustrating—it's an itch beneath the surface of his skin that he can't scratch, one that only grows worse no matter how many times he tells himself that it doesn't even exist, that it's simply a physical reaction to spending so much time with a hot guy. A hot guy with legs for days, broad shoulders, thick hair he could card his fingers through until they disappeared and a way of looking at him sometimes that makes him believe he is the beating heart at the center of the universe.

"This is becoming a problem," he thinks aloud, cursing inwardly when Jake quirks an eyebrow at him. Thinking more quickly than he's generally able to, he adds, "I, uh... I don't think I can leave this view, you know."

"I know what you mean," Jake says, straightening up with a sigh. "But I'm exhausted and I'd rather not fall asleep halfway along the Brooklyn Bridge, so..."

"Yeah, let's go."

They ride the R train from Forty-ninth to City Hall, sharing earbuds and listening to uplifting songs about the city that make Aiden smile at Jake's reflection in the opposite window. His good mood settles warmly over him, helps keep out the evening chill while they buy hot dogs from one of the vendors in the park and step onto the Brooklyn Bridge, where he spots a gay couple walking hand in hand.

"We should hold hands," he blurts before he can stop himself, feeling all at once as if he's twelve years old.

Jake stares at him for a long moment and asks, "Why?"

"What do you mean, 'why?' Because we're *here*, and we *can*, that's why."

"My hands are still all greasy from—"

Aiden rolls his eyes and grabs Jake's hand, holds on tightly and leads him onto the bridge. They are silent as they walk in the cool night, and Aiden feels suddenly grateful for the quiet, for the fact that he can walk hand in hand with Jake without feeling like he's overstepping some boundary or crossing some line—between him and Jake, or between them and the rest of the world. It's a blessedly uncomplicated moment and Aiden revels in it, giving Jake's warm hand a reassuring squeeze and earning an uncharacteristically shy smile in return.

"Wow," he breathes at the center of the bridge, where Jake gently unclasps their hands and they look out at the spectacular light show before them.

Tom Fruin's *Watertower* stands proudly atop a building that houses a collection of artists' studios on Jay Street, its lights switching and undulating from within the multicolored stained-Plexiglas structure, a monument to the ten thousand water towers in the borough of Brooklyn.

"Now *that's* something I'd put in a movie," Jake says quietly, after Aiden has spent a few minutes trying to find any sort of discernible pattern in the light sequence.

Aiden grins and asks, "What would we film here, Valentine?" It's an old game of theirs, one that started back in high school and became a tradition.

"I'd work it into the title montage, maybe?"

"No, this place is worth more. I mean, look at it. It's a work of art—totally worthy of the moment the two leads finally get over themselves."

Jake bites his lip for a moment. He seems to consider something as he straightens, chin tilting upward almost imperceptibly. Aiden knows that look.

"So, okay... it's a gritty romance. I'm the one with the drinking problem who'd been doing much better, but fell off the wagon. Everything had been going really well, and then suddenly everything was falling apart around me," Jake says. He closes his eyes, rolls his neck and drops his shoulders, and it's as if he wears another skin entirely. He approaches the side of the bridge and leans his folded arms on the rusted metal plate of the bridge wall, his eyes taking on a faraway quality as he gazes at *Watertower*. Aiden's turn.

"And some wise, well-meaning relative said something pithy and clichéd to me, the guy who's desperately, head over heels in love with you despite all of your flaws. I've been looking for you all night," Aiden says, backing up a few paces and stuffing his hands into his pockets. "I've come here looking for you because it's our place. Oh, and it's raining."

"Obviously. And I'm trying to figure out a way to fix everything I've fucked up, but I just—I just *can't*," Jake exclaims, dropping his head into his hands.

"And then I see you and call out your name."

Obediently, Jake pulls his hands out of his messy blond hair and looks around at Aiden, abject guilt coloring his features. Not for the first time, Aiden wonders why Jake never wanted to be an actor. "I say the obligatory 'what are you doing here' line, of course."

Aiden jogs closer, leaving no more than two feet of space between them, and looks directly into Jake's eyes. He looks tortured, full of regret but still hopeful, and Aiden feels himself fall a little further into their silly, improvised scene. "No words, or an epic Nora Ephron speech?"

"Somewhere in the middle. No music, just the rain," Jake says, and then tentatively reaches out to take Aiden's arms. "You say something, and I try to disagree with you but you steamroll over me. And then, of course, I ask you what happens next."

"Close-up shot, and I tell you that we'll figure it out... *pause*... together," Aiden says. Jake looks down with a hesitant smile, and Aiden—Aiden's assumed character—tenses in anticipation.

"Switches to a profile shot," Jake says quietly, looking at Aiden through his long eyelashes. "*Watertower*'s perfectly framed between us, and we lean in..."

Though he doesn't move a muscle, there's a challenge in Jake's eyes, and for one endless moment everything is at a standstill. Cars and pedestrians alike have stopped in their tracks, the thick clouds overhead no longer move, and even the lights inside *Watertower* are frozen.

"Aiden..."

It's a reverent whisper; Aiden shivers, and that's all it takes. Whatever spell briefly befell them is broken, swept away by the chill breeze that washes over them both, and Jake shakes his head as if to clear it as he steps back. Aiden wants to say something, wants to speak around the lump that sits heavily just above the dip of his collarbone, but Jake is already looking back at *Watertower*, taking a deep breath that makes his shoulders rise.

"Something like that?" Jake asks, his voice strung tight.

Something like that, but something more, Aiden thinks. *Something where I'm not afraid to kiss you because of what it might mean for us, where it's an act of faith—the likes of which I'm not sure I have.*

Aiden clears his throat and hums an agreement he doesn't believe in. Maybe they need to go out, somewhere they'll be forced to interact with other people, and get out of this intense little bubble of two they've formed. They're sinking into new habits that feel somehow old, as if they've always done exactly this but never took the time to wonder if there was more under the surface.

All he knows is that something has to give, and soon.

964 MILES

Day Fifteen: New Jersey

"You want him, don't you?"

"Yes. Wait, what?"

Jake drags his eyes away from Aiden, who is dancing and talking to one of the other engagement party guests, and glances up at Andrew Fleischman, who stands next to him at the bar. Andrew wears a knowing expression, and takes a slow sip of his Negroni while he watches Jake over the rim of his glass.

"Aiden," he says. "You want him."

"No, I—"

"Every time I've looked over at you, every single time, you've had your eyes glued to him," Andrew continues. He slides onto a stool and signals the bartender for a refill for Jake, who has been playing it safe with vodka-cranberries for most of the evening. It's his turn to drive in the morning, and he doesn't want to be hungover. "So why aren't you doing anything about it?"

"That's none—"

"Of my business, I know. Indulge me."

Jake regards him coolly for a moment, this tall, dark and handsome thirty-something professional with whom he's been acquainted for approximately three hours. By rights, neither he nor Aiden should be at this party. *That's what I get for not looking around corners with a mirror,* he thinks, a move which might have prevented being taken to the pavement by two handsome strangers running late for their own engagement party and the wicked bruise that's already blossoming purple and red along his hip.

He wishes he could go back to a far simpler time in his life, when he could just walk away without it being seen as an act of cowardice. Didn't things used to be so much less complicated? They certainly seemed that way yesterday, when he and Aiden spent the whole day wandering the Ocean City boardwalk, checking out the shops and ducking seagulls, and finally heading to the movies to catch a revival screening of *Empire Records.* Before they made a last-minute decision to head up to Hoboken and check out the waterfront, Aiden had threatened to buy him a neon yellow T-shirt bearing yet another awful slogan until Jake reminded him that he could only get away with one obnoxious T-shirt per year.

Except that Jake let his eyes flutter closed each and every time Aiden's arm brushed his at the movie theater, it was as though nothing had changed between them; as though these moments of push and pull that they've been experiencing had never happened; as though he hadn't wanted to take Aiden's face in his hands right there on the Brooklyn Bridge and kiss him until neither of them could breathe.

"We're best friends," Jake says, leaning his elbow on the bar and cupping the back of his head. "We have been since we were six. It just... it wouldn't be a good idea."

"Why not?" Andrew asks, his tone as conversational as if he's simply enquiring about the weather and not the very foundation of Jake's entire moral code.

"I mean... there was a time when I thought that maybe... maybe we'd end up more than what we are, but... I was just a kid. What we have now is much better. He's my best friend, you know? He's the most important person in the world to me, and I can't take the risk of fucking everything up," Jake admits, the words tumbling from his mouth before he can stop them. *Huh. Maybe there's something to this whole confiding in strangers thing, after all.*

Andrew is silent for a moment. He looks as though he's carefully considering something, and as he drinks, Jake decides to change the subject before their conversation starts striking all the wrong chords. "Anyway, this is *your* night. You should tell me the story of how you and Toby met."

"Ha! Okay, well... I'd just moved to the city to be with my college boyfriend, David. He was already living there, had an apartment all set up for us... but I showed up a day early to surprise him, you know? Took fucking flowers and everything, and I walked in on him fucking somebody else."

"Ouch."

"Yeah. It wasn't the greatest start to the day. Anyway, I had nowhere to go; David was the only person I knew in the city, so I just ended up wandering the streets for *hours,* all these fucking bags on my back. I must have looked like such a tourist. Eventually I ended up at this bar, and..." Andrew trails off, his voice growing soft as he looks over at his fiancé, Toby Hillard, who sits talking with two girls at a table. Everything about him is impeccably disheveled, from his wild bird's nest of blond hair to his loosened tie, and he somehow manages to pull it off without looking like a thirty-year-old poser. "And there he was. I walked into this shitty little hole in the wall called The Crow, and he was in the middle of changing his shirt, right there behind the bar."

"Love at first sight?" Jake asks.

"Hardly. He took one look at me and mixed me one of these," Andrew says, tilting his glass. "We ended up talking for most of the night, he gave me a place to crash and got me a job working at the bar for a few months, and it only took me half a year to get my act together and kiss him. The rest, as they say, is history."

"Who proposed?"

Andrew's laugh comes out as a sharp bark, and he wipes his hand over his face. "He did, behind a fucking 7-Eleven."

Jake hesitates, his brow furrowed, and asks, "How does that even happen?"

"Oh, he didn't plan it that way! No, he'd spent a month doing all these things for me... dinners he could barely afford, dropping by my office with a surprise latté, taking me to some of my favorite places in the city... you know, all the usual proposal set-ups. And there always seemed to be something on the tip of his tongue, but he just couldn't get the words out. Of course, I had no idea. We never even talked about getting married before the laws changed.

"Anyway, we were on our way back from another overpriced dinner one night and I was just... I was so *frustrated* with the way he was acting that I just picked a fight with him over the dumbest fucking thing. I don't even remember what it was about now. We stopped for gas, and I just—I had to take a minute to get my shit together, because fighting never solves a fucking thing. So I was standing around, kicking up dirt behind this 7-Eleven and he just came out of nowhere and started in on round forty-six, going on and on about how I'm 'so damn hard to propose to.' And it must have been the adrenalin or something but I didn't even blink, I was like, 'You could ask me right here, right now, and I'll say yes.'"

"And he asked you, and you said yes," Jake prompts.

Andrew grins. "He got down on one knee and just looked at me like he hated me a little bit, and said, 'So will you marry me or not, asshole?' And after I kicked him in the shin for being such a dick about it... yeah. I said yes."

"It's a great story," Jake says, surprised to find that he genuinely means it.

"It's unique, if nothing else."

Jake smiles despite himself, and finds his gaze wandering once more to settle on Aiden, still dancing, surrounded by smiling people and having a good time. He's gone dressy casual tonight, the same outfit he wore for the gig at The Cannery, and Jake watches the way his hips move, how he seems to have grown into himself. When Aiden catches his eye and grins, the low light casting shadows across his face, Jake's stomach drops and he turns back to Andrew.

"Jake, I don't expect you to fully appreciate what I'm about to say to you. I'm not trying to be condescending, but you're fucking young, and you still need to figure out a lot of stuff for yourself," Andrew says, scratching at the stubble beneath his chin. "That said, there's something that my dad always used to say to me, and that was, 'Try everything once, but make the mistakes first. That's how you learn to recognize them.'"

"I don't want to make this mistake," Jake finally forces out, eyes trained on his glass as he wills his thoughts to quiet. He's never been that great at telling lies right to a person's face.

"Is this guy bothering you?"

Seemingly from out of nowhere, Toby is at Jake's other side, and now glances down at him with kind, sleepy eyes and a lopsided smirk. He stands straight and self-assured.

"Not at all," Jake answers, as if all is right with the world and he wasn't just getting his ass handed to him along with a side of truth. "Thank you for inviting us, by the way. It's a great party."

"It's the least we could do after Andrew took you to the pavement downstairs," Toby says, waving him off with a slight wince and a scrunched nose.

"Sorry again about that," Andrew says. "There's fashionably late, there's obnoxiously late, and then there's us."

"It's fine, I promise. I don't bruise *that* easily," Jake quips—another lie.

"Well, if I'm not interrupting, the band's off their break, so I just wanted to see about stealing away my fiancé for a dance," Toby says, and Jake nods.

"Of course, of course."

Andrew stands, holds up a finger to Toby, and leans closer to Jake. In a voice low enough that only Jake can hear, Andrew says, "Things like this are never *really* complicated, you know. It's people that complicate them. So... maybe it's a mistake. Maybe it's not. But think about it."

With one last meaningful glance in Aiden's direction, Andrew takes the hand that Toby offers to him and leaves Jake with his thoughts.

Jake watches the string quartet file back onto the small stage set up in front of the hMAG penthouse's floor-to-ceiling windows. Wondering if Andrew is right, he downs a healthy mouthful of his fresh vodka-cranberry.

Maybe giving in to this thing between us, whatever it is, would be good for us, he muses, running the tip of his index finger around the rim of his glass. Aiden wants it as well, that much he knows, and aside from the fact that it terrifies him just a little bit, maybe it would prove beneficial for them to just give in to it and get it out of their systems.

It won't be out of your system, though, chides a little voice in the back of his head. *You'll only end up wanting more, because you've always been—*

"Shut up," Jake mutters, knocking back the rest of his drink in one gulp as the band starts the first song of its second set to a round of applause.

"You owe me a dance, mister," Aiden says into his ear. His warm breath smells of rum and his hand is light on Jake's wrist. "Can't have you propping up the bar all night long."

"Next song, maybe," Jake says, trying to put it off long enough for the sudden rush of liquid courage to fade away.

"You love this song; don't even try to deny it," Aiden says, cutting Jake off before he can open his mouth to refute the fact. "And I know you have a super-secret thing for The Wanted, so just for tonight, skip the eye-rolling and come *dance* with me."

Aiden's eyes are hopeful in that puppy dog way that Jake finds nearly impossible to refuse, and his willpower slips from his tenuous grasp quicker than sand through his fingers. The beat kicks in as he hops down from his stool and lets Aiden lead him onto the dance floor where the rest of the guests are already gathering, dancing in couples and groups. He takes a steadying breath when Aiden's hands settle on his hips, swaying them in time with his own, and Jake raises his arms and rests his hands on Aiden's shoulders. Yes, this is fine, he can deal with this. This is a safe distance, and Aiden is smiling and happy, and the music is fantastic. Everything is fantastic.

And then Aiden leans in, and every muscle in Jake's body tenses. "That guy by the end of the bar, the one in the corduroy shirt? He's been checking you out all night," he murmurs. "Pretty hot, a good dancer..."

Slowly, in time with the song, Jake turns them so that he can glance over Aiden's shoulder at the man in question. In the brightly spotlit bar, Jake can see that Aiden is right; the guy is watching him, though he doesn't have the temerity to hold Jake's gaze longer than a couple of seconds. He's classically handsome, if a little strong in the jaw for Jake's taste, with thick, jet-black hair that looks as if it was painstakingly sculpted into organized chaos.

"You and I don't often find the same people attractive," he muses, turning back to Aiden and not quite consciously running his thumb down the column of Aiden's neck.

"Not often, no. Maybe we should capitalize, invite him back to the RV with us," Aiden says, wiggling his eyebrows and holding Jake's gaze in a way that, if he didn't know better, would make him think that Aiden is serious.

"Nah. Not really my type."

"Your type is *breathing*, Jake."

"Play nice," Jake says, batting his shoulder, and Aiden just smiles at him and wraps an arm around his waist, forcing them closer together as if it's the most natural thing in the world. He can feel the heat from Aiden's body pouring off him in waves, even through the layers of their clothes and the space between them, and it's close to intoxicating. Aiden reaches behind his own neck to take Jake's right hand, his thumb pressing over Jake's lifeline, fingers wrapped around the back, and Jake only just holds back a yelp of surprise as Aiden dips him.

Aiden rights them, spins Jake out and then back in so quickly that his feet can barely keep up, and it's only when the song grows quiet that it dimly registers that Aiden's chest is pressed to Jake's back, their joined hands crossed over his waist. Jake turns to face him, presses a hand just over his heart, and they circle one another slowly. Aiden's eyes grow darker by the second, his tongue flicks out to wet his lips, and all it would take is for Jake to lean in and close that last gap. Has this always been here, this nameless something that hovers in the air between them, waiting to take hold? They could be within its grip in seconds.

Aiden's fingertips ghost the sides of Jake's neck in the same second that Jake catches Andrew watching them. It's all too much: too much pressure, too much expectation, too much that he stands to fuck up completely. He closes his eyes, exhales sharply through his nose and takes Aiden's hands away.

Things like this are never really *complicated, you know. It's people that complicate them.*

With Andrew's words ringing in his ears like a cheap taunt, Jake does the only thing he knows how to do. He turns tail and walks away, all the way to the restroom, where he locks himself into a stall with fumbling hands.

His entire body is in revolt. The adrenalin that started its typhoon through his bloodstream the moment Aiden touched him is chanting Aiden's name, imprinting it on his every cell, and he can't think, can only hear his ears roaring to a double-time beat.

Jake closes the lid of the toilet and sinks onto it with a shaky sigh, balls his hands into fists in his hair and squeezes his eyes shut until they stop burning quite so fiercely. He feels like the worst human being in history.

What the fuck am I doing? I've never been some ridiculous slave to my feel-ings—I'm Jake fucking Valentine. I fuck all the boys I'd never in a million years trust to keep my heart safe, and that way I'm not forced into keeping theirs safe, either. It's easy and fun and simple. Three essential attributes he would never apply to this thing with Aiden, this intense thing that makes him feel wrong and sordid and, somewhere in the locked file cabinet in the deepest recesses of his heart, also... kind of right.

But Jake has just gotten Aiden back after a barren year of separation. He can't risk it, he just can't.

No, he needs to get himself together. Go back out to the party. Smile and play the gracious guest of two people who quite literally ran into him and paid for their folly with an enjoyable evening and free drinks. Tell Aiden that he had one too many of those free drinks and had to use the bathroom. Put the game face back on and hope to god it's convincing enough, when all he wants to do is tip over sideways and lie on the ground until his heart stops spinning.

"Deep breath, Jake," he whispers. He stands, unlocks the stall door and breathes a sigh of relief when he doesn't find Aiden standing on the other side. He rolls his shoulders, fixes his hair in the tall mirror over the sinks, and with a sanguinity he doesn't truly feel, leaves the restroom to face the music.

1,217 MILES

DAY SEVENTEEN: PENNSYLVANIA

It's surprising just how much distance can exist between two people in a confined space, Aiden writes, his notebook propped on his knee while he waits for Jake to get back from the Longwood Gardens gift shop.

Jake and I almost kissed at the engagement party. It's a thing that happened. And ever since, it feels as if Jake has been doing all he can think of to act like everything is normal between us, when everything is actually as far from normal as it can possibly be. Quite honestly, it feels like salt in the wound. Jake walked away—ran away would probably be a more accurate way of describing it—and made it perfectly clear that he doesn't want me like I want him, and that's fine. It's more than fine; it's great, and absolutely for the best. I wasn't expecting anything more, anyway. He's Jake, after all, and I'm... me.

I was expecting some awkwardness, some avoidance, some dancing around the issue. That's pretty much par for the course with him. What I wasn't expecting was for him to go into complete overdrive and start acting like some maniac on acid. Yesterday was the craziest day, and by the time we got back, every single part of my body ached.

We spent a few hours walking around Philadelphia, starting at the Random Tea & Curiosity Shop on Fourth and then stopping to see the Liberty Bell and Dream Garden. We went out to West Philly to visit the Please Touch Museum, and when we rode the carousel he was two horses away from me.

I found him early this morning, sipping coffee and scrolling through emails on his phone, all traces of his night on the couch already tucked away. He smiled at me like everything was fine, and sure, it's all just peachy. Honestly, though... I'm just pissed. I let my imagination run away with me yet again, and it almost put our entire friendship on the line. It's just a stupid crush, and I need to get over it for both our sakes. If I did it at fourteen, I can do it at twenty-one.

Yesterday was just... a farce, but today has been okay. We sat on the couch and watched Philadelphia, *our PA movie, and it didn't make me feel any better—in fact, all the talk of AIDS and homophobia just made me even more pissed off—but at least I could talk it all out with Jake. He drove us out here afterward, Longwood Gardens, and we delved into a complete deconstruction of the movie, the performances, the subject matter... every issue it brings up that we've talked about so many times before, though neither of us really cared. We just went over it all again anyway, and it felt... blessedly normal.*

Right now, we're on the way back to another Happy-Mart parking lot, much to Jake's—

The passenger door is unceremoniously yanked open, and Aiden almost falls off the couch in his haste to make it appear that he was doing anything other than writing in his journal. He isn't embarrassed; he just doesn't want it to come up.

Thankfully, Jake seems not to notice. He dumps his things on the passenger seat and collapses into the chair behind the cab, giving Aiden a tired smile just as Aiden slips his journal back out of sight into his bag. He wastes no time sliding into the driver's seat and starting the engine, and as he pulls out of the parking lot, he can feel that the edge has worn off. The silence has morphed back into something comfortable rather than awkward, and by the time they pass through Chester on I-95N twenty minutes later with the radio playing a melancholy Springsteen ballad and the sun dipping below the horizon in their wake, Aiden feels almost okay again.

Until his phone trills in the cup holder, and he sees the name flashing on the display: *Dad.*

He has every intention of ignoring the call, reasoning that he's driving and will just call his dad back later, even though he knows that he won't. And then Jake asks innocuously, "Aren't you gonna get that?"

With a sigh, Aiden grabs his earpiece from the dashboard and swipes his thumb across the screen. "Hello?"

"Aiden, hi. I was expecting your voicemail," his dad says; his cheerful tone already has Aiden feeling prickly. "I just wanted to let you know that I won't have to work this weekend after all. The case settled like we were hoping, so we'll have a couple days of real father-son time. I thought I could show you around DC, how's that sound?"

"Sounds great, Dad," Aiden says, teeth gritted, heart sinking. He's been hoping to get away with an evening at most. "Though you remember I have Jake with me, right? So it won't just be father-son time."

"No, I know. Jake's always welcome, you know that. And actually, I wanted to ask you about sleeping arrangements, because Fiona's already got the two guest rooms all set up for you, or you can both stay in one if you're fi—"

"Actually, Dad, I think we're staying in the RV," Aiden interrupts. He tries not to feel the immediate regret at his harsh tone too keenly, adding, "I'm sorry Fiona went to all that trouble."

"Well, you know your stepmom; it was no trouble at all. And the driveway's plenty big enough—"

"Dad, I'm driving, so I should probably..."

"Right, of course, safety first. I'm—I'm excited to see you, Aiden."

"You, too."

"Okay, so I'll see you on Saturday. Love you, son."

Aiden pauses. The words almost spill from his mouth automatically, but he bites them back. "Bye, Dad."

Silence descends again and lasts the twenty minutes it takes to get back to the Happy-Mart parking lot. No sooner has Aiden cut the engine than he's out of the cab. He takes a gulping breath of the fresh evening air and leans against the sun-warmed metal of the RV, to wait until the churning in his gut subsides. Everywhere he turns there is tension, thick as the fog that rolls in off the ocean on cold mornings back in Maine, and it's threatening to overwhelm him if he doesn't just *do* something, already. He sorely needs to decompress, he just doesn't know how; that's what gets to him more than anything.

"I'd offer you a cigarette, but I think we both know how that'd turn out," Jake says, leaning out of the open driver's side door. "You okay?"

"He's just so fucking oblivious, acting like we're best friends," Aiden says. "Ugh. I just... I need to get laid."

"Well, yeah," Jake says, climbing out of the cab and lighting a cigarette of his own. He draws on it slowly, looking at Aiden, and asks, "So why don't you? You could get anyone."

"Can we not have this conversation again?"

"You brought it up. Ade, I'm serious, you don't know what you're missing. And I've seen the way you look at—" Jake stops, cutting himself short, and looks away as he takes another drag.

Oh, if only you'd just finish that sentence, Aiden thinks.

"I've seen the way you look at some people," Jake goes on. "Is this some sort of internalized homophobia thing? Are you ashamed, is that it?"

"No, I'm not ashamed. I'm out and proud, you know that."

"Well, sure, but it's not like you ever act on it. You're not a robot. I mean, everyone has needs. And if *Philadelphia* taught us anything, it's that life's too fucking short."

"Yeah, well, 'needs' are what got you kicked out of that bar when we were here the last time," Aiden says, and Jake's eyes narrow dangerously. "I'm sorry. I didn't mean that; you know I wouldn't ever judge you for..."

"For getting around."

"Jake, I'm just... look, sex complicates *everything*. Okay? I've seen it. I've *lived* it," Aiden says, the old guilt coming back to haunt him with a vengeance, and dammit, he thought he'd put all this shit behind him once and for all. "Sex is the reason my entire family was ripped apart, and I don't—it was my fault, okay? It was *all* my fault, because if I hadn't come out when I did then it all would have been fine, and I can't—"

"Aiden, hey—Ade, look at me," Jake cuts him off. He drops his cigarette and cups Aiden's face with both hands, gently but firmly forcing Aiden to meet his eyes. *"None* of what happened between your parents—no, let me fucking finish. None of it was your fault, you *have* to know that."

Aiden leans into the touch for a moment and attempts a smile, but says nothing.

"I'm sorry," Jake says quietly. "Aiden, I'm sorry. Look... okay, this is what we're gonna do. We're going to head back into the city, find the first bar we can and get absolutely wasted."

"Since when did that ever solve anything?" Aiden grumbles, though the argument is weak—a night outside his head actually sounds pretty good. He sighs and covers Jake's hands with his own—he doesn't want to lose the comforting touch just yet. "Okay. Okay, let's do it. What's the worst that could happen, right?"

"UGH. I CAN'T BELIEVE I had to get all dressed up in the parking lot of a fucking Misery-Mart," Jake gripes.

They're standing outside the famous Woody's Bar, surrounded by students edging gradually closer to the front of the line, and they're close enough to hear frenetic music pounding from inside. Aiden sweeps appraising eyes over Jake's outfit: slim-fit black dress slacks belted just above the hip and a deep purple shirt, sleeves rolled at the elbow, paired with a scooped-out black vest. The only accessories he wears are his Saint Christopher, which makes Aiden smile, and his black leather cuff.

"For what it's worth, you look great," he says into Jake's ear, his voice low. *You look gorgeous, fantastic, breathtaking.* "Me, on the other hand..."

"Please, you look hot," Jake says, waving him off. Aiden's gone casual in his favorite pair of dark-wash jeans—which, he has to admit, do make his ass look fantastic—a sky blue shirt printed with tiny white anchors and a skinny white tie to finish it off.

I'm not here to pick up guys anyway, he reminds himself. *I'm here to dance, to loosen up, to breathe.*

When they reach the front of the line, they pay their ten-dollar cover and head inside. The music is loud, bass thrumming immediately in Aiden's chest, and he drums his fingers on the bar as they wait for service.

He loses Jake to the crowd after four drinks and about half an hour of close-but-not-too-close dancing. Even though he spends a couple songs here and there dancing with a few attractive but ultimately uninteresting strangers, he's fine with being on his own. And the longer the evening wears on, the more relaxed and pliant he feels. Jake was right: This is exactly what he needed.

Arms raised up over his head as he sways his hips amongst the crush of bodies in front of the giant, lit-up equalizer on the wall, Aiden grins when the crowd cheers at the next song and the atmosphere changes almost immediately. The crowd seems to slow down and speed up at the same time, couples moving against one another while the others look around to find partners and bounce along with the unrelentingly fast pace. With its pounding beat and dirty bass line, this is a song made for grinding.

Aiden isn't surprised when he feels a warm body pressing into his back and fingertips dragging down the length of his raised arms. He revels in the contact, leaning into the touch and chasing the fingers for more. Bodies are packed tight around him, the beat pulsing through them, and he feels as if all of them are here simply to bear witness. He can't hear the moan he lets out when he feels a mouth sucking and nipping at his neck but he *feels* it, rumbling up from deep in his chest and vibrating through his entire body. The stranger is pressed against him from head to toe and Aiden grinds back in time with the beat. Arms wind tightly around him—the right all the way around his middle and the left tight against his chest—and he reaches back to bury his hands in the stranger's soft, thick hair, pulling him closer because the way he's worshiping Aiden's neck with his mouth is filthy-addictive.

Aiden opens his eyes and glances down at the stranger's hands as they begin to loosen his tie and work open the top buttons of his shirt, and just for a moment, he freezes. The song blends seamlessly into a quieter, more intimate-sounding one, and the lights come up only to drop straight back down. In the sudden flash, Aiden catches the most fleeting glance of a black leather cuff wrapped around the stranger's pale wrist, the sleeve of a purple shirt rolled to the elbow.

"Ade, dance with me. Come on," Jake says.

The words cut straight through the beer haze fogging Aiden's mind. He lets out another moan as Jake traces the shell of his ear with his tongue and nips at the lobe, and he can't help melting back into Jake's body. "Been watching you all night; everyone has. You're so fucking hot..."

Jake wraps himself around Aiden, seemingly oblivious to everything but the feeling of Aiden's body against his own. He nudges Aiden's thighs apart, taking most of his weight and swaying them from side to side in time with the sudden, insane beat of the chorus.

"I want you so fucking much; you don't even know. God, they've all been watching you and *wanting* you, but you're mine..."

Eyes closed, biting his lips, Aiden grinds down on Jake's thigh and tightens his grip on Jake's hair to keep him right where he is, keep him doing exactly this because this is... this is...

It isn't enough. Maybe there will *never* be enough. But there is only one way to tell, and Jake has moved from his ear down to his neck, still muttering words into his skin that Aiden can no longer hear, only feel the shapes of. Jake is hard against him, moaning into the hollow of his neck with hot breath that smells like whisky. And it really, really *isn't* enough—Aiden *wants,* feels buoyed with the confidence to not only demand but to take and to have and to keep it all locked inside some warm and secret place.

Already aching with need and anticipation, he turns around and looks deep into Jake's eyes, thumbing over Jake's cheekbone and then taking him by the hand.

Getting back to the RV where it's parked just up the street is a blur of shivers in the considerably cooler night air, rushed footsteps and Jake's arm around his waist, teeth nipping at his earlobe every so often. It takes almost everything he has to keep from pushing Jake down an alley and having his way, right there where anybody could see.

When Jake finally steps into his space in the privacy of the RV's bedroom, his stare deep and searching, Aiden says nothing. He doesn't even blink, just yanks his tie over his head and goes to work on the buttons of his shirt. Jake follows the motion with blown pupils and a flick of the tongue that makes him look ravenous. He hooks two fingers into the waistband of Aiden's jeans and pulls him through the mile-sized inches left between them, replacing Aiden's fumbling hands with his own, strong and sure; and this is what bridges the final gap in Aiden's synapses. He's wanted, and it's Jake who wants him—a weight finally lifts from his shoulders, and he lets himself fall back onto the bed.

Jake follows in the next heartbeat and briefly hovers over Aiden, breathing hard as he pushes the shirt from Aiden's shoulders, and for a single, suspended moment he just stares at Aiden's parted lips. Then he leans down, down, past Aiden's mouth, and sucks hard on his neck.

Seconds pass that feel slower than honey, and the ringing in Aiden's ears still holds remnants of the bass they danced and touched to, lost themselves in. In one moment, Jake is all he can feel, all around him, and in the next no warm, firm body pins him; instead, hands divest him of his jeans and underwear in one quick sweep and toss them over the side of the bed.

Jake drops heavily to his knees and slides his arms under Aiden's thighs, so his thumbs press into his hipbones as he yanks him to the edge of the bed. Aiden could swear he feels the slightest stutter in Jake's pulse against his skin just before Jake licks up the underside of his cock and sinks his mouth over the head with his eyes locked on Aiden's.

"God, your *mouth*," Aiden breathes, descending into a moan at Jake's ensuing dark chuckle followed by the quick raking sound of a zipper. Wet heat surrounds him and it is all Aiden can do to hold back from tumbling and disappearing inside the sensation, nothing about it measured or patient but more like the inevitable boil of a gradually heating pot. It's too much, and he can feel the movement of Jake's arm against his leg as he jerks himself off in tandem with working Aiden over as if he's made for it. The thought drives Aiden insane, further into the fuzzy, tingling warmth he feels at the base of his spine.

Aiden pulls at Jake's hair when he feels himself getting close, tugs harder and harder to let him know, because he can't speak, can't say his name. He can't let those four letters slip from his mouth because then this would become something real, something that in his inebriated state he is so much less than equipped to deal with. Jake shakes his head slightly, humming around him, his fingernails digging painfully into the back of Aiden's hip, and Aiden jolts upward with a cut-off groan. He throws an arm across his eyes and presses, presses until yellow blossoms behind his eyelids like oil on water and he comes harder than he ever has in his life, crying out and digging his fingers into the unyielding mattress. Jake takes it all, working him through it with his own muffled moan of arrival until he finally pulls off with a lewd pop and drops his forehead to rest on the inside of Aiden's thigh, his warm breath fanning over the skin there.

"Fuck," is all Aiden can manage as Jake stands, already tucking himself back into his boxer briefs but leaving his pants undone. His lips are the color of a kiss they haven't shared. Aiden sits up and forward, hooks his fingers beneath Jake's vest and pulls limply. "Come here."

"Aiden, I—"

"Just come here."

Tentatively, without meeting Aiden's eyes, Jake climbs onto the bed and they crawl up the length of it together to lie down. Jake presses his damp forehead against Aiden's neck, brushes a single kiss against his collarbone, and shakily exhales.

They are utterly silent, and all it takes is a few minutes for Jake to fall asleep. Aiden isn't as lucky. He stares up at the ceiling until the edges of his vision blur. Eventually he switches off the bedside lamp, wondering if he'll find answers swathed in the darkness.

He doesn't.

1,410 MILES

DAY EIGHTEEN: DELAWARE

Jake surfaces slowly.

At first he feels the body-warmed cotton beneath his fingers; then skin, smooth and heated. Then comes an awareness of deep satiation, the unfettered relaxation pooled inside every muscle and the quiet need to stretch, all chased by the smacking of lips, the taste of stale alcohol and—fries, maybe? He slowly opens his eyes, searching out daylight between the slats of the blinds, but it's still almost dark. Turning, he takes in the sight of Aiden beneath the covers, his blue shirt wrinkled and unbuttoned. He looks more relaxed than Jake has seen him in a long while, and though things between them are still a little strained and he didn't exactly intend for them to bed-share again so soon, he can't help but smile.

Slowly, so as not to disturb Aiden, Jake stretches himself out of bed and retrieves a T-shirt, a soft hoodie and his comfiest pair of sweatpants from the closet at the end of the bed. He leaves the small bedroom, slides the door closed behind him and goes about his usual morning routine, skipping the shower because breakfast is far more important. *Pancakes. Oh my god, pancakes.*

He's sitting in the driver's seat, sipping from a steaming mug of French roast and watching the sunrise break through cloud after cloud when he realizes, *Shit. We're still in the city. On a Thursday morning.* He doesn't particularly want to get caught in the morning rush hour, all infuriating start-and-stop until they hit the highway. *What time did we get back?* Jake can't remember anything after catching glimpses through the crowd of Aiden dancing in front of the equalizer, but he knows they must have gotten back late, and it's barely a quarter after seven.

Deciding to let Aiden sleep, Jake finishes his coffee and plucks the keys from the hook under the kitchen cabinets. Soon enough, he's on the road again.

Aiden finally appears an hour later, bleary-eyed and yawning as he sinks into the passenger seat. He's wearing the same clothes as last night, his shirt only buttoned halfway up. Jake shoots him a brief smile, turns down the volume on the radio and forces himself not to let his eyes linger on the smattering of dark hair on Aiden's chest—though it doesn't seem to matter, since Aiden isn't looking at him at all.

Even as it settles upon his shoulders, Jake tries to push away the sense that something isn't quite right, and says, "You know, I really like this route we're taking. Gets us out of driving all the way across Pennsylvania."

"Small mercies."

"How'd you sleep?"

"Fine. Where are we?"

"About five minutes outside Smyrna. I figured we could find someplace for breakfast, because I'm craving pancakes like crazy no other."

Aiden snorts, shakes his head and looks out of the window at the other cars on the highway.

"What's with you?" Jake asks. "Are you hung over?"

"Do you remember anything that happened last night?" Aiden asks, his voice even.

"Not really," Jake answers slowly, a horrible thought occurring to him as he realizes, *Pancakes. I only ever want pancakes after sex.* Aiden knows this as well as he does. "Oh god, did it happen again? I hooked up with some stranger, didn't I? Fuck."

"No, Jake. You didn't hook up with some stranger," Aiden replies, and Jake breathes a sigh of a relief—not only does he want to avoid putting Aiden in that situation again, he really wants to avoid hooking up with strangers when he knows that any hookup would merely be an unsatisfying substitute for what he really wants and really can't have.

"Thank god."

"Yeah. Where's the aspirin?"

"In the bathroom," Jake says, and smiles to himself a little as Aiden passes by—Aiden is always grouchy the morning after a night out, at least until he's eaten.

Jake, on the other hand, is in such a good mood that the pancake craving doesn't even occur to him again until he's sitting opposite Aiden inside Smyrna Diner, enjoying the spacious yet homey, throwback feel of the place as he peruses the breakfast menu. Aiden takes only a cursory glance at his own before he slumps in his seat and turns to watch the morning drizzle pit-pit-pattering against the windows. Jake begins to sense that edge of tension creeping back in and orders Eggs Benedict and home fries, though he doesn't really understand why.

Something feels very, very wrong, and it isn't until they've driven the rest of the way to Rehoboth Beach and parked by the Indian River Marina that Jake realizes why.

He's on the couch with Aiden's laptop, listening to music and answering emails, when Aiden steps out of the bathroom with a towel wrapped around his hips. Jake glances up once, twice, and freezes in his seat; on the back of Aiden's left hip are four red, crescent-shaped marks.

Pushing through the crush of bodies around him, needing to get to Aiden and show him how much he's wanted, give him everything he deserves. Moving against him, with him, arousal flaring sharply as he lavishes attention on Aiden's skin; wanting to groan every time he brushes against the stubble on Aiden's jaw. Hard, heavy, hot flesh on his tongue and himself in hand, wanting to cry at the relief of finally, finally, finally. Aiden's imploring eyes, curling into his warm body with an arm holding him close and then—

Jake shoots to his feet and swallows convulsively, panic rising in his throat like bile. He—they... *oh, god.*

He doesn't pause, doesn't so much as blink, just takes his music and runs, the RV's side door banging shut behind him as he takes off toward the north end of the marina. He's wearing the wrong shoes for running, doesn't even really own a pair of running shoes, that's Aiden's thing—Aiden, whom Jake sucked off without a thought. *Selfish idiot, you've ruined everything; you've fucked it all up completely and you won't recover from it. It wasn't supposed to be like this; it wasn't supposed to happen like this, and did you even kiss him before you broke all the rules? Of course you didn't. Take, take, take it all, just like you always do, but not from him, never from him because he deserves better and better isn't you.*

"Jake!"

One of his earbuds slips out, but he doesn't care; his feet pound harder on the uneven terrain and he stumbles, arms flailing wildly in front of him. Somehow he keeps going, running faster along the trail until the loop takes him out to the spit of beach lining the shore, the sand little more than fine, weatherworn stones and pebbles and he can't breathe, can't think because it's all around him, the damage that he's done to them and he can still taste—

"Jake, stop!"

The rain is pouring down now and Jake is freezing in just his T-shirt and sweats but he can't stop, can't do anything other than run from what he did because maybe, if he gets far enough away from it so it's nothing more than a passing blip on the horizon, he can ignore it, get past it, act as if it never happened in the first place. But then Aiden draws level with him, takes his arm and yanks him to a stop.

"Jesus fucking Christ, Jake," Aiden pants, hands on his thighs, and now that Aiden is here in front of him, looking at him as if he's utterly insane,

Jake truly feels it. "Are you trying out for the Olympics or something? What the fuck *was* that?"

With shaking hands, Jake pulls out his remaining earbud and turns the music off, winding the cord for a few precious seconds to compose himself. It doesn't work; it only gives the panic more time to overcome him, and he trembles uncontrollably as the rain pelts him full-force.

"Jake, *look at me,*" Aiden instructs him firmly, taking him by the shoulders. His hands are *burning*. Jake can feel those fingers gripping his hair all over again. "Look at me, and breathe."

Inhaling as slowly as he can, Jake says, "I've fucked it all up, haven't I?"

"What are you talking about?"

"Ade, please. You weren't even half as drunk as I was."

Aiden takes a breath and exhales through his nose, shaking his head and shivering when rivulets of water run from the thick strands plastered to his forehead. "Okay, okay, I just..." Aiden trails off, scrubbing a hand over his face, and Jake wishes and hopes and prays that Aiden isn't about to ask if being drunk was the only reason it happened, if Jake meant even one second of it, because those are dangerous questions with even more dangerous answers.

"Just what?"

"Look, let's be honest..." Aiden says, and Jake holds his breath. After a long pause, Aiden cocks his head to the side, quirks his eyebrows and grins. "I've got moves."

Just like that, the tension cracks and shatters. Jake bites his lip. "Such a dork," he mutters, and the ground stops moving beneath his feet.

"Chalk it up to booze, temporary insanity, whatever you want. Let's just forget about it, okay?" Aiden asks. With a deep, shuddering breath, Jake nods gratefully—he's off the hook, even though that voice in the back of his mind that grows louder with each passing day says, *You don't want to be let off the hook at all.* "You're freezing."

"I hadn't noticed."

Wordlessly, Aiden shucks off his leather jacket and tucks it around Jake's shoulders. It smells like rain and spice and home.

"Come on, Jakey. What do we do when it rains?" Aiden prompts. "We..."

"We shop," Jake answers, rolling his eyes as they turn to retrace their footsteps.

"A little bird told me that there's a great outlet mall nearby. And Jake, did you know that in Delaware, you don't pay sales tax?"

"Why no, Aiden, I didn't know that."

"Just *think* of all the awesome T-shirts I could buy for you."

Jake laughs and leans briefly into the arm Aiden wraps around his waist. *This is good,* he thinks. *This is who we are.*

1,534 MILES

CHAPTER 3

DAY TWENTY-ONE: MARYLAND

"Are you really sure about my Halloween costume?" Aiden asks as he idly plucks scales, shaking out his hand every now and then. He hasn't played seriously in nearly two weeks, and though his fingertips ache as new calluses blossom on top of the old ones, the feel of the black cocobolo and white spruce of his father's Baranik Meridian is undiluted magic. It has him itching to grab his journal and scribble down the new lyrics beginning to meander through his mind.

Seated on the overstuffed crimson couch that stretches along the opposite wall of the music room in the Calloways' basement, Jake glances up from the crate of vinyl records he's flicking through. They've been down here since shortly after a surprisingly pleasant dinner with George and Fiona. Surprisingly pleasant seems to be the theme of the visit, and often throughout the day Aiden has caught himself wondering when the penny is going to drop.

"Why? It's fabulous, very Adam Lambert-esque," Jake says. "Much better than your original idea of going as a tube of lube and a condom. I mean, *really.*"

"April told me it made me look like Elmo at a gay bar," Aiden says.

"She's just jealous that she doesn't get to wear a Jake Valentine original, too," Jake says. He pulls an LP from the crate and sets it on the floor, on the side of the crate Aiden can't see. "Besides, why are you worrying about Halloween when it's still weeks away? Unless—oh. You really *are* unsure about it, aren't you?"

"No, no, it's nothing like that. You *know* I love my costume. I don't know; it's just been bugging me ever since she said it."

"Well, you could always go with the Freddie Mercury instead. But don't think I don't know exactly what you're doing," Jake says lightly. He reaches the last LP, flips them back into place and looks Aiden in the eye, bracing his hands on either side of the crate. "You're doing that thing again."

"What thing?"

Jake wiggles his fingers in the air. "That thing where you nitpick at all the things you *think* are wrong because you're just avoiding the big thing that's *actually* wrong."

"Don't know what you're talking about," Aiden mutters to the guitar, focusing on the grain of the wood beneath its perfect layer of varnish.

"Don't you dare give me that, Aiden Thomas Calloway. There's obviously something that you're not dealing with, and you and I both know what it is," Jake says. He stands up, gracefully unfolding himself from the couch, and takes the vinyl he pulled from the crate to the turntable. Within moments the basement is filled with that comfortable crackling, and the timeless big-band sound of an old Rat Pack song pours from the restored phonograph. Jake turns around and holds out a hand. "Care to dance?"

Aiden worries the inside of his cheek for a moment or two, then stands the guitar against the wall and crosses the room. "Where is this coming from, Mr. Valentine?"

"You're going to talk it out, and I'm going to listen, and then we're going to try and figure it out together," Jake tells him, taking Aiden's hand and settling his own on Aiden's shoulder—a small gesture that says, *I've just told you what we're going to do, now you take the lead,* and Aiden appreciates it. "Deal?"

"Sure, but—dancing?" Aiden asks.

"Grandpa Art's eightieth, don't you remember?"

Aiden blinks as the realization dawns—it was right before Christmas, the first holiday season after Jake's father died, and as soon as this song came on Aiden took Jake's hand and forcibly pulled him from his seat. They danced awkwardly at first, but soon found their feet and ended up having fun. It was the first time he'd heard Jake really laugh in four months.

"There it is," Jake says, smiling. "So?"

Without further preamble, Aiden finds the rhythm and starts them off in a simple yet competent foxtrot, watching Jake's face and waiting for realization to dawn.

"I didn't know you could dance like this," Jake says, glancing down at Aiden's socked feet as if to make sure he's not imagining their progress around the room.

"You remember those lessons Mom had me take for cousin Lara's wedding when I was seventeen?"

"I remember coming with you to one and it being the funniest thing I'd ever seen in my life. Still is, by the way."

"Well... I guess I kind of enjoyed it, so I kept going back."

"How did I not know this about you? I mean—wait. *This* is what you were doing every Wednesday night?"

"What did you think I was doing?"

"I just figured you were having your *alone time.*"

"You honestly thought that I scheduled time to jerk off?"

"Wouldn't be the first time," Jake sings-songs, and Aiden groans.

"Once, Jake. *Once.*"

Jake giggles, and Aiden can feel it when Jake really gives himself over to the dance, his arms adopting a pliancy that gives Aiden a little thrill.

The thrill dissipates all too soon, however, when Jake clears his throat and prompts, "So...?"

"So what?"

"You know what. What are you going to do about your dad?"

Though he already knows it will be fruitless, Aiden picks up the pace as the song bursts into the instrumental section, throwing in extra turns and dips and spins in an effort to distract Jake. To his credit, Jake just goes with it until the song calms again. His eyes sparkle beneath the spotlights set into the ceiling;

it's all Aiden can do to keep his wits while Jake is—essentially—wrapped around him. Somehow their dance position morphs into a close embrace, with their arms wound around each other's waists and Jake's hand resting over his heart.

As the song comes to an end, Jake licks his lips and says, "All those procedural crime dramas that your mom loves—when they're looking for the guilty one, where do they look first?"

"What are you talking about?"

"They look for the person running away, Ade."

"Okay..."

"Isn't that exactly what you've been doing ever since it happened?" Jake asks, his voice forgiving but firm. "You've been punishing your dad for something he did seven years ago because it was too big for you to process or forgive at the time. But since then it's only gotten bigger, and now you're just too scared to open the box you shoved it into. Look, he can't undo it. But with all his heart, he's sorry. I can see it in his eyes, and you would too if you just took the time to look."

Jake moves even closer and lays his palm in the hollow of Aiden's neck; Aiden almost leans into the touch, but lets the hesitancy have him.

"Don't waste the relationships that you *could* have," Jake says softly, his thumb rubbing absently just beneath Aiden's jaw. He swallows and adds, "Not all of us get that chance."

"You boys having fun down there?"

Aiden's head whips toward the basement door and the sound of his father's voice. He freezes, feeling all at once as if he's been backed into a corner, while also realizing that Jake is right; he should have stopped running years ago, but never quite figured out what to do with the momentum. It isn't just his father he needs to forgive, either—he needs to forgive himself. Rationally, he knows that coming out to his parents was not a reason for their split and subsequent divorce—but given the fact that he came out a mere three weeks before his mother discovered his father's infidelity, it's always been hard to believe it wasn't partly his fault.

"Yeah, Dad," he calls out, keeping his voice light. Jake's hand has left his neck, and Aiden avoids his eyes.

There's a beat of silence, during which Aiden notices that Jake has switched off the phonograph, followed by footsteps padding softly down the carpeted stairs.

"You mind if I join in?" George asks as he pokes his head through the door. He's changed since dinner and now wears what he calls his "house pants" with a collared polo and a deep blue sweater. Aiden still can't quite get past the gray in his hair. "I've been meaning to get down here again for a while."

"You know, I think I might go find Fiona. She mentioned her roses earlier, and Charlie's always looking for gardening tips," Jake says quickly. With one last, sharp glance at Aiden, he makes a hasty exit.

George steps all the way into the room, clears his throat and gestures to the guitar. "I couldn't help but overhear, when you were jamming before. You play even better than the last time I heard you."

"Thanks," Aiden says, unable to dampen the small thrill in his chest at his father's proud tone. It makes Aiden want to tell him more, tell him everything. "I was, um—I had a band in college."

"Yeah? Let me guess, you were the rock star front man," George says knowingly, seating himself where Jake sat before their dance.

"Well, I wouldn't put it quite like that, but... yeah, I sang and played guitar," Aiden says, grinning sheepishly. "We actually had our last gig together at The Cannery, the day before Jake and I left."

"I bet that place still looks exactly the same."

"Same gnarly old fishers nursing beers under the marlin in the corner, yep."

George chuckles, and things are easy—and Aiden should have known it was too good to last.

"That was always your mom's favorite place, and I could never figure out why. How's she doing, now?"

A body-wide sweep of tension; Aiden tries not to bristle outwardly. "She's fine."

"Did I hear that she just got a promotion?"

It's nothing, Aiden tells himself. It's small talk. Yet he can feel the old anger dredging itself up, churning in his gut and rising, rising, rising, high enough to flood and overwhelm the dam he painstakingly constructed to protect himself from it.

"Yep, three weeks before we left."

"Well, that's fantastic! How did you celebrate?"

"Dinner at the War Horse."

"Ah, another favorite," George says, a note of wistful nostalgia lacing his tone. Then he grows serious, eyebrows drawn down over his eyes. He leans forward in his seat slightly and asks, "And is she doing all right since Arthur passed?"

"Don't you mean, 'Is she back on the meds?'" Aiden asks hotly, staring his father square in the eye. "Because no, she's not. She doesn't need them anymore."

"Well, that's—that's good to hear," comes the mollifying reply. "And how was the, uh... the service? I would have liked to be there to pay my respects, but—"

"Grandpa wouldn't have wanted them even if you'd been invited to pay them," Aiden cuts him off. The room becomes very still.

"Aiden, there's no need to be so rude," George says. His steely tone would usually have Aiden backing down, but this time it only fuels the hot wash of anger roiling in the pit of his stomach.

"Dad, I'm not a kid anymore. You can't just tell me I'm being rude every time I say something you don't want to hear."

"Now, wait just a minute—"

"No, I won't. I'm an adult now—"

"You don't look like much of an adult to me—"

"And that's because you ran away!" Aiden yells, the dam finally breaking. He can feel how hot his face is, feel the adrenalin coursing through his veins, yet he also feels removed from himself, as if he's been taken from his body and made to watch. "You never got to see me *become* an adult because you weren't *there* to see it! You cheated on Mom, and then you ran away because you couldn't deal with the consequences when she found out, and I bet you don't even have any idea how bad it got; how she lost all of her friends; how she had a psychotic break while you were living it up with your secretary in fucking *Rockland*—"

"Aiden, stop," Jake's voice comes from the doorway, and Aiden whips his head around at the sudden intrusion. Jake moves to step forward, but Aiden holds up a hand.

"No, he needs to hear this," he says quietly, and turns back to his father, who is sitting with the fingers and thumb of one hand stretched across his brow, his face mostly hidden from view. Aiden continues, in a voice so low and controlled he surprises even himself, "Dad, what you did almost *killed* her. I lived at Jake's house for *six months* of sophomore year while they kept her in that place full of crazy people to make sure she wouldn't try to kill herself again, and where were you? Why didn't you come back?"

"I was too ashamed." George's voice is gravel-rough and bitten off, and his eyes are tortured when he looks up at Aiden. "There is *nothing* I can do now that will fix what I did to both of you, but you have to believe that I am so, so sorry."

"Not good enough," Aiden says. "I was ashamed of you too, but I still needed you. I *hated* you because of how much I still needed you, even after you broke everything."

In the silence that follows, Aiden pushes past Jake and runs from the room without so much as a backward glance, even when Jake calls after him. He takes the stairs two at a time and makes his way through the pristine kitchen where Fiona poured them lemonade earlier. Passing through the wide archway into the grand foyer, Aiden's feet slide against the smooth maple flooring and the marble of the wide, curving staircase that serves as the foyer's focal point.

He finds his way to the guest room where he left his things, fully aware of the fact that what he is doing entirely contradicts ideas of "adult behavior." The door slams shut behind him and he curses himself for bringing everything inside from the RV before really taking the temperature between him and his father. He stands at the foot of the bed for a moment, fists opening and closing, and then gives in to the urge to collapse face-first on the downy comforter.

He lies there for at least two hours, picking the day apart into its component minutiae as he watches the muted glow of the lanterns outside the window. Wind howls wildly for a spell, the sound of it like blowing across the lip of a bottle, and he can only just hear the music playing quietly from his laptop on the floor beside the bed.

The day had washed over him in bright pockets of time that burned pictures into his mind's eye with crystal-clear precision: the scent of Old

Spice accompanying the first hug he had shared with his father in years; George nervously clearing his throat and suggesting a tour of the house; Jake's thrilled expression when Aiden agreed that it would be a shame to waste such beautifully-appointed guest rooms; Fiona's bright, pleased smile as she shooed all three of "her boys" out the door for an afternoon drink; a window table at Frazier's On The Avenue and the swirling fog of Jake's Grey Goose martini juxtaposed with the startling amber clarity of Aiden's Heritage Bourbon as his dad sipped an orange juice; laughing until his sides hurt and his dad's eyes streamed at one of Jake's perfectly timed Eddie Izzard references on the way back from the bar; giggling awkwardly around the dinner table at Fiona's misapprehension that he and Jake were an item.

The entire day, all of the smiles and the easy laughter, the renewed faith he'd felt blossoming in some deep and forgotten place... now it all feels as if a gargantuan joke has been played on him, and that the person behind it has taken an ice cream scoop to his insides, gouging out every last shred until nothing but a husk is left behind.

Why isn't this more satisfying? Aiden thinks. *I've been waiting years to say all of this to him. Now what?*

He changes into his pajamas and attempts to write an entry in his journal; he tries counting sheep; he even briefly considers jerking off to work out his frustration before thinking better of it—none of it is any use. Time drags on, and Aiden rolls onto his back, pillowing his head on his arms and counting the tiles from the wall to the small chandelier and back again.

The soft cotton of the sheets is too hot against his skin, and they tangle around his legs as he rolls onto his side in search of a cooler and more comfortable position. He isn't even angry anymore, not really. The anger has been overtaken by a deep, encompassing sadness that reminds Aiden of everything he forgot; it was so easy to hold onto the anger for so long that the good things had slipped his mind—his dad's pride in the things Aiden accomplished; his ever-present and slightly ridiculous sense of humor; even his deep, abiding love for throwing Monty Python quotes into everyday conversation. It had all fallen by the wayside. Aiden has *missed* his father, and it's hitting him all at once just how much. He was expecting two days of a bite-swollen tongue and an awkward knot in his throat, and instead, he got his dad back—right before he caused the chasm to widen further. He should have moved on from this long ago—after all, in their own separate ways, both of his parents have—but he has held onto the anger and loss and utter heartbreak for so many years that it's burned into his skin, now; it has become part of who he is, and he's scared of finding out who he might be without it.

Tap-tap-tap.

Aiden throws back the covers, trying to decide if he'd rather see Jake or his dad at the door. He straightens his pajamas and crosses the room, opening the door to see Jake standing before him with his arms crossed over his chest. They regard one another for a long moment. Aiden starts to speak, and within a split second Jake steps forward and places his hand over Aiden's mouth. Their faces are only centimeters apart; Aiden is suspended in the moment, his heart racing in his chest, blood rushing in his ears.

"Aren't you tired of this yet?" Jake asks, his eyes soft as he draws his hand back and leans against the doorframe.

After a pause, Aiden nods. "Is anyone still awake?"

"Fiona went to bed, but your dad's still out on the patio. Aiden, as proud as I was of you for using your words earlier, I think—"

"I know. I know I have to fix this."

Jake nods and steps aside. "I'm going to bed, but I'll be up for a while. Maybe we could watch our movie? I know that *Hairspray* always makes you feel better."

Aiden gives him a tight, crooked smile, murmurs a thank you and makes his way downstairs. Just as Jake promised, he finds George sitting in the middle of the curving taupe couch, one socked foot resting on the upholstered top of the coffee table. Aiden stands awkwardly half in and half out of the doorway to the patio and looks at his father, *really* looks at the man before him, with his usually tidy hair slightly mussed, his eyes bloodshot and beset by dark circles and the wrong kind of lines around his mouth. He looks more tired than Aiden feels.

Slowly, Aiden moves toward the end of the couch and perches on the arm. He glances out over the backlit silhouettes of the roses that border the waist-height wall separating the patio from the yard, and searches for the words.

George sits up straight and leans forward, forearms resting along his thighs, fingers splayed. Cautiously, he says, "Son, about what happened downstairs. Everything you said—"

"Dad, wait," Aiden interrupts, turning to face him but not yet able to meet his eyes. "I'm—really sorry. I completely embarrassed myself, and I was unforgivably rude to you... I usually have better manners than that, I swear."

"Aiden, the fact is that I let you down in the worst way a father can let his son down. I wasn't there for you when you needed me most, and I can't begin to tell you how sorry I am."

"I thought it would feel really great to finally get all of it out, but..." Aiden trails off, worrying his bottom lip between his teeth and scrubbing his hand across the back of his neck. "But things are actually... things are good now, for both of you. Mom has Stephen, you have Fiona, and I feel like I just watched a video of myself as a toddler throwing a tantrum in the middle of a grocery store or something."

"You had every right," George says gently, but Aiden shakes his head.

"No. No, what I said earlier was right. I'm not a kid anymore, so I should stop acting like one."

Aiden knows that his father can't disagree, and he doesn't; silence falls heavily between them like a curtain, tapestry-thick. But he also knows that his father desperately wants to fix what he rent asunder, and Aiden is finally beginning to admit to himself that this is a desire they share.

"Do you miss being home?" George asks. The question throws Aiden off. He considers it for a long moment.

"No. Brunswick... never really felt like home, not even when—when things were good. Before," he says. The words sound stilted and awkward and true.

"Where *does* feel like home?"

"That's what I'm trying to figure out."

"Well, whether you use it or not, you've always got a home here," George says, and Aiden's throat closes. "Do you think we could start fresh?"

Aiden shakes his head, glancing down at the front of his threadbare Bowdoin T-shirt and blinking back the prickle. "No, but—" Aiden stops, looks up to meet George's gaze and says, "I think we can move forward."

George smiles, and his hand lands heavily on Aiden's knee. It's a start.

1,648 *MILES*

DAY TWENTY-TWO: VIRGINIA

"Clouds are coming up on us," Aiden murmurs, eyes trained on his side mirror. "Think we'll outrun 'em?"

Jake glances into the mirror on his side at the dark plumes gaining on the azure stretched out above them and shakes his head. "We might've if you hadn't insisted on using a map instead of the GPS."

"Hey, you were the one who wanted to drive when this was *my* big surprise for *you*," Aiden counters. "At least we're nearly there."

"So what's in Luray, anyway?" Jake asks, taking in the land surrounding the highway that will soon become winter scrub, and the white siding of the farmhouse-style homes beyond it.

"Just keep following the road. And believe me, you're going to love it. Matt and I made Mom and Dad take us, like, once a month. We used to run around the place pretending we were Indiana Jones. Well—Matt was Indiana Jones. I was always his sidekick."

Jake bites the inside of his cheek and controls his expression—Aiden has always been a little touchy about being in his older brother's shadow. Still, Jake knows that despite Matthew's level of self-involvement and his tendency to give Aiden unsolicited advice, he generally means well. "So it's somewhere you can have adventures, then."

"The *best* adventures."

"And Indiana Jones usually ran around in jungles and caves..." Jake trails off, a horrible thought forming from the jumbled mess that took up residence in his mind somewhere in Delaware. "Last time I checked, there were no jungles in Virginia."

"Turn right up here."

"Where—" Jake abruptly falls silent as he pulls the RV to a stop at the red light before the turn. He leans forward over the steering wheel and looks up at the tall green sign topped with something that resembles a stout, misshapen dog bone. The sign's white letters proclaim: *Luray Caverns*. "Ade, seriously?"

Aiden doesn't even seem to be listening; rather, he's grinning out the window like one possessed, giddy with the joy of being somewhere that, Jake realizes, represents only good and happy things. As the light turns green and Jake slowly swings the RV to the right, Aiden bounces in his seat and shoots Jake a radiant smile.

"Does it really feel *that* good to be back?" Jake asks.

"It really does," Aiden says, leaning so far forward over the dashboard that his seat belt locks. "You'll come exploring with me, right?"

"Just so long as I don't have to wear a fedora," Jake answers, hoping against hope that whatever tour they're about to embark upon does not involve episodes of total darkness. "I'm not nearly swarthy enough to rock that look."

Aiden laughs at that and continues smiling as they park and make their way past the tall walls of the Garden Maze and into the visitor's center. Once he has handed over their tickets and signed them in with no small measure of glee—all of which Jake observes with a half-amused, half-trepidatious smile—they're met by a girl who looks no older than a college freshman. She's tiny, five feet tall at most, with mousy brown hair tied back into a ponytail and ice blue eyes set deep in a face full of freckles. Over a plain white button-down tucked into a pair of skinny khakis, she wears a hunter green blazer, its chest pocket embroidered with the words *Luray Caverns* over the tagline, *What will you discover?*

Hopefully, the way out, Jake thinks, *or failing that, the gift shop. I'll buy Aiden something tacky and obnoxious to pay him back for dragging me into the middle of all this nature.*

"Hi, guys! I'm Jen," the guide introduces herself, her ponytail swinging from side to side as she looks between them. She balances her clipboard on her hip to shake each of their hands in turn.

"I'm Aiden, and this is Jake," Aiden says, shooting her a charming smile.

"Happy to have you both," she says brightly. "Have either of you visited us before?"

"He has," Jake says.

"He isn't really much for nature, but I'm hoping to change that," Aiden chimes in, bumping his hip against Jake's.

"Honestly," Jen begins, leaning closer and lowering her voice conspiratorially, "I *hate* nature. But that's the great thing about this experience, because it's more about the history and what *you* take away from it.

"Now, we're pretty quiet around here today, and usually they don't run the tours without at least eight people," she continues. Out of the corner of his eye, Jake sees Aiden's shoulders droop. "But since you guys are the only booking for the next hour or so, I don't see why we can't just go do our thing."

"Great!" Aiden exclaims, and turns a thousand-watt grin on Jake. "What do you think?"

Jake looks at him, taking in the flush of hope in Aiden's dark eyes and the slight twitch in his fingertips as he brings his hands together and clasps them in front of his chest. Already beginning to feel his resolve crumble, Jake glances around the brightly lit and inviting visitor's center. The snapshots of the caverns adorning the walls spark a somewhat foreign sense of intrigue in him.

"All right," he says. "Let's go."

THE CAVERNS ARE MAGNIFICENT. Jake finds himself unexpectedly enthralled in each and every room; and despite Jen and Aiden's repeated attempts to draw him into their chatter, he pays almost no attention to their animated discussion of the history of the place. He's strangely spellbound by its quiet, natural grandeur, and by the time the tour is nearly over, his neck aches from looking up.

"Told you this place was magical," Aiden says, his voice carrying over the harmonies resonating from the Great Stalacpipe Organ. Jake can feel the lower notes reverberating deep within his chest, and he shoots Aiden a genuine, humbled smile.

"You were right," he concedes, quickly adding, "but please don't do the told-you-so dance. We're still in a cave."

"I swear, you guys make one of the cutest couples I've ever seen," Jen says, and Jake turns to her in alarm.

"Oh no, we're not—I mean, we're..." Aiden trails off.

"Yeah, no, we're—we're just friends," Jake agrees. The words taste stale.

"But... crap. I'm sorry," Jen says, glancing down at her clipboard and back up again. "It's just... you guys, with all your sniping at each other, and the—the *looks*, you know, you're like one of those adorable married couples and... and I'm just going to stop talking now."

The organ's music fades for a few moments as the song ends and another begins, and Jake can feel Aiden's eyes on him during the pregnant silence. He doesn't dare look back. Since Rehoboth Beach, they've each retreated to their separate trenches. Whatever lies between them has become a no-man's land, to be traversed carefully—if at all—and with no small measure of trepidation. And most definitely not in a damned cave.

"Only as awkward as we let it be," Jen finally says with a bright smile, and as she inclines her head to lead them on through the next archway, Jake breathes a sigh of relief.

When they're in the final room of the tour, all lingering traces of awkwardness swept away, Aiden turns to Jen and asks, "Do you guys still do the same thing with the lights in here?"

"*How* do you keep remembering this stuff?" Jen asks incredulously, and Aiden shrugs with a grin.

"What thing with the lights?" Jake asks.

"We usually finish out the tour by turning off all the lights and letting people experience true darkness, and what it would have been like for the first people to discover the caves," Jen explains. Jake tenses. "Really get a feel for it, you know? I mean, there's nothing else like it. Usually there are two of us with a group, and one of us will go switch off the lights while the other stays down here, but since there's only one of me, can I trust you guys not to go insane and start creating havoc?"

"Of course," Aiden answers, waving her off.

"Alrighty, then. I'll be back in a couple minutes," Jen says. She turns on her heel, strides toward the exit and calls over her shoulder, "Stay put, guys!"

Jake lets out a nervous chuckle and tries to square his shoulders and hold his head high. It isn't that he's afraid of the dark. On the contrary, he's always found a solitary peace when enshrouded in it. Spending three pitch-black minutes in the middle of a cave, on the other hand...

"Hey. You okay?" Aiden asks, stepping closer and searching Jake's face.

"I'm fine. Forewarned is forearmed, right?" he jokes feebly, and Aiden's brow furrows.

"Are you sure? I can call her back and—"

Darkness falls as sharply and quickly as the blade of a guillotine, and Jake's head snaps upward almost involuntarily; a gasp catches in the back of his throat. He turns his head from side to side, suddenly feeling as if it isn't just the light that's gone, but his sight as well. Never before has he experienced this kind of complete, oppressively encompassing darkness, and after a few seconds it seems to close about him.

"Jake?" Aiden asks. His voice is loud, as if he's mere inches away, but Jake could swear that they were standing farther apart just a moment ago. "Jakey? You okay?"

"Mmhmm," Jake manages, his own voice sounding louder than usual. It's as if the darkness acts as an amplifier, a giant bowl in which every rustle of fabric and distant trickle of water winds him up tighter and tighter. He doesn't even have the deep melodies of the organ to focus on anymore. He wraps his arms around his waist, closing in on himself as even the sound of his own breathing becomes louder and he hears Aiden shift from one foot to the other.

It's cold down in the caves, far colder than the cloudy yet mild day outside; even so, Jake's palms begin to sweat as he thinks about how far underground they are. His breathing becomes shallow, as if oxygen is hard to come by. He feels a pressure in his chest; his heart races. He panics and gasps for air. He presses his palm to the base of his throat to try to counter the sensation of a band squeezing him. It's suffocating; and he can't breathe. He can't—

"Hey, hey," Aiden whispers, taking Jake's hand in the darkness. Jake's heart races even faster. His heartbeat is deafening. Surely Aiden can hear it, hear the effect a mere touch has even when Jake is panicking more than he can process. "It's okay, Jakey. I'm right here, just come toward me, okay?"

Jake follows Aiden's words, shuffles closer as his breathing becomes harsher and harsher. Clear air in his lungs is an almost forgotten sensation; he chases after it, though that seems fruitless. A roaring whoosh tears through his head. He only dimly registers Aiden pulling him closer, flush against his body; his fingers card through Jake's hair. Jake's forehead presses against Aiden's temple.

"Just focus on me, okay? Just focus on me," Aiden whispers as he sways them there. "Breathe, sweetheart. Breathe for me."

Jake closes his eyes and tries to focus on their movement, back and forth, tries to turn it into a dance in his mind, but there is no discernible rhythm and every time he thinks he's found one to count along to, it evades him again and his breathing keeps on stammering, stammering. And just as he's beginning to feel lightheaded, Aiden starts to hum: quietly at first, almost too quiet to hear even in the utter silence of the cave, but the melody forms and grows until Jake recognizes it, until Aiden finds its rhythm and sways them in time.

It's a silly childhood song, one that they used to sing in kindergarten, but it helps. Back and forth, slowly in and slowly out, back and forth, slowly in and slowly out; degree by degree, Jake gets his breathing under control. He comes back to himself, wrapped around Aiden: an entirely different kind of containment, one of safety and care that takes him back to when he was a boy of six and the very first time they watched *The Lion King* together. Jake had had no idea what would happen when the antelope began their stampede, that Mufasa would be killed, and Aiden had held his hand and then all of him, keeping him together just as he is doing now.

Aiden's singing stops short as light floods back into the cave, and for the first time since taking his hand, Jake feels the slightest tremor in Aiden's body. They sway on the spot for one moment more, until Aiden clears his throat and smooths his fingers over Jake's hair. Shakily, Jake exhales the last breath he took, feels it flow warmly between them.

He opens his eyes, still unwilling to move so much as an inch, and wonders if a kiss on the cheek to say thank you would be a step too far into no-man's land.

"Are you okay?" Aiden whispers, and Jake nods, finally shifting his weight back onto his own two feet. The hand Aiden worked into his hair slides down the side of his neck and brushes off his shoulder, taking warmth with it. "Sure?"

When Jake doesn't respond, Aiden ducks to look searchingly into his downcast eyes. The space between them is dense with tension. Aiden unconsciously licks his full lips, and Jake scrabbles for something to say instead of watching the movie reel unfurling in his head: a swell of music, or maybe none at all, lighting at just the right dim and atmospheric level and Jake rocking forward to crush his mouth to Aiden's, fists grasping the front of his leather jacket.

"Do you think *Parks and Rec* was right about cave sex?" he asks, simply blurting the first thing that comes into his head. Immediately, he wants to slap himself across the face.

"I don't know. Do you wanna find out?" Aiden counters, his tone innocent and earnest, yet somehow still loaded.

"Walked right into that one," Jake says, letting out a tremulous chuckle and stepping completely out of Aiden's hold. When he glances up and sees

Jen approaching from around the corner, he says, "Come on, let's go find the gift shop. There's probably an obnoxious T-shirt that I can get for you."

"Virginia is for lovers?" Aiden asks, and Jake smiles thinly.

"Something like that."

1,779 MILES

DAY TWENTY-FOUR: NORTH CAROLINA

More and more, Aiden notices what he has decided to call "Jake-isms," things that haven't registered before. They're little things, really: the way Jake gazes out of the passenger side window and holds the tip of his left thumb between the thumb and forefinger of his right hand, pressing and rolling until the flesh turns white; how he over-stretches and rolls his shoulders when reaching for a glass on the cupboard's top shelf and sighs at how obviously good it feels; the fact that their every conversation these days is a surprise, and never truly finished.

"We really should try and figure out what the point of our documentary is," Jake says, half turning to Aiden as they stroll through the Downtown Market in Asheville. The statement comes out of the blue, but is spoken as if their discussion about this very topic didn't already end over three hours ago. With a sly grin, Jake adds, "You know, other than two cute film grads touring the United States."

"I was kind of hoping that we'd just come across the perfect idea," Aiden replies. "And by 'we' I mean 'you,' since you're the one who's been doing the most filming. Setting up the shots, checking the lighting..."

"It takes time to get the perfect shot, Ade. You know that. And besides, it's all good practice."

"What are you doing with all the footage, anyway?"

"Well, I was thinking about setting up some kind of blog for the trip, just dumping it all there and sending the web address to people back home. What do you think?"

"I think it's a great idea," Aiden says and nudges Jake's shoulder. "Let me know if you need help setting it up."

"Nah, I can do it. You're busy with other stuff anyway," Jake says, nudging him right back. He rolls his eyes at Aiden's blank expression. "I've seen you writing in that notebook of yours. Don't worry! I didn't peek."

Aiden shoots him a grateful smile and sighs in relief. He can't imagine what Jake's reaction would be if he ever read what Aiden has been writing. His insomnia has gotten even worse since Delaware—he tries not to dwell on that particular link too much—so his entries have been longer and more in-depth. Just this morning he sat on the couch, knees drawn up to his chest to try to hide what he was doing, because he couldn't stop writing without finishing his thought. Meanwhile Jake danced around the kitchen as he made breakfast, hips swaying sensuously to the beat of whatever was playing on the radio. The flow of his movements was without discernible end, as if the song was his dance partner, leading and turning and dipping him across the kitchen with such fluid grace that, had he not known otherwise, Aiden could have sworn that Jake had been dancing for years.

Writing it down didn't help this time, he scrawled, his words a hurried mess bordering on the poetry he'd written in high school before discovering a way to set it all to music. *I'm still thinking about Virginia. It sparked off my old sense of adventure, only this time it isn't a* place *that I want to explore... it's the way this man can make one subtle shift in the darkness and have me shivering; he moved and I was gone, wanting to run cartographer's fingers over his shoulder blades, the planes of his chest, and down, down, down. I hope and wonder.*

Aiden's face colors at the memory—it's all very well to write words no one will see, but another to face the object of his inspiration with those words still echoing in his mind. He swallows hard and his eyes land on a stall farther up the way, where a small African woman sits surrounded by wooden tiles and wall hangings. The words still play upon his mind as they draw closer to her, and his mind circles back to the wondering—*always* the wondering; wondering whether it would be weird if things between him and Jake weren't at all awkward; if instead they just fell into one another as if it was something they were always meant for, as if their love was bought and paid for years ago and they were only just beginning to grow into it.

The bright yellow of the woman's clothing is in stark contrast to the muted earth and wood hues surrounding her. Her face is weathered, dark freckles litter her cheeks and crowds of lines at the corners of her wide mouth and deep-set eyes betray decades. Her gaze briefly sweeps across Jake and lands upon Aiden, boring into him with such intensity that he feels as if she can see straight into his heart and pick out the four letters he's sure are forming there.

"What are your names?" she demands, her English heavily accented.

"I'm Aiden, and this is Jake," he says.

"I am Nanyanika. They call me Nan," she says, gesturing around herself and offering her hand to Jake. After he shakes it, she offers it to Aiden and holds on when he tries to let go. "You belong, yes?"

Aiden exchanges a perplexed glance with Jake and repeats, "Belong?"

"You are his," Nan says, looking between them. "He is yours."

"No," Aiden says, shaking his head. "We're not together, we're just friends."

"Hmm. 'Just friends.' I hear this a lot," Nan says, dropping Aiden's hand and reseating herself on her stool. From beneath her simple wooden workstation, covered in a deep green cloth patterned with the same esoteric symbols that surround her, she pulls two small paintbrushes and a pot of what looks like black ink and gestures for them to sit down.

"It's true, you know," Jake says, crossing one long leg over the other and loosening his thin scarf a little. "We've been best friends since we were six."

Nan shakes her head, her shoulders slumping as she says, "They come to me to see their life and never believe. They keep their eyes closed on *purpose,* don't *let* themselves see. They think good means scary. So you have come to me to see your life, yes?"

"Um," Aiden says articulately, and looks at Jake.

"Yes," Jake answers her, his curiosity written on his face.

Aiden has to admit that, though he's never been much for spirituality, he's intrigued.

"Sleeve up, arm out," Nan commands, and Jake quickly complies, stretching his arm palm up across her workstation. She dips one of the paintbrushes into the inkpot, loosely holds Jake's wrist with her free hand and, without ever taking her eyes from Jake's face, begins to paint. "I paint three things; past, present and future. We see what come out after."

Aiden watches in silent amazement; Nan can't see what she's doing, but three symbols quickly take shape in a shock of black against the Jake's pale skin. He swallows; they've often talked about getting tattoos, musing over placement and what they would be, but they've never actually gone ahead and done it. Seeing the marks on Jake's skin brings Aiden a shiver.

"I come from the Ashanti in Ghana, and these symbols are the *adinkra.* Very important to my people and tell us many things," Nan says, finishing the third symbol with a deft flick of her wrist and looking down at her work. She points to the first symbol, closest to Jake's hand, which looks like a ladder. "*Owuo atwedee...* you have death in your past, yes?"

Jake raises his chin and nods almost imperceptibly. Nan gives his wrist a light shake.

"This is why we paint past so close to your hand, so you can let go. You get weak if you hold on for too long," she says, and quickly moves on to the second symbol: two swirls forming a heart. "This is good sign. *Sankofa*; mean you are learning from your past." Of the third, a diamond with an X at its center that forms four more, smaller diamonds, she says, "*Eban*, for your future. For you, this is sign of love and security."

Aiden watches Jake trace the tip of his index finger around the *eban* symbol, and blinks when Jake agrees with Nan's earlier sentiment, murmuring, "They *are* important. I wish they were permanent."

Nan shakes her head and points to the past and present symbols. "Very soon, you let go of this. Present become your past," she says, sliding her fingers toward Jake's palm. "Your future become your present, and you get new future. You move forward, don't get stuck."

Jake nods and, seemingly satisfied, Nan releases his arm and holds out her hand for Aiden's. He hesitates only for a moment before settling his wrist onto her palm. She doesn't start painting straightaway, as she did with Jake; she seems to sift through the innermost workings of his mind until she finds the things she's looking for, whatever they are, and it takes all his willpower not to break the eye contact.

"You are running," Nan says simply, and Aiden finally feels the wet press of ink against his skin. "But not away, and this is most curious thing about you. I think you were running away, but now, no. Now you are running *to*."

Aiden's gaze slides to his periphery but he doesn't dare look at Jake—not now, not when every look is loaded, like a powder keg packed to the brim and just waiting for the slightest spark to ignite it. They carry it between them as if it's a tangible thing—slowly circling a flame—and Aiden is losing purchase all the while.

"This is not usual, not usual," Nan says as she sits back, and Aiden realizes that the soft bristles of her paintbrush have ceased their movements against his skin. He takes in his three symbols: his past could almost be a basic

Celtic knot; his present is something like the letter X, and his future... is the same as Jake's. "I see *mpatapo* for past, which is peacemaking. You stopped fighting. This explain running. For present, you have *fawohodie;* this mean you are free. Yes?"

Aiden nods dumbly, struck by the accuracy of Nan's insights.

"And your future, this not usual at all. This lead you same place as 'just friend,'" she says, her downturned mouth twisting into something that could be a wry smile. "But for you, *eban* is sign of home and love as one."

"Maybe there's some cutie back in Brunswick waiting for you," Jake murmurs, nudging Aiden's shoulder.

Nan shakes her head, gesturing emphatically to Aiden's future symbol. "Home and love, see? They are same thing," she declares. After a pause that feels too awkward, she sighs heavily and stands to reach one of the displays of small wooden tiles that hang around her stall. Both Jake and Aiden stand and watch as Nan retrieves two tiles bearing the *eban* symbol. She holds them between her palms, closes her eyes and says, "But you will *not* see, not yet. You keep your eyes closed and complicate things. So you take these, and work for them."

Jake pulls out his wallet as Aiden takes their tiles, but Nan waves him off. "Come back and see Nan when your future is present," she says, and for a moment that wry smile is back and Aiden can't quite figure out whether she just wants to see them again, or if she wants to be proved correct in her thinly-veiled predictions.

"Thank you," Jake says, and half turns to leave before seeming to think better of it. Instead, he reaches up, unpins the antique brass brooch from his scarf and holds it out to her. "May I?"

Nan nods, her slightly raised eyebrows the only outward sign of her surprise, and Aiden watches as Jake fastens it in place over her heart. He tweaks it until it's straight, and explains, "It's a turtle, for longevity."

"I have lived long time already."

"And I hope you still have a long time left."

"You should keep him," Nan says to Aiden with a significant look.

"Thank you," he says almost distractedly, too many thoughts turning over in his mind to form one coherent string.

"It was lovely to meet you," Jake adds, and Nan inclines her head.

"You both run *to,* see what happens," are her final words before she sits down again and puts away her brushes and ink.

When they are far enough away to be out of earshot, Jake whirls on Aiden with a bewildered look. "That was *insanely* weird, right? It wasn't just me?"

"I don't know. She seemed to have us figured out," Aiden says with a shrug he doesn't quite believe.

"The past and present stuff, maybe," Jake concedes. "But the future stuff... I mean, *you* know I'm not really into relationships, and... and what was all that about you 'running to' something?"

"No idea," Aiden says. He takes a deep breath and tries to shake Nan's words and the weight of her gaze, but he can still feel it, lingering along with the words ringing in his ears. *Now you are running* to. When he looks back, however, all he sees is a soft smile as she runs her fingers around and around the turtle pin. "That was nice. What you did for her, with the brooch."

"She wouldn't let me pay her," Jake says nonchalantly. "Even if she sells it, at least she didn't completely waste her time."

"It was still nice," Aiden says, prodding him in the side until he smiles. The sun finally breaks through the thick bank of cloud that hangs heavily above them, and Aiden raises his hand to shield his eyes. "I'm starving. Wanna check out that café further up?"

"Actually, do you mind if we head back?" Jake asks. "I found a pasta recipe I've been dying to try. Plus, I need to catch up on a few emails, and since the park has Wi-Fi..."

Aiden grins and rolls his eyes fondly. "Lead the way."

2,151 MILES

DAY TWENTY-FIVE: SOUTH CAROLINA

"I won't be long," Jake says, cutting the engine and unclipping his seat belt. "Just wait here for me?"

"Where are we?" Aiden glances through the windshield at the other cars in the parking lot.

"Just something I need to see," Jake mutters. He grabs his phone from the dashboard and repeats, "I won't be long."

"Jake, stop." Aiden reaches across to take his arm. "Why are we here?"

Jake pauses, takes a deep breath and lets it out slowly. Gently, he slips his arm out of Aiden's grasp. Just before he opens the door and hops out of the cab, he says, "This is Mom's alma mater."

He walks quickly up Greene Street, following the directions he pulls up on his phone and hoping that Charlie hasn't chosen today to check their progress on the GPS. It's a beautiful, sunny day, but Jake struggles to feel the warmth beating down upon him as he makes his way closer to the campus proper.

The two events that led to Jake cutting through downtown Columbia instead of heading straight to Sesquicentennial State Park were individually inconsequential, a pair of fleeting reminders of the past he tries not to think too much about, stings to the heart and mind as ultimately temporary as raindrops slowly rolling from roof tiles. Together in quick succession, however, they were another matter entirely.

It began with the Stevie Wonder song, cutting a swath through the radio static as they passed the state line. Stevie's voice was as full of mirth and joy as it was when Jake sat at the kitchen table, still young enough that his feet didn't quite reach the linoleum, watching his parents dance; and later, when he sat with his mom as she laughed with her hands on her heaving belly while Charlie tried to teach their dad proper turnout.

He had reached over to change the station but withdrawn at the last moment, letting in the wistful pain and feeling it instead of pushing it away. His grip on the steering wheel remained tight until his fingers ached.

Then, the first time they had passed a sign for the University of South Carolina bearing the legend, *Go Gamecocks!* Aiden said, "Oh my god. It's too easy, right?"

"Way too easy," Jake replied offhandedly, before doing a double take and craning around as they sped past. Another memory of his mom—shuffling around the house with a cold, the long sleeves of her USC sweatshirt hanging over her hands—rose to the forefront of his mind and left him short of breath. He remembered crawling up onto the couch beside her and tracing the letters on her sweatshirt with the tip of his index finger as a rerun of an old *American Bandstand* episode played in the background; he asked for a story, and she told him about the fountain where she first met his dad.

Dappled sunlight plays across the street, and Jake glances up at the blue sky through the trees and squares his shoulders; he can already hear that very fountain over passing cars and small groups of chattering students. As he leaves the cover of the trees and sunshine breaks over him once more, he wraps his arms around himself and crosses the terrace in long strides.

Standing at the edge of the fountain, he expects to feel a sense of closure or peace. It never comes. He has only memories of stories told to him, not memories of his own. This place means nothing to him anymore, even though one day many years ago it seemed like a magical promised land.

Exhaling deeply, he sits down on the edge of the low wall that borders the fountain and runs the tips of his fingers back and forth through the cool water, trying and failing to keep his mind blank.

"Excuse me," comes a gruff voice from somewhere above him. Shielding his eyes against the sun's glare, Jake sees a man who looks like a professor approaching retirement age. His hair and mustache are light gray fading into white, and he's clad in a tweed jacket one would expect to see on any stereotypical movie professor. With a genial smile that reminds Jake of Grandpa Art, the gentleman gestures to the wall next to him. "Would you mind if I sit?"

"Of course not, please."

"These old legs are certainly not what they used to be," the man says in a mild South Carolina accent as he sits down. He regards Jake with appraising eyes. "You're not a student here, are you?"

"What gave me away?"

"Ah, I'm just good with faces." After a pause, the man holds out his hand. "John Goldman, professor of psychology."

"Jake Valentine, nice to meet you."

"So what are you doing here, Jake? Did you just come for the fountain?"

Jake rubs his palms up and down his thighs, buying himself a moment before he has to answer. It's the same every time—the throb and stutter in his heart, the thickness in his throat—and he swallows convulsively. "My mom went to school here. Until I saw the road signs, I'd forgotten."

"She couldn't bring you herself to show you around?" John asks.

"She died when I was seven," he says, steeling himself to give the same explanation his father recited by rote to every last person who had called their house in the weeks afterward. "She and my dad were on their way back from a Lamaze class one night, and they hit a patch of ice and spun out of control. Dad was fine, just a couple bruises, but there just... wasn't anything they could do for her."

"I'm so very sorry to hear that," John says gravely. "And she was pregnant?"

"With my baby sister. There were... complications, and they couldn't save them both so they tried to save Mom, but... her heart stopped, and they tried to do compressions but she had a—a punctured lung—"

"Jake," John says, his hand a heavy and unexpected comfort on Jake's shoulder.

Jake reaches up to wipe his eyes and finds them dry. He hasn't cried since that night, after the light from the open doorway spilled out around his dad's crumpling silhouette and the world as he knew it ended with only a handful of shattering words. "How could I have forgotten that this is where she went to school, where she met my dad?"

"It's an easy detail to forget, given how young you were when she passed," John says, ducking his head to catch Jake's gaze. "You remember other things instead, I'm sure."

"I try not to." He blurts it before he can even think about it, and at the terrible truth of his own words he feels utterly ashamed—he spends even more time trying not to think about his father. *What does that make me?*

John is silent, and with a huff of grim laughter Jake returns his gaze to the breeze-rippled surface of the water in the fountain, the wobbling outlines of pennies that have been tossed there with wishes to ace a final or get the girl or win the lottery.

After a long pause, John clears his throat and asks, "Jake, if I might ask... how old are you now?"

"I just turned twenty-two."

"Don't you think that's an awfully long time to be carrying this pain around with you?"

"I don't know what else to do with it," Jake says, wondering why it's so easy for him to unburden himself to perfect strangers and so ceaselessly difficult with someone he's known since almost before he can remember. "But I think it's... I've turned into someone I don't want to be."

"Do you have a penny?"

Jake meets John's eyes with a quirked brow and, at his impassive expression, decides to humor him. He reaches into his pocket and draws out a quarter.

"Good, now stand up and face the water," John instructs him brightly, contradicting his earlier words by practically jumping to his feet, and Jake wonders if the man already knew or was able to see something in him as he happened by. When Jake is standing, John gestures to the water. "Make a wish."

"Do I get twenty-five?" he jokes, turning the quarter over and over between his fingers.

"No. But you do get a chance to do something that I think you probably don't do all that often."

"Which is?"

"Put a little faith in something. In yourself."

Jake pauses at that. "Am I really that transparent?"

"More of a mirror, actually," John replies mildly, but there is a sadness in his tone that lends weight to his words. "Whenever you're ready, go ahead."

"What do I wish for?"

"Whatever you most want for yourself."

Jake looks out at the water, at the spray from the three jets set along the center of the fountain and the white wall bordering it, and lets his gaze slide up and away to the benches nestled in the shade of the crepe myrtle trees, whose branches hang heavily under the weight of their pink blossoms. He can almost picture his mother here, the incarnation of her that he never knew—a dress, leggings, slouch socks and Keds—handing off a stack of thick textbooks to his father and smiling, smiling, smiling.

I wish to be what he needs me to be, Jake thinks, suddenly flashing on Aiden, that night in Philadelphia, splayed out underneath him and waiting for a kiss that Jake was unable to give. Aiden would need all of the person he chose to love, and Jake doesn't know how to let someone have all of him when *no one* ever has. With the hope that he will learn, he flips the coin into the water where it disappears with a soft *plink.*

"Now make it come true," John says. He glances down at his watch and turns to face Jake squarely. "I'm afraid I have a class in ten minutes, so I should be on my way."

Jake nods and wraps his arms around himself again, but suddenly feels as if he doesn't need to hold himself together quite so tightly. It's an alien sensation, and he doesn't know how to process it.

"What made you stop and talk to me?" he asks.

John smiles at him and says, "You look like one of my favorite students."

"Well... thank you. For listening," Jake says sincerely, hoping that his sparse words convey so much more.

"Of course. Take care of yourself, Jake," John says.

As John walks away, Jake takes a long last look at the fountain and turns back the way he came. His thoughts fall into quiet reminiscence, and he recalls trips in the car that seemed endless, remembers sitting in the back seat and convincing himself that the car wasn't moving, that the buildings and trees were chasing one another past the windows while Stevie Wonder played quietly and his parents held hands over the center console. As the trees and buildings move slowly past on his way back to the parking lot, he lets himself wonder if they were holding hands that night, if they broke their grasp or held on more tightly when they began to skid.

Crossing the street just past a small Catholic chapel, Jake sees Aiden standing in the shade of a tree at the entrance to the parking lot, his hand raised in a small wave.

Jake smiles and waves back.

When he reaches the RV and pulls himself up through the open side door, Aiden is dropping tea bags into two white mugs. The kettle is switched on, the water bubbling. Jake leans against the doorframe for a moment and just watches, reminding himself of his wish. *I wish to be what he needs me to be.*

"How was it?" Aiden asks, glancing over his shoulder.

"Strange, and... okay," Jake says, pushing himself upright and walking closer, his fingertips trailing along the countertop. "It was okay."

"Sure?"

The kettle boils, and as Aiden reaches for it, Jake impulsively takes his outstretched arm and pulls him into a tight hug, pressing his forehead to Aiden's temple. A moment or two passes before Aiden reaches up to wind his fingers in Jake's hair, just as he did down in the darkness of the cavern in Luray, and as he does so, Jake presses a fleeting kiss to his cheek.

It isn't much, or even close to enough, not yet. But Jake is on his way.

2,323 MILES

Day Twenty-eight: Georgia

Every once in a while, Aiden acutely feels the blessing of having Jake Valentine in his life. This—their second day in what he thought would be Savannah but actually turned out to be Atlanta—is one of those times.

When they left Columbia yesterday, Jake turned out of the Sesquicentennial State Park with a smile the brightness of which Aiden could barely remember him ever sporting before; and when Aiden retrieved the trip folder from the glove compartment to look up their destination zip code for the GPS, Jake's arm shot out and clamped the folder shut, dragging it across to his own lap. He wasn't quick enough, though—Aiden had already seen the booking confirmation for Stone Mountain Park in Atlanta.

"Atlanta?" he asked. "But isn't Savannah right on the way to Florida?"

Jake groaned and shoved the folder back at Aiden. "It was supposed to be a surprise since the dates worked out so well, but you might as well know."

Aiden reopened the folder and flipped straight to the "GA" divider. His eyes went wide when he saw the tickets. "Jake, are you serious? I thought Pride was always in June."

"Most places it is, but Atlanta's so hot in the summer that they have theirs in October. You've never managed to make it to one before, so..."

"Oh my god, *marry me*," Aiden breathed, so excited as he took in the folder's colorful contents that he forgot his words a second later.

And now here he is, still a little headachy from Kiki by the Park last night but loving every single second of his first-ever Pride event. They've been standing on Piedmont Avenue—across the street from The Flying Biscuit Café, where they ate a grotesquely large breakfast—for over three hours already. The crowd, thousands strong, cheers as music blares over a PA system and the first of the floats approaches from the other end of the street, crossing a road that's probably called Peachtree, judging by how many of them there are. He and Jake are shoved up against each other, Aiden behind and slightly to the right with one hand at either side of Jake on the railing. It's an almost a perfect mirror of that magical night in Providence, the memory marred only by his near misstep. He's beginning to think that perhaps now, perhaps soon, it won't be such a misstep after all.

"*This* is what you've been missing out on all these years," Jake tells him. "Do you love it?"

"I love it," Aiden says, and he can't help it; he winds his arm around Jake's waist and rests his forehead on Jake's shoulder. Jake only tenses for a moment before he relaxes into the hold, leans back against Aiden and threads their fingers together across his stomach. Aiden grins into his shoulder, loving this newly affectionate side of his best friend—it's only a few days since Jake visited his mom's old college, but ever since that peck of a kiss in the kitchen, he seems to be making an effort to touch more; a glancing nudge at Aiden's thigh as Jake got up to go to bed after their movie; a brief squeeze of his arm as they waited in line for brunch at Café Strudel; a fleeting brush across his lower back as Jake edged around him in the narrow walkway to take his turn in the RV bathroom.

Aside from this driving Aiden slowly and quietly crazy with desire, a softly tingling buzz in his bloodstream, it makes him feel... special.

The crowd goes wild as Atlanta's police and fire departments proceed by, red and blue lights flashing. Following their progress, Aiden catches the gaze of the tall-dark-and-handsome man next to him, rainbow stripes painted down his neck and arm. The guy gestures at Jake—who is looking the other way, craning his neck to see the floats coming down the street—and gives Aiden a thumbs up and a wink. Aiden can't help but grin even wider.

"Today is perfect," he says into Jake's ear, and resists the urge to nuzzle his neck.

"I knew you'd love it," Jake says, and save for the occasional whoop or cheer as each float goes past, they settle into the comfortable quiet they've always been able to fall into together.

The parade is an hours-long riot of color, sound, light and laughter that holds Aiden's attention rapt. He takes in floats for Bubbles Salon, Chi Chi LaRue and the Swinging Richards. He is awed by the number of families marching under a PFLAG banner and proclaiming their love for their queer children and relatives, and the huge, bright turnout from Atlanta's Gay-Straight Alliance. The longer the parade goes on, the more intoxicated Aiden feels by the very air surrounding them, filled with love and acceptance for everything that they all are. It's one of the headiest feelings he's experienced in a long time.

As the parade begins to draw to a close, a strange hush falls over the crowd farther up the street. Still holding onto Jake, Aiden turns them sideways and leans over the railing to get a better look.

"It's Angel Action, like they did for Matthew Shepard up in Laramie," Jake says, and Aiden realizes what he's looking at: a procession of angels, everyone dressed in flowing white robes and holding boards emblazoned with the names and faces of LGBT teenagers who committed suicide as the result of bullying and victimization.

All at once Aiden's giddiness fades, and sadness and melancholy settle over him like a well-worn jacket. Finding it hard to watch the angels as they pass by, he drops his forehead to rest on Jake's shoulder again and pulls him close.

After a moment, Jake turns to face him. "I know what you're thinking about," he murmurs, his hand a gentle pressure lifting Aiden's chin to meet his gaze. "Don't."

"I should have been there. If we hadn't had that stupid fight—"

"Ade, it was a couple of bruises. Nothing I couldn't handle," Jake says reassuringly, but when Aiden closes his eyes he can still see purple rage blossoming across the freckled skin of Jake's cheek and jaw, the steel in Jake's eyes as he looked at the contents of his rucksack strewn across the dirty floor of their high school locker room. "Besides, you came back for me."

"It still shouldn't have happened," Aiden mutters darkly, shaking his head and looking at his shoes.

"Need I remind you that it got him expelled? At the very least, maybe he thought twice before doing it to somebody else," Jake says. "Will you please look at me?"

Aiden does, and after a pregnant pause, Jake grins and shakes him by the shoulders until he's smiling, too.

"I was *lucky* to have you, Aiden Calloway," Jake says. "Look at all those poor kids who didn't have someone like you, a best friend who wanted to fight their battles for them."

"You're right," Aiden agrees, something settling in the pit of his stomach even as he does so. *There's that word again: friend.* "I was lucky to have you, too."

"I know you were," Jake quips, and turns back around to watch the end of the parade.

Aiden breathes slowly, trying to rid himself of the sense of deflation overtaking him. Watching the passing faces of teenagers who thought they had no one at all, he knows they really are amongst the lucky ones; and only a few hours ago, at the beginning of the parade, Aiden felt extra thankful to be able to call Jake his best friend, too. *Am I really willing to put all of that at risk?*

He wants more; he's had one taste and it isn't nearly enough. But for now, the ball remains firmly in Jake's court. This is why, when Aiden gets into bed tonight and Jake slides his own warm pillow over to Aiden's side of the bed, Aiden won't crowd Jake's body with his own and pepper the skin of his bare shoulder with kisses.

This is why, when Aiden feels Jake pulling away from him to wave at the final group in the parade—scantily-clad men in black booty shorts and thigh-highs, wearing black angel wings and bearing signs offering free hugs—he simply loosens his grip and lets Jake slip from his arms.

"Hey! Hey, over here!" Jake calls out, and one of the angels saunters over. His light brown hair is styled up and away from his face, bringing all the focus to his piercing blue eyes and the sweep of rainbow colors accenting his prominent cheekbones. Inclining his head toward Aiden, Jake tells the angel, "My friend here could use a hug."

"Is that right? Aren't you enjoying the parade, sweetheart?" the angel asks, raking his gaze down Aiden's body.

Heat fills Aiden's cheeks, and he raises his hands a little. "I'm—no, I'm having a fantastic time, I don't need a free hug—"

"How about a free kiss, instead?"

Before Aiden knows what's happening, broad, sun-warmed hands cup the sides of his neck and soft lips alight upon his own. For a handful of moments, he lets himself get lost in the feel of the angel's mouth, lips gently working his own open with increasing pressure until Aiden is kissing him back and almost moaning into the sensation, *finally, finally,* and he can taste cinnamon gum—but Jake hates cinnamon, this isn't right, what is—

Aiden hears Jake clear his throat, and in a blink the kiss is over. As he pulls away, the angel presses a condom into Aiden's slack hand—if that isn't just the tackiest thing ever, he doesn't know what is—and with a suave grin, says, "I'll find you later, tiger."

"Oh my god," Aiden breathes as the angel turns away to rejoin the parade.

"He can't have been *that* good," Jake scoffs, and Aiden almost steps back as he sees that same steel in his eyes. Jake crosses his arms over his chest as he watches the crowd of angels continue down the street; the almost sheer fabric of his white T-shirt stretches over his upper arms, and Aiden swallows.

"No, I mean—" Aiden lowers his voice. "He told me he'll find me later. He's headed for the park. I need a disguise!"

"So you don't—" Jake stops and drops his gaze. Aiden watches as a small smile quirks the corners of his mouth for a passing moment. Then Jake's expression clears, and he looks back up. "I think you'd make a very fetching Batman. They probably have face-painting in the park, actually."

The crowd has begun to filter into the street and march behind the end of the parade toward Piedmont Park for the rest of the day's Pride events. Letting the whim take him, Aiden grabs Jake's hand and links their fingers together. It feels like the Brooklyn Bridge all over again. "You know, if you want to go full Bowie, I won't stand in your way. I know you have an addiction, but it's really kind of adorable."

Jake silently swings their joined hands between them and circles Aiden's palm with his thumb, another one of those new little things he does that makes Aiden feel as if he's been thrown a curveball and doesn't quite know what to do, other than smile at Jake for just a little too long and with a little too much hope.

2,541 MILES

CHAPTER 4

DAY THIRTY-ONE: FLORIDA

"Ugh. Is there no such thing as 'behind closed doors' anymore?"

"What?"

"Come look at this."

From his vantage point in the RV's open doorway, hands wrapped around a mug of hot tea, Jake watches the couple making their way back from the beach. The girl's shoes hang from her fingertips and her long turquoise skirt billows around her, the lower third of it either tie-dyed or soaked with seawater, Jake can't tell. The guy with her stops every few paces to bury his hands in her shoulder-length blonde locks and kiss her as if nobody is watching.

There probably isn't anybody else watching, aside from Jake. And Aiden, of course, when Jake feels the gentle press of Aiden's chest against his shoulder blades; not close enough, but not far enough, either.

"You don't think they're kind of cute?" Aiden asks.

"I think I'm surprised they don't burst into flames, being out in broad daylight and all," Jake says with a sniff, and sips his tea.

Aiden leans against the doorframe and looks at him pointedly, arms crossed over his chest. "So you're telling me that if someone kissed you like that, you'd really give a shit where it happened."

"I can safely say that if someone kissed me like they were trying to eat my face, I'd make for the nearest exit."

"I think you're jealous. The heat is getting to you."

"It's not the heat at all. It's that we had to stop at yet *another* Misery-Mart, this time with homeless people living inside, and also that I'm a great kisser, and watching *that* makes me want to throw up."

"A *great* kisser, huh?" Aiden drawls, and Jake could kick himself. The all-day sunshine and humidity has done little for his mood since they arrived in St. Augustine yesterday, but it has done wonders for Aiden, and currently he seems to be in the mood for teasing. Jake can almost hear the rest of the conversation unfold before they've even had it; the trap is already set. *How does he always manage to get under my skin like this?*

"I've had good feedback," he says as nonchalantly as possible, sipping his tea and glancing back out of the doorway.

"Show me."

"What?!" Jake splutters. He wipes a few stray drops of tea from his chin as he regards Aiden with an incredulous look. "You can't be serious."

"Oh, I'm very serious," Aiden counters, drawing himself up to his full height and dropping his arms to his sides. "Lay one on me."

"If I remember correctly, you've already had one laid on you in the past few days," Jake says hotly, and turns on his heel to take his mug to the sink. He lifts the lid and unceremoniously dumps out the liquid, suddenly not remotely thirsty. He rinses his mug quickly and notes Aiden's silence but chooses not to comment further; it was already a low blow to bring up *that* kiss, since Aiden neither instigated it nor professed to enjoy it, but it's been playing on Jake's mind since Sunday.

Specifically, the way Aiden's eyes fluttered closed after a second, the twitch in his hand as if he wanted to reach up and pull the angel closer, and—what stung the most, a jagged cluster of razorblades at the base of Jake's throat—how the muscles in his jaw clenched and tightened when, just for a moment, he kissed the angel back.

He's been running hot and cold ever since, flirting shamelessly and then keeping his distance so subtly that Jake can't call him out. It's damnably frustrating and a great part of the reason for Jake's sour mood.

"Jake."

Deep breath. "What?"

"I didn't mean to make you uncomfortable."

"You didn't," Jake says, turning and bracing himself on the counter behind him. "And hey, what happens on the road trip stays on the road trip, right?"

"That's what we agreed, yeah," Aiden says.

After a pause, Jake says, "I might go for a walk. Seems a shame to waste such a beautiful night."

"Even with the humidity?" Aiden asks with a nod to Jake's upswept hair, which has begun to droop despite regular reapplications of hairspray.

"Ah, it's done for anyway," Jake says, gathering up the soft blanket draped across the chair behind the cab. Aiden still stands in the open doorway, hands behind his back, and Jake smirks as he approaches him. Wanting to mess with him right back, just a little, he crowds into Aiden's personal space, parts his lips just so and lets his gaze linger on Aiden's mouth the perfect fraction of a minute too long. "I won't be long. Movie when I get back?"

Aiden's lips purse in a smile. Jake is already on the second step when he hears him murmur, "Sure."

Jake makes his way down the beach, bare toes digging into the fine sand, and takes a deep lungful of fresh ocean air. The sun has just dipped below the horizon, and the spill of colors in the sky is fading into a deep cornflower blue. Venus is rising in the west. Despite the humidity, it's the second beautiful night in a row, and he walks until the RV is well out of sight and he is alone on his little stretch of shore.

After spreading out the blanket and sitting down, he pulls his phone from his pocket and turns it over and over in his hands. He needs to talk to someone, to work his way through the mess of muddled feelings before it overwhelms him. April is the only person in his group of friends back home who wouldn't tell him how much she's judging him, but he knows she's about to go onstage somewhere in Brooklyn. And the issues between him and his sister tend to crop up no matter what they talk about; he doesn't have the energy for another argument with her. Yes, the distance is doing them some good, but the water hasn't flowed under the bridge just yet.

The only other person he can think of is Aiden—and therein lies the problem. His thumb swipes back and forth, back and forth across his phone, clearing the screen of apps and then restoring them, until he catches sight of the camera icon. He pauses for a moment before tapping on it and going straight to the video capture option.

Squinting into the harsh glare of the flashlight when he turns his phone around—there's no way it'll pick him up otherwise, so he'll have to live with the dreadful *Blair Witch* effect—he gives the camera a little wave.

"It's October seventeenth, and we're in St. Augustine, heading down to Key West tomorrow," he says. "We had a four hundred-mile drive in from Atlanta on Monday, which was exhausting. Today we checked out some of the local tourist stuff, including this old hotel that has a café in what used to be the deep end of the pool. Then we wound up back here at the beach. We haven't been doing very much, really."

Jake pauses, recalling his conversations with Andrew and Professor Goldman and how easy it was to open up to them as strangers; he pretends that he's talking to them now, and takes a deep breath.

"Aiden's been acting weird. More than usual, I mean. Back at Pride, one of the Free Hugs Angels kissed him, and for a second he looked like he was really into it, which—it hurt. And I wish it didn't. The thing is, and I keep saying this, we've been best friends for so long that... I don't want to risk everything we have, but right now I'm at the point where every time I look at him I want to kiss him, and it should be weird, right? It should be weird to think about him that way; it used to be!

"I don't know what to do," Jake says miserably. Finding himself with no further words, he turns the phone around and ends the recording, blinking as the impression of the flashlight seared behind his eyes fades. "I don't know what to do."

"HAVE YOU EVER NOTICED how phallic Florida looks?" Aiden asks the next day, glancing at the map Jake had printed and stuffed into the folder along with their campground booking.

"Is that all you ever think about?" Jake asks irritably. They've been on the road for the entire day, contending with freeway traffic and passive-aggressive drivers; now it's nearing sunset and he's almost reached the limit of his patience.

"Look at it," Aiden says, waving the map in front of the steering wheel. "No wonder they call it 'America's Wang.' Anyway, you're one to talk."

"As I was *saying*," Jake intones, "everything happens for a reason."

"Come on, Jake. You don't believe in any of that."

"No, you're misunderstanding me," Jake says, frustrated. *Why do we always seem to be on separate pages these days?* "You *know* I don't believe in any of the spiritual stuff, but I do believe that everything happens for a reason. History, simple as that. Z wouldn't have happened without Y, which wouldn't have happened without X, back and back."

"So what you're really saying is that there isn't actually any such thing as history," Aiden says, and Jake nods with a smile.

"Right. Because one way or another, history is always present."

They lapse back into silence as Jake concentrates on navigating narrower streets and then the campground. They park, check in and jump down from the cab with sighs of relief, stretching their cramped joints and muscles. When they turn onto South from Duval Street, Aiden takes Jake's hand and links their fingers together and Jake's pulse skitters.

He knows he's been subdued since last night, lost in his own indecision and unsure of what to do next. He's made peace with the fact that he wants so much more of Aiden than he gets—and took in Philadelphia. What's really getting to him is that although he has recollections of what Aiden feels like, the weight and measure of him, he knows nothing of the taste of Aiden's lips, or the pressure and temperature of his mouth.

He also knows that Aiden has taken note of his shifting mood—it's clear in that same expectant tension Jake has noticed with increasing frequency since Rhode Island. Perhaps even before then, were he to trace it back. *No Z without Y, no Y without X, no X without—*

"Wow," Aiden says.

Before them stands the tall, anchored concrete buoy declaring the ground beneath their feet the southernmost point in the continental United States and Key West "Home of the Sunset." The sky behind it is appropriately smeared with pink and orange and yellow, as the sun lazily descending in a halo of palest blue.

"Take a picture!" Aiden exclaims with all the excitement of a child; and he stands next to the buoy and grins, bracing himself against it with one hand, his left foot crossed over his right. After Jake has captured Aiden's brilliant grin and forwarded the picture to Aiden's mother, he notices a group of four teenagers a short distance down the sidewalk, crowded around a boom box that plays loud pop music. Watching them twirl and offer one another exaggerated bows as one song finishes, Jake smiles, lamenting the loss of his more carefree days.

One of the girls catches his eye as the punchy, melodic intro to Ellie Goulding's "Anything Could Happen" begins to play, and she winks at him and shakes her shoulders back and forth. Jake laughs and shakes his head, gesturing over his shoulder at Aiden because it's easiest. She follows with her eyes, looks Aiden up and down and calls out, "Right on, man."

With a little wave, Jake circles behind the buoy and lets it cast him in shadow, continuing to watch the group dance while Aiden stares out at the ocean. Jake listens to the song, lets its beat and ebb ground him a little. Second only to film, music is his great love, and this song... this song is actually kind of perfect.

Because anything really *could* happen, couldn't it? What if what happened in Philadelphia wasn't a total mistake, but simply the prelude to Jake finally listening to what his instincts have been telling him for weeks? *What if, what if, what if...*

"What are you doing? Come see this!" Aiden calls out.

Jake takes a deep breath and steps out of the shadows. Aiden is silhouetted against the fading sun, the light picking out the auburn in his hair, and as he stretches his arms up over his head, one finger hooked through the woven bracelet he bought earlier, he grins out at the horizon. Jake feels as if he's watching Aiden through brand new eyes; he knows that there is rescue in those arms. Suddenly he wants to fall into them and hold on until he feels safe.

Aiden turns away from the vista, pushes his sunglasses up on top of his head and looks down at Jake, his eyes sparkling with warmth and light. He leans forward and holds out his hand, and he looks... beautiful.

Jake takes Aiden's hand and steps up onto the wall. The building repetition of the lyrics leading to the chorus wraps him up in recklessness and resolve, because this is it, isn't it? This is the real movie moment, to which the rest pale in comparison. Providence was a premature disappointment; the Brooklyn Bridge belonged to two people who never existed; Philadelphia was a rushed and disastrous taste, nothing more. The simple fact is, Jake doesn't want to leave any more missed opportunities in his wake. He wants Aiden, pure and simple.

Every time we came close, every near miss, every mistake I chose not to make has led to this, hasn't it?

No Z without Y.

The music explodes and so does Jake's desire—his stomach leaps as he hooks three fingers into the collar of Aiden's T-shirt and crushes their lips together in a kiss that makes the hairs on the back of his neck stand up.

It only takes a moment before Aiden is kissing back, inhaling sharply through his nose as he presses forward, his hands flying up to frame Jake's face. It is pressure and give in perfect balance, exactly what Jake has been wanting but not letting himself have—until now, the wall of their friendship has stood strong between them, but as Aiden's lips part, the bricks tumble down on top of them both and Jake pulls back.

"Fuck," he whispers, looking away as Aiden's eyes open. "I'm s—"

"Don't you dare," Aiden orders him. He cards his fingers through Jake's hair and yanks him into a messy, hungry kiss that burns in its intensity, teeth catching Jake's bottom lip. Jake scrabbles for purchase, loops his arms around Aiden's neck and pulls him flush against him, and all at once he feels a click, a slot back into place, a page turning.

Aiden breaks the kiss and says, "RV. Now." He takes Jake by the hand, pulls him down from the wall and back onto the street. Jake's heart pounds in his chest as they run hand in hand back to the RV, and he barely keeps pace. Two kisses and he suddenly feels as if he's standing on the edge of the world, the ground beneath his feet tipping, tipping, tipping him over the edge into a giddy sense of oblivion; and with the drama of the moment broken as he hears whoops and catcalls from the group of teenagers, he grins up at the sky.

No sooner is the door to the RV closed behind them than Aiden's mouth is back on his, his tongue tracing the line of Jake's lips before plunging inside. They stumble sideways up the steps, the inside of the RV growing darker in the fading daylight. Aiden pushes Jake up against the bathroom door, links their fingers and presses their hands into the wood at either side of Jake's head.

"This is finally happening," he says, his voice holding a note of desire that Jake has never heard directed at him; it makes him shiver. "No going back?"

"No going back," Jake says, pushing his hips forward into Aiden's and whining in the back of his throat.

"Fuck, okay," Aiden whispers. He presses himself even more tightly against Jake, and both of them moan at the contact and friction. Then Aiden pulls Jake into the bedroom and flicks on the light.

Jake pushes Aiden onto the bed and looks at him, takes in the blush of sun on his skin and the front of his shirt, rumpled where Jake gripped it in his fist. The impatient fire dies but the heat remains, and with his eyes locked on Aiden's, Jake slowly moves onto the bed, his knees at either side of Aiden's hips. He leans forward, traces Aiden's bottom lip with his index finger and bites back a groan when Aiden sucks it into his mouth—exactly what Jake had wanted him to do on that overtired, hazy night in Vermont.

Have we always been waiting for this?

Jake's lips take the place of his finger, and he cups Aiden's jaw to feel the shift and clench he's been picturing since Atlanta. The kiss is slow, and the sounds Aiden makes in the back of his throat hit Jake like pinpricks. He kisses Aiden harder, savoring the taste of his mouth, while Aiden's hands grip and squeeze his sides, moving up and underneath his shirt. Jake gasps into his mouth at the firm, strong touch.

"God, why haven't we always been doing this," he whines, rolling his hips down onto Aiden's and pressing their foreheads together, mingling their breath. Aiden groans low in response. He tugs Jake's shirt up over his head and tosses it, then lets his fingers drift over Jake's nipples and down over his ribcage.

Jake shivers and surges forward to recapture Aiden's lips. He's never kissed *anyone* like this. He's rushed with everyone he's ever been with, even his first, and he feels as if he's learning all over again. Sweet tremors chase one another up and down his spine and tingle all the way up into his lips as Aiden kisses a new life into him.

They undress one another in increments, trading until there is nothing left of them but skin and flesh and Jake's hips working circles into Aiden's. Aiden falls backward on the bed, taking Jake with him; his fingers grip the back of Jake's neck like a lifeline, and every time his eyes open, they stare straight into Jake.

"Ade—shit," Jake manages, the sensation beginning to build in his fingers and toes.

"Come on, Jake," Aiden says, his pace quickening, his cock dragging against Jake's, palms kneading into the flesh of Jake's ass as his back arches off the covers.

"Are you—you close?"

"Fuck—yes, just don't... Jesus, don't stop, I've—I've wanted this..."

"Tell me," Jake pants into the hollow of Aiden's neck, sweat beading at his temples, and he spreads his knees wider, thrusts down harder, chasing and chasing and chasing.

"Couldn't—ah—get Philly off my mind, you... the way you looked, fuck, I—*Jake...*"

Aiden's entire body tenses as he comes, a soundless cry in his slack mouth, and Jake bites down hard on his collarbone as he winds up and up, coiling tightly and then unspooling like thread.

The comedown is a calm Jake has never felt. Aiden's hands find Jake's face to pull him closer and their lazy lips fit together and slide apart. Jake climbs off Aiden carefully, collapses onto his side and pushes his face into the pillow, blood rushing through his head in a buzz that dulls everything else.

He looks at Aiden and finds him smiling.

"Tell me something," Aiden pants, his chest—gloriously, gloriously bare and oh, is Jake going to take his time mapping out every last dip and contour—rapidly rising and falling as he tries to catch his breath. Jake gazes at him through heavy-lidded eyes, props himself up on his elbow and looks at Aiden expectantly. "This *is* just about the sex, right? There isn't anything more to it, anything you wanna tell me?"

Of course there's something more, you idiot, Jake wants to say, but the three seconds he hesitates let that old fear back in, and it's just enough to slot a couple of bricks back into place.

His heart hammering in his chest, he meets Aiden's eyes squarely and forces out the words, "No. What happens on the road trip stays on the road trip."

3,408 MILES

DAY THIRTY-THREE: ALABAMA

Aiden's first time was a mistake.

The guy's name was Tyler Pace, and he was one of Aiden's roommates in London, an intern in the same program. He wore a sort of uniform, T-shirts in muted colors under a boxy black blazer and ratty jeans that would have appalled Jake. He had small black gauges in his ears and his bright red hair was shot through with blond, shaved at the sides and styled on top in a messy approximation of a James Dean pompadour. A pair of thick, over-sized black hipster glasses with red arms obscured his hazel eyes, and there was always a pair of Skullcandy headphones around his neck blaring Irish folk rock.

Tyler appeared, at first, to be a patchwork of personalities all clamoring for dominion over one body; an enigma who kept mostly to himself, and only ever spoke when spoken to or when he had something particularly important to say. All of Aiden's questions went unasked, and he contented himself with being mostly in the dark, even though Tyler's eyes sometimes lingered on him as if waiting for him to speak.

Aiden scoffed every time Lucy told him that Tyler had a crush on him.

The night they slept together, a few days before Christmas break, Tyler knocked on Aiden's bedroom door mere moments after Aiden disconnected from a blazing Skype fight with Jake. The walls in the flat were old and thin, and everyone probably heard Aiden's placatory tone escalate into angry yelling, louder and louder, until he told Jake that he was glad he wasn't coming home for the holidays before hanging up and dropping his head into his hands.

"Everything all right there?" Tyler asked in his lilting Irish accent when Aiden opened the door. Perhaps it was the concern in his voice, perhaps it was the way his eyes kept dropping to Aiden's mouth, or perhaps it was the fact that he was Jake's polar opposite—whatever the reason, Aiden stepped forward and kissed him.

One thing led to another, and even though Tyler was sweet about it afterward, something changed irrevocably between them. Aiden suddenly began to notice the absence of Tyler's lingering looks. Tyler started talking to him more and more, but never about anything real, and Aiden realized that the mystery surrounding Tyler had been nothing more than the unresolved tension between them.

The second time it happened, Aiden was drunk and in pieces over the news of his grandfather's death. On Tyler's part, it was probably no more than a pity fuck. That was what it felt like: quick, messy, a race to the finish.

With Jake, it lasts for hours. They trade a litany of deep kisses, get lost in one another over and over until they are both spent and Aiden falls asleep with Jake's face buried in the hollow of his neck.

When Jake finally pulls up to the campground's dump station in Ozark the next evening, the sun has long since set. They've been on the road from Key West all day, driving in two shifts and stopping for only an hour in Gainesville. They're both exhausted, not only from the miles they've covered, but also from lack of sleep.

Silence envelops them as Jake switches off the engine, stretches his arms up over his head and rolls his wrists, and Aiden has to remind himself that he actually has permission to look now. So he does, taking in the lean lines of Jake's body and picturing the miles of lightly freckled pale skin that he knows lie beneath Jake's shirt and jeans.

If it weren't for his exhaustion, Aiden might feel compelled to do a victory dance or something equally embarrassing.

"What are you looking at?" Jake asks around a yawn that he stifles behind his hand. Everything about him screams tiredness, and Aiden reaches over to let the backs of his fingers drift over Jake's cheek.

"You, sleepyhead," he says, smiling fondly when Jake leans into the touch. "Do you think you'll stay awake long enough to watch our movie?"

"I'll be fine once I've had coffee and stretched. God, I *ache*," Jake says, turning sideways in his seat and dropping his cheek onto the headrest.

"Go stretch. It's my turn to empty the tanks. Don't be too jealous." Jake wrinkles his nose and Aiden asks, "Aren't you jealous at *all?* Hoses, gauges, *and* disposable gloves? I'd be jealous."

"If I had the energy, I would be side-eyeing you so hard right now," Jake murmurs, his eyes drifting closed.

"Hey, come on. Up," Aiden says, taking Jake's hands and pulling him to his feet. Jake sways then finds his equilibrium and offers Aiden a weak but grateful smile. Quite unable to resist the impulse, Aiden rocks forward and catches Jake's sleepy, slackening mouth in a fleeting kiss that is both a request for and promise of more. He knows he's playing a dangerous game, particularly in light of what Jake said last night, but he can't yet find it within himself to care. What lies between them has a time limit on it, now—an expiration dated the day they arrive back in Maine—and until then Aiden is going to take whatever he's given.

Leaving Jake and his soft smile, Aiden grabs his phone from the dashboard and heads outside. A loop of Coldplay's "Clocks" soundtracks his work, reminding him of tenth grade, when he learned the piano riff by heart and played it so often that, one Sunday morning after a sleepover, Jake told him he'd been drumming it in his sleep.

He makes quick work of emptying the tanks: first the black water, then the gray, running water rinses in between. He finishes the job by dumping a liberal amount of treatment into each tank, then rests his palm on the side of the RV for a second and thinks of his grandfather.

"You were so proud of this RV," he says quietly. "Hope I'm taking good enough care of her, Grandpa."

A chill in the air sends him back inside. He leans in the doorway to the bedroom, watching Jake sprawl on the bed. Jake says, "If there was even the slightest spill, you're sleeping on the couch."

Aiden grins and sets his phone down by the bed. The song still plays softly. Jake is stretched out on his stomach, still in his clothes. Half of his face is pushed into the pillow and he regards Aiden through one bleary eye.

"Coffee?" Aiden asks.

"Mm... no. Too comfy."

"Massage?"

"Oh my god. *Please.*"

Chuckling, Aiden climbs onto the bed and straddles Jake's thighs. He blinks and swallows as he gently tugs Jake's shirt from the waistband of his jeans; skin, miles of it, and he's allowed to look and touch and savor every inch.

He rubs his hands together to warm them and starts with Jake's shoulders. Jake melts beneath his ministrations almost immediately and lets out a positively obscene groan of pleasure.

"That feels *amazing,*" he says. Aiden gently begins to work out a knot at the top of Jake's shoulder blade. "If I'd known you were so good with your hands, I might not have taken so long."

"Why *did* you take so long?" Aiden asks, careful to keep his tone light and conversational.

Jake pauses, and then simply says, "It was totally weird. And then it wasn't."

"Obviously I just became too hard to resist," Aiden says. He pushes Jake's arms up so that he will wrap them around his pillow, and then drags the heel of his own hand up the length of Jake's spine, leaving a light flush of red in its wake.

"Well, you—oh, *right there*—you took your time as well."

"What do you mean?"

"WaterFire? The Brooklyn Bridge? Come on, Dan."

The nickname falls from Jake's lips so easily, as if it hasn't been years since he last used it—seven years, in fact; Jake's father had latched onto the nickname as well, and Jake stopped using it after his passing—and Aiden feels a rush of fondness in his chest. He eases off on the pressure for a moment and lets his fingers drift back and forth across the breadth of Jake's shoulders.

"And what about Delaware?" he asks carefully, knowing that he probably isn't going to get any answers, not with this wall already here between them. It's translucent—almost invisible, really—but tangible and daubed with the words, *Boundary line, please do not cross.*

"Can we just... forget Delaware?"

"Sure," Aiden says, though it will take a long time for him to forget that fear he'd seen in Jake's eyes. Changing tack, he leans forward and presses an open-mouthed kiss to Jake's shoulder. Against Jake's skin, he murmurs, "Something else I'm curious about, though."

"Oh?"

"What number am I?"

A beat, a shift, and then, "Thirteen."

"Lucky thirteen," Aiden says with a chuckle. He sits back and presses his thumbs into the base of Jake's neck. "It was what, four before I left? Wow. I really *was* cramping your style."

"No, you—mmm, that's good... it wasn't ever like that, not really," Jake says. "You were enough."

Aiden breathes in slowly, leans his weight onto his thumbs and works out the knots in Jake's muscles. Jake shudders underneath him when the tension finally dissipates, and this time when Aiden leans forward, Jake hooks his arm around Aiden's neck, dragging him down to lie next to him.

"Better?" Aiden asks. Jake turns onto his side, looking remarkably livelier than before, and nods. "Good."

"Was last night a one-time thing?" Jake asks suddenly, and Aiden blinks dumbly at him.

Carefully, he asks, "Do you want it to be?"

"No," Jake says. "Do you?"

"Not when you were the least terrifying you've ever looked, this morning. No fire, pitchforks *or* death."

"Be serious."

"No, Jakey. I don't want it to be a one-time thing."

Flashing a wicked smirk, Jake pulls himself on top of Aiden and places his hands on either side of his pillow. A glint of mischief in his eyes, he leans down to murmur against Aiden's lips, "So what do you propose we do about that?"

Aiden surges upward to drag Jake into a deep kiss, shivering as Jake cups his jaw and lets out a breathy little hum. Without pulling away, he blindly reaches out to switch off the song he still has playing on a loop—he doesn't want to hear it anymore. He just wants Jake.

4,171 MILES

DAY THIRTY-FIVE: MISSISSIPPI

"...Heading out west, you'll find Denver and Phoenix—"

"Aiden," Jake whines, cracking an eye and searching for Aiden's face in the dim light.

"North to Billings, you might see Lansing, too," Aiden continues, his voice coming softly from somewhere behind Jake. Limbs heavy, with what feels like Herculean effort, Jake manages to prop himself up enough to turn his head to face the other way, where Aiden is stretched out next to him on top of the covers. A wide smile stretches his full lips; Aiden links their hands, singing, "And don't forget about the south, the joy of Clarksdale—"

"It's Jackson, not Clarksdale," Jake corrects him, voice raspy and still thick with sleep.

"I know. But we're *in* Clarksdale, now," Aiden says.

"We are? You drove the rest of the way?" Jake asks, stretching. Aiden shrugs. "What time is it?"

"Almost midnight," Aiden says, and unlinks their hands to trace a fingertip along the line of Jake's brow. "How's your head?"

"Better. Remind me not to watch movies in the dark," Jake answers, and buries his face in his pillow to stifle another yawn. He shivers pleasantly when Aiden's hand drops to his neck, a sensation that he steels himself against chasing; it's late, and they have plans.

"I've never noticed just how many freckles you have," Aiden says absently, dotting them with his fingers, and Jake chuckles as he turns onto his side and tucks his arm under his head.

"Remember that time you stole your mom's eyebrow pencil and drew them all over your face because you wanted us to be twins?"

"God, don't remind me. I looked like I had a rash."

"And then she went *white* when she saw you and started chasing you around with the thermometer," Jake says, shaking with laughter. "I haven't thought about that in *forever.*"

"Thank heaven for small mercies. You used to give me hell about it," Aiden says. "Anyway, Sleeping Beauty, time to get up. We don't wanna be late."

As Aiden starts to move away, Jake catches his hand and pulls him close to press their lips together in an impulsive, sweet kiss that feels somehow timeless, as if he's known how Aiden kisses for far longer than three days.

Has it really only been three days?

Aiden sighs into the kiss, and a tension Jake didn't even know was there drains from his muscles. Just before he climbs off the bed, he whispers, "Later."

Jake rolls onto his back and lies there for a moment, listening to the sounds of Aiden moving around the RV. Music is playing, something with a dark, catchy, synthesized riff that Jake recognizes from the playlist Aiden brought back from London, and he almost starts to hum along until he catches himself. Shaking his head, he throws off the covers and walks around the bed to the small, mirrored closets set along the back wall of the bedroom. Out of the closet on the far left, he pulls a simple white T-shirt and a thick red and black plaid jacket. With a rueful smile at his own reflection, he plucks once at the front of his threadbare shirt—the one Aiden bought him for his twentieth birthday, charcoal black and bearing the slogan *Don't need a permit for these guns,* with arrows pointing left and right—and pulls it over his head.

He catches Aiden watching him in the mirror, calls out, "Later, Casanova," and carries on dressing himself, trying to put all thoughts of "later" out of his mind.

Sex with Aiden is... Well, it's *sex* with *Aiden.* On the surface, at least—and that's where Jake wants to keep it: nothing deeper, no hidden meaning underscoring every word and look and movement and absolutely no mentioning just how dangerous it is to do what they're doing. He doesn't want to examine too deeply, for instance, the pleasant buzz that pools in his limbs whenever he catches Aiden looking at him as if he hung the moon and hand-dotted the sky with stars. That verges way too closely on something he doesn't want to be, something he's never been to anyone. He's the player, the quick fuck, the sure thing, and he likes it that way.

In his second year of college, he tried the whole relationship thing with a guy called Max whom he pursued for a while—and who *insisted* on dates first. Jake managed to stick it out for eleven months, having fallen hard and fast into something that was like love but which he never wanted to give himself over to fully. It would have been easy, but it would also have felt a little like dying; there was love from Max, but too much, like being smothered instead of wrapped up.

And then, after a week of fighting about Jake's numerous shortcomings, Max decided to show Jake just how well he was meeting expectations. Jake showed up at Max's apartment with his favorite white tulips and a promise to do better on his tongue only to find that Max had already found someone else.

The next day, Aiden received the email calling him to London for his internship, and Jake learned once and for all what he was really worth.

He wasn't so vain that he thought Aiden's leaving had anything to do with him, of course, but it seemed so very, very easy for Aiden to leave him behind—both on the day he left and during the course of their year apart.

Before that year, Jake took Aiden for granted. He knows it, and so does Aiden. Jake has always been content enough to spend time alone—he needs it more than anything, at times—but the memory of the crushing loneliness he felt with Aiden so far away keeps him grounded, and grateful to have him back. Jake has to hold onto their friendship at all costs, and push everything else into the corner of his mind where he keeps all the things he never wants to think about.

"Jake, are you—? Whoa. You look nothing like yourself," Aiden says as he comes back into the bedroom, cutting short Jake's melancholic reminiscences.

"That's the point," he replies shortly, appraising his appearance in the mirror before turning to Aiden. "We're in the South, after all."

"Yeah, but—" Aiden starts, but Jake cuts him off with a swift kiss.

"Are you gonna serenade me?" he asks, gesturing to the guitar slung across Aiden's back.

"Wouldn't dream of it," Aiden says. "Come on."

They're parked just a short walk from the crossroads, but with the light chill riding the night breeze, Jake is grateful for his thick jacket.

"So what does 'Jack Jones' mean?" he asks after a minute or so.

"Huh?"

"It was one of the lyrics in that song you were listening to."

"Oh! Uh... it's Cockney rhyming slang for 'on my own,'" Aiden explains after a moment. "It's this sort of dialect, I guess, in London. But instead of making up new words for things, they just used other words instead. Like, instead of a cup of tea, they'd ask for a cup of 'Rosie Lee.'"

"That seems kind of... ridiculous."

"It is! God, I had the worst time trying to understand Tom when I first got over there."

"Which one is Tom, again?"

"The one who wants to be a music supervisor."

"With the double-jointed thumbs?" Jake asks, trying to sort the faceless names. He heard so many stories about Aiden's friends from London over the summer that it was like being there and yet not, as though he knows them but never will—not until they each rise to the top of their respective fields, like everyone else who studies under Serafino.

"No, that's Steve. He's also the one who turned me on to that song."

"Cinematographer, right?"

"Yep. He's got nothing on you, though."

Jake smiles down at his Chucks for a moment, letting the good feeling overtake his frustration surrounding 'the whole London thing,' as he refers to it—it still stings, even now—and capitalizes on the opportunity to change the subject. "As much as I love film, it's kind of nice *not* to have to talk about it constantly. You know? Not having to dissect and deconstruct every single little detail."

"Even though that's exactly what we've done with every movie so far."

"But we don't *have* to. We don't have term papers or projects riding on it anymore."

"It's just easy, right? Going at our own pace."

"Another reason I'm happy we're doing this."

"But the main reason's the sex, right?" Aiden asks, leaning over conspiratorially.

Jake smiles and ducks his head. A curious sense of modesty has been settling over him since Key West. "Of course."

"Look, there it is!" Aiden says, pointing ahead to a fairly nondescript triangular traffic island at the intersection of Highways 61 and 49. Out of a clump of trees rises a large sign: an image of three guitars, their color drained under the orange of the streetlamps, above the legend *The Crossroads*. There are no cars on the roads, and save for the wind, it is silent.

"It's like we're the only two people in the world," Jake thinks aloud.

Aiden gives him that look again, the one that electrifies Jake's very blood, and pulls him across the street to stand beneath the sign. "So what would it take for you to make a deal with the devil?"

You, Jake thinks, and mentally shakes himself. *Get it together, idiot.* "Right now? Probably taking a bath in a real bathtub. What about you?"

Without missing a beat, Aiden answers, "A box of Double Dip Crunch."

"Really? I never tried it," Jake says.

"It was only the greatest cereal the world has ever known," Aiden says, and sighs heavily. "They had something similar in London, but it wasn't the same."

"Did you feel more at home there than you do here?" Jake asks, watching the way Aiden rubs his thumb along his forefinger. It's something he only does when talking about London, something that gives him a distinctly dichotomous air, as if there are two separate versions of him: the one whose heart belongs to London, and the one whose heart belongs to this nomadic life and the search for home.

"I haven't ever really felt at home anywhere," Aiden says. "But I feel more at home this side of the ocean."

Jake smiles wanly and buries his hands in his pockets with a shiver. "I believe you owe me a serenade, good sir."

"And I believe I told *you* I wouldn't dream of it," Aiden replies, but he's already swinging his guitar around and flexing his fingers. "How about some blues, since we're here?"

"I don't know; wouldn't that be bad luck? It's a good thing we're not here on Halloween, with all the spirits walking the earth," Jake says, casting an exaggeratedly spooked glance around.

Aiden simply smiles, pulls a guitar pick from his pocket, and begins to play Robert Johnson's "Ramblin' on My Mind." He seems to settle into the song's unusual rhythm almost effortlessly, and all at once, Jake can see the change that has taken place in him. It's subtle; something in the way he's held himself just a little taller these past couple of days. *Like he used to,* Jake thinks. There was so much tension in his stance when Aiden performed with The Cogs at The Cannery that he almost leaned forward over the edge of the stage; it was as though he was still trying to convince Jake to go, even though he'd long since agreed. Now, Aiden's chin is tipped up, his shoulders are down and that old shine is back in his eyes. He's just Aiden again.

As he sings, he circles Jake beneath a tree, pushing him against it; despite Jake's small height advantage, Aiden seems disarmingly tall. Below the dark cover of the leaves, his eyes are nothing more than dark smudges, and yet Jake can feel them locked on his own. Aiden begins to strum more softly, and his voice drops to little more than a whisper.

A few seconds after Jake's back hits the trunk of the tree, Aiden winds up the song and its last notes fade into the charged air between them. He's breathing heavily, matching Jake exhalation for exhalation, and Jake reaches forward to gently push the guitar out of his hands. As easily as if they've been doing it for years, Aiden hooks his arms around Jake's waist beneath the flannel of his jacket, and his cool hands find their way to the skin at the small of his back.

"How's that for a serenade?"

Jake's huff of laughter is far shakier than he'd like. "I don't think you can serenade someone with the blues unless you're Eric Clapton."

Aiden inches closer and rocks forward to whisper into Jake's ear, "I'll sing you a love song if that's what you really want."

Caught between a spike of fear and wide-eyed eagerness, Jake forces a grin and asks, "And what would the Cockney rhyming slang for that be? 'Rama lama ding dong' or something?"

Aiden pulls back. His expression deadly serious, he says, "'Turtle dove ding dong,' actually."

The tension breaks with an almost audible *snap* and Jake's loud laugh rings through the empty roads surrounding them. "Ridiculous," he says, and tips up Aiden's chin to kiss him. Blistering heat seeps through Jake's clothes, skin, flesh and muscle, all the way down to his bones.

4,590 MILES

DAY THIRTY-SIX: TENNESSEE

"You've reached Alice Cooke. I'm currently unavailable, so please leave your name and number, and I'll return your call as soon as possible."

"Hey Mom, it's me—"

"Sweetheart?"

Aiden smiles, sinks back into the couch and watches the world go by through the window opposite him. "Hi, Mom," he says.

"Well, if it isn't the prodigal son," she says, and Aiden grins even wider. It's been a week or so since they last spoke; any longer and she would have put out an AMBER Alert.

"How are you?" he asks.

"Happy to hear from you, honey."

"And Stephen?"

"You know your stepdad, always working," she says, and Aiden can almost picture her waving a dismissive hand. "But he never misses dinner, and I always have flowers."

"Glad to hear standards aren't slipping just 'cause I'm gone."

"Don't you worry, honey. He's still terrified of you," she says, her voice dripping with exaggerated reassurance, and Aiden suddenly feels a pang of longing to stand with her at the kitchen island, chopping vegetables and talking about hurricanes. "And you? How are you and Jake doing?"

"We're fine," he says. "Hey, am I catching you at a bad time?"

"Not at all! No, I'm just finishing up a few reports, so I've been letting my calls go to voicemail."

"Any big storms heading in?"

"Sunny skies here, but there's something forming out in the Caribbean that we think might get upgraded to a tropical storm soon," Alice says, a note of barely masked excitement in her voice. Aiden knows very few people who love their job as much as his meteorologist mother does. Ever since she completed her training as a SKYWARN severe weather spotter, she's gone in to work each morning with a brightness about her she hasn't had in years.

"Yeah? Where's it headed?"

"We don't know just yet; we're waiting for the NHC to confirm, but we should have a report by five. Anyway, enough about the *weather*! Where are you boys?"

"Mom, we're on the way..." Aiden begins, pausing for effect, "to Graceland."

"Graceland," Alice breathes. "Oh, honey... will you take lots of pictures for me?"

"Of course. I know how you love Elvis," Aiden says fondly. "I'll get you something from the gift shop and send it home next time we stop at a post office."

"You're a good boy. I've loved getting your postcards so much."

"I try."

"So what have you been up to this week? Anything exciting?"

Aiden bites his lip, wondering how much to tell her. For years, she's been hoping that he and Jake would "end this silly 'just friends' charade," but despite the many times they've had sex by now, they aren't boyfriends.

"Honey?"

"I'm here, sorry," he says, shooting a glance toward the cab. He stands up from the couch and takes the phone into the bedroom, slides the door mostly closed behind and sits down heavily on the bed. "Mom, Jake and I... we're, um..."

There's a long pause on the line, and then, "Are you boys being safe?"

"Mom!" Aiden yelps indignantly, his face growing hot.

"Oh hush, honey. I have a right to ask," Alice says.

"Yes, Mom, we're being safe," Aiden grumbles.

"Good. Now tell me *everything!* I've been waiting *years* for you two to get your acts together!"

"Mom, we're not... *together,* we're just..." Aiden trails off and swallows, hard. He clears his throat and, feeling as if he's telling a bald-faced lie, says succinctly, "We're just seeing how things go."

"I see. Well... if you're happy for you, I'm happy for you," she says, her words stilted but reassuringly warm. "Just be good to each other, you hear me? I've seen you two apart and it's not pretty."

"Oh my god, please don't be talking about the fishing trip," he says. "I was *seven,* Mom."

"No, I just mean that I've seen it from both sides, and... it may not be entirely healthy, but being apart isn't good for either of you, and I'd hate to see you get your hearts broken if this isn't what you both want."

"What do you mean, you've seen it from both sides?"

"While you were in London," Alice says, as if it's the most obvious thing in the world. "We had Jake and Charlie over for dinner every Saturday night. He just looked so sad, honey, especially when you weren't able to make it home for Christmas. After that... most weeks he'd go up to your room after dinner and I'd hear him listening to that song you love—the one from that Zooey Deschanel movie."

"'Sweet Disposition?'" Aiden asks, swallowing hard against the sudden fracture in his mind. He looks at the mostly closed bedroom door, a single beam of light peeking through from the living area, and remembers lying on his single bed on Christmas Eve last year, listening to "When I Fall In Love" on a loop for two hours. Jake will never admit to a soul that it's his favorite song, but Aiden knows better—if only because Jake turns it up every time they play it on Brunswick's oldies station. "I, um... I didn't know about that."

"Well, of course you didn't, honey. Jake wouldn't want to upset you, and I'm sure he knew you were missing him just as much," Alice says. "But that's why I'm telling you. I just want you to be happy."

"I'm trying," Aiden replies. Quiet suddenly falls around him, and he clears his throat again. "Mom, I think we're here so I'd better get going. We've got tickets for the tour and all, so..."

"Don't forget about those pictures," she reminds him.

"I won't. Love you."

"I love you too, honey."

Aiden hangs up, feeling miserable, confused and peculiarly buoyant by turns. As he emerges from the bedroom, he catches sight of Jake standing in the cab, leafing through the folder from the glove compartment and extracting printouts for their booking with the Memphis-Graceland RV park and the tour of Graceland. His look is subdued again: straight-leg, vintage wash jeans and a nondescript white T-shirt under a black military jacket with small epaulettes on the shoulders. When he turns around, Aiden sees that he's added a small pin above his chest pocket: the American flag.

"Aren't you laying it on a little thick?" he asks.

"We'd be stupid not to take precautions," Jake says with a shrug, neatly folding the sheets of paper in his hand as he comes closer. His eyes drop to the front of Aiden's slim-fit black button-down. "I like this shirt on you. I don't think I've seen it before."

"I got in London," Aiden says without thinking, and his stomach tightens as Jake's eyes cloud for a moment and the shadow of a frown whispers across his features before it is swallowed by a tight smile. He wants to make that smile stretch from ear to ear, make Jake grin and laugh and be goofy and dumb, like he used to on the first day of every summer break when they went to the Brunswick Diner to split an ice cream sundae for breakfast. He steps forward and cups Jake's face in his hands, watches as Jake's eyes slip closed as if he knows exactly what's coming, and kisses him firmly on the mouth. It still makes Aiden feel as if he's tilting sideways, the feeling of Jake's soft lips against his own, the way Jake yields and returns the pressure in equal measure; and for a moment he revels in it.

"What was that for?" Jake asks breathlessly when Aiden pulls back, dropping his hands to his sides.

"I just... wanted to kiss you."

"Any particular reason?"

"That was Mom on the phone before," Aiden says. "She told me you used to go over for dinner sometimes, while I was away."

Jake's features harden and Aiden's stomach drops; the last time he saw that look on Jake's face was over Skype, when Aiden told him he wasn't coming back for Christmas.

"What else did she say?" Jake asks, his tone measured and so tightly controlled that Aiden knows it would be a mistake to say more. Instead, he takes Jake's hand and tries to link their fingers, but Jake gently pulls out of his grasp. "What else did she say, Aiden?"

"Nothing," Aiden lies. "She just told me about the dinners. Jake, I'm—"

"Let's not talk about it."

"Jake, come on, I—"

"No, Aiden!" Jake yells, rounding on him with fire in his eyes. Aiden takes half a step back, hands raised. "Last year was one of the worst years of my life, and I don't want to talk about it with *anyone,* least of all you!"

"Well, I think we *should* talk about it," Aiden says firmly.

"Why?" Jake asks, spreading his arms wide and letting out a laugh that sounds half-hysterical. "Why, so I can tell you about all the nights I spent waiting by my phone for a call or an email that never came? So I can tell you about going over to your house and up to your room to listen to your favorite song like I was a fucking dog pining for its master? So I can tell you about how much I *hate* myself because I can't listen to you talking about London or your internship without hating *you* a little bit, too?"

Aiden's tentative, newfound sense of bravado is suddenly gone, broken by the dawning realization of what he put Jake through by not being there for him. At the time, Aiden had told himself that it was probably better for Jake not to hear about all of the amazing things he was doing and learning, considering that Jake had applied for the same internship—conveniently forgetting, of course, that Jake would have his own stories to share.

"You hate me?" he whispers, eyes trained on the stupid flag pin.

Jake sighs heavily and his shoulders drop. He wraps his arms around his middle and says, "Dan, of course I don't hate you. I just hate what last year did to me, what it turned me into."

"What is that supposed to mean?"

"Look, let's just..." Jake shakes his head and ducks to look into Aiden's eyes with what appears to be an attempt at a reassuring smile. "Let's just go. We're almost late for our slot. Okay?"

He rubs both hands up and down Aiden's arms, and Aiden returns his smile as best he can while believing he's caused an irreparable rift in their friendship.

What if that's what this is? He thinks as he follows Jake out of the RV. *What if I caused this chasm to form between us, and the only way for us to fill it now is with sex?*

What if this breaks us both?

Although Aiden manages to remember to take plenty of pictures, the tour almost completely passes him by. While Jake looks fully engaged by the tour guide, following everything she says with the kind of rapt attention Aiden only ever saw him display in their Golden Age of Hollywood lectures, the musty smell of the house is too close to the scent of the hallway of his building in London, and try as he might, Aiden can't put any of it from his mind.

They progress through the tour quickly. Aiden barely takes in the grand mirrored staircase in the foyer, the clean, crisp white living room with its fifteen-foot couch, the dark wood and light countertops of the kitchen or the royal blue accents of the dining room. The billiard room, its walls covered in patterned fabric, only draws his full attention when it elicits a small gasp from Jake and excited whispers from the other members of their group. Upstairs in the jungle room, Jake leans over to murmur something about how Elvis had hotel rooms remodeled to look more like home while he was on the road. Aiden only nods, not trusting himself to open his mouth lest a litany of apologies fall from it; they are far too little, far too late.

He and Jake never apologize to one another. Rather than say, "I'm sorry," Jake drove to Yarmouth to get Aiden a loaf of his favorite sourdough from Rosemont Market to make up for the one he ate when he was high. Rather than say, "I'm sorry," Aiden stayed up all night to help Jake rewrite a paper, the only copy of which had literally been eaten by Stephen's dog. Rather than say, "I'm sorry," both of them arrived at their dorm room at the same time, carrying DVDs and bottles of Cuervo, and burst into laughter that swept away any lingering vestige of their disagreement about the cleaning schedule.

Once the tour is over, the glitz and shine of the vast array of posthumous awards in the racquetball building already fading from Aiden's mind, the tour guide leaves the group in the Meditation Garden behind the main house, where they quietly pay their respects at the graves of Elvis and his closest family members.

He and Jake make a slow circuit of the garden's small pool, watching the clear blue water and listening to the steady splash of the fountains. By the time they circle back around to stand at the foot of Elvis's headstone, the rest of the group has moved off.

Jake stands with his arms crossed over his chest as he regards the smooth, dark stone and the tributes of flowers, flags and stuffed animals. As Aiden looks on, Jake removes the flag pin from the front of his jacket and places it on the corner of the marble. He straightens up and sighs.

Aiden glances around surreptitiously, checking to see that no one is in immediate earshot, and buries his hands in his pockets. He rocks back and forth on his feet a little to the rhythm he silently counts off, and when he hums the first line of "Always On My Mind," it's barely audible to his own ears. His voice grows louder as he settles into the tune that has always seemed to him as if Elvis somehow turned a physical ache into music. He keeps his gaze trained on the water beyond the headstone, and in his peripheral vision he sees Jake freeze. He wonders if Jake is thinking of all those times they apologized but didn't, those times they showed it instead of saying it.

At the chorus, Aiden turns to look at Jake, and his voice wavers a little at the shock, bewilderment and turmoil in Jake's eyes, a storm of deep green. Aiden pulls his hand from his pocket and reaches out to brush his knuckles against Jake's hip.

"I was?" Jake asks thickly.

"Of *course* you were," Aiden says. And then, because it feels important to say the actual words in a way he never has before, "I'm so sorry."

Jake bites his lip. Then, faster than Aiden can register the movement, he throws his arms around Aiden's neck and whispers into his skin. "Thank you."

"I told you," Aiden says quietly, wrapping his arms tightly around Jake's waist.

"Told me what?"

"That I'd sing you a love song if you wanted me to."

Jake sighs and shakes his head, murmurs, "Don't ruin it, Dan," and all at once, Aiden is harshly reminded of their agreement.

What happens on the road trip stays on the road trip.

Just then, he catches sight of a heavyset, middle-aged man approaching the headstones and regarding their embrace through dangerously narrowed eyes. Reminded of exactly where they are and how careful they have to be, Aiden thinks quickly. He gestures to the man in his arms and, with an exaggerated eye-roll, explains, "He's a *big* fan."

The man quickly averts his gaze and nods abruptly. Jake steps back; he does not need to see for himself to whom Aiden is speaking. He clears his throat and makes a show of wiping his dry eyes, biting his lip against the grin Aiden knows must be threatening to break free. It makes him feel somehow lighter, as if things are back to normal... as if he can do this.

"Come on," Jake murmurs in a low voice, inclining his head toward the house.

"Gift shop?" Aiden asks knowingly.

"I'm sure it's all gold and sparkly, and so tacky-fabulous that we'll spend hours there."

Aiden chuckles, motions for Jake to lead the way and says, "Let's go."

4,661 MILES

DAY THIRTY-NINE: KENTUCKY

"Holy *hell*," Jake pants, collapsing against the pillows with a breathless laugh. The back of his hand drifts over the expanse of Aiden's chest and keeps slow time with the mellow song playing in the background. Up until five seconds ago, he didn't notice there was music playing. "Goddamn your no smoking in the RV rule, seriously."

Aiden hums under his breath. His eyes slip closed as he says, "Don't say anything. Just bask."

Smiling lazily, Jake lets his gaze drift toward the ceiling and concentrates on getting his labored breathing under control. It feels like the only thing he *can* control these days; but the curious thing is, that doesn't bother him as much as he would have expected.

The moment he decided to give himself over to Aiden back in Memphis, standing at Elvis's grave of all places, things began to fall into place. He has already noticed how free they have become with one another.

Like we used to be, he thinks, *only now, we're more. And if we can't be everything, at least we're more.*

"I believe, Mr. Valentine, that you promised to show me a good time tonight," Aiden finally says, his words punctuated by a stretch of his arms over his head, a motion Jake follows with tired eyes.

"Forgive me, Mr. Calloway, but if what just happened isn't a good time," Jake says, shifting closer and capturing Aiden's mouth in a firm kiss, "then I don't know what is."

"Come on, Jake. You know exactly what I'm talking about," Aiden says, eyes shining even in the dim evening light.

"Hmm. Nope, can't say that I do," Jake replies, unable to hold back the grin creeping along the curve of his mouth.

"I have ways and means of making you talk, you know," Aiden says slowly, and before Jake has the chance to put up a fight, Aiden rolls them over so that he straddles Jake's hips. The thin sheet covering them slips away as Aiden leans forward and takes Jake's wrists in his hands, stretching Jake's arms above his head and holding them there. Their faces are mere inches apart and Aiden simply stays there, his warm breath fanning over Jake's slightly parted lips.

Jake cranes upward to kiss him and Aiden pulls away, eyes still locked on Jake's, stirring the puddle of fiery want in Jake's belly again. He lets out something between a whimper and a groan.

"Okay, fine, you win," he acquiesces, and when Aiden does nothing more than blink down at him, he wriggles a little in his grasp. "What, do you want it in writing?"

"No, I just didn't think you'd cave so soon. I had a strategy," Aiden says, and loosens his grip.

"Oh, a *strategy*," Jake repeats, sitting up as Aiden climbs off him. "And what did this *strategy* involve?"

"Tickling you until you begged for mercy."

"You wouldn't dare."

"Wouldn't I?" Aiden levels him with a fervent look.

Jake sighs in defeat. He sits up and swings his legs off the mattress, bends down in search of his underwear and asks, "So what kind of good time are you looking for?"

It is quiet for a moment, and then the mattress dips behind him and he feels Aiden's bare chest press against his back and strong arms wrap around his shoulders. Aiden presses a kiss just behind his ear and announces, "You're taking me dancing."

"I am, huh?" Jake asks, and lets his eyes slip closed as he leans back into the embrace.

"Yep. Bar Complex. It's downtown," Aiden says.

Abruptly, the warmth of his body is gone as he clambers off the bed and walks to the closets. Jake tilts his head and watches as Aiden pulls out a fresh pair of underwear, feeling voyeuristic but not troubled by it as he would have been—and, admittedly, frequently was—at the beginning of the trip. Now, he enjoys the view, takes him in with appraising eyes: Aiden is as willowy as ever, but toned, and he holds himself differently, chin parallel to the ground and back straight. In this regard, Jake can't hate London quite so much; Aiden struggled with body and confidence issues throughout high school and even college, and the fact that he came back to Jake as he is now makes Jake feel simultaneously proud of the man Aiden has grown into and a little bitter that he couldn't watch him blossom.

Aiden catches him looking and shakes his ass from side to side. Jake laughs and finally pulls himself together enough to join him, bumping Aiden's bare hip with his own. He separates himself from Aiden by opening one of the mirrored closet doors and beginning to pull outfit options, and behind the safe barrier of wood and glass, he lets his urges take over and mouths the words to the chorus of the song still playing by their messy, rumpled bed.

By THE TIME THEY GET to Bar Complex, the dance floor is already heaving with people. Jake takes Aiden by the hand and leads him through the crowd; his pace matches the heavy, pulsing beat of the music. The song is winding up as he finds a spot and turns to Aiden, slips his hands to Aiden's waist and pulls him close.

Just for a moment, Jake lets himself get lost; Aiden is pressed against him from chest to thigh, and his eyes drift closed. Just for a moment, everything slows: the ghostly drag of Aiden's fingertips along Jake's arms as he moves them to rest atop Jake's shoulders; the rise and fall of Aiden's chest against his, only thin layers of slate blue and blood red cloth separating them; the sensation of something slotting into place as Aiden grips his hips and brushes his lips over Jake's collarbone. Just for a moment, he lets himself belong to Aiden completely.

Yet he's grateful when the moment passes, the intensity of it close to over-whelming until he shakes his head and focuses on moving with Aiden to the beat of the next song, which he immediately recognizes from his early teens. Judging by Aiden's grin as he wraps his arms around Jake's waist and rocks him from side to side in a parody of a high school prom slow dance, he recognizes it, too.

Feeling bold—at least, bolder than he did within the confines of the RV—Jake points at Aiden and mouths along with the chorus.

"Where have I heard this before?" Aiden asks.

"Shaun's party, freshman year of high school," Jake says, close to his ear. "Remember when you were so excited that he invited you because you had that *huge* crush on him?"

"I didn't—I hadn't even come out freshman year!"

"That didn't exactly stop you from spending the entire party mooning at him across his basement."

"No, there's no way that actually happened," Aiden insists. He spins Jake out to face the crush of bodies around them and pulls him back, wrapping one arm around his waist and the other around his chest. Momentarily, Jake flashes on another club like this one, dancing with Aiden in front of a neon equalizer, words falling from his mouth quicker than he can register them.

Both of them are getting appreciative looks from the guys in their vicinity, but they all seem content to do nothing more than watch, and Jake gets the sense that this is the kind of place where, if you've got someone practically wrapped around you, you're left alone.

Leaning back into Aiden and resting his head on his shoulder, he says, "You're remembering it all wrong, you know. You had that huge crush on Shaun because he had, and I quote, 'the *best* smile.'"

"Sweetheart, I didn't have a crush on him. I had a crush on *you*."

Abruptly, Jake turns in Aiden's arms and stares him down. He doesn't believe him for a second. "That's not funny."

"Wasn't meant to be."

"You didn't even know if I was gay!"

"What? Of course I did. Don't you remember what I told you when you came out to me? That I'd known since the night of that party, when you couldn't take your eyes off Tom from jazz band?"

"But you—you learned guitar so you could take over Tom's spot after he graduated! I thought... wasn't it just an excuse to spend more time with Shaun?"

Aiden shakes his head, his expression growing more serious by the second, and Jake can't hold the gaze. The last line between them is still a fine one, and he has to walk it carefully. He drops his eyes to the front of Aiden's shirt, where the flashing neon lights tint its crimson fabric every color there is.

"I learned guitar because you wouldn't stop talking about how awesome guitarists were. I thought you liked Tom and I wanted to make you like me instead," Aiden says. "And look how well *that* worked out. I *still* lost out to Brandon Flowers and Adam Levine, those assholes."

Like air rushing in to fill a vacuum, the tension breaks and Jake bursts into laughter, burying his face in Aiden's shoulder to keep from doubling over.

"So what did this crush of yours involve?" he asks when he finally catches his breath.

"We were fourteen, Jake," Aiden says. "And besides, you never would have looked at me. You were always gorgeous, even back then. Totally out of *my* league."

"One day, I'm gonna buy you a decent mirror," Jake says, rolling his eyes. "Anyway. Tell me."

It's moments like this one, when Aiden looks at Jake through his thick eyelashes and smiles almost shyly—like he's so pleased, like Jake just made his entire day—that remind Jake how very, very fine that last line is.

"Mainly, um..." Aiden trails off, and Jake looks at him expectantly. "Mainly taking you out for ice cream, holding hands with you... all that cutesy teenage stuff."

"Back when you were still wearing your Ninja Turtles shirts?"

"Careful. I could totally break those out again."

"Please, those shirts wouldn't fit you now. Unless you were *trying* to look like a rent boy," Jake muses, running his hands over the breadth of Aiden's shoulders and trying to find the skinny, awkward little teenage boy he remembers beneath the flesh and musculature. He's still there somewhere, buried far below the bravado and cracked façade, and while Jake doesn't particularly miss the persistent confusion that comes with early youth, he misses how simple some things used to be.

Yet he wants to have this new thing and keep it, every look and touch and kiss, and *not* think about the indelible expiration date stamped on it. It seems too much like something he's been waiting to discover his entire life.

"What, you don't like that look?" Aiden teases, eliciting a fresh round of giggles.

"Well, I guess I could be persuaded," Jake replies, and trails his hands down to Aiden's waist to tug on his belt loops. "God, look at us. Look at *you*. We grew up."

"We did."

"And now we have this."

"And this," Aiden says, punctuating his words with a firm, fleeting kiss, "is much better than ice cream."

Wrapping his arms tightly around Aiden's neck, Jake returns the kiss, all open mouth and dipping tongue, his teeth nipping at Aiden's bottom lip, leaving impressions of himself behind. The club is almost stiflingly hot, and sweat beads at his temples, but he pulls them deeper into the crowd. Later, when they're danced out and he has let Aiden get him hard and drive him crazy with want, he'll take Aiden by the hand, lead him out of the club and back to the RV. They'll shed the layers of their history; and from the first touch to the last second before Jake succumbs to sleep, he will once again, for a brief time, let himself belong to Aiden completely.

And as one song fades into the next, beats seamlessly flowing together, lights pulsing in time and bodies packed tight and sweaty around them, Jake reminds himself of what he thought earlier, lying spent in bed next to Aiden: *If we can't be everything, at least we're more.*

5,086 MILES

CHAPTER 5

DAY FORTY: WEST VIRGINIA

Aiden's feet rest on the dashboard, the passenger seat tipped back as far as it will go, and he sings along under his breath to the chilled-out, happy song playing on the radio. The RV is parked at the Clark Pump-N-Shop in Huntington, and through the open driver's side window, Aiden watches Jake paying for something—hopefully the Fruit Roll-Ups he says he's been inexplicably craving since waking up.

Jake climbs in, swinging himself into the seat with a plastic bag dangling from his fingers. He tosses a brightly colored package into Aiden's lap, and Aiden picks it up, regarding it curiously.

"Beef jerky?" he says.

"So much beef jerky," Jake mutters, pushing his sunglasses up on top of his head. "There was almost an entire wall of it."

"Did you get your Fruit Roll-Ups?"

"No, but I did get Swedish Fish, so that kind of makes up for it."

"Swedish Fish make up for *everything*."

"And that's why I got extra for you."

"My hero," Aiden says, feigning a swoon and earning himself a smile.

A moment settles between them in which they do nothing more than look at one another comfortably and without expectation. Just when Aiden has finally sunken into it, Jake gestures toward the radio and asks, "Can *you* drive, *darling?*"

Aiden nods and pulls his seat upright, easily switching their places without either of them needing to step outside. It's true that space is limited, but the RV still beats spending three and a half months in a car or an SUV.

It isn't long before Aiden is merging back onto 64 and absently tapping his fingers on the steering wheel. Jake briefly disappears into the back, and when he drops into his seat again, he holds a thick journal. It's worn and weathered; the spine is cracked and the pastel green fabric is wearing thin at the corners, and Jake handles it with reverence.

"So I've been meaning to show this to you for a while," he says. "And now probably isn't the most opportune time, I know, but I haven't been able to stop thinking about it since this morning."

"What is it?"

"It's Mom's art journal," Jake says, turning it over in his hands. "Dad found it when he was cleaning out the attic a few weeks before the accident, and I guess he thought I should have it. He told me that whenever she was sad or stressed out, she would take out this book, sit in his chair and just draw for a while."

Aiden smiles, imagining Daisy's small frame, an island of warmth and color against the brown leather of William's chair, her pencil moving in swift strokes and scratching, scratching, scratching. It doesn't seem like a borrowed memory. "What kind of stuff did she draw?"

"There's flowers, our house, some abstract stuff... everything, really. I got it out because ever since we went to see Nan, I've been thinking more about getting a tattoo. I figured maybe I could find some ideas in here, get one of her drawings tattooed on me or something. Anyway, I came across this one picture..." Jake trails off and flips the book open to a page he's marked with a small, torn strip of paper. He leans across the space between them, holds the book just next to the steering wheel and gestures for Aiden to take it.

Eyes flicking between the time-yellowed pages of the book and the mostly clear road ahead, Aiden looks at the pencil drawing. It's a startling likeness of two little boys, sitting next to one another on a couch and sharing a plate of what looks like carrot sticks and apple slices. One has light, neatly combed hair and sits with his legs crossed, clutching a stuffed animal. The other has a mess of long, dark, tousled hair and his legs dangle off the edge of the couch, one slightly raised as if he's kicking his feet up and down. The boy with dark hair is gazing at the other with such a look of happiness and adulation that it makes Aiden's breath catch in his chest. It's them. It's *him,* looking at his best friend—a real best friend, just like he'd always wanted—the one he adored from the moment they met.

"Oh my god, this is—"

"Aiden!"

His gaze shoots upward just in time to see a deer running out onto the highway; instinctively, he wrenches the steering wheel to the right and slams the brakes.

It isn't anything like in the movies or the books. Nothing goes into slow motion; he only has time to react. They come to a screeching dead stop on the shoulder. Aiden's heart races double time in his chest; his knuckles are white.

"Shit. *Shit!"* Jake says beside him.

Aiden scrubs a shaking hand over his face, flexes the other on the steering wheel as the engine idles. He swallows against the acrid burn at the back of his throat and blinks up at the ceiling of the cab, willing his eyes to stop stinging.

"Oh my god. Oh my *god,* Aiden, I'm so sorry. I'm sorry, it was my fault, I'm—"

"It's fine. Just... give me a minute."

Slowly, Jake reaches across and unfurls Aiden's fingers from the steering wheel, entwining them with his own instead. Aiden glances over and sees Jake's other hand clutching tightly onto his Saint Christopher. They trade shaky smiles, and wordlessly switch places.

BY THE TIME THEY GET to the Fox Fire Campground in Milton, ominous rainclouds have swept away every last vestige of the sunlight that poured into the RV all afternoon, and Aiden's hands are still shaking. Jake hasn't said a word since they traded places, and at first, Aiden was grateful for a little silence in which to collect himself. But the longer it has stretched on, the more vivid his imagination has become, conjuring up multi-angle shots of wreckage and explosions and blood on the windshield.

The rain begins to fall just as Jake cuts the engine, and as the edge of his tension finally wears away, Aiden lets out a trembling sigh.

"Charlie texted me to say that Governor LePage signed an emergency declaration," Jake says, glancing at his phone. He's referring to the tropical storm that Aiden's mom told him about when they were on the way to Graceland. It's since been upgraded to a hurricane and given the name Sandy, and most people they know back in Brunswick have been in regular contact even though the authorities don't anticipate nearly as much damage as is anticipated farther down the East Coast.

"They're saying she'll hit on Tuesday, right?" Aiden asks.

"Early on Tuesday, yes."

Jake climbs out of his seat, pulls Aiden up and leads him to the chair just behind the cab. Then Jake kneels next to Aiden and reaches up to cup his face with both hands. For a moment neither of them moves a muscle, and then Jake pulls Aiden down into a bruisingly tight embrace.

"I'm sorry," he whispers again when he pulls back, his eyes dark green and clouded with anxiety.

Aiden shakes his head. "Will you please kiss me?"

The rain pounds against the windshield, casting dappled shadows across Jake's freckled skin that blur together as he leans to claim Aiden's mouth. Aiden clasps his hands behind Jake's head and pulls him closer, opening his mouth and tasting Jake's surprised hum.

Aiden never sits in the chair behind the cab; he hates the feeling of the world coming at him sideways when he can barely deal with it head-on. But he can make an exception for Jake, who climbs on top of him to straddle his lap. The heat between them chases away the persistent, cold dread in his veins. Jake gives Aiden even more than he takes, slowly thrusting his hips down and lavishing attention on his neck, his fingertips digging into Aiden's shoulders. A Ben Howard track from Aiden's mellow playlist wraps him up in the easy sounds of a soft, steady guitar and an earthy, melodic voice singing of cold and shelter and coming home. Everything is sensual and slow, so slow.

Aiden doesn't want slow. He wants—*needs*—fast, and lasting.

"Jake," he begins, voice tailing into a moan as Jake sucks hard over his pulse point; the sharp burst of an ache under his skin spikes into a twist at the base of his spine. "Jake, fuck—*why* don't we have any condoms?"

Jake all but freezes and pulls away slowly. "It's a little late for that, don't you think? We've sucked each other off how many times at this point?"

"What if I want you to fuck me?"

"I've been fucking you all week."

"You know what I mean," Aiden says, rolling his eyes even as a thought occurs to him. "Don't you top anymore? Is that it?"

"No, I top. Exclusively, actually," Jake says, and rubs a hand over his face. "I was just... surprised, is all."

"Why?"

Jake pauses briefly, then climbs out of the chair and retrieves the plastic bag from the floor of the cab. Sheepishly, he pulls out a box of condoms and a small bottle of lubricant and holds them out for Aiden's inspection. The golden yellow glow of the RV's interior lights picks out a faint pink high on his cheekbones, and Aiden can't help but let out a peal of laughter that settles warmly in his stomach.

He leans over to take Jake by the wrist and pull him back into his lap, and his hands rub over the jeans wrapped around his thighs. "Give it up. You're inside my head, aren't you?"

Jake ducks his head, grinning, and drops the items into Aiden's lap.

"What took you so long?" Aiden asks, rocking his hips up and eliciting a pleasant hiss from Jake.

"Even after this past week, it's still a big deal and I wanted it to be... I didn't want it to mean nothing," Jake says.

"It wouldn't," Aiden says, cupping Jake's face and forcing his gaze upward. "It *doesn't*."

Jake hums and leans in once more, but Aiden stops him with just the tips of his fingers, pressed to his chest. Voice firm and full of conviction, he says simply, "I want you to fuck me."

"Okay. *Okay*," Jake breathes, and surges forward to catch Aiden's lips in a deep, plunging kiss.

They shed their clothes even more quickly than usual, only losing contact for a couple of seconds at a time, and Jake's hands are everywhere, as if he's trying to climb inside Aiden's body and take up residence. This is Jake as Aiden has never experienced him: silently frantic and communicating only through breath and touch.

Somehow, in the process of climbing out of the chair to rid Aiden of his jeans and underwear, Jake stumbles and pulls them both down onto the floor, Aiden on top of him and breathing heavily.

"So graceful," Jake mutters with an almost nervous giggle. "Probably a sign we should take this to the bedroom."

Aiden shakes his head, eyes locked on Jake's as he rocks down hard, biting his lip against a groan—the drag of his cock along Jake's is imperfect friction, and so far from enough. "Fuck me right here."

"Jesus, Aiden." Jake hooks his leg around Aiden's waist and flips them over, making fast work of grabbing for a chair cushion and sliding it, still warm, beneath Aiden's hips.

And then, in a single, seemingly endless moment, Aiden looks up at Jake and takes stock of being spread out beneath him, waiting and wanting. He can feel pasts and futures colliding, annihilating each other until there is only this. It feels like coming home.

There's no turning back, and Aiden will not falter. Jake kisses him while snaking long, slick, practiced fingers inside him, slowly coaxing Aiden open with whispers of encouragement breathed between slack lips.

It's so different from what he remembers. With Tyler it was messy, fumbled, and ran the knife-edge between pleasure and pain. There were no reassuring words or careful motions. Tyler hadn't been expecting a virgin, after all, and Aiden didn't tell him until afterward—and he is a muddled, half-forgotten shade.

"Okay?" Jake asks as he finally draws his fingers out and away, and Aiden whines low in the back of his throat at the sudden emptiness. He shifts, scoots his hips forward and up, watches as Jake tears open a condom and rolls it on, his cock flushed and ready. Wordlessly, Jake winds his damp fingers behind Aiden's knee and lifts his leg to rest on his shoulder, presses a softly smiling kiss to the skin of his ankle.

Aiden takes a deep breath and forces away the strain that courses through his veins, the clamoring for more, and nods; Jake begins to push into him and Aiden closes his eyes, focusing on the blunt, full pressure of Jake sinking farther and farther inside him in one long, smooth motion until Jake's mouth is close enough for Aiden to lick his way into.

"Okay?" Jake asks again, eyes glassy, pupils blown.

"You're sweet," Aiden says, "but I really just need you to fuck me now. No holding back."

Jake pauses, a quirk at the corners of his mouth and a challenge in his darkened eyes, and says, "You asked for it."

With that, Jake pulls almost all the way out and drives quickly back in, his hips slamming into Aiden with a slap of skin on skin. The fullness is exquisite, and Aiden arches his back and scrabbles for purchase where there is none to be found. When Jake curls his arm around Aiden's thigh and takes his dick in hand, stroking him hard again, a litany of half-formed words begins to fall from his mouth, eyes screwed shut as Jake fucks him over and over and over.

"*Aiden,*" Jake breathes, and hearing his own name is suddenly too much, the vowels stretched taut around them both, and Jake... Jake is some fire spirit made of heat cells that crack and break Aiden apart until he is reduced to nothing but this, this writhing, dizzy mess on the floor of his RV, every muscle drawn up and waiting on the brink.

"All week, ever since—fuck, I've wanted this all week..." he manages, and forces his eyes open because he has to see, to watch, to catalog this beautiful and all-too-fleeting moment.

His heart hammers in his chest and he can barely breathe; every time Jake moans and fills him up again he is as winded as if he's just finished a sprint. Aiden chases his release, gaining ground with every twist of Jake's hand on the upstroke. He's *never* felt this wanted.

"Just... just a little—little more," he pants, pleading as if Jake will deny him—but he doesn't. His pace quickens, and strands of damp hair stick to his forehead.

Aiden comes with a broken-off jumble of a sound and Jake follows not two seconds later, shuddering and trembling, his teeth biting almost too hard into the flesh of Aiden's calf. When he carefully pulls out, Aiden closes his eyes, blindly pulls Jake to his chest and tries not to feel the loss too keenly.

"Was it worth the wait?" Jake asks, his voice cutting through the haze of Aiden's sated drift.

"I think this is what they mean when they say 'blissed out,'" Aiden says.

"I don't know how we're going to get any driving done from now on," Jake says, head bobbing on Aiden's chest as he shakes with silent laughter.

"Right? I mean... *God*," Aiden replies. He presses a lazy kiss to Jake's damp hairline and holds him close.

"Not quite, but close enough," Jake says. "We should probably move."

"Or not," Aiden says, eyes drifting closed, limbs heavy. There will be time later to move, clean up, and lead each other to bed; for now, he just wants to be.

He feels Jake curl closer and brush a kiss over his nipple as he winds an arm loosely around Aiden's waist. Rain still pounds dully on the roof of the RV, and Jake's contented sigh is only just audible. The last thing Aiden hears before falling asleep, a light tone of surprise behind Jake's words, is, "It means something with you."

5,229 MILES

DAY FORTY-THREE: OHIO

As far inland as it is, Ohio is not spared the effects of Hurricane Sandy as it gets closer and closer to making landfall on the East Coast.

Jake pulls his heavy jacket tighter, crosses his arms over his chest and leans into Aiden; he revels in the extra warmth when Aiden puts his arm around his shoulders. The rain falls in fine droplets, soaking them through, and the wind whipping around them makes it feel even colder.

The weather seems to have done nothing, however, to dampen the spirits of those lined up outside the Value City Arena, eager to get inside and watch Ohio State play Walsh University. The line stretches all the way around the building and moves at a glacial pace. Aiden grows bouncier and more excitable the closer they get. Jake wishes he could muster the same enthusiasm, but his feet drag and he has to work overtime to distract himself even slightly from... well, everything about this situation.

"You look like someone just kicked your puppy," Aiden says, nudging his side.

Jake plucks at the collar of his gray shirt—borrowed from Aiden's closet; it's a bad fit around the shoulders—and gestures at a group of Walsh supporters farther up the line. "Their colors are red and gold. Why couldn't we have supported the... Chevaliers, or whatever they're called?"

"Cavaliers," Aiden corrects him, obviously struggling to keep a straight face. "You can't wear Cavaliers colors, Jakey. It's Ohio; we have to support the Buckeyes! They're the state team!"

"I don't care who they are; you made me wear gray. You know it washes me out." A particularly strong gust of wind pushes him back on one foot, and he braces himself. He lets out a great sigh and buries his face in Aiden's shoulder. "I can't believe this is the only thing to do in Ohio on a Monday."

"Did you speak to Charlie, yet?" Aiden asks into his hair, and Jake feels a kiss amongst the words. It lifts him. A little.

"No. Let me try her again," he says, and fishes his phone out of his pocket. Droplets of rain obscure the screen almost immediately.

He's been trying to reach his sister on and off all day, wanting one last check-in before the hurricane hits, but every time he's called, he's received a busy signal. This time, to his relief, the call connects, and Charlie picks up on the fourth ring.

"Hey, Jakey," she says, her voice sounding crackly and far away. "Is everything okay?"

Jake lets out a breath, belatedly noticing that he's been holding it. "I'm fine, we're both fine. I mean, it's cold and raining, but otherwise fine," he rambles. "What's going on back there?"

"Nothing much. Everyone's staying home and they pulled all the boats in yesterday, so it looks like people are just waiting for it to pass. That's what we—what *I'm* doing, at least."

Jake's mind finally quiets and he closes his eyes. Conversations between him and his sister have been tepid at best; feeling genuinely worried for her is a little surprising, and very welcome. *Maybe I'm a "Real Boy" after all*, he thinks.

"Okay, so you're safe?" he asks. "Will you go down to the basement if things get really crazy?"

Sounding surprised and touched by his concern, she says, "Jake, you don't need to worry about me. We—I'm gonna be just fine."

"Is Martin with you?" The pause on the line is so long that Jake checks that the call is still connected. "Sis?"

He hears a sharp inhalation. Charlie finally says, "We broke up."

"Oh," Jake says hesitantly, surprised and relieved in a different way.

"Yeah. *Oh*," she says.

Pretending he can't hear the tremor in her voice, Jake pauses and bites his lip. "I won't lie, I'm not *un*happy about it—"

"Don't, Jake—"

"But are you okay?"

"I'm fine," Charlie says, a hair too quickly and far too brightly. "I'm fine, just leave it alone."

Jake kicks the ground before deciding that a straight-up, left-turn change of subject might be for the best. "The storm isn't supposed to hit us too badly, right?"

"Jake, *seriously*. I've got plenty of food and water, we still have electricity, and—"

Jake stands up straight; static crackles through the phone. "Sis?"

"Just carry on having fun—in ag—over the week—"

"Charlie, can you hear me? Charlie!"

With one last explosive crackle, the line clears and Charlie's voice comes through uninterrupted. "Oh, before I let you go, I actually need to run something by you."

The unbroken sentence allows Jake to relax again. Running a hand through his wet hair and turning his face up to the rain, he closes his eyes and asks, "What is it?"

"I've been thinking that... maybe I could go back to school," she says.

"Charlie, are you kidding? That's great!" Jake says, and smiles at Aiden, who looks back at him with a bemused expression. "Why would you need to run that by me? You know I've always said you should go back and finish."

Though the line is clear, Charlie's voice grows a little hesitant. "Well, Caltech isn't exactly cheap. I'd have two more years and everything I've managed to save up would barely cover books."

"Okay, so..."

"I think we should sell the house."

"You think we should *what?*" Jake asks without thinking, sure he's misheard her.

"Hear me out," she says, all hesitation gone as her words spill out in a pleading rush. "The mortgage is finished now, and all the money I got from

Dad is tied up in the shop. Gary can't afford to buy me out of my half, so... doesn't it just make sense?"

Jake shakes his head, sending rainwater trickling down his neck, and leans a hand on the wall for support. If he didn't know it was just his knees shaking, he'd think the ground was falling away beneath him. It might as well be. "Charlie, we can't. We *can't*; we grew up in that house! Can't you just... you're co-partner, wouldn't that cover tuition?"

"I ran the numbers myself," she says, and Jake can almost see her sinking back into the couch, the couch they all used to sit on together, drawing her knees up to her chest and tracing patterns on her thigh. "I'm the only who has time to do my pieces and train the newbies. We'd probably have to bring in two people to replace me, so... it just wouldn't work. This is the only way I can come up with."

"There *has* to be another way," Jake snaps, pushing all the finality he can into his words. "We're not selling the house."

"Jake, there *isn't* another way. I mean, if you wanna come up with a plan then be my guest. But I'm telling you, I've looked at this from every angle I can think of," she says, her voice just as firm. "We could get tenants, but both of us will probably end up hundreds if not *thousands* of miles away, so how would we check in on them or do maintenance? And it's not like you can buy me out—"

"I could petition, get the money released early, like you did," Jake protests.

"Come on, Jakey," she says softly. "There's only one reason I got access to mine, and you know exactly what it is."

"I know," Jake says, sighing. Aiden looks at him with concern, and Jake tries to smile back with a reassurance he doesn't feel.

"Anyway, I had the house valued, and it wouldn't be enough," Charlie continues. "Plus, we might already have a buyer, so—"

"Wait," Jake interrupts. "What buyer? How long has this been going on?"

"Only a couple months—"

"A couple *months*? And you did all of this behind my back?"

"Jakey, it's not like that. Just wait and—"

"No, *you* fucking wait," Jake says, stepping away from the wall and turning his back on the line, the rain, the goddamn basketball game, all of it. "You tell me we need to sell the house I fucking grew up in, the house that's all we have left of Mom and Dad, and this was all happening when I was still there?"

"I'm not *telling* you to do anything, I'm just asking for your help," Charlie says, her voice raised; she sounds exactly like their mom did when she was letting them have it for misbehaving. "Don't you want me to be able to finish school?"

Fury makes his vision go red. "Don't do that, Charlie. Don't you *dare* try to guilt-trip me into this."

"Jake... it's time you figure out a way to let go of Dad. It's been seven years—don't you think you need to move on? This could be—"

Nausea washes over him, and he can't listen anymore. He disconnects the call and walks back to Aiden on shaky legs. They're almost at the front of the line now, he notices. As deliberately as he can, he leans into Aiden and buries his face into Aiden's neck, breathing deeply and trying to keep from vomiting all over him.

Everything seems to speed up; momentum is building around him and carrying him along as if he is in the eye of a storm, the middle car of a runaway train. The most unsettling part, however, is not the sensation of speed—it's that he doesn't know where he is going. All at once he wishes he were back home in Brunswick, sitting on the couch with Aiden opposite Charlie in their father's ancient chair, laughing hysterically as they all try to come up with the most outrageously incorrect answers to questions on *Jeopardy*.

Everything used to be so much simpler, he thinks. A rush of nostalgia sweeps over him, and he imagines the sound of a videotape rewinding, the way the machine churned into high gear after ten seconds or so; the click of jewel cases as he thumbed through CDs at Studio 48; the beeping and scraping of a dial-up modem.

Warm fingers wrap around Jake's wrist and Aiden asks, "Are you okay?"

"Not really," Jake answers dully. "Charlie wants to sell the house, I still have that fucking crick in my neck from sleeping on the floor the other night, and everything was better in the nineties."

"All right, come on," Aiden commands softly, taking Jake by the shoulders and hauling him upright. Jake doesn't have the energy to argue. "So why was everything better in the nineties? Because the way I see it, we've got a hell of a lot more now than we did back then."

They crowd under the awning above the doors to the arena, sighing as a blast of heat from inside thaws them out a little. Grateful that Aiden didn't ask about the house, Jake asks, "Like what?"

"High-speed Internet, iPods, cell phones, DVDs—"

"No, those can't be separate things. Those all come under the category of technology," Jake interrupts. "I defy you to name one thing that wasn't great about the nineties."

Distracted, Aiden hands over their tickets and they both submit to the security screening, but as soon as they're through and following signs for the game, he triumphantly announces, "Scrunchies."

"Something relevant to *us*, Dan."

"Lack of equal rights."

"Point. What else?"

"Not being able to use the Internet when someone was on the phone."

"And what about all the books, the TV shows, the *music?*" Jake counters, dredging up long-forgotten memories. "You were *all* about alternative and ska in the nineties; don't think I've forgotten. And another thing—"

"Okay, okay, oh my *god*," Aiden exclaims, laughter running through his words. "I get it. The nineties were awesome. You win, Twentieth Century Boy."

"Thank you," Jake says smugly. Winning a ludicrous argument shouldn't feel as good as it does, but he'll take every little victory, every tiny lift in his spirits right now.

It's stiflingly hot inside, and he takes off his jacket and folds it inside out over his arm. All too soon, however, and almost without thinking, he takes out his phone and starts pulling up the news and weather reports he's already checked countless times. He can feel the tension seeping back into his body, but he's unable to stop himself from scrolling through news report after news report.

"Couldn't have done that in the nineties," Aiden mutters, and when Jake ignores him, Aiden takes the phone from his hand and pockets it. With a reproachful glance, he says, "You're going to drive yourself crazy. Let's just go watch some basketball and I promise you'll forget all about it."

"Doubtful," Jake says, unable to hold back a note of petulance. Still, he gives in and hooks his arm through Aiden's as they head inside the arena. "But fine. Let's do it your way."

Once they find their seats and the players jog onto the court, Aiden smiles and cheers with the crowd. By the time Jake has figured out who he's supposed to be cheering for, though, the game is already starting.

Jake doesn't understand the game, or why they keep having time-outs when it would be over that much sooner if they just kept playing, and though Aiden tries to be helpful by explaining the rules, none of it sticks. He's trapped in Charlie's words, sentences playing over and over in his mind like a broken record.

A player dunks the ball. *It's time you figure out a way to let go of Dad.* The ball zooms back up the court. *It's been seven years.* A Cavalier intercepts it and passes it to a teammate. *Don't you think you need to move on?*

Doesn't she see that I can't?

There are thousands of people in the arena, a sea of gray and red all screaming and cheering for whichever team they've come to support; the atmosphere is stifling, too much for Jake to stand. When the announcers finally declare halftime, he almost cheers. He's up and out of his seat before he can think; he needs to find somewhere to be quiet, even for just a minute. Their seats are in the center of the row; the noise in his head is so loud that he doesn't hear the insults people are probably tossing his way as he trips and stumbles and pushes past them, following signs that point toward the exit and then to the restrooms.

It's time you figure out a way to let go of Dad.

"Shut up, shut up, shut up," he mutters, bursting into the restroom and closing the heavy door. It's blessedly empty. He crosses to the sinks and runs the cold tap so he can splash some water on his face, his jaw, the back of his neck.

At last the heat starts to recede from his face and he can lift his head again. Feeling like every movie cliché ever, Jake regards himself in the mirror with his hands braced on either side of the sink. He can hear music playing outside, one of Charlie's favorites from a time when there was always music in their house, before the pervasive silence that came when she sold all their dad's old records and he wasn't able to do a thing to stop it.

Something tugs at him, that same runaway-train sensation he's been experiencing all day, and he suddenly aches to sing along with the song's lyrics. Resisting the urge to open his mouth and sing is a thing at which Jake has become practiced—at least outside the confines of his room in an otherwise empty house. This time, however, he drops his gaze to the gleaming white porcelain of the sink and, without preface or preamble, begins to sing—shakily at first, but stronger with each note change.

Where he'd expect his throat to close, words soar. His mouth doesn't go dry as the lyrics trip out. His breath doesn't shorten; instead his ribcage expands to let in more air, as if it hadn't always tightened whenever he heard so much as the opening notes to a song he liked. He sings—*sings!*—all the way through the chorus and the second verse, buoyed up and up, rising, *flying* over the notes and into the second chorus. *This* is what he's been building toward. This is where his glorious runaway train has been taking him.

The door swings open. The music dies in Jake's throat and he turns to see Aiden step inside, both of their jackets folded over his arm and concern plain on his face. He doesn't speak, but keeps his eyes on Jake. Jake can almost feel them, like a touch of fingertips.

"I had to get out of there," Jake finally offers with an aborted gesture toward the door. "I'm sorry."

"Don't be," Aiden says, closing the distance between them and kissing the side of his neck. Mouth still lingering there, he asks, "Feel like talking about it?"

Jake can almost feel the words print themselves on his skin in an invisible breath.

He drags his thoughts back to the moment. "There really isn't much to talk about. Charlie wants us to sell the house and I don't," Jake says, thankful that Aiden knows him well enough to understand what he's really saying.

Aiden's arms go around him and Jake melts, the tension finally draining away. Without thinking, he says, "Let's just stay like this forever."

"In the restroom?"

"Like *this*," he repeats, squeezing his arms around Aiden's waist and pulling him closer. "I could stay like this forever."

Aiden doesn't respond, and in the silence that falls, Jake realizes what he's just said, his treacherous heart getting the better of him yet again. He's been trying to keep a better handle on himself, especially since Aiden's confession in the club in Lexington—trying to reason that he's only getting so attached because Aiden's the only constant he has right now.

Clearing his throat, he steps back and tugs his shirt straight. It's still too big around the shoulders, and Aiden laughs at the face he makes.

"Come on," Aiden says. "Let's head back."

5,383 MILES

DAY FORTY-FIVE: MICHIGAN

His spirits high, Aiden turns this way and that, looking over his outfit in the mirror: tight black jeans that hug his ass and thighs, a simple, fitted black tank and the oversized red feather jacket Jake made especially for him. In the hopes of achieving a devil-may-care look, he has outlined his eyes in smudgy black eyeliner and styled his hair a little more messily than usual. He glances at himself one last time and decides that he's met his objective; he looks good, and feels ready to get onstage and sing his heart out.

Aiden is calling his plan "The Reclamation Project." He and Jake will go to The Alley Bar in Ann Arbor, where Hugh and April's open-mic live karaoke band is playing, and somehow he will get Jake onstage to sing. He's banking on the fact that Jake has never before backed down from a challenge, and hoping against hope that Jake won't break that streak, even with something as contentious as his singing.

His plan has been forming ever since he caught Jake mouthing song lyrics as they readied for their night out in Lexington. It solidified even further when he heard Jake sing during halftime at the basketball game; Aiden had almost gone under, then, as a wave of fondness and excitement crashed over him. Following a brief text exchange with April, his plan has become ironclad.

Now, Jake stalks out of the bathroom, looking every inch the glam rock star in a plain white tank, skinny leather pants and a leather jacket with studded shoulders. He's completed the look with an electric blue star framing his left eye and pink streaks in his hair. Aiden feels as if he's had the air punched out of him, and all thoughts of The Reclamation Project are driven from his mind.

"What?" Jake asks.

"Happy Halloween, indeed," Aiden says, gesturing toward Jake's outfit. "I see what you mean about the pants paying for themselves."

"Best money I ever spent," Jake quips, sashaying as he moves closer. He tugs gently on the shoulders of Aiden's jacket, smooths his palms down the front and asks, "This still fit okay?"

"Perfect. It's perfect," Aiden breathes, taken by how the blue makeup has brought out the depth in Jake's green eyes.

"If only we didn't have somewhere to be..." Jake trails off, scanning Aiden's body from head to toe and shaking his head.

He and Jake are in considerably brighter moods than the past two days. Hurricane Sandy has been and gone. No major damage was sustained at either family home back in Brunswick, and Aiden received a text from his dad just before dinner to report that he and Fiona were safe and well, having gone to their cabin in Saint Mary.

"Well," Aiden begins, ducking his head and looking up at Jake from beneath his lashes, "we've still got fifteen minutes."

Jake raises an eyebrow, and his eyes land on Aiden's mouth. "Excellent," he murmurs, and pushes Aiden backward into the bedroom, kicking the door shut behind them.

HALF AN HOUR LATER, as Aiden's phone buzzes angrily in his pocket, they walk into the bar. It looks packed almost to capacity, with people crowded around tables decorated with black candles and along walls strung with cotton spider webs. Not a single person is dressed in everyday clothes; as Aiden scans the crowd, he counts four zombies, three mummies, a Captain America and an Iron Man, a Daisy Duke, a banana, five witches in various stages of undress and the Eleventh Doctor. The atmosphere thrums with the low undercurrent of a thrill that Aiden can only attribute to Halloween parties—something caught between loud fun and an irrational, suppressed fear.

"Elmo!" comes a croaky voice to his right, and Aiden grimaces.

"Hey, Flower," he greets April, turning at the same moment Jake does. She seems to have made the most of her red hair, which is styled into curls that perfectly offset her skintight Black Widow costume.

"I've missed you guys so much!" she exclaims, and lets out a peal of laughter as Jake grabs her around the waist, picks her up and spins her around. Aiden feels a rush of excitement—at the very least, Jake's good mood is promising.

"*What* is up with your voice?" Jake asks.

April rolls her eyes and tucks her hair behind her ears. "I have fucking laryngitis, so I can't sing. That's why we're so happy you came tonight, because we were wondering—"

"No," Jake interrupts. "April, you *know* I don't sing."

"Honey, I gave up on you a *long* time ago," she says, before turning to Aiden and shooting him a significant look. "Actually, we were hoping that you'd open for us. Remember the show at The Cannery when Will's grandma was in the hospital?"

Aiden nods, smiling at the memory of that show. He had a blast performing with them, even more so than with The Cogs, and he can't wait to get onstage with them again.

"Of course I'll open for you," he says. April grins and stands on tiptoe to kiss his cheek.

"Are you guys drinking?" she asks, nodding in the direction of the bar.

"Yeah, we're parked right out back," Jake says.

"Then the first round's on me. You're seriously saving my ass," she says, folding a twenty-dollar bill between two fingers and holding it out over the bar. One of the bartenders—dressed all in red with a plastic pair of devil horns atop his spiky brown hair—is before her in an instant, and she orders three tequila shots.

While the bartender lines up the shots, Aiden asks, "So where are the guys?"

April rolls her eyes again and says, "Probably all smoking in the courtyard. I had to come *inside* just to get a minute of peace. Can you believe that?"

"What's up?" Jake asks.

"Oh my *god,* it's just... I love these guys, you know I do. But spending every goddamn day with them in a freaking bus is..." April trails off, shaking her head. She raises her glass to Aiden and Jake and downs the shot in one swallow without so much as a pull at the corners of her mouth. Aiden and Jake follow suit. "I mean, Will had to go home because of his grandma, so we're down a singer anyway, and... okay, take today for example. Hugh has been up my ass about taking my fucking medication, which, I've been on birth control since I was fucking fifteen, okay? I know how to take a goddamn pill. Liam's barely spoken to Ethan all week since he made some sort of joke about Green Day, I don't even know what. Drake's constantly pranking the both of them and now he's trying to recruit the rest of us, and Marcie's been freaking out all fucking day because the guys are trying to get her to sing tonight."

Aiden lets out a low whistle and signals the bartender for another round. Jake's face twists in sympathy.

"I'm sorry, honey," Jake says, squeezing her arm.

"Just... I know you two have your magical rainbow connection or whatever, but *seriously*. How do you stand it?" April asks, eyes flicking between them.

Jake shoots Aiden a questioning look, and he shrugs in reply. They haven't exactly discussed whether they're going to tell anyone about their "arrangement," and though he spilled the beans to his mom, telling one of their friends is an altogether different matter.

Their look must last a fraction too long, however, because April steps closer to them and scans their faces with wide eyes. A slow, satisfied Cheshire cat grin blossoms across her face, and as she leans back against the bar, she asks, "How long?"

"It, um... depends," Aiden says, and looks to Jake for guidance.

"It happened in Philadelphia, and then again in Key West," Jake says succinctly. "And practically every night since."

April crosses her arms over her chest and announces, "Well firstly, there is no fucking way I'm having sex with *any* of them."

"Not even Marcie?" Jake asks, nudging her side.

"Please. She's not even out back home; I'm not about to make things even more complicated."

"But you've liked her for so long—"

"And *secondly*, Jake Richard Valentine, since when am I not the first person you text when you add a new ass to the pile?"

"Maybe since the invention of your I-told-you-so dance?"

"Wait," Aiden interjects, turning to April. "You said this would happen?"

"July fourth. I thought I was gonna have to get a fucking bucket, the amount you were drooling over each other," April says.

Before Aiden has a chance to dwell too long on her words—or the way Jake ducks his head and avoids Aiden's eyes—April checks her watch and nods toward the end of the bar, where the band's equipment is set up on a small stage. "Come on, time for us to do our thing."

Jake's fingers coil around the back of Aiden's neck and pull him close for a bruising kiss. He captures Aiden's bottom lip between his teeth and pulls off slowly, then whispers into his mouth, "Break a leg, rock star."

With a bitten-off groan, Aiden leaves Jake at the bar and follows April through the crowd. The rest of the band files in from the courtyard, and each member greets him with a hug or a smile as they rush to take the stage. Once all of them are in place, the lights dim and the noise in the bar dies down as all heads turn toward them.

Breathe, Aiden reminds himself. He finds Jake's face at the back of the crowd just as Ethan begins to play the introduction to their opening song, Robbie Williams' "Let Me Entertain You," and the lights come up.

"Ladies and gentlemen, zombies and ghouls," he says over the synthesized piano, spreading his arms wide. "We are The One with the Band, and we're thrilled to be here in Ann Arbor!

"We're a live, open-mic karaoke band, and we'll be opening and closing the show for you. You'll find copies of the song list around the bar, and we'd love for you to get up here and rock out with us. So don't be shy about putting your name down; just hand your slips to either me or Mystique here," Aiden continues, gesturing to his right where Marcie stands ready at her own microphone, her trumpet by her side. "For now just sit back, relax and let us entertain you."

The crowd applauds politely, some cheering and raising their glasses as Liam strums his guitar and brings a rousing edge to the music. One hand curled around the mic, locking eyes with Jake, who is slowly pushing his way through to the front of the crowd, Aiden begins to sing.

His voice soars over the music, the lights burst into life and Hugh joins in on the drums. And now his true rush begins. He grins at Marcie as she provides his backing vocals—she sounds fantastic, and her young and soulful voice lends the song an added depth.

Aiden spreads his arms wide again and circles his hips, making love to the song and the crowd throughout the second verse and chorus. Performing comes to him like breathing, and whenever he finds himself on a stage, he morphs into the best possible version of himself: free, unencumbered and purely in the moment. He lets go of Aiden Calloway and all of the issues he has with himself, and grabs hold of the only thing that's left: the music. He only experiences a similar feeling when he's directing, watching the action come together right before his eyes and knowing that he's witnessing creation.

The audience is jumping by the time Aiden sings the final refrain, his feet spread, hands beckoning them closer. He circles behind Marcie and nudges her toward center stage for her trumpet solo, clapping his hands over his head as she brings the house down and the song to its end.

Applause erupts, and after taking a brief bow, Aiden picks a slip of paper from the handful he was given by crowd members during the latter half of the song. Handing the rest to Marcie, he says into the mic, "The first brave soul we're welcoming to the stage this evening is going to give us his take on AC/DC's 'Thunderstruck.' Please give it up for Mark!"

He's practically carried through the crowd after he hands over the mic. Jake and April flank him all the way to the bar, where he drinks deeply from the bottle of water shoved into his hand and pauses to throw an arm around Jake's neck and kiss him firmly on the mouth.

"How was I?" he asks, voice raised over the none-too-shabby singing.

Jake's eyes glitter under the bar lights, and his smile is just as bright. "Dan, you were *amazing*. God, I've missed watching you perform."

"Seriously, Aiden. Pure sex," April agrees, nodding furiously. "If both of us weren't gay, I'd tell you to watch out."

Aiden laughs, and they settle onto stools at the bar to take in the evening. He probably won't sing again until the time comes to close the show, and he has at least two hours to convince Jake to sing. Now is the time to sit back, catch his breath and continue nudging.

After five more songs, including a truly awful version of "Livin' On A Prayer" that makes Aiden wince, Jake grimace and April lament the fact that she can't magically turn her water into wine, Marcie takes a break and approaches them almost shyly, her eyes trained downward. When she reaches them, Aiden pulls her close.

"What can I get you?" he asks her, trying to catch the bartender's attention over her shoulder.

"Oh, um... I'm good, thanks, I have water onstage," she says, glancing up at him from under her thick brown bangs. "You were *so* good up there, Aiden. Did I do okay?"

"Are you kidding?" Jake interjects. "You were fantastic! And not just your trumpet solo—which was *incredible,* by the way—but that voice! Why haven't I ever heard you sing before?"

"I don't know," Marcie says, twisting her fingers together. "I mean, I'm the trumpet girl, right? No one looks at me and thinks I could be a singer."

"I'm just sad that *I* was the one singing lead and you had to be backup," Aiden tells her. "You should be front and center."

"You really mean it? Because I've been thinking that maybe I *could* sing a whole song by myself."

"Do it. Oh my *god,* you have to do it," Jake says.

"Is it that song I heard you practicing with the guys this morning? Is that why they wanted you to sing?" April asks, and when Marcie nods hesitantly, she adds, "Then get up there and tell Hugh. Right now."

"I just... it's *terrifying!*" Marcie exclaims, though her voice barely rises. "I don't know how you guys can do it all the time."

"Honey, if you bring even a fraction of what you brought to the song we opened with, you'll blow everyone away," Aiden assures her, squeezing her shoulder, until at length she smiles up at him and nods.

"Okay, I'll do it," she says. "Although... April, will you come up onstage with me? Like, not to sing... I'd just feel better if you were there."

"Of course I will. Hey, maybe I can give Liam a break and take over guitar," April says, looping her arm through Marcie's. "Come on, let's go tell the guys."

Rather than watch the girls weave their way toward the stage, Aiden watches Jake: His eyes follow Marcie with a look so wistful it makes Aiden's stomach churn. For the first time, he wonders if he's doing the right thing or if he should just let it drop. He doesn't need to push Jake even further, not when he's been making so much progress on his own... but there's an itch under his skin, an almost primal need to hear Jake sing, see him completely let go, and he can't help but bump Jake's hip with his own when Marcie takes her place front and center.

"I bet you the next three tank dumps that you could never get onstage and do what she's doing," Aiden says carefully. He inclines his head toward Jake, but his eyes are fixed on Marcie as she slips almost visibly out of her own skin and into that of a performer, as if she's becoming her costume.

"I bet you the next three tank dumps and a week's worth of cooking that I could," Jake replies, his tone holding the merest edge of a challenge.

"Prove it," Aiden says.

"What?" Jake asks, turning to face him. "No, I... you know I can't sing."

"It's not that you *can't*, it's that you *won't*," Aiden says, and points to Marcie. "Five minutes ago she was shaking, and look at her now."

The song is a bouncy Ella Riot track with an eighties vibe, and Marcie bounces with it as she sings her way into the chorus. Aiden snakes an arm around Jake's waist and says, "Come on, let me pick a song for you."

"Why are you pushing this?"

"Because ever since we left Brunswick, it's like I've been watching you wake up again. We both know that you'll feel better if you do it, and I think you *want* me to push you."

Slowly and deliberately, Jake raises his bottle to his lips and takes a long drink, his eyes on Marcie as she dances and spins and jumps across the stage. Holding his breath, Aiden waits him out.

"Sometimes I really hate that you know me so well," Jake finally says, leaning into him. "I... okay. What song did you have in mind?"

"'Payphone' by Maroon 5," Aiden says, exhaling, barely able to believe his plan has worked. "Do you know it well enough to sing it?"

Jake nods once, promptly downs what remains in his bottle and walks off in the direction of the restroom, leaving Aiden by turns excited and confused. Thinking better of following Jake right away, Aiden grabs a slip from the bar and scribbles:

Jake Valentine, Payphone by Maroon 5

He walks to the stage and hands the slip to April. Her eyes go wide as she reads it—she obviously didn't think the plan would work, either—and she gapes openly at him. Aiden simply shrugs and heads to the restroom.

Jake is washing his hands, the sleeves of his jacket rolled to the elbow. He's clearly stalling, and Aiden suddenly wishes that he'd thought to bring him a shot.

"I stopped singing," Jake says quietly. "And you know why."

Aiden crosses his arms and leans against the wall. "Because she wasn't around to sing with you anymore."

"After she was gone, it... I could always talk; that was fine. You *kept* me talking. But whenever I tried to sing, it just... nothing came out," Jake says, and heaves a deep sigh. "What if I'm terrible? It's a *really* hard song."

"You're going to be great, I know it."

"Will you sing backup for me?"

"Of course I will. Come on, Twentieth Century Boy. Let's go."

Jake freezes and looks at him, something unreadable in his eyes. "What did you just say?"

"I... let's go?"

"No, no, before that."

"Twentieth Century Boy," Aiden replies, regarding him curiously.

For whatever reason, the new nickname seems to light a fire under Jake and he grabs Aiden's hand and runs out of the restroom with him in tow. Marcie has just finished her song and is taking a bow, her audience applauding, whooping and catcalling. Jake breaks away, makes a beeline for April and whispers something into her ear. Her face lights up, she spreads the message to the rest of the band and before Aiden knows it, she's at the mic. "We've got a *very* special Halloween treat for you. I've known this next performer since my first year of college, and while I've always had my ideas about him, I've never heard the little fucker sing. Ann Arbor, about to rock the house with T-Rex's 'Twentieth Century Boy,' please give it up for Jake Valentine!"

Taking his place at the backup mic with Marcie, Aiden grins—he should have known. Jake glances at Aiden over his shoulder, his face set in a stoic expression tinged with defiance; as April begins playing the song's dirty, catchy intro, Aiden watches Jake grab the mic in one hand and the stand in the other.

When Jake starts to sing, arching his back and twisting to the side to look straight at him, Aiden stutters over his backing vocals. Jake practically growls into the mic; his lower register is unpracticed and throaty but strong and raw. If Aiden made love in his performance, Jake is laying himself at the foot of an idol.

He takes the mic from its stand and stalks toward Aiden like a predator with its prey in sight. Jake sings the last line of the chorus right into Aiden's ear—then he's gone with a shake of his hips, strutting across the stage in those obscenely tight leather pants, turning back just once to blow Aiden a smug kiss. He looks alive, more alive than Aiden has ever seen him, and he's never been so sexy.

Jake picks out a member of the crowd, to whom he sings a line or two, before moving on and doing it again. By the time he reaches the final chorus of the song they're all begging and screaming for him, even some of the guys. Aiden watches them with a tight ball of possessiveness in his gut. He wants nothing more than to grab Jake, run with him back to the RV and spend hours showing him that he, Aiden Calloway, is the only one who knows how to undo him.

Jake belts out the final chorus, one arm raised and a foot stomping in time. Marcie steps up for her trumpet solo to close the song and Jake begins to thrust his hips to the beat—if it were anyone else it would look ridiculous, but this is Jake Valentine: tall, beautiful, yoga enthusiast, incredible in bed and, apparently, secret rock star. Aiden sends up a silent prayer of thanks that he's wearing such tight jeans, because he's nearing the uncomfortable stage of hard and the last thing he needs is a roomful of strangers seeing exactly what Jake does to him.

As the song ends, Jake punches the air. The crowd cheers louder and longer than they have for anyone yet—they want sex and Jake has given it to them, pure and undiluted.

Feeling suddenly exhausted and needing a moment to collect himself, Aiden scrambles from the stage and pushes his way to the bar, where he asks the bartender for two glasses of water. As surreptitiously as possible, he reaches down to adjust his jeans just enough to relieve some of the pressure. One way or another, Jake is going to be his end.

Drinking deeply from his glass, he catches a flash of pink and blond in his peripheral vision and turns to see Jake rushing toward him with a dazzling smile lighting his face.

"Jake! Holy hell, you were—"

Jake reaches forward and grabs Aiden by the front of his jacket, hauling him into a fast and crushing kiss; when he pulls back, hands trembling, he whispers "Thank you" over and over again against Aiden's lips.

Heart clenching in his chest, breathing heavily, Aiden cups the back of Jake's neck. Jake presses his forehead against Aiden's temple, and all Aiden can dazedly think is, *Mission accomplished.*

5,569 MILES

DAY FORTY-SIX: INDIANA

Much to Aiden's dismay, Pawnee does not exist in the state of Indiana.

Wanting to preserve as much of the magic as possible—as much magic as there is to be found in Indiana, at least—Aiden had declared a rule about the state: Neither he nor Jake were allowed to plan what they would do when they got there. They would simply visit the town of Pawnee—the setting of Aiden's favorite TV show, *Parks & Recreation*—and figure out the rest later.

When the GPS told them, however, that there were towns by that name in Illinois, Oklahoma and Texas, but not in Indiana, their lack of plans proved to be something of a problem for Jake. He took control of the navigation and located a campground in Portage before setting about finding them something to do nearby.

"Have you ever thought about directing a post-apocalyptic disaster movie?" Jake had asked, scrolling through an article on his phone.

"Only always," Aiden replied; and so Jake had decided to program the GPS to direct them to the derelict Union Station in Gary.

The station is a husk. Boards block the main entrance, but getting inside is a matter of simply walking through a large gap. Jake finds himself in awe of just how much wreck and ruin can exist inside a single building while its exterior shows only blemishes. The main hall is littered with debris, obvious—yet old—fire damage lines the walls near the roof, and a lone armchair sits off-kilter in the center of the room, its powder blue upholstery shredded.

He and Aiden separate to walk opposite sides of the perimeter—or as close as they can get to it given the thick scattering of wood and metal. Halfway along, set into the wall and almost indistinguishable from the dirt, is a simple paneled door, inconspicuous save for the rusted padlock holding it shut. Jake is just reaching out for it when Aiden calls out, "Hello!" from across the floor. A frantic flapping sound comes from the other end of the hall, and Jake looks up to see a pair of crows make a hasty exit through a hole in the roof. The echoes of Aiden's voice reverberate in a way that makes the hairs on the back of his neck stand up.

"So, Mister Big Director, what would we film here?" Jake asks, glancing across at Aiden.

"Well, I know you mentioned the post-apocalypse thing earlier, but... couldn't this place make for the ultimate feel-good movie?"

"Are you joking?"

"Not at all. Think about it," Aiden says, gesturing around the hall and turning to face Jake. "Couple of architects discover this place and decide they should restore it to its former glory?"

"Okay, I could get on board with that," Jake concedes. Wood creaks above his head in the breeze that whips through the exposed interior, and he keeps talking to stave off the sensation of a ghost at his back. "So who are these architects? And why are they in *Gary*, of all places?"

"The location doesn't matter; they could be anywhere. What matters is this place. Don't you remember when we went down to Biddeford to explore that abandoned nursing home?"

"I don't follow."

"You said that you'd always thought about buying some old, abandoned place and restoring it," Aiden says.

Jake stops in his tracks and blinks at Aiden, his brow furrowed. Though it takes him a second, he *does* remember.

Both seventeen, they had wandered through that old nursing home for hours, scouring the place for something quirky or interesting to take home. The only thing they found worth taking, the place having undoubtedly already been picked apart by other urban explorers, was a vaguely creepy wooden marionette that Aiden insisted was probably valuable. It wasn't, not even a little bit, and after a series of somewhat spooky but ultimately—in Jake's opinion—explicable events, they ended up ritualistically burning it at one of their friend Josh's Hellraiser Bonfires.

As they climbed back out of the first floor window of the nursing home, Jake had told Aiden what he'd been thinking for the past hour: "Wouldn't it be cool to restore this place, or make it into something different? I've always thought about doing it. It's kind of sad that it's just empty, don't you think?"

Now, Jake shakes his head. "*How* do you remember that stuff? I'm the one who's supposed to be good with details."

Aiden shrugs and crouches to examine something on the floor. Jake tries to distract himself in a similar way, but this is another moment, in a lengthening series of moments, that brings into startling focus exactly how damaging what they've started could prove to be. Jake has been letting himself get carried away, giving in too often to the need to glut himself on the touching and kissing and intimacy, and he's beginning to forget how to rein himself in. The worst part is that he's also losing the will to care.

"I've gotta get some life into this place," he sings to break the tension, and it still strikes him how unfamiliar his own voice sounds.

"Been livin' here too long, at too slow a pace," Aiden responds, smiling as he stands and turns to cross the expansive floor.

"I'll wake up tomorrow just the same as today."

"But tomorrow will be different, 'cause that's when I'll say..."

By the time they meet in the middle, Jake mirrors Aiden's warm smile; they're somewhere they aren't supposed to be, and a frisson of rebellion races the length of his spine as they sing in unison, "This could be new, could be new, it could be all brand new. Just open your eyes and you'll see it, too."

"That song is the *worst*," Aiden groans. "Can you believe I actually wrote that crap?"

Laughing giddily, Jake takes Aiden's arms and wraps them around his own waist. "So tell me more about these architects."

"Well, I figure one of them is kind of down and out, you know? One last job before he gives up and becomes a professor, or something."

"And the other?"

"Young prodigy, obviously. Fresh out of college and answers the other guy's ad for a collaborator."

"So they clash from the beginning, but against *all* odds, end up complementing one another?"

"Hey, they're clichés for a reason," Aiden says with an easy grin. "If you think about it, that's sort of like us, with how many times we've argued about film techniques. And somehow everything we worked on together turned out great."

"That's because we're a very special, and very rare, breed of awesome," Jake says.

"Come on, there's more to it than that."

"Well, sure there is. We've been best friends since before we could tie our shoelaces. Everything had to dovetail at some point, right?"

"Of course, but that's not..." Aiden trails off and drops his gaze, unwraps his arms from Jake's waist and takes his hands instead. Jake waits, rubs his thumbs over Aiden's knuckles, and thinks, *Don't say it, Dan. Don't say it, please don't say it.*

And then Aiden looks up at him with so much fondness and torture in his expression that Jake hears a click in the back of his mind, feels himself splinter and begin to peel apart like damp wood, because... he's in love with Aiden.

Jake Valentine is in love with Aiden Calloway.

The moment hangs, silently suspended between them, disturbed dust motes floating around, and it takes everything Jake has not to reel back from it. He bites his lip and looks away, lacking the trust that he will not prostrate himself at Aiden's feet and make declarations and promises he could never possibly keep; as soon as he even tries, all of what is good and right between them will be dashed, he's sure of it. *This* is why he should have repeated to himself over and over, *What happens on the road trip stays on the road trip.*

Carefully, keeping his face as neutral as possible, Jake opens his mouth. He's cut off by a sharp crack overhead, and he and Aiden both look up just in time to see a thick wooden roof beam break off the ceiling and fall straight down toward them.

He's knocked sideways and lands heavily on the floor, pain flaring sharply along his ribs. He lies still for a moment, listening to the echo of the deep, resounding thud the beam left behind. When he finally breathes out, blood rushing in his ears as his heart pounds, his exhalation disturbs the dust.

Aiden groans somewhere behind him, and Jake staggers to his feet, clutching his side as he stumbles to where Aiden lies on the other side of the beam. Pain is etched into every line on Aiden's face and his eyes are screwed shut as he cradles his arm to his chest. Jake's hands tremble as he cups Aiden's face.

"'m fine," Aiden mumbles before Jake can say anything. "It just glanced off me, I'm fine."

"Jesus," Jake breathes. He drops his forehead to rest against Aiden's and twists to press a kiss to his lips, his heart stuttering when Aiden takes one of Jake's hands in his own.

"Are you okay?" Aiden asks, pulling back to search Jake's face, turning it this way and that.

"I'm okay, Super-Dan," Jake replies with an almost hysterical giggle, and then the reality hits him all at once—what if Aiden had been a second too late, or if neither of them had noticed at all. "You just... you just saved our lives."

Adrenalin courses through his veins. Aiden leans to kiss him again, the pressure fierce and almost too much. "Are—you sure—you're okay?" Aiden asks him between kisses.

He doesn't answer right away, suddenly feeling as far from okay as possible. He's never felt more powerless. Finally he nods, wriggles out of Aiden's grasp and pulls him to his feet. Aiden takes Jake's hand in his own and intertwines their fingers with a gentle squeeze, and Jake flashes on that same hand sliding across a tabletop in Provincetown.

This time, Jake doesn't refuse; on the contrary, he holds on for dear life.

JAKE IS BACK in the old train station, but he can't remember how he got there. The interior looks completely different, still a husk, but as if it's been used recently. The grout between the white brick tiles on the lower half of the walls has turned gray and brown; the wood of the benches is worn and faded. The beige flooring is cracked and raised in places, and in the upper corners of the room, black mold mottles the walls. The ceiling is stained, but intact.

He expects to feel a sense of trepidation and foreboding, but all he feels is an overwhelming sadness that this place has been forgotten. Aiden's grip on his hand is tight, though Jake can't recall if it's been there from the start or if it has only just appeared. He runs the fingers of his free hand along the backs of the benches, pressing into the dust at intervals and leaving behind fingerprints.

They turn toward the padlocked door, the floor before it free of debris, and walk in a beam of sunlight that pours in from behind them. Jake's shadow stretches in front of him, but Aiden's is cast to the side.

"I brought you something," Aiden says, his voice hushed, and they stop in the middle of the aisle as Jake turns to face him. Out of his pocket, Aiden draws an old-fashioned brass barrel key and presses it into Jake's palm. "Don't be gone too long, sweetheart."

Before Jake can ask what he means, Aiden softly kisses his jaw, and is gone.

Jake weighs the key in his hand, trying to learn the measure and balance of it. While old-fashioned in design, not a single mark tarnishes the brass. A knocking begins, which sounds as though it's coming from behind the paneled door; Jake strides toward it, fumbling to fit the key in the lock as the knocking grows louder and more insistent.

Silence falls suddenly; the only sound that slices it apart is the ominous creak of the door swinging wide open. The closet beyond is darkened, the air inside thick with age, its only contents a small, dainty music box on the floor in the center of the room. The box is of a simple design: almost square, about six inches wide and four inches deep, the dark wooden lid inlaid with a crescent moon, two stars and two musical notes. Slowly, Jake winds the silver handle and opens the lid. Inside, a pearlescent ballerina turns in circles to the somber, despondent tune of "The Scientist" by Coldplay. All at once, Jake thinks of a kiss that never was, that should have been, that would have canceled out all other kisses.

Lying on the bottom of the music box is a single train ticket, printed with Chicago as the destination. Carefully tucking the still open music box into the crook of his elbow, he pulls out the ticket and studies it, thinking, *I know what's in Chicago.*

Stepping out of the closet and toward the window in the waiting room, Jake sees a train beginning to pull out of the station. He rushes outside into blazing sunlight; an electronic screen suspended from the corrugated iron shelter tells him that the train is bound for Chicago.

"You missed it," Aiden says, appearing at his elbow.

"I missed it," Jake repeats.

"There'll be another one," Aiden says, an easy confidence in his tone, and suddenly he's sitting on a bench and patting the seat next to him.

"But isn't this where I'm supposed to be?" Jake asks as he sits down, perching the music box on his knees. Aiden's smile is even brighter than the sunshine that lights up the platform. He settles his arm around Jake's shoulders.

"You'll come back, sweetheart. You always do," he says, tilting Jake's face toward his. "I know you'll always be waiting for me."

"But what do I do until then?" Jake asks, imploring, even as Aiden closes the gap between them. Aiden smiles as their lips brush, and—

Jake wakes up, jerking upright with a gasp, wondering where he is. His phone is beeping, and after shutting it off, he sinks back against his pillows, scrubbing a hand through his messy hair. There's a cold, empty space in the bed next to him, and he glances over to find a note on Aiden's pillow that reads, *Cupboards empty, went out in search of breakfast and ice packs. Back soon.*

It's too hot, and Jake unceremoniously throws off the sheets tangled around his legs. He clambers out of bed, grabs his phone and stumbles to the closet for his yoga mat. Humming absently under his breath, finding solace in the simple pleasure of *finally* being free to let the music flow out of him, he spreads out the mat in the living area and begins his warmup stretches.

The dream preys on his mind even as he tries to push it away. *I never remember my dreams. Why this one?* It's as if he had been gazing at a surrealist painting, trying to discern the meaning behind it, and someone had come striding up to him and hit him over the head with it. He can still hear "The Scientist" playing, as clearly as if the music box were sitting right before him, and as he stumbles over an easy stretch that he could normally perform in his sleep, he growls in frustration.

It's the seven-year-old memory that he tries not to let surface too often lest it swallow him whole; the memory of what happened the day his father died, before Jake knew that anything was amiss.

Aiden was wearing those canary-yellow pants of his that Jake outwardly professed to abhor but secretly loved on him, particularly against the deep blue of his favorite comforter. Jake's dad was working out on the boats; with the thunder rumbling outside and rain pounding heavily, Jake thought he would probably be home early. When the words on the tip of his tongue finally became too urgent to hold back anymore, Jake threw down his pen in the middle of their Coldplay-soundtracked study session. In a tremulous voice, Jake confessed his deepest, darkest secret: "Dan, I think... no, I *know*... I'm gay."

After trading Jake's confession for his own, Aiden tilted Jake's entire world-view by shyly asking, "Would you... I mean, since we're both... we could make out, if you want."

Eyes wide, face flaming, Jake asked, "What?!"

"Kidding! I was totally kidding," Aiden said, sitting up straight and grabbing Jake's hands. There was a pause, and Jake couldn't help looking at Aiden's mouth, blushing even harder when he thought about all the times he'd gotten off thinking about his best friend. "Unless..."

"Unless what?" Jake whispered.

"Would you... I mean, can I?"

Without letting himself think about what it might mean, Jake nodded. Aiden moved closer, his tongue darting out to wet his lips as he leaned in. Jake's heart began to race; he was about to get his *first kiss,* from none other than his best friend in the whole world... and just as his eyes fluttered closed, he heard a knock on the front door.

Afterward, they never spoke of it again. The matter was too big for them to make sense of, let alone address. The knock on the door had been two police officers coming to tell Jake that his father was dead. They reverted to what they had always been to one another: best friends, pillars of support, nothing more. And in the years since, Jake has learned to give up on his feelings, learned to keep people who look at him *that* way at arm's length. It's just easier.

Jake reaches over to his phone and hits shuffle. As he sinks into a relaxed Sun Salutation, he lets the music regulate his breathing and guide his thoughts: *I am not in love with Aiden. I don't fall in love.*

Moving through a series of simple poses, working purely on muscle memory, he doesn't allow himself to wonder if that missed kiss should only have been a *near* miss, if they'd been supposed to revisit it soon afterward and make something of it, if what they've always shared is love—love that at first didn't know it was love, and is now trying to be.

It doesn't matter, Jake thinks, *because it's not love.*

More than anything, he's angry with himself for getting so caught up, for losing sight of what they actually have, for idealizing and dreaming and wishing. He dislikes the person he became while Aiden was in London, but he likes this version of himself even less. What has he become, mooning after his best friend like a love-struck teenager? There is no way he's in love with Aiden, or that he's been in love with Aiden all along. The very notion is laughable at best—how could one person be *that* stupid? He isn't that person at all; Jake Valentine is nothing if not in complete control of himself. Calling it "love" when it's just a mix of tension and sex and vacation is wrong... calling it "love" gives Aiden the power—real, terrible power—to break him.

I'm just out of my element, he thinks. *All I need is to step back, recalibrate and remember who I am.*

He can still feel the thick, crisp paper of the train ticket between his fingers, and as he moves from a high lunge to a low one, bringing his hands together in front of his chest with his eyes closed, he knows where it will happen.

Chicago.

5,780 MILES

DAY FORTY-NINE: ILLINOIS

During their second year of college, Aiden and Jake took the same video editing class to fulfill one of their core requirements. The final project of the semester was to create a short film using a well-known song in the style of a music video, but either flip or reinterpret the original meaning of the song.

Aiden chose "Mr. Brightside" by The Killers, an intense and electric song about jealousy, possessiveness and cheating. Within a week he had papered the college with posters headlined, *If You've Ever Been Cheated On, Help Out a Fellow Student by Reading This!* It was a dirty tactic, but he got an overwhelming response. His idea was to film students from all different majors and areas of the campus lip-syncing the song, and edit it to tell the story of an aftermath devoid of closure, of lingering trauma and of the fruitless wish to one day get even.

No matter how Aiden begged, Jake refused to participate in the main part of the video, insisting that Aiden retain his artistic integrity by only using subjects who had actually been cheated on. He did, however, agree to perform his fire poi routine as part of the video in order to give it the atmosphere of orchestrated yet raw chaos Aiden was hoping to achieve.

On his last day of filming, Aiden was out on the quad looking through some of his footage when Jake found him. He looked troubled, and at first Aiden thought nothing of it; Jake had been bitching about the difficulties he was having with his own film for days.

And then Jake said, "You don't need to double up on April's lines anymore," and Aiden froze.

They filmed Jake's lines that same day, and later, Aiden's professor praised him for the surprising yet effective artistic choice of making the mesmerizing fire poi performer the last shot of the video and, therefore, the overall subject of the video's story.

In those days, Jake talked about getting even with Max, coming up with elaborate revenge plans that, for whatever reason, he never saw through. Now, the closer they get to Chicago, where Max moved after graduation, the more nauseous Aiden feels. He knows exactly what's going to happen, and is powerless to stop it. Momentum is building behind it, driving a wedge—however temporary—between them, and as they turn into a residential neighborhood, Aiden can't help but think of the look in Jake's eyes in his two close-up shots in the video. The light in them was muted, overtaken by something resigned and incommunicably sad; it was a look Aiden had hoped he would never see again.

Until they were almost hit by that wooden beam inside the train station in Gary, he hadn't.

It has stayed there ever since, even yesterday as they pounded the pavement and toured the sights of Chicago proper. Jake was quiet. His eyes didn't light up the way Aiden had been hoping and expecting they would when they took pictures of their distorted reflections in The Bean, and he was almost unresponsive during lunch at the top of the John Hancock building, even when Aiden attempted to start another game of *What Would We Film Here?* It was then that Aiden realized exactly what Jake was doing, and wondered if a little of the light in his own eyes had been snuffed out.

Jake cuts the engine outside a small, cozy-looking brick house with a hunter-green front door. He turns to face Aiden, but Aiden trains his gaze on a spot somewhere in the middle distance, for what can he say? What can he *do? Nothing. There's nothing,* he thinks. *Jake's going to do whatever he feels like he needs to do, regardless of whether I give him a reason not to. What reason could I even come up with, anyway? It isn't like he owes me anything—maybe in another life, he would. Maybe in another life, we wouldn't even be here.*

"I'm staying in the RV tonight," he says gruffly, picking at a thread on his jeans.

"I thought you might," Jake says, and then, hesitantly, "How did you know?"

Aiden snorts derisively and shakes his head. "The last time we did anything was back in Michigan. You're warming up. I get it."

"Dan..." Jake trails off, his voice soft and tinged with regret.

"It's fine," Aiden says, and unclips his seat belt. "Come on. Let's go."

He's halfway to the door when Jake grabs his arm and spins him around; Jake kisses him roughly, pushing his fists into Aiden's hair, and it feels like a preemptive apology that Aiden doesn't have the wherewithal to brush off or turn down. Instead he kisses Jake back just as forcefully and sucks in a breath of hollow air when he pulls back. He bolts from the RV before he has the chance to do something he'll regret, like lock the door and drive off with Jake little more than a hostage.

The front door opens before they even make it up the steps, and *god*, Aiden forgot just how intensely he dislikes everything about Max Whitley, from his overly preppy fashion sense and his too-white teeth to his perfectly styled jet black hair and the slight curl of disdain permanently tugging at his upper lip.

"Jake! Aiden! Man, *so* good to see you guys again," he greets them, jogging down the steps and pulling them both into a semi-awkward hug. Merely being in his presence is enough to remind Aiden of how lost Jake was with Max: happy but not his happiest, trying for something like what everyone else had and ultimately being betrayed when he didn't "measure up." While Aiden knows Jake was never in love with Max, he might have been on his way to it—and when Jake loves, he does so fearfully, and holds on with everything he has. It isn't something to be taken lightly or thrown away, and that is exactly what Max did.

"Good to see you, too," Jake says.

"Let's go catch up, huh?" Max asks, though he leaves no room for argument as he motions them both inside, and Aiden doesn't miss the way his piercing blue eyes rake up and down Jake's body as he passes by.

Aiden grits his teeth and says nothing—a practice he employs for the two hours Jake and Max spend catching up. He speaks only when spoken to, and just nods along the rest of the time. He knows he's acting like a child, but can't seem to help it. Moreover, he doesn't particularly want to.

At least there's beer, he thinks upon finishing his third bottle in as many hours. The buzz in his limbs is the only pleasant thing about the evening's rapid fade into darkness—which apparently takes with it the need for things such as personal space and decorum.

They're sitting in Max's living room, three walls painted a neutral cream and the other a deep red that frames the large plasma screen. Before Aiden can protest, they're watching *The Breakfast Club*—the very movie that he and Jake decided would be their movie for Illinois. He didn't think he could be any more pissed off, but the movies are *their* thing, not to be shared with anyone else. Especially not Max fucking Whitley, and especially not this movie, which they've watched so many times that Aiden has long since lost count.

He tries to focus all of his attention on it nevertheless, but his mind seems to have become a wasteland of regrets and the dozen men before him, who all took advantage of the opportunity he's missed time and time again. He coils deeper and deeper within himself, and the more beer he sucks down, the more things feel terribly, terribly wrong. So he keeps drinking.

When he looks over, he can see Jake and Max's fingers brushing in the ever-decreasing space between their thighs. Then Max has his arm around Jake's shoulders, and Jake's eyes flutter closed, and he lets out a pleased hum as Max noses along the side of his face.

Aiden squeezes his bottle so tightly he's surprised it doesn't shatter, and leaps up as if the couch has burned him. Max and Jake spring apart, and if it weren't for the terrible wave of nausea coursing through him, Aiden might laugh at the way Max almost cowers behind Jake. He always has been a complete chickenshit.

"I'm leaving," Aiden manages to grit out between clenched teeth, eyes boring into Jake, who doesn't quite seem able to meet his gaze. "I'll be in the RV. You can come find me when you're done here."

He pauses for a moment, waits for Jake to say something, to stand up and take his hand and walk right out the door with him, before turning on his heel. Head held high, he strides out of the living room, down the hall and out the front door, slamming it behind him for good measure. "Ugh," he groans, scrubbing a hand over his face as if he can wipe a sudden rush of flashbulb imagery from his mind's eye: Jake's bare torso; Jake biting the very corner of his bottom lip; Jake smiling wickedly as he wraps his fingers around Aiden's cock. Jake, Jake, Jake, doing all the things they've been doing together but doing them with Max instead, a person who undoubtedly knows his way around Jake's body just as well as—if not better than—Aiden does.

The thought makes him itch, and he berates himself as he paces the length of the RV, studiously avoiding even a glimpse of the bed. *So fucking stupid, so fucking blind. You're an idiot, Aiden Calloway. An idiot who can't keep your best friend from doing something that'll end up hurting you both.*

Finally, he collapses onto the couch and pulls out his phone. He hits shuffle, neither knowing nor caring what song is about to start, because it's all just noise anyway. Minutes pass—ten, sixty, Aiden loses track—and given how much he's had to drink, he should, by rights, be far drowsier. When the song from the first time Jake fucked him begins to play, however, it shocks him back into wakefulness and West Virginia; sense memories tear their way along his body and he buries his hands in his hair just to give them something to do. It's no use. He's pissed off and frustrated and, with images of Jake rising unbidden on the backs of his eyelids, Jake's moans ringing in his ears, he's getting hard, uncomfortably so.

He hits shuffle again before giving in entirely and roughly shoving his hand into his briefs.

It doesn't matter what he listens to—for some reason, all he can see is that stupid music video. Aiden remembers every last frame of the damned thing—by the end of the editing process, he had never wanted to listen to the song again. But right now, as he works himself into a frenzy of frustration, running after his release as if it is being dangled in front of him, it seems oddly apropos. The video cycles in his mind, Jake's fire poi routine flashing circles behind his eyes, the faces of every single student he featured coming back to haunt him.

In less than a minute he's panting and grunting, not caring what noise he makes because he just needs to be done. Jake's face is the only one with any clarity amongst the blur of frame after frame, angle after angle spliced together until the video in his mind is no longer a chaotic and beautiful performance, but a nightmare.

His back arches with an almost painful snap when he comes, an abandoned cry of Jake's name wrapped around his tongue and the final frame of the video frozen in the forefront of his mind. It's that look he'd never wanted to see again but, for some perverse reason, suddenly can't get enough of: the thunderous gray overtaking the usual deep green of Jake's eyes, a look that Aiden knows he would never deliberately put there himself.

"Fuck. Fuck, fuck, fucking hell," he whispers, half-sobbing and shuddering as he grinds the heels of his hands into his eyes.

For a count of five he lets himself be lost, breathing raggedly, making no attempt to stave off the bile burning the back of his throat. *One,* he counts. *You have more with him than anyone else ever has. Two. So get it together. Three. Don't be a slave to how you feel; today you barely stopped short of pissing all over him. Four. He has the right to do whatever the fuck he wants. Five. You still have a right to be pissed off, but he's not yours to claim. He's made that clear.*

Then, calmly, he turns off the music, quickly changes into clean underwear and sweats, sits back down on the couch and closes his eyes just for a second.

The next thing he's aware of is the engine of the RV rumbling beneath him, but Aiden doesn't bother to move; a quick check of his watch confirms that he slept for a little under an hour, and his head is already throbbing.

It's twenty minutes before Jake pulls the RV into a spacious parking lot somewhere—Aiden hasn't exactly been paying attention, and he's finding it difficult to care all that much—and switches off the engine. Aiden looks up in time to see Jake walking quickly toward him; he jumps up from the couch and takes three steps back, and Jake stops in the middle of the living area, hands opening and closing at his sides.

"I'm sorry," Jake whispers, and Aiden's stomach gives a painful lurch. "I'm so sorry, Dan, I couldn't—"

Aiden resists a perverse urge to laugh and looks Jake squarely in the eye. "All this for a fuck-and-run?"

"Dan, it wasn't—" Jake starts, but Aiden holds up his hand.

"Don't," he says, moving toward the bedroom and turning his back. "Just don't."

5,810 MILES

CHAPTER 6

DAY FIFTY-ONE: WISCONSIN

Jake (8:53 a.m.) – *[Sent to: ALL CONTACTS]* Have you voted?

April (9:12 a.m.) – Yes, dummy. Remember we all did our absentee ballots at the same time?

Toby (10:32 a.m.) – We managed to coordinate lunch breaks so we can head over together. Thanks for the reminder!

Marcie (11:01 a.m.) – Of course! Thank you so much again for all your help with the door-to-door this summer!

Eric (11:11 a.m.) – Got my sticker and everything. And now, we wait.

Aiden (12:59 p.m.) – Finally on my way back. Got into a debate with a Romney supporter. They were out of the sandwich you wanted so I got you an Italian Club instead. Need anything else while I'm out?

Zoe P. (1:44 p.m.) – IMG_20121106_9368.JPG

Zoe P. (1:44 p.m.) – Voting lines around the block! :)

Alice (4:54 p.m.) – Never realized all of this driving around would be so exhausting! Don't know how you two do it! Getting them all to the polls has been worth it, though, even if just for some of the characters I've met today. Give Aiden a hug from his momma.

Charlie (5:02 p.m.) – Just got off work and heading straight to the polling station. Good luck tonight, Jakey. Give me a call soon, okay? We need to talk about this house thing.

Aiden (6:00 p.m.) – Where are you? It's starting.

Jake smiles crookedly, anticipation fluttering, and pockets his phone. He stands outside Madison's, a bar on King Street, having a much-needed moment to himself after what has been a thoroughly crazy day. The evening air is cool and he breathes as he would if he was doing yoga inside the RV with his mat stretched out in front of the couch where he has slept for the past two nights.

Before Chicago, Jake thought that going there and being with Max was at least partly about closure, but it wasn't really about that at all—it was about proving something he thought he knew about himself but that turned out to be a gross mistruth. It was an itch that he'd needed to scratch, but when Jake had Max sprawled out on top of soft, pristine covers and looking up at him with his penetrating gaze and lecherous smirk, Jake couldn't do it. And he had tried, *god,* how he had tried. The mortification still smarts. And then, after he ran back to the RV and drove them far enough away that he stopped wanting to throw up, he saw the hurt in Aiden's eyes and his stomach flipped like a pancake, and he knew without question that he had fallen in love with Aiden, sometime beyond memory.

Today, he and Aiden have reached some sort of unspoken détente. Over the summer they both spent time volunteering for President Obama's re-election campaign, and the excitement over all of their efforts hopefully coming to fruition has put a firm moratorium on mostly everything else.

He sighs once, allowing himself a moment's grace. Somehow he will make things right between them, but tonight is not the night.

When he steps inside, Aiden waves him over to the bar with a rueful half-smile.

"Have they called any yet?" he asks, sliding onto an empty bar stool next to him and taking a sip of the cocktail that Aiden slides over.

"Indiana and Kentucky for Romney, Vermont for Obama," Aiden replies succinctly. He tilts his head toward Jake but does not look away from the screen over the bar playing NBC News; he rests his elbows on the bar, clasps his hands and absently chews his thumbnail. Tension radiates from him in waves. Tentatively, Jake slides his hand over, fingers splayed and wiggling to catch Aiden's attention. It feels a little as it did back in Provincetown: a hand reaching out for more where there has never *been* more. Only this time, it's Jake trying to push back unturnable tides.

When Aiden finally takes his hand, though, Jake thinks that maybe together they can do it.

"What about Question One? Any news?" he asks, referring to the bill on Maine's ballot that, if passed, will grant marriage equality to same-sex couples.

Aiden shakes his head and takes a large gulp of his beer, then grabs a napkin and wipes his mouth. "What if—"

"Dan," Jake interrupts. "This is our year."

At last, Aiden gives him a real smile. After he briefly leans into Jake's touch, and after Jake bites his lip against the urge to kiss the smile wider, they join hands again and settle in to watch.

The hours pass at a crawl, and tension grows as more and more people filter into the bar. Despite the air conditioning and the cool temperatures outside, it quickly becomes hot; and before long, the scent of beer and body odor permeates the air.

At seven p.m., they cheer as Maine is called for Obama along with Illinois, Rhode Island, Connecticut, Delaware and Maryland. At eight-thirty, the entire bar erupts in triumphant whoops as Wisconsin goes blue. And at ten fifty-four p.m., when early results show marriage equality ahead in Maine, Aiden's unfailing grip on Jake's hand suddenly becomes so tight it almost hurts. Uncomfortable under the weight of his scrutiny, Jake shifts in his seat and signals the bartender for another round.

At length, Aiden asks, "Do you think you'll capitalize on it?"

"On what?" Jake asks, pulling out his wallet. "On marriage equality?"

"Yeah, if we get it."

Making a face at him, Jake nudges over his fresh bottle of beer. "Of course we'll get it. This is our year."

Aiden takes a fast pull from his beer. With a tight smile, a quizzically furrowed brow and a humorless laugh, he asks, "Why didn't you answer my question?"

"Because I don't know."

"Why not?"

"Aiden, *Jesus*," Jake exclaims.

"I'm just curious."

Taking a deep breath, Jake squares his shoulders and says, "Maybe. I mean, I'd like to think there's someone out there who could put up with me 'til death do us part, but..."

"There *is* someone, you know," Aiden says, as matter-of-factly as if he's commenting on the weather.

"What are you saying?" Jake asks slowly.

Aiden takes a long, deliberate drink from his bottle and meets Jake's questioning look. "There *is* someone who can put up with you. He's been doing it for seventeen years already."

"I don't understand what you're trying to say," Jake says weakly, his stomach twisting into a tight knot. *There's no way he can be saying what I think he's saying. Not with the rules. Not after what happened in Chicago.*

"Just that," Aiden says, his voice infuriatingly mild.

"What about you?" Jake asks, shifting in his seat to face him.

A barely there smile has the corners of Aiden's mouth twitching, and at length he responds, "If the time was right, if he was the right guy... yeah, I think I'd like to get married."

"Proposal?" Jake prompts, resting his chin in his hand.

"Something simple," Aiden answers, looking thoughtful. "Quiet and intimate, just the two of us. Not on an anniversary or a birthday or Christmas. *Definitely* not on Valentine's."

"You or m—him?" Jake forces out, quickly covering his slip and clearing his expression as much as he's able. He can't keep letting his mind run away with his tongue, he *can't*—it feels too much like cheating himself. He clears his throat. "Would you be the one getting swept off your feet or the one doing the sweeping?"

"I haven't ever really thought that far ahead," Aiden admits, picking at the label on his beer bottle where condensation is causing it to peel away from the glass. "Either way you end up pretty vulnerable."

"Isn't that the point of love, though? Being vulnerable but being okay with it?"

"No. It's being vulnerable but trusting the other person not to betray that vulnerability."

Jake finds himself nodding even as this hits him with blunt, bruising force. It's an unexpected segue, but a segue nonetheless.

Not a second after he opens his mouth to speak, the bar erupts in a cheer. Jake's head snaps up to the television, where he sees a smartly dressed blonde anchorwoman. She holds her earpiece and says, "Once again, that's Iowa, California, and Washington for President Obama. I'm just waiting for confirmation..."

A quiet envelops the inside of Madison's, and Jake leans over to press his forehead to Aiden's temple; his eyes slip closed. Aiden squeezes Jake's knee and leaves his hand there; Jake covers it with his own and takes a deep breath.

"And with two hundred and seventy-four electoral votes, we are now calling this election for President Barack Obama."

The force of Aiden's hug, arms thrown tightly around him with Aiden's face buried in the hollow of his neck, almost topples Jake from his stool. He grabs the bar with one hand to right himself and then holds Aiden tightly, thoughtlessly pressing a kiss into his hair.

Looking around the bar, he sees other couples and groups of friends hugging, exchanging high fives and fist bumps, and two girls by the door to the restrooms are wiping away each other's joyful tears. The group of students sitting over by the electronic jukebox is playing celebratory music. Jake grins despite himself, lets himself revel in the simple, uncomplicated, unbridled elation of the moment.

Aiden has always been so expressive that Jake has never had difficulty reading the emotions on his face—an exaggerated downward quirk of his mouth when trying not to laugh; a tilt of his head and furrow of his brow when giving sympathy; a slight but unmistakable widening of his eyes and a flush of anticipation in his cheeks when turned on—but when Aiden breaks their hug, clears his throat and settles his hands on his thighs as though he doesn't know what to do with them, Jake has no idea what's going through his mind. The water is flowing quickly between them instead of under a bridge—does he need to divert it or build a bridge over it? At this point, either action looks likely to require a Herculean effort, with skills he can't be sure he possesses.

The rest of the evening passes in a blur, exchanging goodwill and congratulations with the other bar patrons as they all wait for Romney's concession and Obama's acceptance. By eleven fifty-nine p.m., in the midst of the merriment surrounding them, Jake has almost forgotten about Question One.

One minute to midnight, and the new ticker at the bottom of the television screen suddenly reads, *Breaking News*. Jake sits up straighter on his stool, his hand automatically gravitating toward Aiden's. A replay of Romney's concession speech cuts to the same blonde anchorwoman. Her makeup looks as if it's been retouched.

She smiles as she reports, "And while we're waiting for President Obama's acceptance speech, this evening Maine has made history as the first state to vote by referendum to back marriage equality."

It's as if he and Aiden have formed their own private vacuum; sound ceases to exist, and the air feels hard to come by. Jake feels tremors in Aiden's hands, almost imperceptible at first but growing until he shakes violently, his eyes still glued to the screen.

"Hey," Jake says, squeezing his hand. "Hey, look at me. Dan, *look at me*."

Even in the dimmed light of the bar, Aiden's eyes swim and shine, and for a moment he looks as if he doesn't recognize Jake. Then his expression clears, and he pitches forward to take Jake's face in his trembling hands and kiss him, softly and tenderly, like a first kiss at the end of a first date and the beginning of the rest.

God, I love you, Jake thinks, stretching into the kiss and welcoming the feeling of Aiden's lips skating over his own in long stretches, not caring that they're in public and acting like the very people he professed to hate back in Florida.

Aiden inhales sharply and breaks away, eyes remaining closed for a moment. Jake glances to their left and catches the bartender watching them with a wry smile.

"I'm guessing you guys are from Maine?" he asks, taking their empties and putting them behind the bar. At Jake's nod he continues, "Champagne's on the house if one of you proposes."

Aiden snorts derisively, and it all comes screaming back. "Unlikely, when we aren't even together," he says with a weariness that Jake hates with every fiber of his being.

"Could've fooled me," the bartender says, and moves off to serve some customers down the bar—or more likely refuse service, considering the way they practically fall over one another.

Jake is surprised to find that the assumption doesn't irritate him. The way he and Aiden interact, he can't blame someone for thinking they're an item.

"Told you it was our year," Jake says, and Aiden shoots him a quick smile. He looks freer than he has all night; Jake thinks, *Maybe the tide is turning anyway.*

5,957 MILES

DAY FIFTY-TWO: MINNESOTA

"Oh my g*od,*" Aiden wheezes between bouts of laughter. Jake is still splayed out on the shiny, waxed wooden floor of the lane, holding his stomach, his eyes watering from his own giggling. "This was the best idea *ever.*"

They're at the Bryant Lake Bowl in Minneapolis, a place that somehow manages to be a restaurant, bar, theater and bowling alley all at once. They have most of the bowling area to themselves, the only other people there a group of six hipster-looking students occupying the lane at the far end. Aiden had immediately fallen in love with the atmosphere of the place: warm and accepting, somewhere to get out of his head and cut loose for a while.

"Okay, okay," Jake says breathlessly, struggling to his feet and brushing off the seat of his pants. He squints as he looks at the pins. "Did I even hit any?"

"Gutterball," Aiden calls out, raising his voice to carry over the music.

"What was it again?" Jake asks as he walks over in time with the beat, and Aiden glances down at the dog-eared, laminated card titled, *BLB Crazy Bowl.*

"One-Eyed Jack," he says. "You have to turn around twice, cover one eye with your hand and bowl. That's how you ended up on your ass."

"Right," Jake replies, green eyes sparkling with some of that light Aiden has been missing. He checks the scoreboard. "Look who's winning. Two games to one."

"So *weird,* since I haven't beaten you since we were sixteen," Aiden comments, prodding him in the side and leaning in to say against his lips, "Stop letting me win."

Jake sashays away with a wink and a wiggle of his hips, retrieving another bowling ball as he goes. Aiden bites his lip and thinks, *There you are. I missed you.*

Aiden watches Jake almost follow the instructions from the laminated card, rapidly spinning twice and covering both eyes instead of one, as instructed. He sends the ball rapidly spinning into the gutter and, sure enough, ends up on his ass for the second time in a row. His bright, musical peals of laughter are infectious, and Aiden leans on the backs of chairs for support as he staggers over to help him up.

The teenagers at the other end of the alley are dancing and spinning one another in time with the song's stringed refrain, and Jake glances over at them as Aiden holds out a hand to help him up.

"Dance with me," he says, and Aiden complies immediately. It's almost too easy to assume a loose waltz position and let Jake lead them around in a slow dance that is more a shuffle of their feet than any discernible set of steps. He drops his head to rest on Jake's shoulder, inhaling the scent of his cologne and letting the music carry his heavy limbs.

Jake hums along to the vocalizations over the strings, and the vibrations tickle Aiden's cheek. He thinks, *The thing is, I'd be yours in a heartbeat if you asked. I'm already yours. Aren't you mine, too?*

"I've missed us like this," Jake murmurs, reminding Aiden that no, Jake *isn't* his. Lips brushing the outer shell of Aiden's ear, Jake says, "I've missed *you.*"

Aiden abruptly breaks their hold. Without meeting Jake's eyes, he asks, "Can we get out of here?"

Jake pauses. His hands slowly fall to his sides. "Sure. Let's go."

They'd left the RV in the parking lot of a grocery store only a few minutes' walk away, and Aiden wastes no time jumping into the driver's seat. He's pulling out of the lot before Jake has fully closed the passenger side door, and he sighs inwardly in gratitude when Jake remains silent.

It's a mere five-minute drive to the waters of Lake Calhoun, a straight shot up Lagoon Avenue, but to Aiden it seems unending. Anger charts a fiery path through his veins—he needs to be near the water, to look at it moving under the light of the half-moon and let its perpetual nature ground him again. It isn't Maine, it isn't the ocean, and it certainly isn't getting answers to all of his unasked questions, but it will have to do.

Jake seems to realize that Aiden needs some time alone and doesn't try to follow him out of the RV. Aiden's footsteps make dull thuds as he slowly walks the couple of blocks down to the lake and along a narrow dock that juts out into the water. He sits down at its end, crosses his legs and closes his eyes.

The night is fresh and uncomplicated, the water calm and still, but his head is a mess of threads tangled up in music and movies and sex. Aiden places his palms flat against the dock at either side of his body in an effort to give the anger somewhere to drain, to worm its way through the wood and down into the water where it will dissipate... but the encumbrance of his own unmet expectations presses down on him like a tangible weight he can't shrug off.

He isn't surprised when he hears the distinctive click of Jake's boots approaching.

"Dan?" he asks from a few paces back. "What's going on?"

Taking a deep breath, Aiden lets his eyes slip closed, just briefly, before standing to face him. Quietly he asks, "What are we?"

Jake sucks a breath in through his teeth and closes his eyes. Aiden's rage crests, and he lets the wave take him.

"I'm serious. Why are we doing this? Am I just your safe option because I'm here and willing?"

Jake stares him down with a look that makes Aiden want to step back. "In what universe would you be *anybody's* safe option?"

"I'm a pretty safe option for *you*," Aiden retorts. "It's not like you have to commit to anything with us, because you already laid down the rules, right? Only I think I missed the part where you get to go fuck your asshole ex-boyfriend just to *prove* that all this means nothing to you."

Jake stares at him with an incredulous expression. "You can't be serious right now."

"Oh, I'm deadly serious."

"You *really* think the reason I...*fuck*, Aiden. Do you even know me at all?"

"You know what? These days, I'm not so sure," Aiden says.

"Look, Aiden, it wasn't about *you*," Jake says, shaking his head and biting his lip. His brow furrows, and Aiden waits. "It was... all I wanted was one time with him that ended on *my* terms. Mine. I wanted to choose whether or not it happened, how it went, when to walk away."

Aiden considers this for a moment. "So you needed closure."

"Yes," Jake says, the relief in his tone almost palpable, but Aiden isn't even close to understanding why he did what he did.

"Why would you want closure that in *any* way gets him off, too? Tell me how that even works in your head, because I'm at a loss," he says.

"I know it's fucked up, that *I'm* fucked up—"

"Yeah, you are," Aiden interrupts. "You know, ever since this whole thing started—no, ever since I got *back,* you've been like a different person. Sometimes I feel like I barely know you at all."

"That's because I *am* a different fucking person!" Jake shouts, throwing his arms out to his sides. The sudden outburst makes Aiden take a step back. "And I said I'm sorry! What more do you want from me?"

Anger rising up in him yet again, Aiden walks forward, grabs Jake's arms and looks straight into his eyes. "I want you to tell me that this *is* just a road trip thing."

"What? Of course it is," Jake says, trying to wriggle out of Aiden's grip.

"Then why don't I believe you?" Aiden presses.

There is a long, awful pause in which Jake meets his eyes, the moonlight highlighting the frown lines around his mouth and between his eyebrows. And then he asks quietly, "What changed, Aiden?"

"What do you mean, 'what changed?' Nothing's changed."

"When did you fall for me?" Jake asks, his voice rising, and Aiden's stomach drops into his shoes.

"Stop it," he says, finally releasing his grip on Jake's arms and turning away. "This isn't about how I feel or don't feel about you. This is about *you* being selfish and reckless and a complete *idiot* for thinking any good would *ever* come of getting back into it with Max fucking Whitley."

"I wasn't getting back into it with him, Jesus!"

"Then what *were* you doing?"

"I was trying to prove to myself that *I* wasn't falling for *you!*" Jake screams.

His words echo around them, and then a terrible silence falls as Aiden just stares at the rapid rise and fall of Jake's chest, at the wideness of his eyes. Aiden shifts from one foot to the other. He opens and closes his mouth, wanting to ask so many questions but unable to give his voice to any of them.

Jake stuffs his hands into his pockets, drops his head and mumbles something that Aiden doesn't catch.

"What was that?"

"I didn't *fuck him*, Aiden." When Jake lifts his chin, his eyes flash with hurt and anger. "Fuck, I knew my opinion of myself was low, but I thought—I thought *you* thought better of me, at least."

"Jake." Aiden's voice is a relieved breath on the wind, all of the venom and fight suddenly gone. "What was I supposed to think? You let me believe—"

"I know, *I know*," Jake says. He covers his face with his hands and mutters, "I'm an asshole."

Aiden steps forward and tears Jake's hands away, takes a deep breath, and kisses him. He swallows Jake's surprised whimper, licking hungrily into his mouth. He can feel Jake's hands flail before they settle, one against Aiden's chest and the other molded to his neck. And he can feel the crack in Jake's armor widening.

I can wait, he thinks. *I can wait for you.*

"Aiden, I—stop for a second, just..."

"Okay, okay, I'm stopping," Aiden says, pressing his forehead to Jake's and cupping his jaw with both hands as they breathe each other's air.

"I don't want to fight with you," Jake murmurs, his breathing ragged. "That's not us; it's *never* been us."

"I know, I know," Aiden says quickly, all the fight in him gone. "I'm sorry, I just got so—"

"I know. I've been putting up with it for nearly seventeen years, remember?" Jake reminds him in a tentatively wry tone, and Aiden can't help but smile. "Can't we just... be happy with this?"

"What you did—what you let me *believe* you did—was really, *really* shitty," Aiden says.

"I know. I know, Dan, and I'm so sorry."

"But okay."

"Okay?"

"Okay," Aiden says with a shrug. "We can be happy with this."

"And we—" Jake stops, clears his throat and momentarily drops his gaze. "We have to remember that we're friends first."

Aiden hesitates. "One condition."

"I'm listening."

"I know you well enough to know that you were—you would have been safe," Aiden begins, searching Jake's eyes and receiving a nod. "But, look… we've been going out a lot and sure, we always look out for each other, but what happens if one of us isn't around? What if we get too drunk to remember to be safe?"

"Well, not that I really want to think about that, but sure, it's not *impossible*," Jake concedes, shifting from one foot to the other. "What's your condition?"

"If we're doing this, then it's just us," Aiden says. "No one else. Deal?"

"Deal," Jake agrees, nodding and holding out his index finger for Aiden to hook around his own.

Aiden pauses, blinks and asks, "Just like that?"

"I think you're right. So, yeah, just like that."

"Okay, then," Aiden says, and taps his lips. "Here."

With one eyebrow raised, Jake steps forward and seals the deal with the requisite kiss, settling his arms atop Aiden's shoulders. Aiden immediately pulls him closer, trying and failing not to smile against his mouth.

This is what we are, he thinks. *But… maybe.*

6,231 MILES

DAY FIFTY-FOUR: IOWA

"Have you ever had one of those moments where you look at your life and just think, 'What the hell?'"

Smiling, Jake glances around the inside of the barn. Everything is rustic and light; roof beams are strung with fairy lights and globes. They are surrounded by tables dressed in white, russet and laurel green, with baskets of apples and greenery serving as centerpieces. Wait staff, dressed almost casually, clear away the last remnants of dessert and serve cups of hot cider.

Jake leans forward in his seat and takes a sip from his cup. His tongue darts out to chase a droplet at the side of his mouth before he answers, "Pretty much every day."

"Seriously, though. What the hell? This day has been insanely surreal," Aiden says.

It started as they drove along I-80 from Des Moines on their way to the KOA campground in Adel.

It was an unseasonably warm day for Iowa in November—or so the morning weatherman said. Jake pushed his sunglasses higher up on his nose as he turned to look out the window at the rolling fields passing them by. There wasn't much to see, given that most harvests had already taken place. All that was left behind was tilled earth, resting before the freeze of winter. It was like watching a piece of the earth fall asleep, and were it not for the few other vehicles ahead and the suit-clad man walking along the side of the road trying to hitch a ride, Jake could probably have fallen asleep with it.

"Look," Aiden murmured, gesturing to the hitchhiker, who was waving wildly at each car and truck as it passed. Something about the man seemed somehow... familiar.

"No way," Jake said. "We are *not* picking up a hitchhiker."

"He doesn't exactly look like a hitchhiker, though," Aiden reasoned. "He's wearing a suit."

"Oh, so he dresses up to kill people, how thoughtful," Jake replied. "Just keep driving, Dan."

They were almost passing the hitchhiker when Jake realized why he looked familiar: it was Andrew, one half of the couple whose engagement party they had attended back in New Jersey.

And now, hours after giving him a ride to the wedding ceremony for which he was running late—"Long story short, major freakout last night, disgusting amounts of booze with the guys, and apparently they all thought it would be fucking *hilarious* to drive my drunk ass out to the middle of a field and leave me without a car or a cell phone"—Jake finds himself seated just to the left of the head table, dressed in his Sunday best with Aiden beside him, both of them half-jokingly named the guests of honor.

"Insanely surreal" is probably the best way of putting it, Jake thinks.

"Ladies and gentlemen," a voice comes over the speaker system, ambient music fading. Jake turns to look at the head table, where both grooms are on their feet and Toby speaks into a microphone. "Andrew and I would just like to begin by thanking you all for coming here to be with us today. We know it was a bit of a trip for most of you, so we really appreciate you being here. And to the New Yorkers: We're not even a little bit sorry for making you spend the afternoon at the Hillard family farm, so suck it up."

Laughter breaks out in the back of the room, and Jake can't help but smile at Toby's easy humor. His blond hair is styled a little more neatly than usual but is still messy, and he's dressed in a charcoal gray suit offset by the light green of his waistcoat. The microphone is in his right hand, and his left clutches Andrew's.

"All of you know the story of how we got together, and of course Andrew's told *everyone* our proposal story," Toby says, and groans break out around the room. He glances at Andrew with a lopsided grin and quietly continues, "It's been, um... it's been a long journey to get here. To be honest, I didn't know if I'd ever be able to have this. Not just because of the person I fell in love with and where I come from, but also just... me.

"And then one night, he walked into that awful bar and changed everything," Toby says. He takes a deep breath, and Jake, watching him blink rapidly, almost fails to notice when Aiden takes his hand. "Andrew, you've taught me to ask and to answer, to wait and to fulfill, to love and to be loved. My life began when I poured you that first Negroni, and I don't want it to ever end.

"Thank you for finding me; thank you for seeing me, and thank you for sticking around even after you tasted my awful Eggs Benedict. Most of all, thank you for agreeing to be my everything," Toby says. Andrew cups the back of his neck and tugs him down for a brief kiss.

Feeling like an intruder, Jake looks away and meets Aiden's lingering eyes. Nowadays, he's used to that look of radiant warmth on Aiden's face—he missed it after Chicago, and it only came back after Lake Calhoun.

Since their fight, Jake has coasted on being on the road with a wonderful man, transcending time and obligation and the need to be somewhere. Though he's tethered to something that he is beginning to realize is bigger than either of them, it no longer feels like a chokehold constricting his air supply—instead, it feels like roots.

"Always has to set a high bar," Andrew mock-grumbles into the mic. Jake hears low chuckles from around the room. "I have a laundry list of people to whom I'm grateful, but there are just a few I'd like to thank in particular:

"Mr. and Mrs. Hillard, thank you for managing to pull off a summer wedding in November—and in *Iowa*, no less! This place looks beautiful, and Myra: I'm sorry I ever doubted you," Andrew says. "Stu and Jeff, thank you for being the best groomsmen we could have asked for, even if you did leave me in the middle of a field last night.

"Jake and Aiden, our guests of honor..." he says, pointing toward where they sit, "How the *hell* did you end up being in exactly the right place at exactly the right time?"

"Superpowers!" Aiden calls out, raising his and Jake's joined hands in a semi-triumphant gesture. Jake flushes at the coos he hears from the back of the room.

"Well, thank you for saving me from having to hitchhike *all* the way here. The facilities were top notch," Andrew continues. "And finally, one last thank you to my late father. He taught me that you have to make the mistakes first so that you know how to recognize them, and..." Andrew trails off, snakes his arm around Toby's waist and speaks directly to him, "I know it took me making a *lot* of mistakes first, but once I knew, I knew.

"I love you," he whispers into the mic, and drops a kiss on the corner of Toby's mouth. Jake squeezes Aiden's hand, though he doesn't quite know why.

One of the groomsmen—Jake can't remember which—stands and takes the mic from Andrew to announce the first dance. As Andrew leads Toby to the middle of the dance floor, their matching rose gold wedding bands catch the light of the globes strung above, and all of the guests turn to watch as Diana Krall's version of "I've Grown Accustomed To Your Face" from *My Fair Lady* begins to play.

"Wasn't this your parents' first dance song?" Aiden asks quietly.

Jake sits up straighter in his seat and the black and white wedding video playing in his mind's eye comes into sharper focus. The smiling couple twirling each other around is suddenly so real to him that he can almost reach out and feel the fabric of their wedding finery. His mother's best friend Sarah sings on a tiny stage erected in the backyard of his grandparents' house, and the only source of light spills through the French doors off the dining room, casting long shadows that stretch into the saplings lining the fence.

He opens his mouth to speak, but finds himself without words.

"What's *your* first dance song?" Aiden whispers into Jake's ear, and Jake shivers as the hairs on his arms stand on end beneath the fabric of his hastily pressed, white button-down.

"No idea," Jake replies. He watches Toby and Andrew begin to turn on the spot, their arms wrapped tightly around one another's waists. They exchange indiscernible words and soft smiles.

"Me neither," Aiden says, and Jake fixes him with a raised eyebrow. "I guess it's just something you figure out together, you know?"

"I guess so," Jake says. He fiddles with the cuff of his shirt and glances at the two grooms again. They look as though they've already left the barn, as though they're dancing in their own walled-off world.

It makes Jake think of the RV, where nothing exists but him and Aiden and the asphalt ahead.

The song ends and the guests applaud Toby and Andrew as they take their bows in the center of the floor. The music bleeds into an upbeat number Jake doesn't recognize, and he's just beginning to think about going in search of more cider when he sees the grooms exchange a glance and make a beeline toward him and Aiden.

"I think I owe you a dance," Andrew says, holding out his hand. Jake looks at it uncertainly for a moment, remembering the pinpoint precision of Andrew's insight the last time they talked privately, but before he can say no Andrew adds, "As a thank you."

It's just one dance, he thinks, and moves onto the floor with him. Andrew's hold is loose; his hands are bigger than Aiden's, and he has a couple inches' height on Jake. He feels as if he's in the wrong arms, but brushes it off.

"Thank you again for what you did today," Andrew says as they begin a quick approximation of a foxtrot in time to the beat of the summery song.

"We couldn't exactly just leave you by the side of the road," Jake replies.

"Well, no, but... everything needed to be perfect today, and you two really helped make that happen," Andrew says quietly as Toby and Aiden pass by on their left. "Toby, he... the reason I got so drunk last night... he has OCD. It's much better than it was when we first met, but last night he had to flick the lights twenty-four times before he left the house. It hasn't been more than four in about a year, and I just... you know?"

Jake nods; he can't quite imagine himself acting differently in the same situation. "In that case, I'm even more glad we found you."

Andrew smiles and falls silent. Jake glances across the dance floor, catching a wink that Aiden throws his way. The song is fun and flirty, and it tugs at Jake more than he would have expected, capturing his attention and focusing it all on the way Aiden moves with another partner: not too close yet not too far apart, something not quite clicking in their rhythm.

"You still want him, huh?" Andrew asks wryly. Jake meets his gaze, but stays silent. "I know I'm not wrong."

"No, you're not wrong."

"But you still won't do anything about it."

"There you're wrong," Jake corrects him.

Andrew's eyes flick between him and Aiden a few times, and then his grin cracks wide open. "How's that working out for you?"

"We're figuring things out," Jake says at length. "It's complicated."

Andrew scoffs and rolls his eyes. "I keep trying to tell you—"

"It's not complicated, I know."

"No, it's not. Do you love him?"

"I'm trying not to."

"Why?"

"He deserves better," Jake says, "and I'm not so good at trusting people with my heart."

"But Aiden's not people," Andrew points out, and all of the reasons Jake has been conjuring sputter into darkness, as if the words have suddenly become his enemy, loaded with meaning he never intended them to have. Why is he biting his tongue and feeling only the pressure? Why is he biting at all?

Somewhere in the darkest corners of his mind—the ones he rarely feels brave enough to explore—he knows. No matter how much stock he sets in movies and television shows, the characters and their journeys to love and redemption and happy endings, fairy tales rarely happen in real life; and though this wedding could be described as one, they certainly won't happen to him. He's known that ever since he was eight years old, after all, when a boy in his class called Zachary became the first breath of air after the long, suffocating grief of his mother's passing.

Zachary flushed Jake's handmade Valentine's Day card down the toilet while their classmates looked on, jeering and calling Jake names he still doesn't like to hear. He bit his tongue then, the sharp pain pushing back the sting in his eyes, and he's never really stopped.

The song speaks of memories and Sunday mornings and summers spent listening to Bob Marley, and once more Jake glances over at Aiden—just in time to see Aiden and Toby stop dancing. Aiden steps back with an almost stricken expression on his face. Andrew seems to notice as well, and they both start to step toward the two men but catch themselves at the last second, exchanging a sheepish grin and shrugging it off. Jake will probably get the story later, and with Aiden and Toby taking up the dance again after a moment, it's easy to do the same.

"Answer me one thing," Andrew says. "Was it a mistake?"

Jake bites his lip and considers the question. Maybe it's being surrounded by so much happiness and love; maybe it's the image of his parents dancing in the faded light; maybe it's even the burn of Aiden's gaze from across the room...

"I thought it was, at first," he finally answers.

Andrew nods, seemingly satisfied, and Jake lets himself relax into the final few bars of the song. Andrew thanks him for the dance and leaves him with a smile to take Toby's sister's hand just as she's trying to leave the floor. Toby himself is standing with Aiden in the corner closest to the speakers, one hand on Aiden's shoulder. It reminds Jake of Aiden's brother Matthew.

When Aiden finds him a few minutes later, Jake is admiring the table of wedding favors—packages of green apples, homemade caramels and hot apple cider mix, all wrapped in plastic and tied up with twine.

"I can't believe you're *still* wearing this bracelet," Jake says. He hooks his finger beneath the woven black cord around Aiden's right wrist and gives it a gentle tug, admiring the different shades of green in its solitary, banded bead of malachite.

"It's lucky," Aiden tells him. "Green is lucky."

Jake smiles, and in an effort to distract himself from just how good Aiden looks with his tie loose and shirtsleeves rolled to the elbow, he asks, "So what other dances do you know? I'd bet money that you didn't just stop at ballroom dancing. Maybe salsa? Latin? *Line dance?*"

Aiden pauses for a moment, looking as if he wants to talk about something else but thinking better of it. "I know the tango," he says, fiddling with one of the favors.

"You know the tango," Jake scoffs. "Sweet, naïve, awkward, seventeen-year-old Aiden learned the tango? I'll believe that when I see it."

"I'll do you one better," Aiden counters, drawing himself up and grabbing Jake's hand to drag him back onto the floor as a low, sensual piece of music begin to pour from the speakers.

"This isn't exactly tango music," Jake says.

"Think you can keep up with me?"

"I know how to tango."

"Not like this, you don't," Aiden says, and pulls Jake into their opening position. It's a close embrace—a striking difference from what Jake learned in his dance elective. He's used to arching his upper body away from his dance partner while maintaining contact at the hip, but Aiden has the position almost in reverse, their chests flush against each other and heads close. Seeming to notice his trepidation, Aiden says, "You learned the ballroom tango, I think, but this is the Argentine."

Jake quickly picks up that the Argentine tango is an almost completely improvised dance that relies on the follower picking up on the lead's cues. Aiden guides him through a simple *sistema cruzado,* and although the concept feels foreign to him after learning the fundamental ballroom choreography, Jake finds that it's easy to follow Aiden's movement. His is a body Jake knows; his arms feel so right around him that he wonders again how he could possibly be wrong.

But I was wrong about Max, and that sometimes felt right, he thinks, improvising with a sudden rush of flirtatious courage and hooking his foot around Aiden's calf, dragging it upward. He leans back into a controlled drop; Aiden leads them backward for four steps in time with the beat, and as the song swings down into its chorus, Jake straightens and takes the lead in order to surprise Aiden with a dip of his own.

With Aiden's dark eyes shining in the light, his chest heaving and limbs pliable, Jake suddenly understands as he never did with his class partners why the tango is described as an overtly sexual dance.

Their movements grow in speed and complexity, and Jake starts to notice that guests are moving off the floor and forming a circle around them. He feels momentarily embarrassed that they're stealing the focus, but they can't very well stop now. Imbued with the same alien confidence he found onstage in Ann Arbor, Jake shows off by embellishing a simple step with a *pasada*.

"I'm impressed," Aiden says, smiling when they go back into a sweetheart walk just before the final chorus.

"Told you I could keep up."

"I never really doubted you," Aiden says, glancing at their audience and leaning close to whisper, "I've always thought that this dance is a little like sex, and we both know you're okay at that."

"Just 'okay,' huh?"

"Well, you know what they say..."

"Practice makes perfect?" Jake supplies. He fixes Aiden with a mock-glare and reminds him, "This, coming from the guy who was practically celibate?"

"Well, you can't deny that I'm a fast learner," Aiden says with a wink. Jake laughs as Aiden pulls him close again and throws a few spins into their steps to give their impromptu audience something to watch. Echoing Jake's own sentiments from the bowling alley in Minneapolis, Aiden says in a low voice, "I've missed us like *this*."

"So have I."

Aiden takes a breath, his hands flat against Jake's shoulder blades, their dance almost lost, and whispers, "I wish..."

"You wish what?" Jake prompts, leading him through a series of crossing, pivoting steps with their chests pressed tightly together and heads held high. When he doesn't answer, Jake presses his forehead to Aiden's temple and whispers, "Tell me."

"I wish I'd told you about the dancing sooner," Aiden says, exhaling, and nods to their rapt audience.

"That's all?" Jake can't help but ask. *When did I stop biting my tongue?*

"That's all," Aiden says, and takes the lead once more, bending Jake back in one final dip to end their performance. The applause is enthusiastic, and in his peripheral vision, Jake can see Toby and Andrew's infuriatingly knowing smiles. When he looks back up, Aiden is gazing down at him with eyes that remind him of harbor lights back home, guiding his way long after nightfall.

6,491 MILES

DAY FIFTY-SIX: MISSOURI

It's only when the nights' shadows begin to extend that Aiden realizes that they've gone beyond the halfway point in their journey.

The sun noticeably rises later and sets earlier now, and he and Jake get used to long stretches of dark drive time, keeping the lights dimmed in the RV after sunset and leaving a pot of coffee brewing almost around the clock. Aiden's mood is still bright, though—brighter even than when Jake finally gave in and kissed him that first time, his lips salted by the ocean air.

So much is changing. So much has *already* changed. But Aiden finds that for once, rather than chase down the new until he can hold it in his cupped palms and turn it this way and that, now he is content to pick up the new only when it has almost passed by without notice.

"What are you waiting for?" Toby had asked during their dance at the wedding. This was seemingly out of the blue until he continued, "I see what you guys are trying to do, and I respect that, but seriously, what you have is too special to just piss away like this. So what are you waiting for?"

Aiden had stepped back, needing to know that he could still bolt if he wanted to. But instead he composed himself, took up the dance once more and simply answered, "Him. I'm waiting for him."

Now he glances over at Jake, asleep in the passenger seat, and smiles to himself. He's been driving for hours; his body is stiff, and his eyes feel dry, but a pleasant sensation is growing in the back of his mind, like the slow awakening of a creature in hibernation—something about the approaching winter drawing it out rather than sending it into a deeper sleep. Aiden doesn't know what it is, and usually the not knowing would drive him to distraction; but not now.

Jake jerks upright in the passenger seat; his body goes rigid and his hand flattens against the window. Aiden winces in sympathy as Jake rubs his eyes and relaxes back into his seat with a shudder.

"Bad dream?" he asks.

"It was like—" Jake begins in a sleep-choked rasp and stops to clear his throat. "It was like some weird version of *The Hunger Games,* but with congressmen. You were there for some reason. And there was *so much blood.*"

"Ugh," Aiden says. He suppresses a shiver and turns his attention to the GPS. "Well, we're almost there."

Jake grabs the GPS from its holder, studies it intently for a moment and then programs something into it. When he returns it to the dashboard, the Kathy Bates sound-alike whose voice they still haven't bothered to change instructs, *"In half a mile, turn left onto Legion Road."*

In answer to Aiden's questioning look, Jake says, "You'll see."

When they pull up outside The Dam Bait Shop, the headlights cast the faded wooden storefront in a harsh shade of yellow. Aiden gives Jake a sidelong glance and asks, "Are you sure this is where we're meant to be?"

"Yes," Jake says, offering no further explanation.

"But it's a bait shop."

"Yes, Captain Obvious, it's a bait shop."

"So... what are we doing here? Are you taking me on a romantic fishing adventure or something?"

"There's no such thing as a romantic fishing adventure, Dan," Jake says with a sigh. Turning in his seat, he gestures toward the bait shop and explains, "This is where Dad brought me when I was seven. After Mom."

"Is that why you wanted to come here instead of Joplin?" Aiden asks gently, reaching over to intertwine their fingers.

Jake looks at their joined hands and glances out the windshield once again, his brow furrowed. "Let's go," he says, exhaling and giving Aiden's hand a single, light squeeze.

They drive on quietly. Aiden merges back onto US-54 and pulls into River View RV Park ten minutes later. The night is quiet, the air a little damp from the afternoon's thunderstorm. While Jake stays still in passenger seat, looking lost in his own thoughts, Aiden makes quick work of getting them signed in and around to their parking spot.

After retrieving two blankets from the hall closet, Aiden shrugs into his thick Bowdoin hoodie and grabs Jake's sweater from the back of the couch. Jake is in the process of stretching out his arms and legs when Aiden approaches him, and as he takes in the blankets, he raises an eyebrow at Aiden in question.

"Grab your phone and meet me on the roof," Aiden says, shoving the sweater into Jake's hands and turning on his heel.

"The roof?" he hears Jake ask, but the door closes behind him with a deep click before he can answer. Instead, he makes his way to the back of the RV, tosses the blankets over his shoulder and climbs the ladder. The metal is cold under his hands, and the night carries a chill breeze that makes him grateful for the hoodie.

He spreads out the blankets and sits down; he only has to wait thirty seconds or so before he hears Jake gasp in the sudden cold. Aiden grins down at him from his vantage point.

"Are you crazy?" Jake grumbles, craning his head back. "It's fucking freezing."

"The RV walls are high and hard to climb," Aiden challenges him, remembering childhood nights when it was all he could do to get Jake into Matt's long-abandoned tree house.

In the little slices of moonlight cutting through the clouds overhead, Aiden can see Jake work his jaw for a moment before moving around to the ladder and replying, "Stony limits cannot hold *me* out." When Jake has climbed high enough to see over the top of the RV, he grabs Aiden's wrist, pulls Aiden toward him and whispers against his lips, "Or dorks like you, apparently."

Something twists and swoops in Aiden's gut as he kisses Jake, parts his lips and tastes peppermint. It happens at the oddest of moments, this sensation of being suspended, weightless and timeless in a world grown quiet save for their matching heartbeats. When he pulls back, he sees faint tremors in the cotton of Jake's fitted T-shirt that betray the racing heart beneath.

"Come on, sweetheart," Aiden says, scooting back to make room.

With a grace in his long limbs that Aiden often envies, Jake pulls himself up onto the roof and arranges himself between Aiden's legs, sitting with his back pressed comfortably against Aiden's chest. Aiden shakes out the second blanket and wraps it around them both. His breath comes out in barely visible puffs of white.

"So are you going to tell me what we're doing up here?" Jake asks.

Aiden doesn't answer for a moment. He takes Jake's phone and, as he scrolls through his extensive library, counters, "Are *you* going to tell me what's up?"

Just as Aiden finds the song he's looking for—"Swingset Chain" by Loquat, a mellow acoustic track with a dreamy, reminiscent quality that has been a staple of theirs for years—Jake exhales heavily and pulls a cigarette from the pack clutched in his hand. He lights up and draws deeply, pulls Aiden's arms snug around his waist and shrugs a little. "Just a few more ghosts to exorcise," he says, and drops his head back onto Aiden's shoulder. "Do you remember when Dad came to get me and Charlie that April in 1998?"

"When you'd been staying at my place?" At Jake's nod, Aiden adds, "Of course I remember."

"Well, this is where he brought us. Lake Ozark," Jake says. "The drive down was so... I was so *pissed* at him for leaving for three months and then just coming and taking us away like we'd been at your house for a sleepover or something. Charlie was so happy you'd think all of her Christmases and birthdays happened at once, but I barely spoke to him until we got to that stupid bait shop.

"We were looking at the fishing poles, and he was talking to us about them, you know, telling us which ones were better," Jake says, pausing to take another deep drag from his cigarette and flicking the ash over the side of the RV. "And then he just looked down at me and said, 'So which one do you want, Jakey?' And suddenly it was like, 'Oh. I still actually have my Dad. I didn't lose him *and* Mom.'"

"You came back different," Aiden says quietly, pressing his lips to the hollow of Jake's neck.

"It was the first time in three months that I didn't feel like I'd lost everyone."

"You always had me."

"You with your Band-Aids," Jake reminds him, elbow gently nudging his stomach.

With an almost startling clarity, the image of a seven-year-old Jake screaming at the sky appears in Aiden's mind's eye. When William gave him the news about his mother, Jake bolted from the house, Aiden at his heels because he knew exactly what Jake was thinking: Simba's dad talked to him from up in the sky, so Jake's mommy would too, right?

"Dan, why isn't she up there?" Jake demanded, but there was nothing that Aiden could think of to say. What *could* he have said that would have made it all better? It wasn't like that time Jake fell off his bike in the front yard and his knee got all bloody. There was nothing to clean up or put one of his cool dinosaur Band-Aids on.

The first time Aiden saw Jake again after the funeral, however, he took one of those Band-Aids and stuck it onto Jake's shirt right over his heart. He did it every time Jake got sad until they were thirteen.

"Why did you stop doing that, by the way?" Jake asks, as if reading his mind. "It always cheered me up, no matter how crappy I felt."

"Are you feeling crappy right now? Because we have Band-Aids, you know. They're just the regular kind, but—"

Jake twists around and kisses him firmly. His eyes sparkle in the moonlight when he pulls back. "No. Right now, I'm happy."

Aiden wants to ask, *Is it because of me? Are you happy with me, will you let me keep making you happy? Will you trust me with your heart if I promise that you can?*

Instead, he shrugs it off and says, "Me too."

"Good," Jake says. "So what *are* we doing up here?"

"We're going to listen to a little music," Aiden begins. "We're going to huddle for warmth like the penguins do, and then we're going to make cocoa, because I don't know about you, but I'm completely over coffee right now. And then maybe we could watch our movie. Or we could have sex. Your choice."

Jake laughs; the sound is melodic yet too loud in the stillness of the night. "Is 'all of the above' an option?"

"Always. Why? Do you want to go inside already?"

Jakes one last drag of his cigarette and tosses it over the side. He tugs the sleeves of his sweater down over his hands and settles back against Aiden. "Maybe in a little bit. It's nice up here."

"I do have good ideas sometimes."

"Those Band-Aids were the best idea you ever had, you know."

"I wanted to take care of you."

"You always have."

6,830 MILES

DAY FIFTY-NINE: ARKANSAS

"Just got a text from April," Aiden murmurs from the passenger seat. "She wants to know what songs we want to do solo for the gig this Saturday."

"Must be the text I just got, too," Jake replies, having felt his phone vibrate against his leg a moment ago. "What did you choose?"

"It's a surprise."

"Did she send over those two new ones yet?"

Aiden nods and taps a response. "Yeah, I just got the email. How crazy is it that they're writing their own stuff now?"

"Well, the only one they've written is the one she wants to close the show with," Jake corrects him. "The other one she sent is a We Are Scientists song. But yeah, it's crazy. I mean, they've *never* been serious like this before. In fact..."

"What?"

Scratching absently at his jaw, Jake considers his words. "When we talked yesterday, April kept mentioning Alaska being the last big show, and then she was saying that not everyone is joining in on writing the new material. I don't know, it just, it got me thinking."

"Thinking what?"

"I think they might break up after this tour. Or, if they don't break up, a few of them will start a new band," Jake says. He sits forward in his seat, resting his forearms on the steering wheel, and as he glances out of the windshield and catches sight of the blue and white sign declaring, *Welcome to Arkansas, The Natural State,* he says, "All right, we're in Arkansas. Crank it."

He catches Aiden's affectionate smile in his peripheral vision, and within moments Johnny Cash's distinctive throaty voice is pouring from the speakers. Aiden taps his thumb and drums his fingers against his thigh, singing along quietly and harmonizing to Johnny's timeless vocals.

"Why didn't you go into music?" Jake asks, and lowers the volume.

Aiden looks thoughtful for a moment. "A lot of reasons. I mean, you know I love film and directing."

"Right, but you love music just as much, if not more. And you're just as good at that."

"I don't know, I guess... it was Dad's thing, you know? He had his lawyer band, no matter how lame they were. I kind of wanted to distance myself from all that, and you were doing film, too."

"Don't tell me you took film just because I was taking it," Jake says, shooting him a look.

"Narcissist," Aiden teases. Jake sticks out his tongue in response. "Wouldn't it have been weird, though? Doing different things after growing up doing everything together?"

"Probably would've been healthier, not gonna lie."

"Well, anyway. If I'm honest, it was *one* reason... just not the *whole* reason."

Jake nods, mostly to himself, and they lapse into silence. After a few moments, Jake turns the volume back up, unsure what to do with this new piece of information. He's beginning to think that Aiden is approaching a crossroads. It's been a subtle shift, so much so that Jake is only just starting to notice that Aiden no longer discusses their movies with his usual passionate analytical fervor. Instead, he tends to focus on the sound and music, picking out pieces of the score that strike him as either particularly fitting or at odds with the scene.

Noticing that the skin of his left arm is starting to feel tight, Jake lets it drop from the window and murmurs absently, "I think my arm is getting sunburned."

Aiden glances at him. "Want me to take over in a little bit?"

"Maybe," Jake says. "Hey, do you remember that time I got sunburned at Hampton Beach and you ended up icing my legs for me?"

"I still don't get how you can burn through SPF seventy in an hour," Aiden replies, shifting in his seat to turn and face him.

"It's called being pale," Jake tells him. "We can't all have beautiful, model-quality skin that doesn't even know what a sunburn is."

"Beautiful, huh?"

"Shut up."

"No, really, tell me more," Aiden says, leaning on the arm of his seat and propping his chin in his hand.

Jake remains silent—usually this territory warrants exploration, but while driving it is decidedly perilous.

Aiden goes on, "Because, you know, 'beautiful' is probably how I'd describe your skin, too."

Jake scoffs, and yet in the pause that follows, knowing he's taking the bait but quite unable to resist, he asks, "Since when?"

"Oh, since... Alabama, maybe? Is that where we were when I gave you that massage?"

"I think so."

"Well, either way, since then. Let's just say I was really glad when you said you didn't want it to be a one-time thing."

"You were, huh?"

"Yep. Otherwise, I wouldn't have gotten to figure out all these things about you."

"What things?" Jake asks. He wants to kick himself as soon as the words are out of his mouth.

"Oh, I don't know..." Aiden trails off, stretching his arms over his head. He seems to consider his words carefully, and Jake licks his lips with a dry tongue. "That tongue, for instance. I mean, I'd never have known you can do more with it than just tying knots in cherry stems.

"And we probably shouldn't talk about exactly *what* you do with it," Aiden continues, his voice hushed, as if he's speaking in riddles and prayers. "We also probably shouldn't talk about how badly I've been hoping you'd drive off the road for the last hundred miles so I can drag you back to bed."

"You wouldn't exactly have to drag me," Jake says, clenching his jaw and tightening his grip on the steering wheel.

Aiden chuckles to himself, low and dirty, and turns his gaze out of the window. But the seed is planted in Jake's mind, and while they drive on with only his Johnny Cash playlist and the rhythmic hum of wheels on asphalt to soundtrack their progress, his thoughts drift.

Growing up, Jake always felt as though he looked at the world more closely than everyone else. He seemed to pick out the tiniest details and take mental photographs to remember them by: the single droplet of water left on a window long after the rain had passed; the almost invisible, hairline crack in a cup from his mother's tea set; the drooping end of the tinsel where, try as he might, he couldn't keep it wound around a branch.

Yet Aiden is different. The mental images Jake takes of him are far more sensory: the curve of his cheekbone under Jake's thumb, the softness of the skin behind his knee, the taste of his lips in the last seconds before he falls asleep. They're tied up with the panoramic shots: Aiden dancing under pulsing lights, the only enticing thing in a sea of what *should* have been enticing; Aiden splayed out and spent, a sheen of sweat covering his back after his third orgasm; Aiden waking up with pupils already blown wide, pulling Jake on top of him for lazy morning sex somewhere in the middle of Kentucky. These are the most precious pictures he's ever taken.

By the time an hour has passed, Jake is uncomfortably hard in his jeans; he can't focus on any of Aiden's comments about Arkansas being Happy-Mart country or Hot Springs supposedly having its own red light district. Instead, he focuses on the lips and eyes and hands that know exactly how to undo him, and he's almost frenzied in his craving.

His frustration hits its peak when Aiden glances over and, upon noticing Jake's predicament, does nothing more than toss him a knowing smirk.

"You fucker," Jake says. "You know exactly what you're doing, don't you?"

"Who, me?" Aiden asks, all wide-eyed and innocent. "The guy who was practically celibate?"

"Oh my god, shut up," Jake says, and finally decides to act on his instincts. He drives them off the freeway, following the signs for Buffalo River National Park and barely keeping to the speed limit. He winds tighter and tighter until they're finally parked and he grabs Aiden by the wrist, yanks him upright and leads him to the bedroom without so much as a word passing between them.

In almost a parody of their night in Philadelphia—a hazy picture in his mind that blurs around the edges—Jake pushes Aiden down onto the edge of the bed and leans over him.

"What do you want?" Aiden asks.

"This," Jake says, gesturing down at himself, "is your fault. So I want you to shut up."

"Shut up and... what? Just take it?" Aiden asks, and when Jake nods, his brown eyes grow darker with the hint of a challenge. He smirks again, lifts his chin and says, "Make me."

Jake lets out a noise between a growl and a groan, pitches forward and kisses him with no finesse whatsoever, sloppy tongue and lazy lips. Even as Aiden puts on a show of struggling against Jake's grip around his wrists, he hooks his legs around Jake's waist to pull him closer, still daring him to chase, challenging him to deliver and betting that he won't in the world's most willing game of cat and mouse.

With only a few breaks in contact, reluctant to give up a single second of the release he's been craving, Jake manages to strip them both entirely naked. As he settles his body over Aiden's, his teeth raking the skin of Aiden's neck, he feels Aiden's limbs go intoxicatingly lax for a fleeting moment and it almost makes him want to stop, catch his breath and make this last.

Jake pulls back to drink him in, rests his crossed forearms across Aiden's chest and lets them bear his weight. *You really are beautiful,* he thinks, tracing one fingertip along Aiden's bottom lip... and then Aiden raises his head off the sheets just far enough to whisper against Jake's mouth, "Do something useful."

With that, the moment passes as quickly as it came, swept away by the heat and fire that boil Jake's blood.

"*Useful?*" he manages, screwing his eyes shut as Aiden's cock drags along the length of his own; this is an appetizer when he wants a five-course meal. He pulls Aiden farther up the bed, straddles his hips and holds him down with one hand. "Fuck you, Aiden Calloway."

"That's the idea," Aiden says without missing a beat. His roguish grin defies Jake to resist, and Jake has had just about enough.

"You know what? I told you to shut up."

"And I told you to make me. But if you're not *up* to it—"

Jake puts his hand over Aiden's mouth, locking eyes with him as he moves to straddle his chest. He waits until Aiden blinks up at him with wide, humoring eyes and nods. He works the tip of his index finger between Aiden's lips and tugs his mouth open, holding himself just out of reach and reveling in the heat of Aiden's bare chest against the skin of his thighs.

When Aiden rears up far enough to lick across the head of his cock, it's like relief painted onto his skin, second by exquisite second. Aiden sinks his mouth over the tip and sucks hard, his eyes fluttering shut. A moan vibrates through Jake's sensitive flesh and up, up, up, a puddle of warmth tingling in the pit of his stomach.

Jake's breath stutters in his chest when Aiden slowly pulls off with a barely there graze of teeth along his shaft before going back to working him over at an agonizing pace that is nowhere near close to enough. Jake begins working his hips back and forth, tangling his fingers in Aiden's hair and pumping his cock between Aiden's stretched lips; he spirals at the sensation of tight, wet warmth around him, driven further with each snap forward.

He finally pulls back when his thighs begin to shake. His breathing is labored. Aiden looks up at him with a smug expression and licks his lips.

"I hate you," Jake exhales raggedly, but he can't help the traitorous smile tugging at his mouth.

"Evidently," Aiden agrees, schooling his features into an exaggeratedly sympathetic expression. "Why'd you stop?"

Jake moves back far enough to free Aiden's arms only to grab his wrists, pin them at either side of his head and fix him with a look. "Because I'm not letting you off the hook *that* easily."

"*Oh,* so you were about to... right. I get it," Aiden teases.

Jake shakes his head. "You just don't get it, do you? You need to *stop talking.*"

With that, he climbs off of Aiden, flips him onto his belly and holds him there with one hand on his back while he palms a condom and their three-quarters empty bottle of lube from the nightstand. Aiden's muscles shift beneath his overheated skin and, after rolling on the condom and slicking up, Jake can't help but scratch his fingernails along Aiden's spine, leaving bright red trails in his wake.

"You don't need to—"

"I know," Jake interrupts firmly. They've been doing this every night for the past week, and their prep routine gets shorter and shorter every time. He presses an open-mouthed kiss to Aiden's shoulder as he leans over him and winds his hand back into his hair, damp with sweat at the nape of his neck. He nudges Aiden's legs apart and presses in slowly; Aiden lets out a stuttering breath that sounds like long-awaited release.

Jake knows Aiden's body well; how much he can take, how far he can be pushed—these are the secret parts of him that Aiden has allowed him to learn, has given freely even though it's probably far more than Jake deserves. But being wrapped in this velvet heat expels all such thoughts from Jake's mind as he drives into Aiden over and over, holding him down by his head and shoulder. Aiden takes it all so beautifully, muscles contracting and loosening beneath Jake's grip.

"I... fuck—harder, *please...*" Aiden begs, the words a broken moan that settles at the base of Jake's spine; the bundle of nerves there fires sparks through his every cell. Jake bites his lip against a loud groan; he's losing control at a rapidly accelerating rate and won't be able to hold onto himself much longer.

Instead he holds onto Aiden, hooking his hand under Aiden's arm and up over his shoulder; the skin turns white where his fingers press into the flesh.

"Jake, please, *please—*"

He covers Aiden's mouth with his left hand, unable to take anymore. Aiden is undone, so utterly undone that it spurs Jake on, faster and faster until his hips jerk forward of their own volition and he has to press his forehead to Aiden's temple to block out the look in Aiden's eyes, so open and vulnerable and brimming with something that can't possibly be.

Aiden bites down on Jake's third finger as he comes, tensing and clenching around him, and it's that shock of pain that pushes Jake over the edge, a debauched grunt the only sound that leaves him as his body bursts outward and back in on itself.

With the little strength he has left, he manages to carefully untangle himself from Aiden, get rid of the condom and collapse onto the cool, welcoming sheets.

"Old man," Aiden whispers into his ear, the mattress sinking beneath his weight as he lies down next to Jake and draws circles on his upturned palm.

"There's only a hundred days between us, lest you forget," Jake reminds him, and turns onto his front. "I can still kick your ass."

"I think you just did," Aiden says, chuckling mostly to himself. A comfortable quiet falls, the only sound that of their matching labored breaths as they both regain their equilibrium. Jake can just feel Aiden's fingertips tracing patterns on the skin of his back; the ghost of a touch, but still there. "Your freckles are fading."

"Hmm?"

"I said your freckles are fading."

"Good. I hate them," Jake says.

"I bet I could make you like them."

"Remind me that we don't need to buy any more coffee for you."

"Yeah? Why's that?"

"You're the only person I've ever met who's buzzed *after* an orgasm, and it makes me hate you a little bit. You neither need nor deserve coffee," Jake rambles. He doesn't care if he's making sense, not when his body feels both leaden and weightless.

Aiden chuckles again, and Jake hears him fumbling through one of the drawers in the nightstand for a moment before letting out a triumphant, "Ha!" and moving across the bed to straddle Jake's waist. He winces a little at a jolt of sensitivity, and soon begins to feel a tickling drag across his neck.

"What are you doing?" he asks.

"Making music," Aiden answers vaguely.

"Wait, are you—are you *drawing* on me?"

"Shh. I'm in my creative space right now."

"*Such* a dork," Jake mutters, but pillows his arms on his head and lets his eyes slip closed—Aiden can't be dissuaded when he's in this sort of mood, and Jake doesn't have the energy anyway. "You writing lyrics, too?"

"Do you want me to?"

"Hmm... yeah. Write me a song I can wear."

He imagines himself looking down on them from above, Aiden bent over him, picking out melodies on wavering staffs and covering Jake's skin with quavers and half-measures and treble clefs until he feels as if he's made of Aiden's music.

Could you capture me in four minutes? he wonders idly, feeling himself drift toward sleep. *What about ten? Five hundred, twenty-five thousand? Would you have me for that long? Longer?*

He comes around some time later, fuzzy-eyed and cotton-mouthed, his cheek pressed against Aiden's chest. He can hear Aiden's heartbeat, a steady *thump-thump* in his ear, and when he looks up, he sees a soft smile playing about Aiden's lips. He has pulled the laptop onto the foot of the bed, and *Walk The Line* is paused at the very beginning of its opening scene: a gray, desolate shot of Folsom Prison in Represa, where one of Johnny Cash's many legendary performances took place.

"What are you so happy about?" Jake asks, rubbing at his eyes.

"I just love movies like this. I mean, I know the story's been changed and exaggerated in places, but still... we're watching *history*," Aiden says, picking at a loose thread on the comforter. "What if you met your soulmate but you were already with someone, like Johnny and June? Is there anything sadder? Someone's heart's going to get broken whatever you do."

Jake swallows thickly, hearing that line from the movie playing in his head, and somewhere in that dark corner of his mind, he knows what Aiden is *really* asking. It's what they do in this boundary-pushing pas de deux of theirs. But Jake can't say it, can't offer up his bleeding heart and ask Aiden to tell him he doesn't love him, like the June to Jake's Johnny.

"It's sad," he agrees. "But everything worked out for the best, in the end."

"Right," Aiden replies obliquely, and gestures toward the laptop. "Shall we?"

Jake nods, and taps the space bar with his foot. He shakes off Aiden's words. They've decided to be happy with this—they made a deal, and Jake intends to hold up his end. Whether it is enough is a question to which he doesn't need the answer, because... because being cradled against Aiden's chest, wrapped up in his magic words and velvet heart with the afternoon light fading into dusk, Jake feels as complete as he can imagine feeling.

This is already enough.

7,028 MILES

CHAPTER 7

DAY SIXTY: LOUISIANA

"Okay," Aiden says, setting everything down onto the blanket and sitting back. "We have beignets, we have hot cider and we have about fifteen minutes before we should start seeing them."

"Merci beaucoup," Jake replies, his diction barely flawed, and accepts the small cup of cider that Aiden pours for him. Jake's eyes remain on him as he sips, tipping his head back a little to expose the long column of his neck as he swallows.

Aiden licks his lips and busies himself in transferring their warm beignets to paper plates. A pleasant fizzle of anticipation simmers beneath his skin; all day, Jake has been throwing every single trick he possesses at him, as if he's still trying to pay him back for Arkansas.

Which was unintentional. Mostly.

"We should come back here one day for Mardi Gras," Jake muses absently, taking a bite of his beignet and glancing at the sky. Save for a few clouds lingering in the distance, it's a crystal clear night—perfect for watching the Leonids as they skitter through the stars.

They aren't the only ones sitting on the roof of an RV—it seems as though almost everyone in the Pontchartrain Landing Park is out tonight. The sites are all in a line overlooking the still waters of the marina, and the other campers are gathered in couples and groups, laughing and eating and listening to music.

They arrived at the park just after sunset, bellies full of creole jambalaya and crawfish étouffée from the French Quarter. People were already on top of their vehicles, singing raucously along to the dark, sultry *True Blood* theme playing from someone's car, the girls all dropping their chins to hit the low notes. Jake took it all in with a barely concealed sigh and rolled his eyes when Aiden joined in.

Then they both heard mention of a meteor shower, and suddenly everything made sense.

"Wow," Aiden says after taking a sip of his own cider. The apple and spices burst fruity and sharp over his tongue, and he licks his lips so as not to waste a single drop. "Can you get the recipe for this from Toby?"

"I think it's his mom's recipe, but I can ask," Jake says. "It's pretty special, right?"

"Let's just say, I'm glad we got extra," Aiden murmurs. He reaches out to thumb away a few specks of powdered sugar at the corner of Jake's mouth. Eyes lingering on Jake's, he sucks on the tip of his thumb.

"What are you doing?" Jake asks, exhaling. He wraps both hands around his cup and links his fingers.

"Exactly what you've been doing all day," Aiden replies with a grin, just as the group of girls three vehicles away starts playing the *True Blood* theme for the third time this hour.

"Oh my god," Jake mutters. "Is this a thing people just *do* in Louisiana?"

"Good news," Aiden says, reaching into the pocket of his hoodie and producing his phone. He offers Jake one of the earbuds. "We also have music."

"You're my favorite," Jake sing-songs, and Aiden smiles as he scrolls through his playlists, hitting play on the one titled "Mellow Magic."

"Lie down," he says. With a little maneuvering, they manage to arrange themselves so that they're lying on their backs, stretched out in opposite directions, heads pillowed on each other's shoulders as they look up at the sky and wait for the show to begin.

At least, Jake is looking up. Aiden is regarding the silhouette of Jake's profile against the marina lights. The scent of his cologne still lingers faintly around his collar and coils into Aiden's senses, wrapping him in a phantom of home.

They've been on the road for two months, with less than seven weeks to go. Aiden can almost hear the clock *tick-tick-ticking* their seconds away, and he wants more than anything for their road trip to go on far longer than another forty days if it means that they get to stay caught in this snow globe that they themselves shake, over and over and over until the slant of the land sends them sliding all too closely to the truth: This isn't just a road trip thing.

"You're going to miss it if you keep staring at me like that," Jake says, shifting onto his side and propping himself on one elbow. "What's got you so preoccupied?"

"Do you remember that night you drove us out to Coffin Pond?" Aiden asks after a moment.

"I drove us out to Coffin Pond lots of times, Dan. You might have to narrow it down a little."

"The day you got your license," Aiden clarifies. "When we saw the SWAN comet and named your car."

"Odette! I miss that car," Jake says wistfully. "What about it?"

"We've got less than seven weeks left," Aiden says, and pauses to clear his throat. "Don't you think it's time we named the RV?"

Jake hums a little, reaches up to scratch the side of his jaw, and says, "I propose 'Leona.'"

"Leona?"

"Odette for the SWAN, Leona for the Leonids."

"Leona," Aiden repeats, rolling it around in his mouth as he shifts to mirror Jake's position.

"Do you think your grandfather would like that?" Jake asks.

"Yeah. Yeah, I do," Aiden says. "Leona it is."

"You're going to make this a thing, aren't you," Jake grumbles with a long-suffering air. "Do I have to go get that bottle of champagne and smash it against the side?"

Aiden lets out a bark of laughter and, surroundings be damned, leans forward to press his lips to Jake's.

"Aiden," Jake whispers into his mouth, his hand cupping Aiden's jaw so firmly that he doesn't know whether Jake is pulling him closer or pushing him away. Eventually his patience wins out; Jake drops his elbow and pulls him over, giving in with a soft moan. The angle is awkward at first but Aiden makes it work, shifting so that he can part Jake's lips and dip his tongue inside. He tastes like cider and sugar.

Tick-tick-tock, he thinks. *Down counts the clock.*

Loud cheers startle them apart, and Aiden looks up to see the first of the night's meteors streak across the sky. What would he wish for, if he let himself wish? More time, of course, but that is a given. Or perhaps... perhaps not for more time. Perhaps instead, he would wish to *stop* time, right here and now, so that he could live suspended in this moment until he was ready to say, "Take me to the next place, and the next, and I'll go wherever you want me to follow as long as my heart is in your hand and your hand is in mine."

"Do you ever wish you could stop time?" Jake whispers.

Aiden glances down at him. "Mind reader."

"One of my many talents."

"If you could freeze-frame any moment from your life, which would it be?"

Jake considers the question for a long moment. "This one's up there, but... I think I'd have to go with getting up on that stage in Ann Arbor. I could live in that one 'til I'm old and gray."

"You'll never be old, Jakey," Aiden assures him, and tries not to feel disappointed that Jake didn't pick a moment featuring him.

"What, you think I plan on dying young? I have *way* too much visual magic to work in my lifetime, thank you very much," Jake says primly, and loops an arm around Aiden's neck. His blunt fingernails scratch just underneath Aiden's jaw, and he asks, "Will you still be there, Band-Aids and all?"

"What do you mean?"

"You remember in *Benjamin Button*, when he was getting older but his body kept getting younger, until Daisy had to take care of him because he couldn't take care of himself anymore?"

"Yes..."

"When I'm that old, will you still take care of me?"

"Well, I'm not—"

Aiden stutters and stops. He wants to make a joke, tell Jake that he's not in love with him as Daisy was with Benjamin, but for the first time, it occurs to him that what he feels for Jake is way more than the adolescent love he thought it was—something that he'd grow out of, like a pair of sneakers. On the contrary, he realizes, this is something he has been growing into.

Nothing about the moment is remarkable, and yet everything is. *Is this—is he—it?* Aiden wonders numbly as he tries to trace it all back to something, some logical point that would explain how being a teenage boy infatuated with his flighty, amazing, unpredictable best friend had turned into something irrevocable. But he can't—Jake has long since stolen his heart, and Aiden thinks that maybe it hasn't ever really been his own, not since they were riding bikes to the end of Merrymeeting Road before even learning each other's names.

His daze is broken when Jake taps the side of his head and says, "It's a simple question, *mon ami.* What's going on in there?"

At that, Aiden's throat closes up for an entirely different reason. That word, '*ami.*' A friend: all Aiden was before, and all he will go back to being after they return to Maine.

"Of course I would," he finally replies in a bitten-off voice, and manages a tight smile. "Band-Aids and all."

"Aw," Jake says, and when he leans up to kiss Aiden again, it feels as if Jake has somehow reached past him and up into the ebony sky, stealing meteors to breathe into Aiden's veins. When he pulls back, teeth nipping at Aiden's bottom lip, he asks, "Are you cold?"

"Not really."

"It's chilly up here. Let's go inside."

Aiden nods silently and floats through packing up their cups and plates and blankets. Barely any of it even registers when all he can think is, *I love you.*

Jake's smile disappearing past the edge of the RV as he climbs down the ladder: *I love you.* Jake undressing them both inside the RV, his eyes a dark green storm, his smile faint as he pulls Aiden under the covers: *I love you so much.* Jake kissing him, just once, then pulling Aiden's arm around his own shoulders and resting his head on Aiden's chest: *God, I am so in love with you.*

And I'm so fucked.

"What?" Jake asks, looking up at him. Aiden wants to punch himself in the face. "Why?"

"I'm just... exhausted. That's all," he says, rubbing at his eyes for effect.

Jake sits up suddenly, eyes sweeping Aiden's bare arms and chest. "Dan, you—you're *shivering*; are you sure you're not cold?"

"I'm sure," he replies, and it's only as Jake's gaze catches his own, lingering with a penetrating stare, that Aiden realizes his mistake. He keeps his face as impassive as he possibly can, but Jake's eyes widen infinitesimally, and Aiden knows the game is lost—Jake has been telling him for years that his face reads like an open book in large print. There's no way in hell that he hasn't figured it out.

And yet, instead of bolting or simply turning away, as Aiden expects, Jake's features rearrange into a small smile that doesn't look at all forced. He leans over and presses a drawn-out kiss to the skin just over Aiden's heart. *Why do you have to make it so easy?*

"We should get some sleep. Long drive tomorrow," Jake says, quietly puncturing the tension. He pulls himself into Aiden's side and lays his head on Aiden's shoulder, every point of contact a warm revelation.

"Yeah, okay," Aiden murmurs, winding his arm around Jake's shoulders. He holds on as tightly as he can, brings the moment closer, as complicated and fleeting as it is. With a sigh, he says, "'Night, then."

"'Night, Dan."

7,562 MILES

DAY SIXTY-TWO: TEXAS

"Okay, here goes," Jake says, taking a deep breath and steeling himself. "I know you probably have a lot of questions and this is going against literally everything we said, but Aiden... I'm in love with you, and I think... I think you love me back. I don't know what this means for us, and it's probably the last thing—"

"Who are you talking to?"

Aiden opens the bathroom door and pokes his head inside, and Jake almost jumps out of his skin. "No one," he says quickly, turning back to the mirror and making a show of checking his hair.

"You look fine, come on," Aiden urges him, and grabs his hand to pull him from the bathroom.

"Just 'fine?'" Jake asks breathlessly, tugging on Aiden's hand. "Fine" definitely isn't glowing enough to describe his outfit: a tightly fitting, seagrass green shirt that brings out his eyes; his white double-breasted leather jacket and mulberry purple jeans that hug his ass and thighs. Aiden stops, and Jake turns in a slow circle on his toes, looking at Aiden over his shoulder. "I think you can do much better than 'fine,' mister."

"Jake," Aiden begins, cupping his jaw, "you look about a hundred thousand times better than 'fine,' but if I spend too much longer staring at your ass in those jeans, we'll be so late that by the time we get there the gig will be over. And April will be out for blood if that happens, sweetheart."

And there it is again, that affectionate little nickname Aiden gave him that twists Jake's stomach in a coil of rushing love. He leans down for a fleeting kiss, taking what no longer feels stolen, simply good and easy and right.

"Anyway, it's not like you've said anything about *my* outfit," Aiden chides him in mock-seriousness, and performs his own spin. "Well?"

Jake takes him in, in his pale gray swallow-print shirt, black leather jacket and cuffed dark-wash jeans. The shirt accents the breadth of his shoulders and the nip of his waist perfectly, and the jeans show off his toned thighs. It's a good outfit, something that he might have worn in high school if he hadn't been so obsessed with his comic book shirts.

"It's kind of like high school you, but better," Jake tells him. "You look really good."

"Having jailbait dreams?" Aiden drawls.

Jake rolls his eyes. "Come on, Mister Punctual. Wouldn't wanna be late, now would we?" With that reminder, he spins on his heel, grabs his phone and keys and sweeps out of the RV with an undeniable spring in his step.

Nothing is going to bring Jake down today, not even the fact that they're parked at a Happy-Mart. He barely gives the sign a second glance as Aiden catches up and they stroll past, making their way into downtown Austin.

"What's got you in such a good mood?" Aiden asks, nudging his shoulder while they walk.

"I'll tell you later," Jake replies.

A little of the day's heat lingers, taking the edge off the cool breeze coming up behind them; for once Jake feels as if he's being carried comfortably along rather than riding the back of a hurricane and holding on for dear life. He feels buoyant, jubilant, excited. His chest clenches every time he pictures that softness around Aiden's warm eyes, the one that spoke of affection and desire and, yes, love. Jake knew that look as soon as he saw it, more transparent than plate glass and plain as day.

Aiden is in love with him, and he loves Aiden back, and now... now it's finally time to come clean.

He's planned it all down to the last painstaking detail: the colors he's wearing—green for luck, white for renewal, purple for transformation—what he's going to say, how he's going to do it. He even texted April to change his song to one that better sums up his feelings. It's going to be a call—and, knowing that his solo performance will come before Aiden's, he can only hope that Aiden will respond in kind.

When they arrive, they find the gay bar a flat one-story building painted sky blue and off-white with a neon sign proclaiming *Cheer Up Charlie's*. The band is already set up under the marquee in the courtyard.

"Disturbing new development," Jake says in a low voice, nudging Aiden's side and gesturing toward where Liam and Ethan huddle together behind the stage, heads too close and smiles too wide as they talk. Liam wears a tie-dyed tee bearing the slogan *Keep Austin Weird*. Jake hopes the choice was ironic.

"Didn't April say they were barely speaking the last time we were all together?" Aiden asks, sounding utterly confounded, and Jake nods.

"Yep. Something about Green Day, I think? Either way—"

"Guys, you're here!"

Jake whips around to be greeted with a hug from April and a characteristically shy half-wave from Marcie before Aiden lifts her off her feet and spins her in a circle. She's blushing when he sets her down, and fiddles with a few strands of hair that have fallen out of her sleek up-do.

"What's with Liam and Ethan?" Jake asks without preamble, and April rolls her eyes.

"Really? *That's* the first thing you ask about," she says, her voice dripping with sarcasm, her hands on her hips. "What about, 'Hi, best friend! It's been too long, and I feel awful about not calling you for longer than five minutes since *Michigan*, and how's your throat now, and oh my god, that outfit looks *incredible* on you!' How about *that*, Valentine?"

"Okay, I get your point, I'm sorry," Jake says, raising his hands in submission. She doesn't look appeased; it is as if she towers over him in her floaty, sky blue maxi dress and black heels. "I *do* feel awful, and that outfit *does* look incredible on you. How *is* your throat?"

"That's better," April says, crossing her arms over her chest. "I'm still getting over it, so I'm just doing some backup singing for the next few gigs. And by the way, the Liam and Ethan thing is your fault."

"What? My fault?" Jake asks, affronted.

"She told them about you and Aiden," Marcie interjects.

"What, and they thought it was a good idea?" Aiden asks, chuckling. His eyes dance with humor as he glances at Jake, slowly looking him up and down. At Marcie's nod, he adds, "Well, it does get lonely on the road..."

April scoffs. "Yeah, okay, *loneliness* was a factor in you two finally getting it on."

"April," Jake warns.

"If that's your story, stick to it. I don't care," she says, flicking her long red hair over her shoulder. Jake's jaw sets and he takes her by the elbow, leaving Marcie and Aiden to exchange a glance as he steers her through the crowd and toward the fence that borders the courtyard.

"I need you to stop," he says, and April just rolls her eyes again.

"Jake, come on. I *know* you, and I know Aiden, and this thing you have going on? Anyone with *eyes* can see that it's more than just—"

"I'm in love with him," Jake interrupts, and it's almost comical the way April freezes, her eyes going wide and her mouth hanging open. "What, like you're surprised?"

"No, I just never thought I'd get you to admit it," she breathes and grabs his hand. "Jakey, this is so exciting! Does he... I mean, of *course* he feels the same way, the way he looks at—oh my god, have you told him yet?"

"I'm planning on doing it tonight," Jake says, gaze sliding to Aiden and Marcie as they talk. Marcie keeps pulling at her fingers and smoothing down the front of her ivory lace sundress, but she seems to be relaxing degree by degree; it looks as if Aiden is managing to pull her out of her shell. "She's really sweet on him, isn't she?"

April doesn't respond, and when Jake looks at her, her face is stony.

"Shit. I'm sorry," he says, but April shakes her head.

"Let's just... not," she says. "I really need to not go there right now."

Is it his own good judgment or the look in April's eyes that betrays her? Against his better instincts, Jake asks, "Did something happen?"

April glances at Marcie one more time and then crouches low against the fence, the bottom of her dress fanning out around her. Jake joins her when she beckons him down and carefully watches her face. She crosses her arms and rests them on her knees, letting out a deep sigh. "We all got drunk after the show last night and she kissed me."

"*What?*" Jake asks, his voice way too loud. They get odd looks from the people standing nearest to them, but he shrugs it off and focuses on April. Quietly, he continues, "Shy little Marcie Stevens got drunk and kissed you? How did that even *happen?*"

"It was almost closing time, and we were sitting on one of the couches inside," April begins. "She had her head on my shoulder, and she was tracing these stupid patterns on my leg, and I was like, freaking out internally because... well, *you* know how it is."

Jake nods, and gestures for her to go on.

"We'd been drinking tequila and I should have known better than to give her that stuff because it always makes her super melancholy, but anyway... she was getting kind of down on herself, and I swear I just said like, one nice thing and the next thing I knew she was all over me."

"What did you say to her?" Looking anywhere but at him, April mumbles something that Jake doesn't quite catch. "Say that again?"

"I told her she's the only girl I've ever fallen for, okay?" she says, her eyes screwed shut and her mouth twisted into a grimace. She opens one eye and looks at him. All he can do is smile at her. "Okay, fine. I was drunk, too. Just shut up."

"I didn't say anything."

"Well, whatever you're thinking, don't. Sappy asshole."

"I just don't see what the problem is, honey," he says, reaching out and putting a hand over hers.

She smiles a little—she knows Jake isn't touchy-feely with most people—but it fades quickly as she says, "She doesn't remember any of it."

Jake laughs humorlessly. "Is she me?" At her confused look, he waves her off—Philadelphia is another story, for another time. "How do you know she doesn't remember? Are you sure she isn't just embarrassed and acting like nothing happened?"

"Please. There's a reason she never declared as a drama major," April says. "Can we just change the subject now? I'd really like it if we could stop talking about this."

"Okay. But if you need me..."

"I know. A five-minute conversation is one phone call away."

Jake winces, but doesn't contradict her; instead he shuffles forward in his crouched position and gives her an awkward hug. She drops her forehead to his shoulder, hugging him back after a moment, and asks, "Are you nervous?"

"I'm a Valentine, honey. We don't get nervous."

April pulls back and levels him with a single look. "Jake, are you *nervous?*"

Jake swallows and gives her a tremulous smile. "Terrified."

"Piece of advice." April gets to her feet. Jake follows as she brushes herself off and adjusts the skirt of her dress, looking up at him with earnest eyes. "Do *not* break eye contact with him when you do your solo. After that, you probably won't even need to tell him."

"You're really sure he feels the same way," Jake says. He feels like a teenager all over again; he can't help needing the extra reassurance.

"You forget that I know what song he picked," April reminds him with a wink, and links arms to lead him toward the stage. "Now let's rock the shit outta this place, and get you your man while we're at it. You game?"

With much more conviction than he feels, Jake nods and says, "Bring it on."

Five minutes later, all members of The One with the Band are assembled: Hugh behind his drum kit, Drake on bass, Liam and Ethan on guitar and keyboard off to Jake's right, Jake at two backup microphones with April and Marcie on the left and Aiden center stage to open. The main lights drop; the only remaining illumination is provided by the giant screen behind them, undulating between deep and pale shades of blue. The crowd noise has died down to a murmur punctuated by a few coughs and cleared throats. It's enough to have Jake's stomach churning with nerves and anticipation.

A single glimpse of Aiden's reassuring smile, and the nervousness is gone.

A fleeting brush of their reaching fingertips, and *Jake* is gone.

There's no introduction this time, simply Liam counting off and strumming the introduction of their opening song. It's fun and energetic, and sure to get the crowd interested. As Hugh joins in and the lights come up, Aiden stands with his feet shoulder-width apart, his back straight, both hands curled around the mic.

He starts singing and Jake watches the crowd fall for him, cheering when he manages to work the name of the bar into the second line. Jake grins and joins in with April and Marcie's over-the-top, cheesy backup choreography. The song is a fantastic choice to open the show—it is bright and bouncy enough to engage the audience but doesn't show off everything the band can do.

During the final refrain, Aiden takes the mic from the stand and struts across the stage, slotting himself between Jake and Marcie and snaking his arm around Jake's waist. They trade lines, calling and responding exactly as Jake's been hoping they would, and when Aiden is back at his mic stand, the song drawing to its close, he breaks his rapport with the crowd to sing the last line directly to Jake.

Shouldn't I be asking you to stay? Isn't that my line? Jake wonders in distraction, half listening as the guys play through the song's final bars and the crowd bursts into applause louder even than in Ann Arbor.

"Cheer Up Charlie's!" Aiden shouts into the mic, raising his arms. "A *very* good evening to all of you! We're absolutely thrilled to be here in Austin, so thanks for having us. We're playing two sets for you tonight, and we've left some song lists scattered around because we'll be inviting a few of you up here to jam with us in the second set, so don't be shy! If there's a song you want to sing, write your name and song on a slip and bring it up to us.

"I'm Aiden," he continues, and gestures to each of the other band members in turn. "Behind me on drums you'll see Hugh; over on guitar and keyboard you'll see Liam and Ethan; on bass we've got Drake; there's April on backup vocals; and Marcie on trumpet.

"And next up, ladies and gentleman, we have Jake," Aiden says, his voice soft around the sound of Jake's name as he motions him over to the mic.

With weak knees and trembling hands, not really knowing how much of it is coming from his adrenalin rush, Jake takes the stand and kisses Aiden's cheek. Aiden's hand momentarily lingers at his waist and then Jake is alone under a spotlight. It's almost as terrifying as the thought of offering himself to Aiden, flaws and all.

Jake watches Aiden climb down from the stage—his anchor, his touchstone, his reason—and glances over at April, who smiles at him reassuringly. It does little for his resurgence of nerves. He can only hope that the song he has chosen to encapsulate everything manages to resonate. The song says it all, and says it all with hope—from his point of view, at least.

Hugh takes up the percussive introduction of Jake's song, and Jake draws in a centering breath. *This is it, Jake. This is where it begins.*

Ignoring April's earlier advice, he fixes his gaze upon the middle distance as he starts to sing—and oh, how liberating it is to do so freely now, without his throat closing up and his words stuttered if they come out at all. This song is soulful; though it isn't the sort of thing Jake is used to singing, and though his upper range is still somewhat unpracticed, he finds it easy to let his voice run over the notes in a comfortable flow. Being onstage and feeling Aiden's eyes on him, singing for him and letting one hand grip the mic and the other drift up into his hair, Jake feels... sexy. Powerful. He can do this.

He sways in time with the flowing beat and notices the crowd getting into it, waving their arms from side to side over their heads. Jake's eyes finally come to rest upon Aiden during the second verse; drawing him in is easy, and keeping him is easier. Their eye contact is charged—Aiden *has* to know Jake is singing about him, to him, *for* him. The possibility that he might not, that he might unwittingly let his lifelong self-confidence issues get in the way, is a thought that Jake quashes as immediately as it occurs to him, lest he let the knot in his stomach travel too far up and make him start biting his tongue again.

The song is a contradiction, and the lyrics illustrate the war that Jake has waged against himself for longer than he will probably ever know, but no more—they could be the worst, but they could also be the greatest. All he has to do is leap, and put aside the fear that Aiden won't be there long enough to break his fall.

By the song's end, Hugh drumming him out with the same rhythm that brought him in, Jake is flying again. He grins and takes his bow, smiles in response to the wink April throws his way and accepts another passing kiss from Aiden as he takes his place in backup once more.

"Just you wait. He's closing the first set with it," April whispers, leaning close enough to bump her shoulder against his as the next song begins. "He's really special, Jakey. He's good for you."

"Yeah, he is," Jake whispers back, and hooks his pinky finger around hers.

The rest of the first set passes in a blur. The stage is a bubble—past the bright lights trained on the band, Jake can hear the crowd, can even see silhouettes beneath the marquee, but he's in a world where nothing exists apart from Aiden and the music. Before he knows it, April is ushering everyone off the stage save for Aiden, Hugh and Liam.

Please, Aiden, Jake thinks as April squeezes his arm. Aiden loops an electro-acoustic guitar across his body and take a seat on a wooden stool before the microphone. *Please tell me you feel the same.*

Aiden begins to strum, picking out a seemingly random tune to bridge the break in music, and leans forward to speak into the mic. "All right, folks, we're gonna take a quick break so you can all recover from how awesome we are... just kidding! But before we go, we're going to play one last song for you. Are there any Barenaked Ladies fans in the house?"

There are some scattered but loud cheers, plus a couple of outright screams from the back. Jake cranes his neck to see a handsome older man with glasses and a bowtie and a woman with dark hair and perfectly applied red lipstick hold their half-empty cocktails up in the direction of the stage, clearly not caring that most of the twenty-something crowd has turned to look at them.

Aiden laughs, and as he begins to strum the opening bars of a song that Jake doesn't recognize, eliciting more screams from the back, he leans forward again and says, "Looks like I'm singing for you guys, then! This one's called 'Easy.'"

When he starts singing, his vocals are bright, upbeat, at odds with lyrics that seem to be telling off the subject of the song, the singer in love with someone who doesn't seem to feel the same way. Jake's blood runs cold. He grabs April's hand and holds on as tightly as he dares.

"What the fuck?" he hisses at her, but she simply holds up a finger, her hazel eyes still trained on the stage, her smile stretching wide.

He follows her gaze. Aiden is still singing, his voice strong and assured and undercut with a tenderness that takes the edge off Jake's anxiety.

What are you telling me? he wonders desperately, and then Aiden begins to sing of someone forgetting what they were hiding for, someone being easy to adore even though they want to run away, and it becomes clear as crystal. It's a response to Jake's call; it's all or nothing; it's a *plea*. Isn't it?

"See?" April says into his ear. "See what I mean?"

Rendered mute, he nods at her, and his heart leaps into his throat when he turns his attention back to the stage. Aiden watches him, smiling and singing with an astounding conviction. The rich, smooth timbre of his voice only grows stronger as he dives into the final chorus, and Jake's resolve increases tenfold. No more fear, no more excuses, no more being afraid of a future he can't possibly know. He's going to tell Aiden that he's in love with him, and Aiden will tell him that he hasn't fallen in love alone, and Jake will finally find out exactly what "I love you" tastes like as he breathes it into Aiden's mouth.

"Thank you, Cheer Up Charlie's!" Aiden cries, wrapping up the song to rapturous applause. Jake glances out over the crowd and can see almost every single person in the courtyard gazing up at Aiden adoringly; he wonders again why this isn't what Aiden does every single night. "We'll be back in fifteen, so don't go anywhere!"

And then Jake is moving, pushing his way back up onto the stage where Aiden is clapping Liam and Hugh on the back in turn, and he takes a deep breath to ask Aiden to go somewhere they can talk in private—

"So what do you think about doing this for a living?" Hugh asks, eyes trained on Aiden, and the floor falls out from beneath Jake's feet.

Aiden openly gapes at Hugh and Jake just stands there, fists opening and closing by his sides, his smile fading

"What do you mean?" Aiden asks.

"The band's breaking up after this tour," Hugh says, "and a few of us are moving to New York to start a new thing, see if we can make it. April doesn't wanna sing lead, Will's staying back home for good now, and we were going to try to find someone there, but dude... we already know you, you fit well with us, you know?"

Jake's ears are roaring, and he can barely hear Aiden's sputtered response. Never has he hated someone as much as he hates Hugh right now. He hates all five feet, six inches of him, hates his stupid red hair and squinty brown eyes and offensively green shoes. He can't even muster the wherewithal to wonder why April didn't warn him and he feels like an idiot, working himself up all night to tell Aiden that he saw the look in his eyes, because now he's witnessing an entirely different look—as if Aiden has seen his entire future flash in front of him, a future brighter than anything Jake can possibly offer. He'll go to New York to start making the music that still lingers in patches on the skin of Jake's back; he'll become the nomad Jake was afraid of when he agreed to come along for the road trip. He's back standing in the shadow of a mountain.

"Just think about it, okay? You don't have to give me an answer now," Hugh is saying with a tone of finality, and as he passes them to join the rest of the band at the bar, Aiden turns to Jake and opens his mouth.

"You should do it," Jake blurts, cutting off whatever Aiden was about to say.

"Oh sure, just waste my entire college education," Aiden replies, but it's too late. Jake already knows that Aiden wants to go more than anything; he's been shifting for weeks already. They'll get back to Brunswick at the end of this trip and it will be over. It isn't as if Jake can just pull up stakes and move to New York—he has a career of his own to think about starting, and the last time he checked, being a groupie wasn't a viable profession.

"Well, like Hugh said… think about it," he manages, pasting on a smile that he hopes doesn't look as fake as it feels. "You're… different when you perform. Something about it just seems right."

Aiden scoffs and shakes his head, and guides Jake offstage with a hand at the small of his back.

As they stand at the bar waiting to be served, Aiden nudges his shoulder and asks, "So what did you think?"

"You were really good," Jake replies, mouth dry.

"Hey, what were you gonna tell me earlier?"

"When?"

"I asked you why you were in such a good mood, and you said you'd tell me later," Aiden says.

"Oh, *that*. Nothing, really," Jake says, affecting an air of nonchalance and turning his gaze on the crowd. *Nothing, except I'm crazy about you. Nothing, except I would do pretty much anything to hear you say that you love me back. Nothing, except I've been daydreaming about what my life will look like in five, twenty, fifty years, and in every single future, there you are by my side, holding not just my hand, but all of me.*

Jake doesn't say any of this. How could he? Aiden deserves to have nothing stand in his way, whatever his decision about New York. He deserves to be free, to have his name up in lights, to not be tied to Maine while Jake tries to figure out where he's going and how he's going to get there.

April catches Jake's eye as she winds through the crowd with Marcie in tow and gives him a questioning thumbs up. He simply shakes his head and scuffs his shoe against the bar's poured concrete base.

"Where do you go?" Aiden asks with a chuckle. Jake cuts off his train of thought and glances at him with a raised eyebrow. Aiden continues, "When you get that faraway look in your eyes?"

"Are you saying that I'm vacant?" Jake replies, dredging humor from reserves he thought pretty depleted.

"No, no. No, it's... you look like you're in this whole other world, someplace I can't find you," Aiden says. He reaches down to link their fingers, and Jake tries not to tense.

He looks down at their joined hands, rubs Aiden's thumb, and says, "I don't go anywhere."

"Not even sometimes?" Aiden presses him.

"Maybe, I..." Jake trails off, finally letting the question bear the weight Aiden obviously intends it to. And he sees that it's true; for weeks he's been skirting the edges of a brave new world, dancing within reach of possibility and metamorphosis, but now comes the reality check. Now comes the break of day, chasing away the artifice and bathing everything in fact. He shakes his head, and finally answers, "No. No, I'm always here. With you."

Aiden smiles, noses along his jaw and whispers into his ear, "Good."

Yeah, Jake thinks sadly. *Good.*

8,072 MILES

DAY SIXTY-FIVE: OKLAHOMA

When they walk into the lobby of the Route 66 in Clinton, it is as if they have passed into a bygone era. Aiden taps his foot to the Rolling Stones' classic rock'n'roll cover of "Route 66" playing over the PA system, and as

Jake catches sight of the classic red Chevy parked in front of the curved windows, Aiden watches him light up.

"Oh my god," Jake breathes, slowly approaching the car with his hands twitching at his sides. "This is a 1957 Chevy Bel Air. What I wouldn't give to own one of these."

"Is grand theft auto a felony in Oklahoma?" Aiden stage-whispers, and Jake casts him a wistful look.

"You'll just have to buy one for me when you wrap your first big budget shoot," he says his gaze full of reverence as he returns it to the vintage car.

Aiden hums noncommittally. For once, he doesn't want to talk about his intended career path—as of late, it has begun to feel like the wrong fit for him. He still loves the prospect of directing, but now that he's no longer surrounded by film day in and day out, he finds that his passion for it is somehow muted, as if someone turned it down with a dimmer switch. But the second Hugh approached him with the idea of fronting the new band and helping to create and perform original music—in New York, no less—something seemed to click.

"Ready?" Jake asks, pulling him from his thoughts. Aiden nods, and after they sign the guest register and pay their admission fee to the chatty proprietor, they set off on their self-guided tour.

Aiden thought the glass-tiled front of the museum looked cool, but it's nothing compared to the content of the museum itself. Each room's theme is a different decade in the highway's history and features exhibits of vintage cars from as far back as the thirties. It's more like an art gallery than a museum. The history in the place is overwhelming and Aiden drinks it all in, his eyes roaming over the old-style gas pumps and a wall full of postcards from all of the states Route 66 winds its way through. The rooms are connected by tunnel-like hallways, the walls plastered with newspapers whose headlines proclaim *MARILYN DEAD; PRESIDENT KENNEDY IS SLAIN* and *THE WAR IS OVER!*

"I'm glad we have Leona," Jake says after they've taken turns posing with the VW camper covered in crazy sixties hippie designs. "I don't think we'd have made it far in one of these."

"Yeah, being on top of each other like that all the time..." Aiden trails off, shooting him a wink.

"Please, like you'd complain about me being on top of you."

"Never said I would."

"In fact, I think it's your favorite thing," Jake continues loftily, bending to examine a model car inside a glass case—a yellow 1967 Ford Mustang, Aiden reads from his position opposite. He glances through the glass at Jake, at the fascinated look in his eyes and the way his deep green irises reflect the yellow of the model car and suddenly take on a unique shade, one that Aiden hasn't seen in nearly fifteen years.

"And what makes you think that?" Aiden asks in a low voice, though there's no one else around.

"After all the times we've had sex, what *wouldn't* make me think that?" Jake asks, though it's more a statement than a question. Slowly, he circles around the case to back Aiden up against it, his brow furrowed as his eyes drift down Aiden's body. He cocks his head to the right, tenses his shoulders and lets out a low "*Mmm.*"

"What are you—" Aiden begins, but Jake silences him with a finger pressed against his lips. Eyes closed, clearly trusting Aiden to keep watch, Jake loops his arms around Aiden's neck and pulls their bodies closer together.

"Fuck," Jake whispers, the fingers of one hand carding through Aiden's hair. "Right—right there... fuck, Jake, harder..."

"Do I really sound like that?" Aiden asks, because there's no way he does, so raw and sexual and... hot.

Jake nods slowly, and his breathing grows shallow and harsh, hitching in his chest. His arms shiver and he crowds Aiden closer to the case. Its corner presses between his shoulder blades.

"Just a little more," Jake pleads, his voice high and desperate, and it's as if all the blood in Aiden's body just *stops* and rushes south. He clenches his fists, thinking of cold showers and dead bodies and breasts and *anything* to keep from having to wait out a boner in the middle of a fucking museum. "Come on, fuck me, make me yours."

"Jake, you have to st—"

When Jake opens his eyes his pupils are blown wide, and Aiden falls silent. Jake leans so close that their lips are a hair's breadth apart, and though his face blurs, Aiden knows that their eyes are locked. "Please, *please...*"

"Someone's coming," Aiden blurts, and Jake abruptly steps back, hands falling to his sides.

As if nothing has happened, he goes back to looking at the exhibits, casting one salacious look over his shoulder and stating, "No one's coming, Dan."

Aiden feels as if he's been knocked over sideways. How could this Jake—his favorite Jake, all sultry tease and subtle love—have eluded him for so long?

What they have is love of a kind; Aiden can see it now. Yet still he waits, because it's all he knows how to do when he has put the object of his affection on a pedestal and he waits for the descent, the press of a kiss that tastes like love, the vowels and consonants that will spell it all out. And really, what reason does he have to think they will? History just repeats itself for Aiden Calloway—at least where his unrequited crushes are concerned. He had mooned over Peter Groves, one of the guys working at the Subway on Pleasant Street, for the entire summer before his internship. He worshiped the guy and never did a goddamn thing about it, because how could anyone reach so high as to touch an idol?

Do you honestly believe that this is just a road trip thing? he wants to ask as he follows Jake through the last hallway and out into the foyer. Aiden watches Jake's fingertips trail along the wall just as they trail along his own skin in the dark clutches of night and wonders, *What if we'd met in another life? What if I were different, braver, more sure that I'm worthy of you? What then?*

"Gift shop?" Jake asks innocently when Aiden catches up with him. "I'm thinking a shirt from this place might not be so bad."

"Yeah?" Aiden asks, his mood brightening.

"Just this once."

LATER, LONG AFTER DARKNESS has fallen and they've glutted themselves on one another, Aiden leaves Jake sleeping. Unable to drift off, he pads out into the living room in socks and pajama pants, pulling on his hoodie as he goes; the nights are turning colder.

He switches on the radio, leaves it on the first station he finds and drops into the chair behind the seats. He catches up on the news and replies to a few emails, none of it distracting him in the way he wants it to. Every minute or so, his eyes drift to the half-closed bedroom door, and he realizes just how lonely it can be on the road.

After a moment's hesitation, he grabs his travel journal and a pen from his bag and flips to the first blank page.

I could probably use some advice, though I probably wouldn't follow it anyway, he writes, then chews on the tip of his pen as he considers his next words. *The thing is... I know that everyone's been able to see it. How I've been feeling, how I've been falling, even if I couldn't. I'll probably have to get someone to clue me in to how they do that one of these days. But the point is that I really don't know what to do about it, any more than I did the night I realized that... that I, Aiden Calloway, am in love with Jake Valentine.*

He stops short, the rest of the blank page sitting there, taunting him as he considers the words he wants to vocalize but can't—fear holds his heart captive, when it should be Jake. Aiden has *thought* them, over and over, at least once per waking minute since the meteor shower, but hasn't spoken them. It was nice, at first, the thrill of something secret and new—old, he keeps reminding himself, but newly realized—to hold close, to keep just for himself. But what at first felt like a feather between his fingers now feels like a weight of responsibility and ruin around his neck.

For a while, I was doing okay, he writes, halting after every other word. *I even kind of thought that Jake might feel the same, or at least be on the way to it. I mean, god, he told me back at Lake Calhoun that he'd thought he was falling for me, which was why he did what he did in Chicago. So it's not like I'd be completely off-base, right? And all day Saturday he kept looking at me like I put the sun in the sky, and I was so sure that he was going to say* something. *But he didn't. I mean... why would he fall for me anyway? He's just... he's* everything. *Everything.*

I talked to Hugh at the gig on Saturday night, and he told me that a few of them are forming a new band once the tour is over and moving to New York to see if they can make it. He wants me to go with them, sing and write, and the first thing I thought was, "What about Jake?" Should I hold on? Should I wait, half expecting to get my heart broken? Should I just take this for exactly what we've said it is, take everything he'll give me and let the timer run out? What should I do?

After Aiden dots his last i and crosses his last t, he closes the notebook and tosses it back into his bag. He stretches out his legs and arms; the deep ache and satiation in his limbs reminds him just how rough they got earlier, and despite the heaviness of what he just put into words, he can't help but smile.

He reclines the chair, curls up on his side with his arm tucked up under his head and closes his eyes. But it's no use—sleep eludes him, just as it did at the beginning of the trip, and writing hasn't really helped. Idly, he wishes that Jake might wake up of his own accord and suggest making cocoa. Aiden can never get it to taste quite the same when he makes it.

Aiden sighs, turns off all the lights and goes to sit in the cab. Resting both arms over the steering wheel, he looks out into the wooded clearing at the semicircle formed by the few other RVs and campers in the park. A group of people is gathered around the fire pit, all paired off. They have blankets wrapped around their shoulders and drink from red plastic cups.

Aiden watches one couple because the man bears a passing resemblance to Jake; the girl he's with says something that makes him laugh, and he looks at her as though she's the best thing he's ever seen.

Aiden and Jake still haven't found the time or place to have a campfire, and Aiden aches to know what it would be like, now that they are... whatever they are. Their campfires used to be legendary, all-night affairs that only ended when the embers died, and Aiden has always been entranced by the inherent romance of sitting by the dancing flames, speaking in hushed voices and with shadowed eyes. There is something intrinsically special about that aspect of their shared childhood, and Aiden longs to recapture it.

Exhaustion settles over him like a blanket of snow. He feels himself being slowly buried beneath it, the only light above him an unattainable one; he can reach up toward it, but the silhouette of his own hand eclipses the source of his warmth. He wonders what will happen to him and Jake if he decides to go to New York. Knowing what he now knows about how his absence during the internship affected Jake, he feels selfish for even considering it. But is it really so selfish not to want to be beholden to something finite? Then again, how can he give up everything they've discovered between them over the course of this road trip, not to mention all that he worked so long for?

A shuffling behind him alerts him to Jake's sudden presence, and warm, sleep-heavy arms curl around his shoulders. "You should come back to bed."

"What's in bed?"

"Someone who won't really mind if you wanna have sex half asleep."

"I was hoping that'd be the case," Aiden says, chuckling.

"It's like one mind," Jake says, squeezing his shoulders before straightening up.

Aiden turns, stands and drinks in the sight of Jake, relaxed as he so rarely is during daylight hours, his Henley and sweatpants rumpled and a blanket wrapped around his shoulders. He looks far more inviting than the mess inside Aiden's head, so Aiden leaves everything behind in the cab—the words, the music, the confusion—and simply lets himself be led.

8,519 MILES

DAY SIXTY-SEVEN: KANSAS

"Aiden!" Jake calls at the top of his voice. It echoes in the stillness of the night. He shrugs, adjusts his backpack and carries on walking, taking left after left after left. Even with the somewhat comforting twinkle of stars above him and his flashlight in hand, the darkness inside the maze remains oppressive.

"'Let's turn off here,' he said. 'It's a maze, it'll totally be fun,' he said," Jake grumbles aloud, shaking his flashlight when it flickers. This has all the potential of a grisly horror movie: two very non-virginal boys lost in a maze in the middle of nowhere, separated because one of them insisted on racing to the middle for their Thanksgiving picnic. Why they couldn't have it inside the RV, where it's warm, and more importantly, safe, Jake doesn't know. What he does know is that he is mostly powerless to resist those dumb puppy eyes of Aiden's, even as he slowly but surely resigns himself to the inevitable end of what they've been doing. This is the beginning of a long, painfully drawn-out goodbye; they will always be best friends, of course, there's no doubting that, but Aiden has the prospect of a new life waiting for him now, and Jake has no right to hold him back from it. He loves Aiden, so as much as the thought leaves him cold, he has to let him go.

Just as he reaches another dead end, his flashlight flickers and goes out. Jake swears under his breath and switches to the miniature flashlight he keeps on his key ring.

It's too quiet so deep in the maze. Jake stops to weigh the benefits of listening to music against the ability to hear approaching serial killers; as he starts to take off his backpack, his phone rings in his pocket at top volume.

When he sees *Home* emblazoned across the screen over a picture of Charlie smiling—a fleeting, candid moment he snapped at a barbecue over the summer when Eric, her best friend from college, was visiting—he answers it immediately.

"Hello?"

"Baby bro!"

Jake grins at Eric's customary greeting. His infectious happiness makes Jake smile every bit as much as if he has just been wrapped up in one of Eric's bone-crushing bear hugs.

"What are you doing in Brunswick? I thought you couldn't make it this year," he says.

"Ah, most of the fam's down in Puerto Rico for the holidays, you know how it is. Thought I'd swing by at the last minute; Thanksgiving doesn't seem right now without seeing you guys," Eric says.

"And how does one just 'swing by at the last minute' from all the way across the country?"

"You get on a fuckin' plane, that's how. Anyway! Happy Thanksgiving!"

"Happy Thanksgiving," Jake says, inhaling deeply and imagining that he can detect the faint scent of laundry detergent and American Crew hair wax on the cold night air. He pictures Eric in their worn-out living room, his linebacker build taking up two seats on the couch and his feet up on the coffee table no matter how often Charlie tells him to get them off. The image warms him a little bit. "Where's Charlie?"

"Walking off dinner," Eric says, with incredulity in his voice. Jake can see him throwing a hand into the air and making a face as if it's the dumbest thing he's ever heard. "I mean, I've got a total food coma situation going on right now, and she had just as many helpings as I did. I don't know how she does it; she must have hollow legs or somethin'."

"How many helpings are we talking, here?" Jake asks.

"Eh... four, maybe? But it's Thanksgiving! Eating crap tons of food is the whole point."

Jake shakes his head, grinning, and sits down on the ground, taking off his backpack and leaning against the hedge. If he keeps walking without paying attention to where he's going, he'll only end up more lost.

"It's really good to hear from you," Jake says, and he means it. Eric has been a Thanksgiving fixture at the Valentine household ever since their dad died, when they sat around with Chinese takeout boxes littering the dinner table, not a smile among them—except on Eric, this larger than life, born and bred Californian, who looked at Charlie as though she was his favorite person. Somehow, by way of a bizarre and slightly concerning stand-up comedy routine that involved spraying his black hair white-blond and heavily outlining his hazel eyes in black, he managed to make them laugh out loud for the first time in two months. "How's life in... *where* are you living now?"

"Oh man, you didn't hear? I'm back home! Californ-I-A, baby."

"That's fantastic! Charlie said you were never really happy in Denver."

"Yeah, I wasn't," Eric says. "Way too far from the ocean."

"I know that feeling," Jake says with a sigh, glancing up at his surroundings and feeling too contained. He traces patterns in the cold, hard-packed earth, closing his eyes and pretending that the dirt is the thick sand on Thomas Point Beach.

"So what the hell is up with this crazy-ass route you and the squirt are taking?"

Jake opens his eyes again, the moment lost. "What do you mean?"

"Charlie showed me the GPS thingy earlier and it looks like you guys are playing connect the dots on a map."

"Yeah, I know. It's a crazy-ass route. It just seemed like if we were going to cover all the states and be able to actually do something in each one, we should do the whole zigzag thing."

"And you're where right now? Kansas?"

Jake's humorless laughter comes out in a puff of white. "Well, right now I'm sitting in the middle of a maze somewhere outside Wichita because Dan decided it would be great to spend Thanksgiving lost, cold and hungry."

"Wait... who's Dan?"

"Sorry. Just a dumb nickname I have for Aiden," Jake explains, his face growing hot.

"Gotcha," Eric says. "You know, Charlie and I totally had a bet going once upon a time. She bet me twenty bucks that Aiden wouldn't figure out that you had that crush on him in senior year, and she's still winning."

Biting his lip, Jake goes back to drawing patterns in the dirt. "She's still so sure that we're going to end up together."

"She's missing you, man," Eric says. "She won't say it, you know how she is. Might as well be British for all that stiff upper lip crap! But I can tell."

A circle, a line through the circle, a triangle around the circle, a square around the triangle, another circle around the square and Jake loses track. "I've been meaning to call her. We... sort of had a fight, when I was in Ohio."

As if he's tiptoeing around whether to bring it up, Eric says, "Yeah, she told me about all this house stuff."

Jake's hand stops moving. "She did?"

"Yeah, we got to talking about the old days, you know how it is. Told me she wants to go back, but she'd have to sell the house."

"Did she tell you all of it?"

"She told me. And I totally get it, man. I mean, I practically grew up in my *abuela's* house and it was a wrench when we had to sell it. But it was all for the best, you know? She wouldn't have wanted us all stuck down in San fuckin' Pedro."

Jake forces his splayed fingers into the earth and grips a handful. It's nothing like the sand back home. He pulls his hand free and wipes it off on his dark pants, not caring whether he leaves dirty smears or not.

His fight with Charlie has been preying on his mind for nearly a month and he's been inching closer and closer to telling her that they *should* sell the house. It's probably time, after all; and other than Charlie and the house, he has nothing left to tie him to Brunswick anymore. But every time he's come close to calling her, a fresh wave of sadness takes him under and he gets lost in memories; his mother's window boxes and hanging baskets full of bougainvillea; the ocean smell that always clung to his parents' bedroom; sharing plates of carrot sticks and apple slices with Aiden in the living room while they watched Saturday cartoons; and all the times he and Charlie built blanket forts or held stuffed toy ballet recitals under the kitchen table.

"You're right," he finally says, scrubbing over his eyes. "I guess... that house, it... it's the last thing we've got left of them."

"Like I said, man. Totally get it," Eric says. "But we've all gotta move on sometime."

It's time you figure out a way to let go of Dad. It's been seven years; don't you think you need to move on?

Swallowing hard around the sudden lump in his throat, Jake says, "I know. I'm trying to work on that."

"Tough stuff, man," Eric says. In the background, Jake hears the unmistakable sound of his own front door closing.

"Is that Charlie?" he asks.

"Yeah, one sec," Eric says, and there are a few seconds of static that sound as if he's covered the mouthpiece to speak to Charlie. When he comes back, he says, "So when're you gonna be down in Cali, huh?"

Jake mentally flips through the binder in the RV. "Mid-December, I think. Can we come by?"

"Shit, I'll be outta town. Big job in DC that month. That's too bad; I coulda shown you around the place."

"We'll make it happen sometime. I miss your dumb face."

"Miss you too, baby bro."

"So tell me, Eric Batista, just when do you plan on marrying my sister?"

Jake waits for the customary laugh accompanied by the usual, "When I get that dirt off my shoulder, that's when!" But it doesn't come. There's a moment of pregnant silence on the line, and then, "One of these days, man. One of these days."

"Wait, wha—"

"Here's Charlie."

"Eric, wait!"

"Jakey?"

One word from his sister, and the light edge of panic he barely noticed creeping up on him fades back into the shadows. Jake smiles. It's good to hear Charlie's voice. "Hey, sis. Happy Thanksgiving."

"You too," Charlie says. "What are you crazy kids up to today?"

"I was just telling Eric that I'm lost in a maze somewhere near Wichita because Dan thought it'd be fun to make me work for my food," Jake says, and Charlie's ensuing chuckle makes him feel a little warmer.

"Yeah, I heard that you're singing for your supper these days."

"You—who told you that?"

"Aiden's mom and I do talk, you know."

Lump firmly back in his throat, Jake starts drawing on the ground again. "She told you about the singing."

"Yep. She told me something else interesting, too," Charlie says, and though she's obviously trying to sound pissed off, there's an unmistakable note of excitement in her voice too. Jake knows that his sister is a patient woman, but that she's expecting an answer to a question she doesn't even need to ask.

"What *exactly* did she say about—about me and Aiden?" Jake asks glumly, not the least bit surprised that Alice knows. Aiden speaks to her at least once a week.

"Nothing much, just that you two are 'seeing how things go,' whatever that means," Charlie says. "Jakey, why wouldn't you tell me something like that? I've always thought we can talk about this stuff."

"We can, sis, it's just..." *Where do I even begin?* "I'm so confused."

"Confused about what? About Aiden? Jake, he's *crazy* about you, has been ever since he was wearing those awful band T-shirts."

"He still wears awful band T-shirts sometimes."

"You know what I mean," Charlie says, adding, "And I know you're crazy about him, too."

"That's the whole problem!" Jake exclaims, getting to his feet and pacing back and forth. "I'm in... I *really* care about him."

"So... *what's* the problem? Everyone knows you've been in love with him for years."

"But *I* didn't know! I didn't know. And it's just... it's *terrifying*," he says, running his free hand through his hair and down his face. A torrent of fear is rising inside him like a tidal wave, and for once, he can't help but let it out. Suddenly, he has his sister back, the girl whose toenails he used to paint while they looked at teen magazines together and rated guys on a scale of one to ten. "What if... what if we get back and he finds someone else, or what if he wants to go back to London, or what if he decides he wants to join April's new band in New York and I'm just left behind *again?* What then?"

"Jakey, I'm only gonna say this once, so listen," Charlie says, her voice low and controlled.

He takes a deep breath and braces himself. "Okay. I'm listening."

"Get your head out of your ass."

"Charlie!"

"I'm serious. So what if he wants to go to London or New York or, Jesus, even *Guam*? What you guys have is special, and it's *rare*. Don't let it go to waste before you even give it a chance."

Her words are meant to comfort him, energize him into doing something about his situation, he knows, but they only make him shiver in a way that has nothing to do with the cold. It isn't as simple as not letting it "go to waste"—he needs to save *something* for himself. What if he takes the leap only to find that there is no net? What if he lets his heart be cradled in Aiden's nomadic hands, only to have it stolen away from him completely while he winds up left with nothing? In five minutes' time—once he tells Charlie that he wants her to sell the house—he won't even have home to fall back on anymore.

"I don't know if it's that simple," he finally says, his voice much smaller than he wants it to be.

"Because you won't let yourself see the end of the movie. You never do," Charlie says, and Jake stops in his tracks. "You're just making the most of the scene you've got in front of you."

That's all I know how to do anymore, Jake thinks, remaining silent.

"Just think about it, okay? Promise?"

Jake nods, feeling as though he's just been hit with a sucker punch to the gut, and says, "I promise."

"Okay then," Charlie says, seemingly satisfied.

Lowering himself down once more beside his backpack, Jake listens to the silence on the line and that of his surroundings: one is unavoidable and the other slightly awkward, and he hates them both. Before he can even think about it, he blurts, "I want you to sell the house." This doesn't exactly have the desired effect—there is yet more silence. "Charlie?"

"You want me to—are you serious?" she asks, her words a disbelieving rush.

Sighing, Jake throws up a hand and says, "Yeah, I am. You were right when you said that it's time. Actually, it's probably way overdue."

"You *have* to be sure about this. And *you* were right, too; I shouldn't have gone behind your back, and I'm sorry."

"No, sis. No. I was awful to you when we talked about it before, and *I'm* sorry," Jake says. Glancing up at a sky thick with clusters of stars that he can barely separate, he takes another deep breath and goes on. "Look, when we... when we lost Dad, you didn't just lose *him*, you sacrificed everything to come home and be the parent. I know how much you gave up just so that I could have some normalcy, and you didn't have to do that.

"That house, it... it's just a place, you know? *We're* the ones who remember all the good things that happened there, so... yeah. Let's do it, let's get you back to school."

When Charlie finally speaks, she's sniffling and her voice cracks. "God, you're such an asshole. Why do you have to be halfway across the country where I can't hug you?"

"Blame Dan, it was his idea," he jokes and smiles at Charlie's laugh, the one that always reminds him of their mom.

"Smack him upside the head for me, would you?"

"Believe me, he's got a lot worse than that coming when I find him. A fucking maze on Thanksgiving, who *does* that?"

Charlie takes a deep, shuddering breath in and lets it out slowly, still sniffling. "So it looks like we have a lot to talk about when you get back."

"Screw talking," Jake says. Now that he's made the decision—not to mention how happy it's made his sister, whom he loves dearly and has missed more than he realized—he just wants to set the wheels in motion. "Let's just do it."

More laughter, relieved and musical, and then, "Okay. Oh my god, oh my god—okay. Okay, I'm stopping, I promise. I'm just... I'm really happy, Jakey. Thank you."

"Thank *you*," Jake says. "Love you, sis."

"You love Aiden, too."

"Oh my *god*. Are you five?"

"Well?" Charlie prompts.

"Yes, Charlotte Anne, I love Aiden, too," Jake finally admits. *Does that ever get any easier to say out loud?* "And... thanks. I'll think about what you said."

"Anytime, little bro," she says. "Now go kick his ass. No one keeps a Valentine from food on Thanksgiving."

As Jake ends the call, feeling comforted and confused and relieved, he notices a string of text messages on the screen.

Aiden (8:01 p.m.) – I just realized that I haven't kissed you all day. It's driving me crazy.
Aiden (8:04 p.m.) – Are you mad at me? You're mad at me. Come let me make it up to you?
Aiden (8:10 p.m.) – Where are you?
Aiden (8:16 p.m.) – Shit, are you lost? This was a bad idea, wasn't it?
Aiden (8:19 p.m.) – Sweetheart?

In spite of everything, Jake's stomach twists pleasantly and he smiles a little. Just as he moves to pick up his backpack and get moving again, something grabs him around the waist and knocks him sideways.

He shrieks and struggles as he hits the ground, panicking and lashing out, but within moments he realizes that it's Aiden pinning him down.

"Asshole," he spits as his anxiety subsides. He pushes Aiden off and staggers to his feet.

"Just came to see what was taking you so long," Aiden says, slinging Jake's backpack over one shoulder as Jake brushes himself off.

"We're in a fucking maze and I got fucking lost," Jake retorts, and tugs his jacket straight.

Undeterred, Aiden takes Jake's hand and leads him out of the dead end. As they make two more left turns and then a right, Aiden almost running in his apparent eagerness, Jake sends up a silent thank you for the fact that—even in the bleakest of places—Aiden always manages to find him.

And then they're out of the maze, jogging across the parking lot toward the RV. All of the lights are on inside, and Jake considers pointing out that, if the picnic is in the middle of the maze, they're going in entirely the wrong direction. He's so cold at this point, however, that the RV is even more welcome a sight than usual.

When they get inside, everything becomes clear. The picnic that Aiden has set up takes Jake's breath away. He has laid out two blankets on the floor of the RV in an overlapping diamond, at the center of which is the brown paper bag of groceries they got from the Whole Foods in Oklahoma City. Next to it are a small stack of plates, two cups and a bottle of hard cider. The setting is lit by tiny votive candles, set at intervals around the perimeter of the blankets.

"So... I'm hoping that this gets me off the hook for letting you get lost in a maze," Aiden murmurs, squeezing Jake's hand. "But I needed to get you out of here while I set up."

"You planned this for me?" Jake asks, swallowing the declaration of love that rises in the back of his throat.

Aiden shrugs and absently scratches the back of his neck. "I figured since we can't spend Thanksgiving with our families—"

Jake cuts him off with a swift kiss and whispers against his lips, "You're my family, too."

Aiden shifts on his feet, shoots him a shy smile and gestures to the picnic. "Shall we?"

When they're seated, Jake between Aiden's legs with Aiden's arms around his waist, Jake pulls the grocery bag closer and finds that Aiden has already made up the turkey, stuffing and cranberry sandwiches Jake suggested this morning. He passes one back to Aiden and carefully unwraps his own to take a bite.

"Oh my god, these are perfect," he says around a moan. The cranberry's sharp sweetness bursts across his tongue and brings out the flavor of the turkey.

"They are pretty good, if I do say so myself," Aiden agrees.

"So," Jake says, setting down his sandwich for a moment and running his fingers along Aiden's arm, "what are you thankful for this year?"

"I'm thankful that Grandpa left me this place," he says, hooking his chin over Jake's shoulder.

"I'm thankful that you came back, and asked me to come on this trip with you," Jake replies.

"I'm thankful that you agreed to come," Aiden says, pressing a kiss just behind Jake's ear.

"And most of all..." Jake trails off, sits up and turns to face Aiden. He takes a deep breath and thrusts his fist into the air. Aiden does the same, and they cry out in unison, "I'm thankful for dolphin-friendly tuna!" Then they collapse against each other in a fit of giggles, just as they have every year since they were fourteen, when Aiden got drunk on his dad's beer and started rambling about everything he was thankful for.

Aiden's expression grows serious, and he places two fingers under Jake's chin and tilts his face up. "I'm thankful for *you.*"

His laughter fading, everything feeling the bittersweet side of too right, Jake kisses the corner of Aiden's mouth. "Happy Thanksgiving, Dan."

"Happy Thanksgiving, sweetheart."

8,766 MILES

DAY SIXTY-NINE: NEBRASKA

The neon lights buzz, flickering almost in time with the strobe lights over the dance floor, and Aiden leans his forearms on the railing of The Max's upper level, sipping his beer slowly as he surveys the crowd. He can see Jake below, swaying in the center of the packed dance floor with a stranger wrapped around him. Every so often, Jake glances up at Aiden and smirks; it's all for show. Aiden knows Jake is his, and though a twinge of jealousy stings his gut, he pays it no mind. Hearing Jake say those words—*Yes, Charlotte Anne, I love Aiden, too*—has caused an abrupt about-face in Aiden's mood. The pedestal suddenly doesn't seem so tall.

Aiden takes another sip of his beer, and his eyes rove the interior of the dark club. He can't imagine anyplace in Omaha better for the LGBT crowd to blow off steam on a Saturday night—or anyone, really, when he takes the ratio of obviously straight couples on the dance floor into account. The place is expansive, with different rooms playing different genres of music; the cover is low and the drinks are cheap. The DJ in this room is playing a mix of dance and pop, and—with the exception of an occasional foray into nineties classics—he seems to know exactly what the people of Omaha want: music to lose themselves in.

The next time Aiden glances down, Jake is nowhere to be seen. Aiden drains the contents of his bottle, leaves his spot and makes his way downstairs to the bar to wait for Jake to come back to him—which, sooner or later, he always does. Aiden can count on at least that much.

Just as he's accepting another beer from the bartender, a familiar hand settles over his own. Jake tips the bottle to his own mouth and drinks deeply, eyes on Aiden as he swallows.

"Having fun out there?" Aiden asks, raising his voice over the music. Jake smiles and leans closer.

"I swear to god, that guy must have a dick about the size of that building we saw yesterday," he replies, and Aiden chuckles. The "Penis of the Plains," as native Nebraskans refer to it, is already a running joke between them.

"Did he warn you, at least?" Aiden asks. "Because that's the kind of thing you have to warn a guy about."

Jake tucks a finger beneath Aiden's chin and answers him with a kiss, then turns his back to the bar and leans on his elbows. Aiden's eyes sweep downward, taking in Jake's clingy olive green shirt, his long legs wrapped in dark waxed jeans and the heel of one foot tapping to the beat.

"Come on," Jake says after a moment, wrapping his fingers around Aiden's wrist. "This song always makes me want to move."

They push their way through the crowd, the press of bodies pushing them close as they walk with the beat. Once Jake has found a spot, he loops one arm around Aiden's waist, while the fingers of his free hand play with Aiden's skinny, loosened tie as he dips himself back.

"You're in a good mood," Aiden observes with a grin.

Jake says directly into Aiden's ear, "I'm dancing with you. Of course I'm in a good mood."

"What, that other guy wasn't keeping you happy?" Aiden jokes.

"You've got *moves*, remember?" Jake answers. He scrunches his face and shoots him a look. "Too soon?"

Aiden shakes his head; Delaware is back far enough in the rearview now for them to laugh about it. "Speaking of moves, mister," he says, "I haven't seen you dip like that since senior prom."

"The classics never go out of style," Jake quips, and circles his hips into Aiden's.

Aiden's hands slide around Jake's ass, giving back as good as he's getting.

"Have you ever thought about being tied up?" Jake says into his ear quite unexpectedly; Aiden groans and drops his head to Jake's shoulder. "Should I take that as a yes?"

"Okay, first, where did that even come from; and second, do we have anything in the RV?"

"It was just something I was thinking about last night. I might have a pair of handcuffs somewhere."

"You don't need to tell me why," Aiden manages, grazing the line of Jake's neck with his teeth.

When he raises his head again, it's to see the lights come up and drop straight back down; he catches the briefest arresting glimpse of dark, wide pupils.

"What about some classic Aiden moves?" Jake asks with a nudge, pulling Aiden back in to himself. "Because I remember a certain sixteen-year-old version of you bringing the jazz band into Mrs. Beck's history class, singing Sara Vermosa to that poor kid—"

"There's no jazz band here," Aiden interrupts smoothly, placing a finger against Jake's lips.

Jake puts his mouth to Aiden's ear and rolls his earlobe between his teeth. In a voice so low Aiden struggles to hear him, he sings, "Baby, sing me a lullaby and I'll be yours..."

"Shut up," Aiden groans, turning to catch Jake's lips in a filthy, open-mouthed kiss.

As the flowing, electric intensity of Goldfrapp's "Strict Machine" coils its way through the crowd, strong hands grasp Aiden's hips and turn him around to face the rest of the clubbers.

Shivering despite his skyrocketing body heat, Aiden again drops his head to rest on Jake's shoulder. He catches the scent of Jean Paul Gaultier intermingled with a tang of sweat, and barely holds back a groan as Jake's arms creep around his middle to pull him closer. "This definitely is not how we did it at prom," he says, reaching back to cup the nape of Jake's neck.

"What do you want tonight?" Jake purrs in a deep, thrilling undertone. Aiden presses his forehead to the heat of Jake's neck, becoming more relaxed as he finds the pattern of the beat and gives himself over to it. Jake's fingers slide between the buttons of Aiden's white shirt and press the skin of his chest; with his other hand, he hooks a belt loop to pull Aiden even closer, almost as if he's trying to fuse them into a single entity made of a symbiotic, rhythmic give and take. They move together as the song continues, so synced to each other that Aiden is suspended in the feeling of body on body. "Tell me what you want."

Aiden winds his fingers up into Jake's hair, scratches lightly at his scalp and tugs so that Jake meets his gaze. He circles his hips back in time with the two sweeps of bass that precede the second bridge; the music sets his every nerve aflame, and Jake's full lips inches closer, closer, closer, until his eyes blur and close. *This* is what Aiden wants.

He wants the feeling of this firm, assured body moving in time with his own. He wants the surprising and welcome gentility of the first kiss, and for it to turn to pure filth soon after. He wants these worshipping hands running the lines and planes of him as his hair stands on end and he surrenders and moans and pours heat into a kiss that sears him with its obscenity. He wants this contact, this touch, this sensation of his axis tilting.

"I want you," he groans into Jake's ear after one last sweep of his tongue along Jake's lower lip.

Jake steps back. *Come with me,* he mouths. Aiden happily takes Jake's hand, follows him from the room and out through the main hallway to the doors of the nightclub complex; as soon as they're outside, they're running. Jake pulls him into a narrow, dark alley, and Aiden hesitates with Jake's hand still tangled up in his own. It's starting to rain, and he takes in deep lungfuls of freezing air to soothe his racing heart.

"Hey," Jake says softly; his thumb rubs back and forth over Aiden's knuckles as he takes a step forward and closes the space between them. Jake tilts Aiden's face with a gentle hand, and with the wind whipping around them, Aiden feels the ghost of a breath across his lips just before Jake catches his mouth in a slow, deep kiss,.

Rain falls in fat drops onto Aiden's skin, and he falls with them, giving himself over entirely. He presses his palms into the small of Jake's back to pull him in closer, and god, he could cry with the rightness of it all: Jake's lips reaffirming a daily claim, Jake's body pressing tightly against him, Jake's love coursing into his own bloodstream.

"Okay?" Jake breathes, and Aiden nods quickly.

Grinning, Jake curves his palm around the back of Aiden's head and pushes him back against the rough brick wall, swallowing Aiden's gasp. Aiden has been growing harder since the dance floor, but it only registers now as Jake's hands, wet with the rain that runs down his skin in rivulets, come to rest on the buckle of his belt and Aiden's hips automatically push forward.

Jake makes quick work of Aiden's belt and the button fly of his jeans. He yanks the jeans to mid-thigh and drops to his knees. Aiden hisses at the sudden cold of the raindrops hitting his newly exposed flesh; his skin is so hot, he's surprised they don't sizzle away into nothingness. Jake wraps hot, damp fingers around him and glances up from beneath thick, wet eyelashes.

Aiden bites his lip when Jake's mouth sinks over the head of his dick, and his back arches forward. The front of his shirt is freezing against his overheated skin. As Jake pulls off slowly, teeth lightly grazing Aiden's length, Aiden's hips cant forward to search out more of the blissful heat of Jake's mouth. Aiden watches as Jake smiles and licks his lips, glancing up at him with a positively wolfish gleam in his eyes. A second after Aiden's eyelids flutter closed, he feels himself being enveloped by that heat; the quick, rhythmic push and drag of Jake's tongue along his shaft sparks simmering flames beneath the surface of his skin, and he curls his fingers into a fist and fucks Jake's mouth in short, shallow bursts of movement.

Aiden drops his chin to his chest and his eyes lock on Jake's; a dark thrill courses through his veins. Jake grabs him by the hips again, pulling Aiden forward to fuck his mouth harder and deeper, and Aiden lets out a guttural groan at the sight of his cock pumping between Jake's flushed lips. He knows he won't last long; he can feel the pressure begin to mount, a trembling in his thighs that only gets stronger with every gentle rake of Jake's teeth, every obscene moan that resonates throughout his body, every time he catches Jake's gaze, still zeroed in on him.

He feels the rush building fast, an almost tangible thing, and he gives Jake's hair two quick tugs.

Jake surges forward, pinning Aiden back against the wall, and the sharp flare of impact in his lower back sends him tumbling over the edge, releasing his hold on Jake's hair and scrabbling for purchase on the brick. As his orgasm tears through him, he cries out in an abandoned litany of obscenities that are consumed by the open sky.

When it all becomes too much, Aiden raises one heavy arm and drags his fingertips along the side of Jake's neck, and Jake pulls off with one final, wet pop. Hands almost numb from the cold and the aftershocks running through him, Aiden drags Jake up by the shoulders and kisses him languidly, open-mouthed and whimpering at the taste of himself on Jake's tongue.

Jake chuckles as they break apart and Aiden pitches forward, dropping his forehead to rest on Jake's shoulder as he tucks himself back inside his jeans with still-shaking fingers.

"Your fucking *mouth*," he mumbles, feeling a rush of warmth as Jake rubs his upper arms. "Where did you learn to give head like that?"

"Practice," Jake answers, grinning when Aiden straightens.

"Can we...? I'm soaking."

"Plenty of dry clothes back in the RV. And a bed, a couch, a floor, a shower..." Jake says, taking a step back and holding out his hand with an expectant look.

Without hesitation, Aiden slides his slick fingers between Jake's. As they head out onto Jackson Street, he sees a group of girls practically falling out of the club onto the street, all singing at the top of their lungs. Oddly, they're singing "Lullaby," the song Jake teased him about in the club: "Baby, sing me a lullaby and I'll be yours, I've been hurt too much and I can't take no more..."

But this doesn't hurt anymore, Aiden realizes. Blinking rain out of his eyes, he wonders, *Is it almost time?*

He's distracted by the lights of an approaching cab. Just as he raises his arm to flag it down, Jake pulls him close to kiss him again, slow and indescribably sweet, and Aiden feels it all the way down to his toes. He only breaks the kiss to fling out his arm and shout, "Taxi!"

Jake holds the door open for him to climb inside and, once they're settled, directs the driver to the Happy-Mart on South Seventy-second with barely a grimace. The cab pulls away, and he whispers in Aiden's ear, "So what do you have planned for me?"

"Well... I hear there's a bed..." Aiden begins, fingers trailing the length of Jake's thigh.

"There is," Jake confirms, his voice a thick rasp.

"And a couch, a chair, a floor, a shower... possibly even handcuffs."

"God, just tell me."

"Sweetheart," Aiden says, cupping Jake's jaw and taking his bottom lip between his teeth, "You have no idea."

9,073 MILES

CHAPTER 8

DAY SEVENTY-ONE: SOUTH DAKOTA

Jake is *flying*.

Not literally, of course—he isn't even driving fast enough to get a speeding ticket—but his mood is so light, he feels as if he is barely touching the ground. He grins like a buffoon as he passes a sign that reads, *Mt. Rushmore, EXIT 2 MILES*. Although it is cold, it's a beautiful clear day with only a few scattered clouds darkening the horizon to his left, and he's surrounded by trees and hilly peaks that undulate as far as he can see on either side of the curving highway.

And everything is capped with a blanket of pure white snow.

Jake pulls into the left lane as he passes the half-mile exit sign and follows the road beneath an arched wood bridge. His smile stretches from ear to ear; Mount Rushmore is one of the great American monuments he's always wanted to see, and he can't believe that he's finally getting to do it. Still exhausted from an almost solid eight hours of driving yesterday, Aiden naps in the bedroom; if he isn't up by the time they arrive, Jake plans to kiss him awake.

Passing by a small strip mall in Keystone, its storefronts decorated to look like saloons, Jake can tell that he's getting close. Around thirty minutes ago he set up his phone in the cup holder with the video camera ready to record, and now he brings his phone out of sleep and hits the red button.

"It's the Monday after Thanksgiving, day seventy-one, and I'm in South Dakota, where it's cold, clear and beautiful," he says brightly, pushing his sunglasses up on the bridge of his nose. "The best part? There's snow *everywhere.*

"I'm usually stationary, I know, but today I thought it might be fun to make a complete tool of myself by recording what I'm sure will be a ridiculous, over-the-top reaction when I first see Mount Rushmore," Jake continues. He pauses as he drives through a tunnel carved out of rock.

"I've wanted to see it ever since I was, oh... seven, maybe? So this is really big for me. I'm just..." he trails off, shaking his head and smiling. "You know, I think there are times in every friendship, every relationship, when you have to just sit back and let everything go but what you have. And right now, that's what I'm trying to do. Because if what happens on the road trip stays on the road trip, then doesn't it kind of follow that whatever happens should be amazing? I think—"

A clutch of breath-held moments and he pulls the RV to a stop in the visitors' parking lot, as close as he can get. For a full minute, he does nothing but slump back against his seat and smile. The cinematographer in him wants to examine every tiny detail, search out every flaw in the time-weathered rock, and celebrate them all.

"Are you freaking out?"

Aiden's voice, a sleepy sort of wry, startles Jake out of his reverie. Aiden stands by his side, dressed only in pajama pants. His knuckles brush Jake's arm as he takes in the spectacle for himself. Jake reaches up to pull Aiden in for a sound kiss.

"You're freaking out," Aiden sing-songs, and stretches up onto his toes. A red blinking light in Jake's peripheral vision distracts him, and he hastily reaches over to stop the recording.

"Come on," Jake says, getting to his feet and tugging on Aiden's arm. "Get dressed. I want a closer look."

It isn't long before they're both bundled up in their winter gear, walking arm in arm through the eerily silent parking lot and beneath the square stone archway onto Grand View Terrace.

Their boots crunch through the snow, and Jake feels a giddy delight build-ing inside him; winter is *his* season, and snow is his favorite aspect of it. Something about snow carries with it a sense of magic. There is no peaceful quiet like that when the snow is falling, and it leaves in its wake a ground reflecting so much light that, as a young child, Jake sometimes wondered if he was walking on the sky.

"Well... I guess it *is* a Monday at the end of November," Aiden comments, gesturing back at the parking lot as they pass between pillars adorned with the state flags. "Although, I did think we wouldn't be the *only* ones here."

"I guess most people are working, or going home to get away from obnox-ious family members," Jake says blithely.

"Like Great Aunt Mildred?"

"She made me eat sprouts, Dan. They taste like farts."

"Oh, I'm well aware. Don't you remember Sproutgate 2005? I didn't talk to Matt for almost a month," Aiden says, shuddering in a way that Jake knows has nothing to do with the cold.

They come to a stop before the low wall overlooking the amphitheater, and as Jake stands gazing up at the four faces towering above them, he catches sight of Aiden brushing snow from one end of a stone bench. He takes the seat Aiden offers him with an exaggerated, gentlemanly bow. Before he can clear a space next to him, he finds himself with a lapful of Aiden: a warm, grounding weight and an arm curled around his shoulders as if it's nothing.

Maybe it *is* nothing.

"Are you still freaking out?" Aiden asks, glancing up at the mountain and then down at Jake. It always strikes Jake how oddly nice it is to have to tip his head back in order to meet Aiden's gaze.

"I was never freaking out."

"You were freaking out a little bit."

"Fine, I was freaking out," Jake concedes. After a moment, he adds, "Thank you."

"For what?" Aiden asks.

"For bringing me along," Jake says. "I mean, who knows when I would've gotten to see this otherwise?"

"I told you, I wouldn't have left without you," Aiden says quietly, his thumb burrowing beneath Jake's scarf and rubbing the skin at the nape of his neck. The moment hangs between them, and Jake can tell that they're both wondering the same thing: *What if we never left Brunswick? What would we be right now?*

Jake returns his gaze to the mountain and says, "I'd love to shoot here. Wouldn't you?"

"Set the scene for me," Aiden says. "What would we film here?"

Two best friends on a road trip, Jake thinks. *Sitting in this very spot and feeling like right now, right at this moment, they're exactly where they're meant to be.*

"Post-apocalypse," he finally replies, and Aiden's eyes widen a little. As surreptitiously as he can, Jake conceals his hand and starts collecting snow. "I wanna see it filthy and neglected, the entire place in ruins, with the terrace back there all overgrown, and the whole place covered in snow, like it is now. I'd want to really juxtapose innocence with horror, you know?"

"Go on," Aiden says, nodding.

"And there are two guys—"

"Naturally."

"All bruised up, guns slung across their backs, looking like they've never seen snow before." Jake looks out over the wall and sees powdery puffs of it falling from the boughs of trees on the hill.

"What happens next?" Aiden prompts.

"They're standing at the wall, shoulders slumped because it's cold and they're exhausted and haven't found shelter," Jake continues, nudging Aiden off so that he can stand. They cross to the wall, Jake's snowball packed tight in his gloved hand. He puts a few paces between them, knowing that he's about to begin World War Three. "It's quiet—all they can hear is the wind howling through the trees. And that's when a song begins to play. Barely there to begin with, but getting louder... and then one of the guys grins at the other..."

"And then what?"

"Duck and cover!" Jake yells at the top of his voice, turning and hurling the snowball toward Aiden. It explodes against the front of his dark pea coat, leaving a splatter of white on his chest and a comically shocked expression on his face. "What, like you really weren't expecting that?"

Aiden brushes himself off and draws his shoulders back. "Battle stations, Valentine. You're going down."

"May the best man win!" Jake calls over his shoulder as he takes off across the terrace, running for what little cover the Avenue of Flags can provide him. Snowball fights are no laughing matter between him and Aiden—the last one they had, back in their second year of college, went on for nearly an hour before Aiden grudgingly conceded victory.

Jake ducks behind the third pillar along the avenue and crouches, packing handfuls of snow as tightly as he can. He has a title to defend and he isn't going to give it up quietly.

"Incoming!" Aiden calls, and Jake glances past the pillar just in time to see him leap through the air and toss a snowball mid-jump.

It misses Jake by a few inches and he hides behind the pillar with his back to the stone, grinning. "You know, if you want to keep the element of surprise then you probably shouldn't announce that you're going to attack!" he calls.

No response comes, and aside from the brief sound of Aiden's heavy boots crunching through the snow, it is silent. Jake gathers a snowball in each hand and cautiously peeks out from behind the pillar, but Aiden is nowhere to be seen. Silently congratulating himself on having the forethought not to wear his other jacket, which is dry clean only, he steps all the way out from between the pillars and waits.

"Come on, Calloway!" he shouts. "I'm not gonna wait around all day while you get up the courage to face me!"

A snowball hits the side of his thigh as Aiden, quick as a flash, darts between two pillars to Jake's right. Jake swears under his breath and follows, but Aiden has already run out into the open space of the avenue. With a quick smirk at the pile of snowballs Aiden has left behind, Jake lobs the ones he's holding at Aiden—both hit him square on the shoulder—and gathers up three more.

"You sounded exactly like your sister just then, you know!" Aiden calls as he scurries off toward Jake's original hiding spot.

"Yeah, and look how her fight with your brother ended up! Epic Valentine Smackdown!" Jake shouts, dogging Aiden's footsteps and following him back out onto the terrace. As soon as they stop zigzagging, Jake takes two of his three shots, landing one on Aiden's back and the other on his calf.

Aiden turns to throw one back, and it hits Jake smack on the jaw. He hisses and staggers backward—the snowball was packed tight, and stings like a bitch. Aiden is by his side almost immediately.

"Are you okay?" he asks, gloved hands cupping Jake's neck and tilting his face up so he can see.

"You never learn," Jake reprimands him, taking his remaining snowball and crushing it into Aiden's hair. He laughs at Aiden's grim expression, kisses him firmly and takes off again.

He doesn't get far, however, before Aiden grabs him around the waist and tackles him to the ground, landing on top of him in the snow and saying with a smirk, "Yield, Valentine."

"Never," he says, softening his voice and his gaze. He has lost enough fights to Aiden's employment of dirty tactics that, if this is about to end, he's determined to get the final shot. Slowly, he slides his wrists from Aiden's loose grip to twine their fingers together. The cold seeps into his hair and through his clothes, and as he looks past Aiden hovering above him, he sees that the sky has turned an ominous shade of gray.

Aiden twists around to see what he's looking at, and Jake takes the opportunity to hook his leg around Aiden's hips and roll them over, hands still clasped together. Aiden's lips are cold, but warm Jake nonetheless when he leans down for a slow kiss. "Yield, Calloway," he whispers, breath coming out in a bloom of white.

"Fine, keep your stupid title," Aiden grumbles, shivering, but a quirk at the corner of his mouth betrays him. "Can we get up now? I'm freezing. And it's starting to snow."

By the time they've brushed themselves off, it's already coming down in fat flakes, and Jake is looking forward to getting inside and feelings his hands burn as they warm up. He looks at Aiden in his pea coat, with the snow settling into his thick brown hair, and remembers him in a short-sleeved T-shirt, standing on a wall in Florida and kissing him as if the world was ending.

"I'm freezing," Aiden repeats, his shoulders up by his ears, his hands buried in his pockets.

"Let's stay here for a second," Jake says, and quickly unbuttons his coat to wrap it around both of them.

"Okay," Aiden says, pushing his arms beneath the thick wool and squeezing Jake's waist.

Jake glances around, watching the snow settle around them. Their tracks are already beginning to disappear. "Listen."

"I don't hear anything."

"Exactly. Isn't this perfect?"

Aiden ducks his head, kisses Jake's jaw where it still stings and hums in agreement.

After a while, Jake unwraps Aiden and takes his hand. "Let's go."

As they make their way across the terrace toward the Avenue of Flags, he glances at the pillar he hid behind; his snowballs are gone. The snow falls in thick sheets, catching in his eyelashes. The footprints they left by the wall are almost filled in, and the bench is covered again.

"Almost looks like we were never here," Aiden says.

9,619 MILES

DAY SEVENTY-TWO: NORTH DAKOTA

"So… just what is it about this place you're taking us?" Aiden asks, reclining in the passenger seat as they cruise along US-85 at a comfortable speed. They're on their way to Williston, North Dakota, a small town Jake is adamant they visit even though it means parking overnight at a Happy-Mart.

"South Dakota," Jake says, pointing to the license plate on the SUV in the passing lane, before he answers. "It's where I got the paperweights."

"What paperweights?"

"The ones I have on my desk. You kept fiddling with them when we first started planning this trip."

"How do—oh, look, *another* South Dakota—how do you always remember things like that?" Aiden asks, as he always does when Jake presents clear recollections of the tiniest details.

"Cinematographers have to be good with details," Jake sing-songs his stock response. "But, um… do you remember when Charlie and I flew out to Bismarck for Grandma Doris's funeral?"

"Yeah, the week before graduation?"

Jake nods, scratching his shoulder and licking his lips. Aiden turns sideways in his seat and leans his cheek against the warm leather of the headrest. Jake has never told him what happened during that trip.

"She... in her will, she left us instructions for this ridiculous scavenger hunt, which was just like her. We ended up at this kitschy little art shop in Williston, and she told us that we had to get something to remember her by, instead of her leaving us something."

"Why'd you choose the paperweights?" Aiden asks, curiosity getting the better of him.

"Well, they're the Tree of Life, and Grandma Doris spent her entire life in North Dakota, like she was rooted or something. And she always kind of reminded me of Grandmother Willow in *Pocahontas,* you know, talking in loose riddles and dishing out life advice like it was her sole purpose for existing," Jake says. His tone betrays a fondness that his words do not.

"How much of her wisdom made it into your valedictory speech?"

Jake laughs. "None of it, actually. Although, I guess, in a way, she was in it. The thing I said about people wanting us to be only one thing—that's how she was. I always felt like she was trying to categorize me."

"God, you rehearsed that speech for weeks. Do you still remember it?"

"Bits and pieces, but not really. I still have a copy of it saved somewhere, though."

"It was a kick-ass speech," Aiden tells him, and quite uncharacteristically, Jake blows him a kiss.

Aiden catches it, and slowly lowers his hand back into his lap as he considers just how out of character Jake has been acting since... well, that's the thing; he can no longer remember when the shift occurred. Perhaps it has been a gradual change, one that he's only able to see now that he is looking back at the beginning.

"Texas," Jake points out quietly, and Aiden just catches sight of the passing truck's license plate. His thoughts turn once again to Hugh's offer, and the prospect of moving to New York to be part of their new outfit. After a few moments pass, Jake breaks the silence by saying, "You've gone quiet."

"I'm just thinking."

"About what?"

"What would say if I told you I was thinking about New York?" Aiden asks, crossing his hands in his lap and thumbing his index finger.

"I'd say tell me something I don't know," Jake replies at length, his tone over-bright. "And I'd say that you should go for it."

"I should—wait, really?"

"What is there to keep you in Brunswick?"

"Well, I—I..." Aiden trails off, his thoughts short-circuiting before they make it to his mouth. *You,* he wants to say, though all at once he realizes that he has no idea what Jake's plans are, beyond his long-held dream of "creating beautiful things." "What are *you* gonna do? After we get back, I mean."

Jake says nothing at first, and mostly dismisses the question with a simple shrug. "Now that we're selling the house, I'm kind of... still figuring out that part."

"Would you come to New York with me?" Aiden blurts, the words tumbling out before he can stop them. He quickly adds, "I mean, don't get me wrong—I love those guys, but I'd go crazy if I had to live with them. I'm gonna need a good roommate."

"I don't know, Dan," Jake says with a heavy sigh. "Honestly, I'm trying not to think too much about what'll happen when we get back."

"Why?"

"Being on the road like this, it's kind of magical, don't you think?"

"Of course."

"I know it has to end, and I know it *will,* but... I just don't want it to."

"Me neither," Aiden assures him. He reaches over and briefly covers Jake's hand with his own, and they fall silent once more. Aiden knows what "I'll think about it" means when Jake says it: The deal is as good as off the table. But there's still time for them to figure everything out. He can sense that the right moment to tell Jake how he really feels is growing closer, as if he's standing on train tracks that are just beginning to vibrate.

Before long, they jump out of the RV into a mostly empty strip mall parking lot. Aiden finds himself hanging back half a step, watching Jake's long legs take the sidewalk in stride, and suddenly he thinks, *What will I do if he doesn't come to New York?*

The thought makes him swallow hard as he follows Jake past the Economart and Country Floral. Aiden has experienced their relationship at both extremes now, and he knows exactly which he prefers. Being without Jake would be like losing a vital piece of himself—had felt exactly like that his entire year abroad, in fact—but being without Jake's heart, however veiled it might be, is unthinkable.

"I... it didn't look like this last time," Jake murmurs as they come to a stop outside a storefront.

The wooden façade is painted entirely black. The display in the front window is a selection of Ray Caesar paintings—surrealist images of women in various poses, some of them displaying animal characteristics, and others that are completely abstract. The silver lettering above the storefront reads, *Moiety: Fine Art for the Discerning Collector.*

It's the last place Aiden would expect to find in a small town like Williston, North Dakota. "Are you sure this is it?"

"Yeah, *Moiety,*" Jake says, gesturing at the sign. Aiden likes the way the word sounds when Jake says it. "It's the same place; it just looks completely different. Before, it was... well, almost the exact opposite. All kitschy and bright."

"Do you wanna go?" Aiden asks. He brushes his knuckles over Jake's elbow, and the stiff canvas fabric of his jacket scratches against Aiden's skin.

"No... no, we came all this way," Jake answers with a sigh, and pulls the door open.

Moiety's interior smells strongly of sage and sandalwood, and its lighting is surprisingly dim for an art gallery; spotlights set at intervals in the ceiling cast fuzzy circles of yellow on the floor between aisles of postcard-sized paintings. One wall is entirely taken up by a nighttime scene of winter-bare trees, and the glossy, dark stain of the floorboards makes Aiden think of his father's cabin at Saint Mary Lake, where they'll stay during their three nights and two days in Montana. A slow, echoing, piano-driven song is playing, and it lends an even darker atmosphere to the already dark store.

Moiety is a place entirely at odds with the other small stores in the strip mall; it sticks out like a bruised thumb. When Aiden says as much, they hear a dark chuckle from the back.

A tiny woman with frizzy, graying hair appears as if out of nowhere. Her thin-framed spectacles hang from a gold chain around her neck, and her bare toes peek out from beneath her floor-length black velvet dress.

"That's because we're the only place with a modicum of culture in this backward town," she says, her voice thin and reedy. The scent of cigarette smoke hangs around her like a cloud as she approaches them, and she looks them over from head to foot. The crooked, toothy smile twisting her mouth sends a shiver down Aiden's spine. "What can I help you gentlemen with today?"

"I was here a few years ago," Jake begins. Aiden can see him drawing himself up a little straighter. "At least, I think I was. It looked completely different back then."

The woman nods, her eyes narrowing and her smile growing wider. "Yes, it *was* very different. Why did you come? I took over from the old owners about a year ago, you see."

Jake hesitates for a moment, seemingly thrown off by her odd pattern of speech. "I came to find something to remember my grandmother by, after she passed."

"And what did you choose?" she asks, her gaze narrowing even further. She steps closer, her head tipped back so she can look Jake in the eye. "The old owners were unaware of how a place such as this should be run, you see. Very *unimaginative.*"

She pauses to clear her throat and Jake says, "A paperweight with the Tree of Life on it."

"Do you know what 'moiety' means?" she asks, suddenly turning her attention to Aiden. He shakes his head and feels as if he's just failed a test for which he's been studying all week. "The owners didn't, either. So laughable, all of the things they *didn't* know. But I'm here, now.

"It means, 'one of two equal parts.' You see? You see why they were so blind, why I had to take over?"

"Oh, yes. Yes, definitely," Jake says, nodding fervently. "How could anyone *not* see?"

The woman throws up her hands with an air of exasperation, places one on Jake's arm and fixes them with a gentler smile, one that almost looks kind. "You are welcome to browse. Now, if you gentlemen will excuse me, I have books to balance."

Without another word, she disappears to the back of the store, passing through a heavy black curtain that sways in her wake.

"What the fuck?" Jake whispers, and Aiden instinctively steps closer to him. "Seriously, what the *fuck?*"

"Is it just me, or—"

"It's not just you. That was *really* creepy."

"Do you wanna get out of here?"

"Can we stay, just for a couple minutes? I kind of…"

"What?"

Jake waves a hand and scans the store. "I had this idea that I'd get another paperweight here, one to remember our trip. If she even has any, amongst all the dead flowers and animal bones we'll probably find."

"Okay."

They make a quick circuit of the store, and among the displays of dark, surrealist paintings they find shelves full of odd ornaments, a box of ornately jeweled pen and journal sets, and finally, by the cash register, the paperweights they're looking for: heavy, glass objects in all sizes, nestled in black boxes lined with white silk.

Aiden watches as Jake picks a globe from the back of the shelf. It's clear as crystal, no bubbles or imperfections; suspended within is a black frosted silhouette of the United States.

"How perfect is this?" Jake whispers, holding it out to Aiden.

"Pretty perfect," he murmurs.

Jake takes the paperweight in its box to the cash register while Aiden scans the rest of the display. Most of the paperweights look like something he could find at Nightshade, the single "alternative" store in Brunswick, where the vast majority of their high school's goth and emo population shopped for their accessories. One catches Aiden's eye: a perfect likeness of a human skull. His eyes linger, and he can't help but shiver. Then he turns his attention to the paperweight sitting to its left: an oval, containing a single bougainvillea blossom.

Immediately, he thinks of Jake's mother and how, on his first visit to Jake's house after they met in the street, he noticed the basket of bougainvillea hanging from a hook on their porch. The basket hung there for months after the car accident, the bright pink flowers slowly turning brown and curling in on themselves.

Just as Aiden resolves to buy this paperweight for Jake, the old woman reappears. She is silent as she rings up Jake's purchase, pulls a glossy black bag from behind the register and gently sets the paperweight inside.

Jake thanks her and turns to Aiden, raising his eyebrows in clear relief.

"I'll meet you outside," Aiden says with a nod in the woman's direction; Jake briefly squeezes his arm as he passes by. He seems not to notice the box in Aiden's hands.

Cautiously, he approaches the register. The woman's dark eyes bore into him with an intensity that makes the hair on his arms stand on end.

"Just this, please," he says, attempting to break the tension.

"Where did you find this?" she asks as she takes the paperweight from him. "I told them to take all of it with them, you see. But they didn't listen, and there was so much waste. Why did you choose this?"

Because it's the least depressing thing in this entire store, Aiden thinks, but bites his tongue. "My friend's mom, she always loved bougainvillea."

"She's dead."

"Yes, ma'am, when he was seven."

"And his father, too," she says, shaking her head.

Aiden blinks and gapes at her for a moment. "How did you—"

"Oh, he's all torn up, that one. You can see it from a mile away."

"I beg your pardon?" Aiden asks, more confused by the second.

The woman sighs with that same air of exasperation, and leans over the counter to grab Aiden's hand with a force he wouldn't have thought possible. "How can you love someone like that?"

"How can I... what?" he asks weakly.

"He's *broken,*" the woman says.

Aiden pauses, carefully considering his response as a wave of indignation crests over him, hot and furious. "With hope," he says. The woman scoffs and releases his hand. "With *faith,*" he goes on, but she just ignores him and continues ringing up his purchase. Frustrated, he leans over the counter and looks her straight in the eye. "With *everything that I am.*"

She regards him coldly for a moment more, and then shrugs as if to indicate that she is finished with him. He pays, takes his black bag and walks away from the counter, anger and defensiveness putting a terrible weight in his step. *Who the hell does she think she is? She doesn't know me, and she* certainly *doesn't know the man I love.*

In the second that his palm settles flat against the door, he hears the woman ask, "That heart of yours. Did he steal it or did you give it?" He half turns back toward her, and she's standing at the end of the aisle nearest the back, looking at him with an almost-kind smile. "I know that they'll come back someday, you see. So I have to keep it everything it can be."

Dropping his gaze, Aiden says, "He stole it first, but I'll give it over and over again if he'll let me."

The expected reproachful response that has him already bristling never comes; when he looks back up, the woman is gone. Mentally shaking himself, he passes through the door and into the bright, cold sunshine outside. Jake pushes off the wall he's leaning against and stubs his cigarette out on the pavement. Aiden feels the anger drain out of him all at once, and it leaves him almost dizzy; Jake seems to sense this, and takes his hand. He leads Aiden away from the store with a concerned glance.

"Are you okay?" he asks when they're halfway back to the RV.

"Just... really, really creeped out," Aiden says.

"What did you get?"

"Something for you."

"Really?" Jake asks. "What is it?"

"Surprise," Aiden tells him, swinging the bag in his free hand. "Do you wanna see it now?"

"Ugh, let's not talking about *seeing things,*" Jake says with a shudder, retrieving the keys to the RV from his pocket and unlocking the side door. He turns around as he climbs the first step and leans down to kiss the corner of Aiden's mouth. "Come on. We've got a movie to watch and a Misery-Mart to suffer."

Aiden hesitates, sparing a single glance back at the storefront.

With everything that I am, he thinks. Somehow, he is imbued with more resolve than ever. Weighing the bag in his hand, he idly muses that perhaps, rather than having bought the paperweight to honor an old memory, he claimed it to anchor a memory soon to be made.

9,976 *MILES*

DAY SEVENTY-FOUR: MONTANA

"Hey, Aiden?"

"Yeah?"

"You're pretty much fulfilling every single lumberjack fantasy I ever had right now."

Aiden laughs as he wipes a forearm across his forehead and then swings his axe to rest on his shoulder. "Lumberjacks, huh?"

Jake smiles coyly, burying his hands in his pockets and descending the cabin's front steps. "We watched the *Wolverine* movie together, remember?"

"Well, sure, but I just thought that was a Hugh Jackman thing," Aiden replies.

"It's *always* a Hugh Jackman thing," Jake says, "but in that particular instance, it was also a lumberjack thing."

Aiden laughs again, and bends to retrieve the last small log from the pile he's been working his way through for the past half hour; as he swings the axe over his head and brings it down to split the log clean in two, Jake watches the muscles of his back and shoulders flex and contract beneath the thin cotton of his black T-shirt.

"How are you not freezing right now? I feel colder just looking at you," he says.

"Manual labor, working up a sweat, all that jazz," Aiden says, and he swings the axe one last time to bury it in the stump. He picks up the log basket and crosses his arms through the wicker handle, carries it up the steps to the porch and nods for Jake to follow.

"I don't think I'd ever get used to this view, you know," Jake murmurs at the top of the steps, moving closer to Aiden and feeling the heat that pours off him in waves. "Thank you for showing me."

Aiden's arm slips around Jake's waist and pulls him closer as they stand on the porch, gazing out at the sun setting behind the mountains. Aiden smells of sweat and cologne and nature.

Their drive up yesterday was brutally long but beautifully scenic, the hardship offset further by the fact that they have another two nights to spend in Aiden's father's log cabin. After falling into bed, watching *Big Eden* and sleeping a solid twelve hours, they both woke up refreshed enough to spend their day on a long walk, taking in the picturesque views and frigid mountain air.

The cabin is 760 square feet of country charm, the likes of which Jake can only imagine finding in Montana, and even the exterior has him itching for a light meter and a handheld camera. On the porch is an oversized wooden rocking chair Jake categorically does not picture himself sitting in while Aiden goes out for a run through the woods five, ten, fifteen years from now. Through the unassuming green front door is a small living room that leads to a rustic kitchen, in which all the appliances are concealed by panels that match the cabinetry. Upstairs is a loft bedroom with a tiny en suite.

No cell service, no Internet and only local stations on the television. At the beginning of the trip, Jake thought this would be two days of board games, nature and hell—now, he knows he couldn't have been more wrong. It's perfect.

"I have something for you," Aiden says, his warm lips grazing Jake's ear. "For both of us, actually."

"Lead the way," Jake says, shivering, and follows him inside.

As Aiden stacks a few logs in the open fireplace and sets the kindling aflame beneath the grate, he says, "So... don't be mad."

"Don't give me anything to be mad about," Jake quips, removing his coat and perching on the arm of the chocolate brown leather couch.

Aiden chuckles weakly. "I got us some pot."

"Why would I be mad about—wait. Where did you get pot?"

"I went out to stretch my legs while you were in the shower yesterday morning, and I noticed a bunch of guys—"

"Tell me you didn't."

"In the parking lot, and one of them called me over—"

"Aiden, tell me you did *not* get us Misery-Mart marijuana."

Aiden stands, wipes his hands on his jeans and pulls a small plastic baggie from his pocket. He holds it between his thumb and forefinger, shaking it back and forth with a sheepish grin. Sighing, Jake holds out his hand and accepts the baggie, pulling apart the re-seal top and inhaling deeply. It's pungent and rich, with a sharper tang than he's used to. With no small measure of surprise, he glances back at Aiden, who waggles his eyebrows and says, "Good, right?"

Letting out another sigh, Jake seals the baggie and hands it back. "We need snacks and live music before I'll even consider this. On principle."

"Methinks the gentleman doth protest too much, but I already have that covered," Aiden announces, and speeds off into the kitchen. Jake just stares after him.

"What do you mean, 'already covered?' How do you have live music 'already covered?'" he asks, poking his head around the open doorway to see Aiden dumping a bag of pita chips into an oversized bowl.

"I've got a bootleg of a show at the KOKO from last year," he replies, his words fast and excited. "There are a few bands I've been *dying* to play for you—this one band, Bastille? Holy shit, you're gonna love them. I actually have a feeling that they're gonna be *huge*—"

Jake silences him with a kiss, pulling back only when he's breathless. He presses his forehead to Aiden's temple and whispers, "Okay."

"No, seriously, it looks like a face!" Jake crows, looking at the map that hangs outside the cabin door and pointing at Montana's western border. "It's the *profile* of a *person*, Dan."

"Do you think it's a thing?" Aiden asks. "Like, do you think anybody ever gave it a name?"

"What, like Steve? The Steve side of Montana?" Jake suggests.

"The Steve side of Montana," Aiden agrees.

Jake giggles and takes another toke on their second joint of their evening. "Why do we never play *Would You Rather* anymore?"

"Because it always ends with awkwardness or dick jokes," Aiden reminds him, barely stifling a snigger as he takes the joint. The smoke is a thick cloud around them where they sit on the porch; it's a still night, and the air is freezing, but with Aiden curled around him on the rocking chair and a blanket covering them, Jake doesn't particularly notice. He doesn't care at all, in fact.

"We played it all the time when we were kids," Jake muses. He glances up at Aiden and slowly works his fingers into Aiden's thick hair. His arms feel pleasantly heavy. "You need a haircut."

"Do not," Aiden says. He bats Jake's hand away and sticks the end of the joint back between Jake's lips. "Don't you remember how long it was when we first met, how curly it used to be?"

"Mm hmm. It looked like a big, fluffy cloud. Like on that old calendar we found up in the attic."

"Do you remember that day when we counted the squares and figured out our birthdays?" Aiden asks.

"Of course I do," Jake replies, smiling at the memory.

The Saturday after they met, Jake and Aiden were in Jake's attic looking through box upon box of books when they found a calendar from 1990. Jake counted along with Aiden, their fingers hopscotching across the squares, and they went from September sixteenth to December twenty-fifth three times to be sure. They got to one hundred every time.

"Do you get twice as many presents, then?" Jake asked him, thinking that it must be great to have a birthday on Christmas, but when Aiden wrinkled his nose, he wondered if everyone asked him the same thing.

"Nope. Mommy and Daddy get me one extra present that's just for my birthday, but nobody else does."

Jake thought that wasn't very fair at all, and tried to remember to ask his mommy if they could get Aiden two presents in December, when they went shopping at the big department store with the pretty Christmas windows.

He tells Aiden all about this now, and Aiden smiles as he drags deeply on the joint. In the dim porch light, Jake watches Aiden's eyes grow dark; Aiden taps Jake's mouth once before leaning down and sealing his lips over Jake's. It's an addictive kiss, and Jake pulls the smoke out of Aiden's mouth and into his lungs, his hands flying up to frame Aiden's face. When he pulls back, he rests his forehead against Aiden's, eyes closed, and lets the dizziness take him.

The rocking chair tips back and forth, back and forth, creaking under their combined weight, and *god,* Jake loves him so much. He loves Aiden's every last cell, and reason only just edges out his wild urge to confess something, anything. He swallows hard, and says, "Tell me something you want."

"To be in two places at once," Aiden whispers, his right hand covering Jake's where it has slipped to rest against the warmth of his pulse point.

"Easy," Jake whispers back, "just straddle a state line. Tell me something real, something you actually want."

Aiden sighs and drops his head, burrows into the hollow of Jake's neck. "I want you to fuck me in front of the fireplace later."

"Later is good," Jake says. "I don't know if I can do anything right now."

"Me either!" Aiden exclaims, bursting into laughter that shakes his entire body. "It's like my dick disappeared."

"What do you mean it disappeared?"

"It moved. To *space*."

"Fuck, I'm so high that that actually made sense," Jake giggles. He takes a deep breath and waves his hand, trying to collect himself enough to ask again. It's no use, though; he's done for. He clutches Aiden and they both laugh until they wheeze, until it's been so long that he has to relight the joint before taking another drag. "Seriously, though. What do you want for your birthday this year?"

"Surprise me," Aiden says.

"You hate surprises."

"I like yours."

"Okay," Jake murmurs. "How is it only twenty-six days anyway? That's less than four weeks."

"Don't," Aiden says, his voice so low and commanding that it sends a frisson dancing up and down Jake's spine. He stifles the impulse to break the tension by attempting to bounce Aiden on his knee or something equally ridiculous.

"Getting cold," he mumbles, burying his face in Aiden's chest and rubbing his cheek against his soft flannel shirt. It feels *amazing,* and Jake can't help but let out a moan of pleasure. Aiden's answering chuckle is a deep rumble in his chest, and oh, every sensation is like a miniature firework bursting beneath Jake's skin.

Time slips by him as Aiden clambers out of his lap and bundles him inside, and before Jake really knows what's going on, he finds himself stretched out on the couch, Aiden sitting cross-legged at one end with Jake's head in his lap. Music is still playing from his phone, the sound amplified by the deep bowl into which Aiden has placed it, but the song has changed—he vaguely recognizes it as "Back Down South" by Kings of Leon. It's sad, heavy and soothing, perfect for his sudden, inexplicable wave of melancholy.

Their zigzagging route around America is coming toward its final stretch. After leaving this cabin—a prospect Jake doesn't want to think about any longer than is absolutely necessary—they will indeed head south, for the last time on this trip. He wants to stay here forever, bury this night in the soil of the flowerbeds lining the cabin's backyard and let enough time pass for something to bloom, something that aches with beauty.

"I had a crush on you in senior year," he blurts before he can stop himself, and just before he screws his eyes shut, he catches a glimpse of Aiden's gaze settling on him.

"Told you I liked your surprises," Aiden murmurs. "Your crush probably didn't involve ice cream and hand-holding, though."

"No, it did," Jake replies, sighing as he opens his eyes. "I mean, it was before Brad, so..."

"Ah, yes. Brad the Great Deflowerer."

"That's not a word. And—"

"It's totally a word."

"And he didn't *deflower* me; I wasn't some blushing virgin."

"Sweetheart, you barely even admitted to jerking off until you were seventeen."

"*So* not true."

"It is! Why do you think I was so surprised when you told me your kill count?"

Jake snorts derisively. "I've said it before: this coming from the guy who was practically celibate before me."

Aiden simply laughs again. He drops his head and gazes down at Jake through his thick eyelashes. "So, about that kill count..."

"Yes?"

"Who was the best?"

"*That* is quite a question. Hmm, let's see..." Jake teases, making a show of tapping his chin and looking thoughtful. He knows the answer, of course, but he also knows that Aiden is fishing for compliments. "Well, there was Brad, of course. I guess I have to look back and laugh, a little bit. But for a first time, he was... nice. It was nice.

"Then—well, you know about Nathaniel. Drunk, don't remember much," Jake continues, wrinkling his nose. "Edward was... mm, Edward was fantastic. And then... Max, obviously."

"So we've covered the ones I know about," Aiden cuts in smoothly. He shifts on the couch, his posture straighter, his eyes more attentive. The fire-light licks over his skin and casts him golden, and Jake wants to say that it doesn't matter, that none of it matters, because Aiden is here and he's the only one that Jake cares about anymore.

But he's started, so he'll finish.

"After you left—literally the day after—I, um... I slept with Ethan."

"Ethan who?" Aiden asks, and then, "Oh my *god,* Ethan from the band?!"

Shamefaced, Jake nods, and Aiden bursts out laughing. "Shut up," he grumbles, reaching up and punching Aiden's shoulder.

Aiden's laughter is already dying; he grabs Jake's arm and brushes his lips across the inside of his wrist. "How did that even happen?"

"I went over to April's and they were all jamming together," Jake says. "All of us went to The Cannery, one drink turned into seven... the next thing I know, we're in his parents' basement and I've got him over his desk."

"Wow. Okay. Okay, so that's five."

"Oh my god, I need a drink," Jake moans, hiding his face in his hands. He takes a deep breath and continues. "All right. Next was Stefan—you know, the Serbian guy from Baxter House? Gave one *hell* of a blowjob. He just, um... didn't have much of his own to work with.

"You know, come to think of it..." he trails off, retracing his missteps through that lost year without Aiden. "There were... four? Four guys after him that kind of all blur together, not that memorable. Then there was James Thompson—"

"Dairy Frost James Thompson?" Aiden interrupts.

"The very same."

"He only came out last year."

"Oh, I know," Jake says, pursing his lips against a laugh and holding his hands up. "We ran into each other on campus, one thing led to another... he made the announcement the next day. I'm not saying I had anything to do with it, but..."

"I wonder how many other guys your dick has forced out of the closet," Aiden muses, earning himself another punch on the shoulder. "That makes eleven, so... Pickup Line Guy was twelve?"

"Interrupted, remember?"

"Then who did I succeed?"

Jake swallows and mentally berates himself for admitting his number to Aiden on that balmy night back in Missouri. "Roberto Mancini."

Aiden blanches, and his mouth drops open. "You fucked *Roberto Mancini?* As in, Roberto Mancini, the guy who almost sabotaged my entire internship proposal?"

Jake averts his eyes. "If it makes you feel any better, he was awful. He dragged me into the shower afterward and practically scrubbed us both raw because, and I quote, 'We must wash off the sin.' And then he tried to wash my fucking hair for me, so that was just... a wonderful experience all around."

After a moment, he feels Aiden relax beneath him. A moment more, and he's shaking with laughter. "Oh my god. *Oh my god.*"

In spite of himself, Jake soon joins in—Aiden's infectious, booming belly laughs are too much to resist. When Jake finally catches his breath, he lets his longstanding curiosity get the better of him and says, "You never really told me, you know."

"About what?"

"About Tyler. How was it?"

At that, Aiden sobers entirely. His eyebrows draw together and his expression darkens. "Nothing. It was just... nothing."

Carefully, Jake asks, "And me?"

Meeting his gaze squarely, Aiden whispers, "Everything."

"Oh," Jake says. He lets his eyes slide toward the flames, lets the music wrap around him anew, lets everything fade except the pleasant buzz in his bloodstream. It's too much—everything is too much these days. The weight of it all is terrifying, but then... but then there is something burning inside of him, too, something stirring, yearning to break free, and Jake only ever feels right when he lets some of it out. Some, but not too much; inches that still feel like miles. "You too, by the way. Out of everyone, it's you."

Aiden slides the tips of his fingers beneath the collar of Jake's Henley and leans down over him. "See?"

"See what?" Jake breathes.

Aiden closes the last of the gap between them, and Jake closes his eyes—warmth and home and *yes*—and in the second before Aiden kisses him, he whispers, "I love your surprises."

10,476 MILES

DAY SEVENTY-SIX: IDAHO

Tentatively, Aiden ducks under the metal flap beneath which Jake is hunkered and crouches low. He surveys the ground around them. Jake's tools are piled in a cluster next to him, and what looks uncomfortably like the guts of the RV are strewn haphazardly by his knees.

"Jakey?" he ventures, wiping his sweaty palms on his jeans.

"Hand me that wrench," comes the bitten-off reply.

Aiden watches the hem of his loose white T-shirt ripple in the breeze and ride up to expose a strip of freckled skin above the waistband of his jeans. If there weren't more pressing matters at hand, he might be content to sit back and enjoy Jake doing his grease monkey routine. Unfortunately, however, there *are* more pressing matters at hand—namely the fact that the RV chugged and sputtered to a stop twenty minutes ago, and now they're stranded next to an abandoned park just outside Roberts.

He puts the wrench into Jake's waiting hand and asks, "Shouldn't we just call Triple-A?"

Jake pauses, arms-deep in the inner workings of the RV, and levels Aiden with a raised eyebrow. "I wouldn't call Triple-A before trying to diagnose the issue unless this thing caught on fire, Dan. At which point, we'd have much bigger problems anyway."

"Just a suggestion," Aiden says, hands raised. He sits to watch Jake work and runs his index finger back and forth under his bracelet.

"If I can't fix whatever it is, then we'll definitely need a professional," Jake continues at length, his words punctuated by small grunts of exertion as he works to loosen something with the wrench. "I made sure that I knew every inch of this lady."

"Son of an engineer, I guess."

"What?"

"Your dad," Aiden says. "Isn't he the reason Charlie wanted to be an engineer?"

"Dad was a fisherman. You know that," Jake says. His voice is tight. He reaches up to scratch his jaw and leaves a thin streak of grease painted onto his skin, like a scar risen to the surface, a protest and a reminder.

"Right, but he used to be an engineer," Aiden says.

"He gave it up after Mom died, remember?" Jake says in a tone that doesn't give an inch.

Deciding to play it safe, Aiden says, "So we know it isn't a blown fuse. What else could it be?"

"Well, I'm pretty sure we ran out of gas, so..." Jake trails off, pausing again and breathing deeply as if to clear his head. He lets out a humorless laugh and says, "Maybe this *is* pointless."

"How so?"

"I was thinking that it was a fractured float, but even if I'm right, I can't fix it." At Aiden's obviously perplexed expression, Jake goes on, "The float is what sits in the gas tank and feeds back to the gauge. Floats expand and contract depending on the temperature, and we've been going from one extreme to the other."

"Sounds like something that'd need replacing."

"Yep. And it's not like we just have one lying around."

Aiden pushes up on his knees and pulls his phone from his pocket, but just as he finds the entry in his contacts, he hears an almighty, metallic clanging sound and suddenly Jake's oil-slick fingers are wrapped around Aiden's wrists, his grip as tight as a vise. Aiden looks up to see Jake's eyes wide and desperate, and the plea in them makes him freeze.

"I can fix it," Jake says, though even he doesn't sound as if he believes it. He licks his lips and scoots closer. "I can fix it, Dan, I swear. I can... I can patch it or something, I—"

"Sweetheart," Aiden interrupts, taken over by his need to soothe Jake even though he's unsure exactly why Jake is this worked up.

As soon as his hand comes up to cup Jake's cheek, the urgency seems to leach from him like a tide washing out before he gets his toes wet. Jake takes his hands away and drops them in his lap, looking down at them as if he doesn't understand how they could have failed him. Dumbfounded, Aiden just looks at him, taking in the bow of his head, the rise of his shoulders and the flatness of his hair. Without its usual messy, upswept style, it makes Jake look all of fourteen again, when he wore it neatly combed to the side, parted an inch or so off-center.

Aiden worries his lip, watches the breeze lift strands of Jake's hair and asks, "What's going on? Ever since we crossed the state line you've been acting like you're just trying to get us out of here as fast as you can."

Jake sniffs harshly, and Aiden's stomach drops like a stone. *You don't cry,* he thinks, and then Jake looks up. His eyes are dry, and Aiden can breathe.

"Make the call," Jake says, and now he's back to avoiding Aiden's eyes, bent double until he steps out from under the metal flap and brushes off the seat of his pants.

Aiden follows and walks around to the other side of the RV. As he speaks to the operator in stilted sentences and half-muddled words, giving their location and an idea of what the problem is, he feels as if he left his mind with Jake.

When Aiden comes back, Jake is looking out at the empty park, arms crossed over his chest, defeat clear in his hunched posture.

"They're sending somebody out. Should be here in an hour, maybe less," Aiden says, breaking the tense silence as gently as he can. "Do you wanna wait inside?"

Jake scuffs at the ground with the toe of his boot and shakes his head, but offers nothing further. It's discomfiting. Aiden isn't used to this Jake anymore; he thought they'd left him behind along with their teenage years. He hasn't seen Jake like this since the months following his dad's death, when there were times Aiden thought that beating his head against a wall would yield better results than trying to get more than two words out of Jake.

As he looks out at the park and watches a circular swing sway in the breeze, he remembers all the weekends they spent at the little place they discovered hidden away down at the end of Thomas Point Beach. It wasn't much more than a clearing behind the tree line, but a tire swing was hung from the branch of a hundred-year-old oak tree, and they never saw anyone else there. To Aiden, it always seemed like an otherworld, so simple that it could have existed anywhere, and they always stayed for hours, messing around on the swing and climbing trees and healing. It was the place where *What Would We Film Here* was born, where they stashed candy—and, later, illicit magazines—in the hollow of that same oak tree; where they went when nowhere else made sense.

This forlorn little park looks nothing like Thomas Point, but nonetheless Aiden thinks, *Maybe.*

Aiden burrows his fingers beneath Jake's arm and takes him by the hand, ignoring Jake's protests and leading him away from the RV— no one else is around this close to sunset, and the RV is locked up anyway. He guides them through the small, unlatched gate and over to the swing.

"Get in," he says, motioning Jake forward and paying no heed to the half-sullen, half-puzzled look thrown his way.

The swing rocks back and forth as Jake climbs in. It's not a tire, but a circular frame wrapped in blue plastic padding with a hammock-style bottom; still, it will do. Jake lies back without being prompted and Aiden moves around to his head, takes a deep breath and gives him a push.

"Did you know that potatoes were first planted in Idaho in 1837?" he asks.

Jake tilts his head back, and Aiden almost laughs; only Jake Valentine could arch one eyebrow while looking at someone upside down and still look formidable.

Because this is the way it has to happen, Aiden continues, "And did you know that potatoes are, like, the *perfect* food? You could eat nothing but spuds for the rest of your life and you'd still get all the nutrition you needed."

It takes a full ten seconds, but it does happen: Jake looks at him and, in a completely flat voice, says, "Spuds."

There it is, Aiden thinks, grinning. "Welcome back."

"I didn't go anywhere, dork," Jake mutters. "Don't think I don't know exactly what you're doing."

"Oh, I'm counting on it."

"It isn't going to work."

"If you say so, sweetheart," Aiden says, and pushes harder, until Jake's head is almost level with his own every time he swings back.

The next—and final—stage is slow to begin. Aiden's arms are starting to ache, but slowly, ever so slowly, Jake unfurls his arms and spreads them, at first gripping the sides of the swing and then, at long last, turning his palms to the sky. On the next push, Aiden sees that his eyes are closed—the signal to stop pushing and just let him swing. They figured all of this out so long ago, and it's so beautifully familiar that it feels as if it could be any other Saturday back in Brunswick.. He moves away, leans up against one of the wooden beams of the structure and smiles as he watches Jake fly.

The air smells metallic, as if lightning is about to strike, but when the swing stops moving and Jake opens his eyes, Aiden forgets all about the darkening sky.

"Good flight?" he asks.

"Great flight," Jake says, and then heaves himself over to the left side of the swing. "Get in."

"I doubt that thing was built for one grown man, let alone two."

"Please?"

Aiden complies. Somewhat awkwardly, they arrange themselves so that Jake is curled into Aiden's chest. Aiden keeps one foot on the ground and gently rocks them back and forth.

"So... this part is new," he says, because it is, and because he doesn't know what to do next.

Jake chuckles, the sound like music, and twists around to look at him, his chin propped on Aiden's chest. "Thank you."

"Wanna tell me what's going on up here?" Aiden asks, tapping Jake's forehead.

"I never told you that Dad was from Idaho, did I?" Jake asks. He's obviously reluctant to speak, but he's doing it anyway, and Aiden feels a rush of pride.

"I guess you already knew about the potatoes, then," he jokes, earning a small smile. "Didn't you say that he and your mom met in South Carolina?"

"After my grandparents got divorced, he and Grandma Betty moved there," Jake explains. "Anyway, it's... being here, it's—"

"It's hard, I get it."

"Yeah."

"Is that why you..." Aiden trails off, gesturing in the direction of the RV.

"No, I—maybe? I don't know," Jake says in a rush. He takes a breath, his eyes flutter closed and in a near-whisper he chokes out, "I wanted to make him proud."

"Jakey—"

"He could fix *anything*," Jake goes on, eyes opening and sparkling with memory. "Do you remember when you brought over your mom's cuckoo clock, after your dad and Matt had that epic fight?"

"God, it was in pieces. I don't think I'd ever seen her that mad," Aiden says, suppressing a shudder as he recalls the look of apoplectic rage contorting her features.

"That was the week before the storm," Jake says quietly, and tucks his head under Aiden's chin. "I sat with him while he was working on it. He was wearing that hideous Christmas sweater that Grandma sent, you know, the one with the reindeer that looked homicidal? The heat was broken and we were freezing our asses off, but when I asked him why he was working on the clock first, he said, 'Son, if a lady needs something she loves fixed and you can fix it, you fix it.'"

Eyes stinging, Aiden blinks up at the sky and holds Jake just a little tighter.

"Sometimes I wonder if he could fix me," Jake says. His light, almost joking tone sounds completely forced. The words pinch Aiden like ill-fitting shoes, and he sits them both up, takes Jake's hand and laces their fingers together.

"You're not a cuckoo clock," he says, trying to keep it easy, but he can't help adding, "You're my Jake."

Jake blinks, and in the next second his arms are wrapped around Aiden's neck and he's kissing him as though his life depends on it, just as he did all the way back in Florida and has done so many times since. Aiden gives it all back, holds onto Jake's waist and pulls him closer, his tongue sweeping along Jake's bottom lip. Despite the heaviness of what they've just been talking about, something loosens in his chest and new energy blazes in his veins; he's started to live for these moments when it seems he manages to say exactly what Jake needs to hear.

"Ugh. Fucking Idaho, man," Jake says when he pulls away.

Aiden puts a hand on his knee. "Don't be so hard on yourself."

"What?"

"I'd say 'promiscuous' rather than 'ho,' that's all," he says, trying and failing to keep a straight face. "Though I guess 'Idapromiscuous' doesn't really have the same ring to it. And kids would forever be misspelling it on tests."

Jake rolls his eyes, but Aiden can see that he's fighting back a smile. It relaxes him a little; the gravity of what just happened hasn't escaped him.

Jake hardly ever speaks of his dad, and on the rare occasion that he does, he never mentions the storm that took his life. Everything about this day so far has been somewhat unsettling, but that most of all, and Aiden wonders what the next curveball might be.

"How long 'til they get here?" Jake asks, and Aiden checks his watch.

"Forty-five minutes or so," he says.

Jake curls into him, pushing him to lie back again with gentle fingertips. "Thank you," he repeats, and then, "Maybe it isn't so bad here after all."

"D'you wanna stay for a while?" Aiden asks unnecessarily, just so he won't blurt out the wash of love that constricts his throat and squeezes tight around his chest.

"Can we?" Jake asks. "It's kind of comfy."

Aiden smiles, nods and kisses his hair. And although it's not completely true, he says, "We've got time."

10,939 MILES

DAY SEVENTY-EIGHT: WYOMING

"Hmm... are you starting to feel better?"

Jake arches his back, hissing pleasantly as Aiden's fingernails scratch over his hipbones. "I'm still fucking sick of driving, and Kathy Bates is still a fucking liar," he says, his words coming out the slightest bit slurred.

"But are—you starting—to feel better?" Aiden repeats, carefully punctuating his words with his rocking, back and forth. Jake is buried to the hilt inside him, and Aiden looks down at him with an expression that says, *I'm accepting none of your bullshit today, Valentine.*

"Yes. I'm—*fuck*—definitely feeling better," Jake answers, and this, coupled with the languor three beers have brought to his limbs, finally makes it all drain away: frustration that they've run out of coffee, with no decent beans to be found anywhere; anger at the GPS for having led them astray and dumped them on the outskirts of a forest near Rock Springs; the constant, dull ache that has plagued his lower back for days.

All that is left is Aiden, tight and slick and burning hot around him— *angel*—gorgeous as he leans back to plant his hands behind him on Jake's thighs—*you must be an angel, sent here just for me*—and rolls his hips agonizingly slowly.

Jake runs his fingers up and down Aiden's torso. There's no rush—there never has to be. Having Aiden above him, riding him like it's the thing he was put on Earth to do, makes him close his eyes and moan through his bitten lips.

There doesn't have to be anything but this, the voice in the back of his head reminds him. His hands trail down to squeeze Aiden's hips—just once, just enough of a signal. Even if Jake were in full command of all of his faculties, he doesn't think he would try to quiet the voice. He doesn't even try to ignore it, simply sinks farther and farther into it to the very core of his pleasure, the crackling energy made just for them. It feels as if the brokenness inside him has been repairing ever since their first kiss; strands are slowly knitting back together in something he didn't even know was torn until Aiden held it up in front of him.

"God bless Wyoming, *fuck,*" Aiden whispers. He drops forward and brackets Jake's head with his forearms.

Breathlessly, Jake says, "I keep telling you, it's not even a real place. It's a state of mind."

"Don't think it was where Billy Joel was singing about, though," Aiden quips, laughing on a ragged exhalation that disappears inside a moan, and *oh,* the feeling of that is two different kinds of wonderful.

"That's—*Aiden*—that's because... fuck, keep doing that..."

"Admit it, Jakey. Wyoming is real. Otherwise, where exactly *are* we right now?"

"North Colorado."

"North Colorado is already a place."

Not missing a beat, Jake chuckles and rolls his eyes, wrapping his arms around Aiden's middle and rolling them over under the thick blanket. *"Really north Colorado, then,"* he says, kissing the tip of Aiden's nose and bracing his knees against the floor of the RV.

"Fine, really—fucking *hell*—really north Colorado it is," Aiden acquiesces. He hooks his legs around Jake's middle, urging him closer, faster, deeper, until Jake feels as if they might fuse into one person. He surfaces, buries his face in the curve of Aiden's neck and licks a sloppy kiss over his collarbone.

He's spinning out. Aiden's hands scrabble for purchase on his back, his shoulders, his neck; Jake pulls back and buries himself again with stronger movement and utter abandon. Always, the chasing—it's always the chasing and always has been, but with Aiden, it's running hand in hand toward something: running toward a horizon that they're painting onto the sky; running toward the next ten years; running toward each other. It's a lie that is too seductive, too easy to believe, too hard to resist.

"Sweetheart," Aiden says, cupping Jake's jaw, "get out of your head and come join me."

Smirking down at him, Jake moves as if to twist out of his grasp but Aiden holds firm, eyes locked on his. Something shifts between them and Jake realizes that he's close, right on the brink, as if he's been falling with the ground rushing up to meet him.

"Eyes on me," Aiden murmurs, his voice half-strangled as he arches and writhes.

Jake swallows. When did Aiden become this? When did he transform into this bundle of sex and want and arcane knowledge, sizzling with electricity that leaves Jake dizzy?

"Don't close your—*fuck,* I'm so close..."

Jake isn't just running, now; he's *racing,* like his heartbeat, pounding Aiden into the floor and winding his hand between them to twist around Aiden's length. He can feel himself crack, leaving shards behind as he moves harder, faster, pivoting and falling into the rich coffee brown of Aiden's eyes until—

Breaking point. Both of them come, slack-jawed and silent, pulsing and trembling, a flatline and a shock back to life all at once. Flashes in Aiden's eyes, light and dark, life and death, love and despair; everything Jake saw in him in Louisiana, and it's too much. He collapses, his limbs shaking and spent, and he silently mouths those three painful little words into the bare skin of Aiden's shoulder.

He carefully shifts them both onto their sides, curling into Aiden with a shiver—his hands are burning, yet freezing to the touch—and still buried inside him even as he softens.

"Shame we didn't start this when it was still warm out," he says quietly, glancing up at the ceiling. It's too soon to look Aiden in the eye again. "We could have been doing this outside."

"Still thinking about July fourth?" Aiden asks, tugging the blanket up under their chins.

"What about July fourth?" Jake asks. Slowly, wincing all the way, he pulls out and gets rid of the condom, then sits up to retrieve two more blankets from the pile on the couch—the heat is on, but it's still cold. He heaps the blankets on top of them until they resemble something of a nest.

"You told me you wanted to have sex outside."

"There's no way I said that. Not back then. How weird would that have been?"

"You did!" Aiden exclaims, his voice loud in Jake's ear. "After the fireworks were done, don't you remember? We were still squeezed into that lounger, and I saw Hugh and Lisa coming out of the bushes..."

"Right," Jake says, nodding as the memory finally resurfaces. He'd been busy trying not to notice the fact that they were lying on their sides in a lounger made for one, and that Aiden's dick had seemed half-hard in his pants. He knows much better now. "And you made The Face, and I told you to lighten up, and then you made The Face at *me,* and I said—"

"You said that you'd wanted to try it for a while. Just to see what it'd be like," Aiden finishes for him, his fingertips ghosting the skin of Jake's arm. "And?"

"Pretty damn perfect, I'd say."

They lapse into quiet after that—or at least, as much quiet as there is to be had in a campground full of other vehicles and groups of people.

Then Aiden takes a deep breath and says, "So... there's this guy I've been seeing for the past month or so."

"Yeah?" Jake asks, inclining his head. "What's he like?"

"Smart, funny, talented... so gorgeous," Aiden says. "It's been going really great, but lately... I'm just really confused."

"About what?"

"About what happens next," he says, and Jake's heart speeds up. "We're not... what we are is not set in stone, and that's fine. It's only been a month, like I said. But this great opportunity has come up for me, and it would mean me going away. I guess I'm just trying to figure out what to choose."

Jake's head is swimming now, the alcohol affecting him even more with his racing heart, and he's suddenly overcome with desperation, reeling and dizzy from his ricocheting emotions. His mouth goes dry and he tries to speak, but words fail him.

"I want the music, but... I love you," Aiden whispers, and just like that, the strands unravel.

I'm not ready, Jake thinks. Fear breaks over him like the waves of a sea in the height of a storm and he's gone again. Aiden is wrapped around him, but so far out of reach; he has instantly tensed at Jake's obvious discomfort, and saying *anything* now is too much of an admission: Jake knows it, and he knows that Aiden knows it, too. So they lie there silently for a few moments, watching each other in the dim light, and Jake thinks, *It's all over.*

Abruptly—too abruptly for it to be the cold or the hard floor finally getting to him—Aiden moves away. Jake swallows, sits up and wraps a blanket around himself. He feels exposed, like a raw nerve expecting to be cut.

"You know, we're *always* listening to music these days," Aiden says, looking out through the living room window. "We used to be able to be quiet around each other, and now it seems like it's this huge, scary thing.

"And do you know why that is, Jake?" he continues, fixing his gaze on him. It penetrates to Jake's very core, as if Aiden can see through his every mask. "It's because ever since we started this, we've stopped knowing how to talk to each other. Every word just feels like it's loaded, now, and... it's because we've always known that this is something bigger than either of us thought it was, but there's so much riding on it that we both just kept our mouths shut and got on with it. But I—I can't do it anymore.

"I'm in love with you."

How can you love me after everything I've done, after Chicago, after all the time I forced us to waste? Jake thinks, openly gaping at Aiden and pulling the blanket tighter around himself.

Slowly, cautiously, Aiden reaches for his hand. "Please say something."

He might feel sober as a teetotaler, but Jake's mind is still clouded by the alcohol, just enough to render him helpless against the urge to draw back. "Why now?"

"It's not like you didn't know," Aiden says, as if it's the most obvious thing in the world, and Jake's eyes go wide. *How can he... he can't know, he can't, he can't...* At his dumbstruck expression, Aiden adds, "You've known ever since Louisiana. I'm not the only one with a face like an open book, you know."

Never has Jake wanted to run away from something so much in his entire life, but his legs are shaking against the floor and he can't trust them, can't trust anything now that the world is on its head. Desperately, he says, "I told you that it... that it meant something with you; can't we just leave it at that?"

"You told me *what* meant something?" Aiden asks, his voice suddenly harsh as he gets to his feet, and both of them are naked and this is *so* not the way Jake wants this evening to end, but everything is exploding, out of his control.

Struggling for words, for coherency, for anything, he sputters, "The... the sex, the... *all* of it."

"Don't you see? That's *exactly* what I'm talking about!" Aiden shouts, shocking Jake into finally scrambling to his feet. The last time he saw Aiden this mad, anger rolling off of him in almost palpable waves, was from three thousand miles away, over a grainy Skype connection.

"You're my best friend; of *course* it means something!" Jake shouts back, looking Aiden straight in the eye. "It means *everything!*"

"Then why not just say it? Jesus, who taught you not to love?" Jake's mouth falls open, and Aiden barrels on, "Was it Brad? Or Max? Was it *me*? What happened to you that made you so terrified of how you feel?"

"Is that really what you think of me?" Jake asks. "You think I'm just some heartless asshole who doesn't give a shit about you?"

Aiden's expression softens. The lines in his forehead and around his mouth smooth out, but all wrong, as if he's drooping instead of coming back to life.

"I don't know what I think anymore," he says, his voice softer than the wind Jake hears whispering past the windows. "This really is just a road trip thing for you, isn't it?"

What if? What if I tell him everything, offer him my bruised heart in exchange for his? What if this is the moment that could begin something new, something wonderful, something that doesn't ever have to end?

But that's the thing, Jake thinks, watching the hope grow brighter in Aiden's eyes the longer he stands there. *All good things have a shelf life—why would we be any different? We have rules for a reason.*

"We had a deal, Aiden," he finally says, dropping his gaze to his feet. "What happens on the road trip—"

"Stays on the road trip. Yeah, I remember," Aiden interrupts, his voice low and dangerously controlled. His shoulders slumping, he turns toward the bedroom, but seems to think better of it at the last moment. He approaches

Jake as if scared he might run away, and stops when they are only inches apart. Two fingers beneath Jake's chin force his gaze upward to meet Aiden's eyes, and Aiden says, "See, the thing is, I don't believe you. We both forgot about that stupid fucking rule, and I'm glad. And you can be as stubborn as you want about it, but I *know* what you feel for me is more than 'best friends.' So until you tell me what you're not telling me, I'm not giving up and I'm not going anywhere. It's out there now, and you can do whatever you want with it."

With that, he rocks forward and kisses Jake tenderly—as he might at any other time, as if he hasn't just fractured the fundamental building blocks of Jake's entire universe—and then walks away without looking back.

Splintered, shivering and lost, Jake just stands still until he loses track of how many minutes it's been.

11,207 MILES

CHAPTER 9

DAY EIGHTY: UTAH

Once Aiden has parked in the sparsely populated lot at the far end of Sunset Memorial Gardens, he scrubs a hand over his face, retrieves the small bunch of daisies from the dashboard and reaches into the glove compartment for the small box of his grandfather's ashes.

Arthur Thomas was born and raised in Moab, where he was married at eighteen to his high school sweetheart, Rose Dixie. When she and Arthur were both twenty-four, she passed away from what would later become known as cervical cancer. Afterward, with ghosts around every corner and no children to support, Arthur left Moab for Richmond, Virginia, to work with a construction company and start a new life.

In his will, he asked that a small portion of his ashes be scattered at Rose's grave.

It doesn't take long for Aiden to locate the plot on the map by the entrance, and, though the cemetery is mostly dark, small lamps set in the ground at intervals keep him on track. Aiden finds the grave and sets about brushing the leaves and debris from the faded stone. His heart aches—with no siblings or children of her own, Rose's grave has been all but forgotten. He runs his fingers over the grooves and depressions of her name, then lays the daisies at the foot of her headstone and gets back to his feet.

"Hello, ma'am," he says. "My name's Aiden. I'm Arthur's grandson."

Standing at the grave of a woman he never knew—that even his mother never knew—Aiden buries his hands in his pockets, at a loss for what else to say. He feels almost like a traitor to the memory of his own grandmother.

"He asked to be brought back to you," he finally says, drawing the small wooden box from his pocket and turning it over in his hands. "We weren't expecting it, but you should—you should know that he passed away peacefully, and he wasn't in any pain."

The corners of his eyes sting and he tips his head back, blinks up at the sky. "I guess you know that, though, if you're up there," he continues, his voice almost a murmur. "Maybe you could tell him that I miss him every single day. And that we called the RV Leona."

At that he falls silent, remembering the taste of cider and sugar on Jake's lips while meteors streaked by. He shakes his head, loosening the memories before they have a chance to take hold, and digs his phone out of his pocket. Clutching the wooden box tightly in his other hand, he scrolls through his contacts to *Mom,* and hits send.

"Hi, honey," Alice answers after the fourth ring, and the brightness in her voice makes Aiden loosen his grip on the box.

"Hey, Mom," he says. "How's the weather?"

"Cloudy with a chance of meatballs," she quips, and though Aiden rolls his eyes, he can't help but smile a little. "It was sunny this afternoon, but it's cold. Nothing much to report. How about where you boys are?"

"It's already dark here, and pretty cold."

"And where is 'here?'"

Aiden squares his shoulders and fixes his eyes on Rose's headstone. "I'm in Moab." After a few seconds have passed with no response, Aiden pulls the phone away from his ear to check that the call is still connected. "Mom?"

"Sorry, honey. I'm here." Her voice quavers, and Aiden can almost see her slowly sink into her wingback chair by the fireplace in the living room. "So you're in Grandpa's hometown."

"I'm at the cemetery. I thought I'd—well, I wanted you to be on the phone with me while I did this. I didn't wanna do it alone."

"Alone? Where's Jake?"

"A yoga class in town," Aiden says dismissively, adding, "we just needed a little space, that's all."

"You boys aren't fighting, are you?" she asks.

"No, we're not fighting. We just..."

"Aiden, you know I can tell when you're lying to me."

"I'm not lying, I just—I don't... I don't know what we're even *doing* anymore," Aiden says, the words rushing out of him like a breath held for too long. "I came clean with him two days ago, told him *everything,* and he just... he hasn't said anything."

"Oh, honey," Alice sighs. "That boy... he carries an awful lot of pain around with him, you know that. And I know how much you might want to fix it, but sometimes you just have to be patient. He'll get there."

"What if he doesn't?"

"He will. You did the right thing in telling him."

"How can you be so sure?" Aiden asks in a small voice; all his most deep-seated fears confront him at once.

The thing is that if he chooses the music, he can't trust that Jake will follow him. He won't just lose everything that they are, he'll also lose everything they could be. He'll lose the twelve-month lease on a shitty, shoebox apartment that they'll both outwardly hate but secretly love, because when they move around, they'll constantly be pressed up against one another, each touch still sparking a thrill. He'll lose every possible future he's imagined for himself with Jake by his side. He'll lose his best friend, the one person with whom he shares everything.

The music won't be worth it without him, he thinks, drawing his shoulders up against the pervasive cold and the realization that nothing else will ever come close. This is not something he knows because he's experiencing the first in a line of loves, but because he knows without doubt that the line consists of one person. Jake is Aiden's first and last, and there's nothing he can do to change it or fight it.

"Because I've known Jake since you two still had training wheels, and I know that he loves you with his whole heart," Alice says, her assured tone cutting into his thoughts. "It's only a matter of time."

"I feel like we've wasted so much time already," Aiden admits. "There were so many times when I could have—"

"Thinking like that isn't going to get you anywhere," she interrupts gently. "And look at how brave you were in telling him. My brave little soldier."

"*Mom,*" Aiden whines.

"All I'm saying is that I'm proud of you. And Jake will come around, just you wait," she says. "Now, you've got something to do for Grandpa. No more stalling."

"I wasn't—" Aiden begins, but stops as he realizes that stalling is at least part of what he is doing. He holds up the small wooden box, examining the intricate Celtic knot on the lid, carved by his own grandfather's hand, and heaves a deep sigh. A breeze picks up, and he knows that it's time. "Do you think I should say something?"

"Only if you need to, honey," comes the soft reply, tinged with a deep sadness.

He carefully unlatches the small metal clasp on the front of the box and opens the lid, averting his eyes even in the darkness. He wants to say something, but he said all of his goodbyes on the day of the funeral with Jake's fingers in the crook of his elbow smoothing the rough edges. The breeze picks up even more, and as he tips the box toward the ground by degrees, words from a William Penn poem he heard long ago come back to him: "For death is no more than a turning of us over from time to eternity."

"I think Grandpa would have liked that," Alice murmurs after a moment, her voice thick. "You run along now, okay? Go and find Jake, and tell him to give you a hug from me."

Aiden nods and says, "Okay, Mom. Love you."

"I love you too, honey."

He hangs up with a heavy heart, pausing as Rose's name catches his eye once more. He feels oddly sorry that he never knew the first woman to capture his grandfather's heart. They had so little time together, but then, as Aiden's grandfather once said, "I'm lucky that your Grandma turned out to be a love of my life. I'm lucky to have had two of those."

Leaving the box on top of the headstone, he turns and makes his way back to the RV, feeling a little lighter for having closed the chapter completely.

Later that evening, when he has picked Jake up from yoga and taken in the flush high in his cheeks, the fluid grace returned to his body, Jake insists on taking over driving duty. It's nearly three hours before he finds out where Jake is taking them, and as they step out of the RV in the middle of the desert, it occurs to him that his mother may have been right.

"One foot here, and the other here," Jake directs him as they stand atop the Four Corners monument. The border of the circle that surrounds the meeting point reads, *Four states here meet in freedom under God*. He has one foot in Arizona, the other in New Mexico. "Now, bend over—"

"Bend over?" Aiden repeats, one eyebrow raised.

"Stop being a pervert and just do it," Jake says.

"I swear to god, if you take a picture of this," he grumbles, but follows Jake's instruction and places his left hand in Utah and his right in Colorado. "What now?"

"Now you enjoy the fact that you're in not just two, not just three, but *four* places at once." He lets the knowledge sink in and take root—he wanted to be in two places at once, and Jake has just given him four.

He stands, brushes his palms off on his jeans, turns to Jake and cups his jaw. He crushes their lips together and lets the kiss set his body aflame, and Jake kisses him back just as fervently.

And then, because he can't not say something, he settles for five words that he hopes convey everything, whispered into Jake's ear like a promise and a prayer: "Thank you. I love you."

11,688 MILES

DAY EIGHTY-ONE: COLORADO

When Jake slips quietly back inside the RV, he finds the living area empty. Sunlight pours in through window behind the couch, and he tiptoes across the beams spilling onto the floor as if he's walking on broken glass.

"Aiden?" he calls, just as his eyes land on a note propped in front of the coffeemaker: *Went for groceries, back soon.* ♥ *Dan*

He feels himself relax. The tension drains from his shoulders as he shucks off his jacket and takes his mom's art journal from the inside pocket.

After they'd gotten settled at the campground just outside the center of Durango, Jake had slipped the journal out of his bedside cabinet and taken it with him on his walk into town. He was convinced that he had finally found the drawing he wanted to get as a tattoo—an anchor with a frayed rope—but when he arrived on Camino Del Rio and looked up at the unassuming *Tattoo & Piercing* sign over the door of Skin Incorporated, he kept on walking.

He spent an hour in Buckley Park, one hand clutching a venti pumpkin spice latté, the other leafing distractedly through the journal while he wished more than ever that he could just pick up the phone and talk to his father.

It's nearly December ninth, Dad, he thought, and lingered over the single drawing of his father that he never looked at if he could help it. He traced around the lines of his father's thick, prematurely gray hair, and stared at the image of his slouched form. His father had his hands in his pockets and wore an old sweater as he stood gazing out of the living room window. *It's been seven years, and Charlie says I have to let you go, and we're selling the house, and I don't feel ready for either. I never got to know you well enough to know that I'm doing anything right, or making you proud, or living like the son of the man I remember.*

He turned the page, and his eyes landed on the drawing of him and Aiden as children. *What should I do, Dad? Did you ever feel so much for Mom that it scared you shitless? Sometimes I feel like I'm just waiting for him to break my heart, because I don't know if I can trust him with it. It's like he's holding it and I'm following him around with my hands cupped underneath his in case he drops it. So what do I do? What if I don't want to go to New York? Would he stay for me? Would he give up everything, even though that's the last thing I want for him?*

And what if I did go with him?

He sighs now as the ache resurfaces, and heads for the shower. The water is almost too hot, but it pounds on his shoulders and back and chases the cold from his bones. When he steps out to towel off, he smiles at the unmistakable shift in the air that lets him know Aiden is back. He hears something fall to the floor, and Aiden swear softly; Jake shakes his head as he pulls on his softest pair of yoga pants and the T-shirt Aiden gave him the day they left Brunswick.

Aiden is sitting on the couch; his laptop is playing a haunting, piano-driven song and his fingers tap the melody against his thigh. Sunlight still pours through the window behind him, and it casts him in the same auburn halo that surrounded him thousands of miles ago, before the kiss that finally changed everything.

There is no describing how important Aiden is to him, for their story didn't begin with a dropped pen or eyes meeting across a crowded room or bumping into one another on a busy street and spilling coffee everywhere—it began with two young boys who made each other feel a little less lost; two young boys who held each other together through thick and thin. Two young boys who should long have felt like brothers but never did. Jake returns Aiden's smile as he looks up, his fingers still playing the keys of an invisible piano. Silently, Jake climbs onto the couch behind him, settling his knees on either side of Aiden's hips and draping his arms around his shoulders. It's comfortable, but something about it also makes Jake need more than he has allowed himself since Wyoming; he ghosts a kiss on the back of Aiden's neck, peeks over his shoulder and watches the lines of muscle in Aiden's arm shift as he mimics the piano riff.

Aiden's arms have held him with tender strength and kept him safe for weeks; Aiden's fingers have learned how to undo him and put him back together piece by shaking piece; and Aiden's hands now hold his heart, flawed and fragile as it is. Jake finds himself mesmerized by the movement, fixated by the sudden, unexpected question of what else Aiden could do, if Jake will only let him.

When he shifts around to Aiden's side, Aiden sets the laptop on the floor, then hooks his hands beneath Jake's thighs and pull him into his lap. Music still permeates the charged air between them, and Aiden meets Jake's kiss midway, his tongue sliding against Jake's almost tentatively.

"Wait, wait," Jake whispers, pulling back and searching Aiden's eyes. "Aiden, I... I've never trusted anyone the way I trust you. You know that, right?" At Aiden's nod, he clears his throat and continues, "And you know that I... the way I feel about you, it's not—"

"Stop," Aiden interrupts, and gently places his fingertips over Jake's mouth.

"We're not gonna do that right now."

"Why not?" Jake asks slowly.

"I didn't tell you because I was trying to rush you, and I wasn't expecting anything. Hoping, sure, but..." Aiden reaches up to trace Jake's cheekbone. "You don't owe me anything. Okay?"

Warmth blooms in his bloodstream, and Jake nods.

"Good. So, for now... please come back to me," Aiden says, dropping his hands to graze Jake's thighs. "Let it go, and just be with me."

Jake pitches forward, falling into a kiss that feels shattering in the wake of Aiden's words. All at once he's five years younger, fumbling and frenzied and trembling under the weight of the things he wants. Aiden's hands are still, now, and heavy on his thighs; he scoots forward in Aiden's lap, pressing into the firm touch and chasing the taste of something sweet that lingers on Aiden's tongue.

He reaches down for Aiden's hands and pushes them back, back, back until Aiden is cupping his ass and holding him right where he is, immobile save for the tight figure eights he makes with his hips. Slow kisses contrast with the movement of Jake's impatient hands as they rush beneath Aiden's shirt and undershirt and push them up over his head.

Though he feels Aiden growing hard beneath him, Jake doesn't know how to ask for what he suddenly wants, and pulls away to catch his breath. Aiden follows, one hand tipping Jake's head back; his mouth is warm and wet on Jake's throat, trailing down to his collarbone.

Opening his eyes and staring blankly up at the ceiling, Jake breathes, "Do you remember what I said to you in West Virginia?" At Aiden's questioning hum, he swallows and adds, "You asked me if I topped."

"And you said exclusively," Aiden says. He works his hand up into Jake's damp hair, but Jake peels it away and brings it to his cheek, and then kisses Aiden's palm.

He stares into Aiden's eyes. "This time, I want you to."

"You..." Aiden trails off, eyes wide. "Jake—"

"Just be with me," Jake echoes, adding in a whisper, "like that. Please."

Aiden looks at him searchingly for a moment, then pulls Jake's legs forward, wraps them around his waist, and carries him to the bedroom. They shed each other's clothes quietly, revealing skin inch by inch, keeping eye contact as much as possible as they let their fingers retrace maps long since drawn. Aiden's hands shake as they trail the length of Jake's bare arms with the lightest whisper of a touch, leaving the hair raised in their wake. Jake licks his lips with a dry tongue, and his eyes close as he finally lets his foundations crumble and gives himself up. It's as easy as falling asleep at the end of a long day, a drift into floating.

Aiden's mouth is soft on his and his hands are everywhere, a breath of skin on skin. He strokes Jake all the way to hardness as they kiss deeply, kisses that are like drowning, falling farther and harder and faster, and breathes raggedly whenever they break apart, as if he too is surfacing for air.

"I love you," he whispers, taking his hands away and swallowing Jake's soft whine inside another kiss. While Aiden moves to the nightstand, sunlight floods Jake's skin and there's nothing but heat. His head falls back onto the pillow and he takes a few deep breaths. He can barely stand this out-of-control cascade, this bone-deep need and vulnerability, this feeling that if he doesn't have Aiden, he has nothing. It hurts so beautifully that he wants to cry.

And then Aiden drops a condom and a small bottle of lubricant onto the bed and brushes his thumb over Jake's lips. With just a nod, it becomes simple. It's him and Aiden—just him and Aiden, like always.

Everything in him loosens, uncoils, and he surges up to capture Aiden's mouth, smiling against his lips as Aiden slowly moves his thighs apart and settles between them. The shift is immediate, the tension is broken, and soon Jake feels one of Aiden's slicked fingers circling him and then slowly pushing inside. He gasps at the soft pressure, full but not to bursting, and Aiden pauses to look up at him.

"Okay?" Aiden breathes the word as if it is a benediction, and Jake wriggles underneath him, bearing down and already wanting more.

As Jake watches, encourages him with soft words and silent nods, Aiden moves steadily; a second finger soon joins the first, and his trembling has stopped.

Minutes seem to pack themselves into seconds, an incomprehensible but pleasant stretch during which Aiden, eyes dark and heavy-lidded, checks and double-checks that what he's doing is still all right. Jake is panting, lost, three fingers twisting inside him and sweat beading at his temples while Aiden brings him back to full hardness.

And then Aiden's mouth covers his, gives him air as he pushes inside inch by inch and mile by mile. The feel of Aiden inside him, and the look in his deep brown eyes when he pulls back—volumes of love and awe—create an ache in Jake's soul, a cut that runs so deep he knows he'll carry it for the rest of his life.

Aiden starts to move, barely at first, and it's a maelstrom of wildfire sensation: Jake's arching back and his fingers curling into the sheets. It's Aiden's half-sobs, half-laughs choked into the hollow of his neck. It's push and pull and give and take, winding and reaching and a burning heat that scorches Jake from the inside out; it's falling apart over and over and knowing that Aiden will catch him.

It's everything.

Jake is too close too soon, but he doesn't have it in him to ask Aiden to slow down; his toes curl, and he breathes only fragments of Aiden's name. Chasing sensation, rubbing against the soft swell of Aiden's stomach, he hooks his arms around Aiden's neck and pulls himself up, pressing his forehead to Aiden's temple just as he screws his eyes shut and lets go completely, Aiden's arm sliding underneath him to hold him up, to cling to him like a lifeline.

Aiden follows him over the edge moments later, panting and gasping and whispering, "I love you," again and again and again. Jake drifts down, locked on those three words and truly wanting, for the first time, to return them. But everything is already too intense; Aiden's eyes water as he pulls back, and Jake's entire body feels like putty. He lies back and pulls Aiden down with him, shaking in the thick air that surrounds them.

Then it's sudden emptiness as Aiden slowly pulls out; damp, unsteady fingers card Jake's hair; a lazy kiss bleeds into another, and another, as Jake's nerve endings recover from overload.

It's Aiden wrapped around him from head to toe, the pulse in his neck rabbit-quick, something unfurling and stretching awake.

And later, much later, when Jake is absolutely sure that Aiden is asleep, it's letting the words roll onto his tongue, their taste heady and dizzying; it's lying stone-still as he considers them. It's looking over at Aiden, arms curled up beneath his pillow and his face peaceful in sleep, and whispering, "I love you, too."

11,772 MILES

DAY EIGHTY-FOUR: NEW MEXICO

"Ready?" Aiden asks, taking Jake's hand and giving it a reassuring squeeze.

They're standing outside Loretto Chapel in downtown Santa Fe. With its snow-covered adobe buildings and unlit *farolitos* lining the sidewalks and rooftops, it seems like some made-up place, nothing like the city they read about on the Internet.

Jake takes a deep breath and leans into Aiden for a moment. "I'm ready."

They push through the heavy wooden doors, which are hung with Christmas wreaths, and stop to take in the pews decorated with greenery and twinkling lights. Carvings of saints stand sentinel amid ornate stonework over the altar, and above them the vaulted ceilings are painted in an intricate, swirling red and gold design. To Aiden and Jake's right is part of the reason for their visit: the miraculous staircase.

"So what is it with this staircase?" Aiden gently nudges Jake's shoulder, his voice low; several people are seated in pews throughout the chapel, heads bowed in prayer. Aiden tries to shake the feeling that he's trespassing— neither of them are Catholic, but this private ceremony is a tradition Jake has observed since the first anniversary of his father's death.

"The story goes that the chapel architect died," Jake begins, walking toward the staircase and running his hand over the banister. "And the builders realized that there was no stairway to the choir loft included in the designs. The Sisters of Loretto prayed to Saint Joseph for divine intervention for, like, nine days straight. On the tenth day, a man appeared.

"He told the nuns that he'd build them a staircase, but that he needed complete privacy," Jake continues. "So he locked himself inside for three months, and as soon as the staircase was finished, he left. No one knew who he was, and they never saw him again."

"And what's the miracle?" Aiden asks.

"The construction," Jake answers. "No nails, no visible means of support... apparently, it still has some people baffled. The Sisters eventually decided that the man was Saint Joseph himself, come to answer their prayers."

"Aren't we gonna go up?"

"You can't anymore," Jake says with a sigh. Aiden follows his gaze to behind the staircase, his eyes immediately drawn to the flickering candles gathered on a high, wide table. A small sign in front of the votives reads, *Light a candle and speak your prayer, and accept the light that it may protect and keep you.*

Aiden crosses his arms over his chest and leans against the pillar just in front of the table, looking out at the rest of the small chapel. Trying to see through Jake's eyes, he quietly asks, "What would we film here?"

"I don't know."

Aiden conceals his surprise—Jake is the one with the visionary imagination, and Aiden is the one who riffs off of it. "Nice place for a wedding, maybe," he suggests, straightening and stretching his arms out in front of him. He deliberately frames a shot badly, knowing that Jake won't be able to resist correcting him—which he does, after a moment, covering Aiden's hands with his own and creating a panning shot that begins at the door and travels across the pews right to the altar.

"Native Santa Feans," he says, his hands lingering on Aiden's.

"Nah," Aiden says. "Two guys who've been in love with each other forever but haven't seen each other in years."

"And, what? They randomly run into each other here?"

"And finally admit everything, yes."

"Why here?" Jake asks.

"This place, it..." Aiden trails off, dropping his hands and looking up at the staircase. "Do you get the feeling that everything would be better if you just stayed here for a while and figured your shit out?"

"It does have something," Jake concedes. His hands are balled into fists, and his knuckles are white. He looks down at his feet for a long moment before finally turning around.

Aiden hangs back while Jake moves over to the table. He bows his head, says his own kind of prayer and thinks back to waking up this morning and finding Jake curled up on the couch, his mom's art journal open and face down on his chest. When Aiden picked it up, he found that it was open to a page featuring a drawing of William, and that was when he realized the date—December ninth, the anniversary of his death.

He sees a small group of children robed in white file into the apse, holding red hymnals. They arrange themselves in what must be their usual formation. A man comes to stand before them, and once they're ready, they start to sing. It isn't a Christmas carol, as Aiden might expect; it sounds more like a haunting lament, and it sends chills up and down his spine. It echoes the sorrow he feels for Jake, for Charlie, for their little family that was ripped apart by one freak storm.

Aiden's eyes sting, and he watches Jake reach for a lighting stick from the small pot in the corner of the table. There's no discernible pattern to the way the candles are lit; flames flicker in clusters and pairs, and though Jake's back is turned, Aiden knows that as he pauses, he's turning the stick over and over in his hands, agonizing over which candle to light because there is no neat line to join. Slowly, his boots quietly clicking against the wooden floor, Aiden closes the distance between them and reaches forward, clasps Jake's shoulders and runs his hands down his arms. Then he gives in and wraps his arms around Jake's waist and hooks his chin over his shoulder.

Jake leans back, curls his fingers over Aiden's, and asks, "Do you think he'd be proud of me?"

"I know he'd be proud of you," Aiden says.

This seems to be all Jake needs to hear; the warmth of his fingers over Aiden's disappears, and he reaches forward to light the stick. Aiden watches him pick a candle in the center of an unlit group and hold the flame over the wick. He lights the one next to it, too.

For both of them, Aiden thinks, and squeezes Jake's waist before stepping around to his side. His skin glows warm in the candlelight, reminding Aiden of WaterFire, of feeling for the first time in his life as if he was on the precipice of something that had the power to transform worlds.

"I wrote a letter to him last night. That's why I didn't come to bed," Jake says, his voice raspy and thick. "Will you help me with it when we get back?"

"What do you need?" Aiden asks.

Jake sucks a breath through his teeth and his shoulders rise as he buries his hands in his pockets. He exhales and says, "To let go."

It's mostly dark by the time they step outside, and it's like walking into a different world—the Christmas lights have burst into life, and the *farolitos* lining the sidewalks and rooftops have been lit as if by magic.

They go to the Blue Corn Café on Water Street and get tipsy on margaritas despite eating more than their fill of tamales and *calabacitas* and *carne ado-vada*, and Jake barely puts up a fight when Aiden buys him a café T-shirt. He puts up even less of a fight when Aiden leads him to the back of the bus that will take them to the campground and spends their fifteen-minute journey holding him, touching his face, kissing his mouth and chasing the scent of Jean Paul Gaultier that always lingers around his throat.

When they get back to the RV, Jake disappears into the bedroom and returns clutching a thin white envelope.

Past a weathered pavilion hung with white lights, the edge of the campground is a low cliff overlooking a gorge. They walk there in silence, holding hands.

They're both dressed in dark colors; the envelope stands out in stark relief, and the moon is bright above them. The wind is strong, and the elevation makes Aiden feel as if he's only filling his lungs halfway. He looks up at the impossible stars—they seem close enough to touch.

He sounds hesitant and stilted when he asks, "What does it say?"

"Too much, probably," Jake says, sounding distant. The envelope is in his right hand, which is also curled around the cold metal guardrail; it crumples as his grip tightens, and the wind roars in Aiden's ears. "Everything I've never... it's four fucking pages."

"It's okay. You don't have to tell me," he says, pressing his hand into the small of Jake's back.

"I came out to him," Jake says. "In the letter. I still don't know how he'd feel about it. Whether he'd be supportive or not... if he'd be proud of me."

"I think he'll probably end up with your boy one day, you know," he hears William say, and as he loiters outside the living room door, Aiden's breathing stops for a second.

"I think you're right. Wouldn't that be something?" Alice says.

William clears his throat. "Has he come out to you and George yet?"

"Not yet, but it's only a matter of time. For Jake, too. They're both working up to it; I can tell."

"Just wait, they'll end up doing it on the same day."

As the memory comes rushing back, long misplaced, yet brighter than the stars above their heads, Aiden closes his eyes. "He knew. I overheard him talking to Mom one day, and he knew."

Even with his eyes closed, Aiden can feel Jake's gaze on him, knows the exact measure of shock that is widening his eyes and dropping his jaw. "You never told me," Jake says.

"I'm telling you now." Aiden opens his eyes and turns toward him, thumbing over his cheek. "And he *was* proud of you, Jake."

"Thank you." The words shudder out of him like a sob. He takes the envelope in both hands and rips it in two, then four, again and again until it's nothing but handfuls of scraps covered in fragments of Jake's crooked handwriting. His eyes are screwed shut. Aiden's heart races. As Jake lets out a long, slow breath and throws the pieces into the wind, Aiden thinks he hears him whisper, "Bye, Dad."

The wind dies down as if all the air has just been sucked from the world. Jake is breathing rapidly, in through the nose and out through the mouth. His hands shake as he lowers them to the guardrail.

"Jakey?" Aiden ventures, motioning weakly toward him; Jake looks at him for a split second that makes Aiden's chest clench painfully, and then takes off faster than Aiden can register, running back down the hill and off into the darkness. "Jake, wait!"

Aiden follows as quickly as he can, and the frigid night air burns his throat and lungs as he vaults over the low fence bordering the campground. He sees Jake silhouetted by the pavilion lights; blood rushes in Aiden's ears and he wants to stop, to lean over and empty the contents of his stomach onto the ground at the sight of the tears he saw in Jake's eyes.

Aiden watches Jake stumble up the steps to the pavilion and crumple to his knees as if in slow motion, hunched over and barely holding himself up, his body wracked with sobs. Aiden feels as though he's suffocating. Guilt roils in the pit of his stomach—he used to wish that Jake would break down like this and purge himself, but gave up hoping long ago. Now, Jake is a volcano, stone undone by heat and sorrow.

Just as he did fifteen years ago, twenty-five hundred miles away under a January midnight sky, he circles in front of Jake and stands there. He's breathing razor blades, and he hates himself for not knowing what to do. Jake's sobs intensify until he sounds like a wounded animal, until he's barely getting air, and Aiden falls to his knees, cups Jake's jaw and forces his head up.

"Look at me," he says. "Sweetheart, look at me. I need you to breathe."

It's been fifteen years, but Aiden still recognizes the wrenching shade of green Jake's irises turn when he cries. It's somewhere between lime and pistachio, the color of sun-bleached grass.

"Get away from me," Jake says, staring him straight in the eye for a moment of stone cold resolve before his face crumples and he manages to get to his feet and wrap his arms around his middle.

"Jake, I'm *sorry*, he—"

"Shut up, just shut up, please *stop talking*, I can't—"

Standing, Aiden moves closer and tries again. "Jake, it's okay. It's *okay*, I understand, you don't have to—"

"Don't," Jake says, his voice ragged. "Don't say you *understand*."

"I lost someone, too," Aiden gently reminds him. "Of course I understand."

"No, you *don't*. And don't think that just because I finally let you fuck me, it means you know every fucking thing about me," Jake spits, looking him in the eye. The words hit Aiden like a slap in the face and he breaks eye contact. His gaze lands on Jake's right hand, where he works his thumb back and forth over the crease of his index finger.

"That's not fair," Aiden says in a small voice, shaking his head and chancing a glance back up.

"Oh, okay, let's talk about *fair*, shall we?" Jake says, rounding on him with fire in his eyes. "It's not *fair* that he got taken away from me just like *that*, like he wasn't my whole world. It's not *fair* that the first thing I think of when anyone says his name is those two fucking cops at my front door in their dumb-ass anoraks. *It's not fair* that I have to carry around this huge, gaping hole in my chest when some days it feels like it's all I can do to put one foot in front of the other. Sometimes it feels like I'm *bleeding* him, Aiden. Do you *understand* that?"

Aiden wraps Jake up in his arms. Jake struggles, but Aiden only tightens his hold until he finally goes lax, still trembling and sobbing.

"I'm here. I'm here; I'm not going anywhere," he whispers, not knowing what else to do. Jake's knees buckle under the weight of his grief, and Aiden doesn't know how to help other than sink to the floor with him.

Taking a deep, shuddering breath, Jake pulls away, wiping his eyes with the back of his hand and looking miserably at the floor. "Aiden, I'm... I'm so sorry. For what I said before, and... all of this," he says, shaking his head and blinking back more tears. His hand falls to his lap, his thumb rubbing over his index finger again.

"You're not Catholic," Aiden blurts.

"What?" Jake asks.

"The whole guilt thing isn't hereditary, you know," Aiden jokes weakly, gesturing to Jake's hand and adding, "Plus, you look like my grandma at church."

Blinking, Jake looks down at his hand as if he doesn't even realize what he's been doing. "Mom had this rosary that I used to hold. After," he explains. He flexes his fingers and sniffs harshly, something in his face shuttering.

"You don't need to wear the mask around me. You know that, right?" Aiden asks.

Jake lets out a hollow laugh. "Are you my therapist now? You took *one* psych class, remember?" he says, but there's no venom behind the words.

"Come on," Aiden says, tugging him to his feet. "Come on back to me."

"I didn't..." Jake stops, and looks at Aiden almost sheepishly. "Okay."

A chill sweeps over them as the wind picks up again, but Aiden doesn't hurry their short walk back to the RV. The moonlight picks out the tears still rolling down Jake's face, and it isn't until they're back inside and passing the bathroom that Aiden realizes one small thing that he can do.

He kisses Jake's hair and nudges him toward the bedroom, and then ducks into the bathroom and rifles through the cabinets until he finds what he needs.

When Aiden enters the room, Jake's shoes are on the floor but he's otherwise still dressed and sitting on the bed with his arms wrapped around his knees. Aiden slowly climbs onto the bed next to him and waits until he unfolds before peeling open the Band-Aid and sticking it onto Jake's shirt, right over his heart. Jake blinks down at it for five long seconds. And then he pitches forward into Aiden's arms as his sobs turn frantic once more.

Aiden can feel the tears seep through his thin shirt and onto his skin; it's as if Jake is made of tears, as if he's been saving them all up for this one night when Aiden can finally reach up, catch him as he tumbles down and hold him together. His chest hurts with the sensation of being needed; it spreads through him and fills him up. And in this moment, with Jake's fingers tightening in the cotton of Aiden's shirt as he cries himself out, Aiden realizes that he doesn't need to be some knight in shining armor, riding in to save the day and make everything better. He needs to be the oak tree in their place at Thomas Point Beach, the pillar of strength rooted to the earth. He needs to be the anchor, the tether, the reason to come back and endure.

When Jake finally falls asleep, Aiden tucks him under the covers and breathes deeply as Jake curls into his usual position. Something about his face has changed; the lines in his forehead are gradually easing out. He looks younger, more at peace... beautiful.

Pulling the door closed behind him in the hope that Jake will just continue to sleep, he makes his way through to the living area with every intention of spending the night on the couch. But then the magnets on the refrigerator catch his eye. Most of them are left over from his grandfather's many road trips; Aiden lets his fingers drift over one in particular, Arizona-shaped and proudly proclaiming in silver and teal, *The Grand Canyon State*.

After the briefest pause, he grabs a bottle of iced coffee from the fridge, pulls the magnet from the door and takes both items with him to the cab. He switches on the radio and the GPS, puts his seat belt on and starts the engine.

He knows exactly where he's going.

12,000 MILES

DAY EIGHTY-FIVE: ARIZONA

Jake wakes up with his breath stinging his raw throat and his eyes still full with the bittersweet ache of catharsis. He's wearing yesterday's clothes, and his face feels like a puffy mess. There's also the matter of Aiden sitting on the edge of the bed, gently pushing back Jake's hair and looking as though he hasn't slept all night.

"Morning," he says, a smile tugging at his mouth.

"Morning," Jake rasps. He shifts under the covers. "What time is it?"

"After seven," Aiden says. "How'd you sleep?"

Jake stretches his arms and blinks. He feels *rested*. "Better than I have in years, actually. You?"

"I haven't slept yet," Aiden says, his hand dropping and tracing the line of Jake's jaw. "There was something I had to do."

"And it took you nine hours?"

"Eight, actually."

"You didn't go out and get lost, did you?"

"No. But I did drink way too much coffee."

"Well, that's nothing new," Jake says, suppressing a yawn and momentarily letting his eyes close. "I'm guessing I'm awake for a reason?"

"Put on the warmest clothes you own," Aiden says, removing his hand, "and meet me at the door in five minutes."

"What's going on?" Jake asks, sitting up and catching Aiden's wrist as he stands to leave.

"You'll see," Aiden sing-songs, his voice cracking with fatigue. With an exaggerated wink, he ducks out of the bedroom, and Jake is left alone.

He stays still for a moment more, stretching out into the warmth of the sheets and listening to the air settle. He feels as if his heart has been cracked open, but instead of wanting to claw himself back together and patch up his fault lines, he wants... Aiden. He wants him openly, honestly, and completely—almost as if Aiden has passed some test neither of them were aware had been set.

Jake glances down at the front of his shirt, peels off the Band-Aid and sticks it directly onto the skin over his heart.

He dresses quickly and simply in thick, charcoal gray jeans, a white shirt and a soft wool sweater, finished with a black scarf and gloves. He's feeling somehow rebellious, as if he needs to be contained—kinetic energy thrums beneath his skin, and the muted colors help ground him. Avoiding his reflection, since his hair is probably an unmitigated disaster, he heads out to meet Aiden, who is bundled up in his pea coat and waiting—as promised—by the door.

The RV is shrouded in darkness, all of the blinds drawn and the lights switched off. It carries the same atmosphere as their teenage "runaway" nights did, when Jake stayed over at Aiden's house and they snuck out for bike rides up to Coffin Pond long after dark.

"Come here," Aiden murmurs. He holds out a hand; the other loosely holds his scarf.

"You're starting to freak me out," Jake says as he approaches. "Seriously, what's going on?"

"Can I blindfold you?"

"I—what?"

Grinning sheepishly, Aiden holds up the scarf. "There's something I want to show you, but I don't want you to see it 'til we get there. It's only a couple minutes' walk."

"We're not in Santa Fe anymore, are we?"

Aiden bites his lip and shakes his head. "Nope."

Jake regards him for a moment before stepping forward and letting Aiden blindfold him. And then, as if it's the easiest thing in the world, Jake lets himself be led: down the steps and out the door; along smooth ground that gives away nothing; then down a gradual incline that leads to an uneven set of winding steps.

The world around him is nearly silent; only the occasional bird sings a dawn song to accompany them. Jake is grateful that there seems to be no one else around while Aiden patiently guides him down the steps. Jake's arm occasionally flails for purchase where there is none to be found.

"How much far—" Jake begins, but stops short when he feels a railing press against his waist. He reaches out and feels the metal beneath his free hand. "Aiden?"

"It's about to start," he replies, dropping Jake's hand and loosening the blindfold. "Are you ready?"

"Ready for wha—"

Bright, dawn-pale sky stretches for miles and miles, all the way to the horizon, and Jake squints against the sudden light. Then, like a blurry long-lens shot suddenly pulled into focus, the landscape resolves itself into buttes and side canyons and giant sprawls of sedimentary rock. Jake's breath punches out in a single, disbelieving huff and a wave of dizziness overtakes him, as if every molecule of oxygen has left his body at once.

"Ready for the Grand Canyon," Aiden says.

A sliver of sunlight appears to the east, and Jake's eyes drink in the pink, purple and orange hues that begin to transform the rock.

"It looks like it's breathing," he whispers.

Aiden chuckles, wraps his arms around Jake's waist and hooks his chin over his shoulder. "Pretty amazing, right?"

Jake turns in his arms and locates the splinters of green and gold in Aiden's eyes that he only sees in the morning light. He presses his forehead against Aiden's temple and tells him, "You make everything else go away."

"Nah," Aiden says and kisses his cheek.

"You do, though," Jake says, pulling back and meeting his eyes. "Everything that happened last night, it... no one's ever done anything like that for me before, and now *this*..."

"I wanted you to wake up to something good today. That's all," Aiden says with a shrug.

Jake wants to tell Aiden that he loves him—the words are on the tip of his tongue, their taste as thick and full as when he whispered them to Aiden's sleeping form in Colorado—but last night still weighs on him. He doesn't want to say it when the cracks inside him still simmer with the fury of sleeping giants; he needs some measure of peace.

So he holds onto the railing and leans back to look over his shoulder at the land beneath the rising sun. Aiden drops his head to rest on Jake's shoulder, his eyes drift closed and a smile plays about his lips when Jake tells him he's missing everything.

"We've already been here for an hour or so. I came up earlier, sat for a while," he replies around a yawn. "And we've got tomorrow."

"I can't believe you drove all night," Jake says.

"Well, you took me to Four Corners," Aiden points out.

"Did you stop anywhere?"

"Yeah, at about two-thirty. There was a Denny's in Holbrook."

"Kinda glad I wasn't awake, in that case."

"Mm. You needed to sleep."

"Thank you. For last night," Jake says, and rests his head atop Aiden's. "And for everything else."

"You're welcome," Aiden says. Another yawn, and Jake can feel the warm exhalation even through his layers.

Clearing his throat, wanting to offer something, he says, "Aiden, you—you know I'm getting there, right?"

"Hmm?"

"With us. You know I'm getting there?"

Only silence greets him, stretching so taut that Jake thinks it might snap back like an elastic band at any moment—until Aiden's arms go limp, and Jake realizes that he's fallen asleep. He allows himself a bone-deep sigh, and then hooks his arms underneath Aiden's and hauls him to his feet.

"You fell asleep on me," Jake tells him as he blinks himself awake. "Literally."

"Did not," Aiden grumbles, rubbing his eyes and giving him a bleary look. "Okay, maybe I did."

"Come on, Sleeping Beauty. Let's get you back to the RV," Jake says, taking his hand and leading him away from the railing.

"Is that my Disney character?" Aiden asks.

"Actually, I'd say Rapunzel. Your hair grows fast enough," Jake replies, and ruffles Aiden's shaggy locks until Aiden scrunches his nose and bats his hand away. His hair isn't really that long, just longer than Aiden has worn it since he was in single digits.

"If my hair were that long, I'd probably look like a hobo," he says, and Jake laughs. As they reach the top of the steps, Aiden tugs on his sleeve and turns back to face the sunrise. Quietly, he asks, "Do you think we'd fly if we jumped?"

Jake glances around at Aiden, at his eyes, closing as the sun's warmth starts to reach them, and says, "Maybe. Soon." He doesn't miss Aiden's beatific smile, his skin luminous in the light of the magic hour. "Now, come on. There's a bed with your name on it."

"So WHERE DID YOU MEET this guy?" Aiden asks as they take a seat on one of the benches behind the campfire.

"At the store, when I went for Advil," Jake replies, resting his head on Aiden's shoulder and inhaling deeply.

Jake had awoken late in the afternoon, after they both slept most of the day away, with dream images still flashing in his mind: an empty dance floor littered with debris; a black gymnastic ribbon that turned to fire when he picked it up and danced with it until everything was alight; walking through the flames toward a glass door. The handle was almost within reach when Jake woke up, head throbbing, abandoned sentiments fizzling on his tongue.

At the Market Plaza store, he ran into Oscar: six-four, with broad shoulders and muscled arms barely concealed by his regulation black polo, white blond hair shot through with deep purple, subtly outlined hazel eyes and an arresting, sultry smile that, only months ago, would have driven Jake crazy.

"We got talking," Jake continues now, "and his best friend's dad owns the place, so they come up every Monday to hang out, spin, blow off some steam. In the summer they put on shows for the kids."

He scans the clearing; rows of benches are set up behind the campfire as if it is a preacher's platform. Five couples are sprawled across the benches and on blankets strewn haphazardly around the campfire, and none of them pay Jake and Aiden any attention; they are transfixed by Oscar, who is halfway through a sensuous fire poi routine set to an intense country rock song.

The poi he uses are made of steel wool so his every weave and reel results in a cascade of sparks, and as the song builds and builds toward a thumping, insane crescendo, Oscar raises his arms up over his head and spins the poi together. Sparks shower down around him, carpeting the ground and eliciting gasps from the girls sitting just in front of Jake with their arms wrapped around one another. Jake and Aiden applaud and cheer along with everyone else, laughing at Oscar's theatrical entertainer's bow. He unwinds the poi from his hands and tosses them to the side as they burn out, and a small, curvy girl with blue curls that bounce as she walks takes his place. She carries two five-pronged pyro fans that Jake eyes enviously, and while she works herself through a few warmups, Oscar jogs over.

"Jake! So glad you came," he says, slightly out of breath. His vaguely Swedish accent melts Jake a little. Oscar shoots him an infectious smile, takes a seat and turns his attention to Aiden. "And you must be the boyfriend Jake was telling me about. I'm Oscar."

"Aiden," he says, shaking the hand Oscar holds out. He throws a look Jake's way that is a mixture of confusion and surprise, and Jake finally understands what it means to wish that a chasm would open up beneath his feet. He prays for a change of subject.

"How long have you guys been together?" Oscar asks, glancing between them with an easy openness. Jake curses his luck.

"You tell him, sweetheart," Aiden says, nudging his side. *Oh, he's just loving this.*

Jake sucks in a deep breath to keep from committing homicide, forces a smile and says, "We've been best friends since we were kids, but things didn't change, I guess, 'til this trip."

"And you guys are from Maine, right?" Oscar asks. "You just got marriage there?"

Jake bristles even more, mostly at the memory of that walking-on-broken-glass night in Wisconsin, and nods with a tight smile. "You were right, by the way," he says, finally finding the wherewithal to redirect the conversation. "That routine was incredible."

"Ah, it's all in finding the right music," Oscar says, waving off the praise and gesturing to the blue-haired girl. She's warming up with a few basic turns and sweeps, waving the fans up and down in a way that makes it look like she has wings. "Now, Hailey is something else. She's an *artist.*"

"Just like Jake," Aiden interjects, and as he winds his arm around Jake's waist, Jake can't help but smile, even though it's been a long time since he's felt like an artist. "I filmed him for a music video once, and his routines are beautiful."

"You're up next, then," Oscar says, slapping his palms on his knees in way too decisive a manner.

"No, I haven't spun for a couple years," Jake says.

"Not taking no for an answer," Oscar sing-songs, and gets to his feet just as Hailey's fans light up, bright as fireworks. Envy bites once more at Jake's insides; he could swear they're the Pyroterra fans he coveted for months when he was still part of his college fire club. "Come over once she's done and we'll get you set up."

"Okay," Jake says weakly, and after Oscar has left them to join a couple of his friends sitting closer to Hailey, Aiden leans over and kisses him under his jaw.

"Boyfriend, huh?" he asks.

"He was about to hit on me." It isn't a lie, but neither is it the truth. "I had to say *something.*"

He feels rather than sees Aiden's small, knowing smile, hears his murmured, "Okay," and the electricity lingering in his bloodstream has him almost jittering with the itch to spin again, to feel every minute shift of the chains as he creates his own escape of patterns and heat and light.

"What if I've forgotten everything?"

"I'll stand right in front of you, if you want. Pretty good motivation not to fuck up," Aiden offers, but before Jake has even rolled his eyes, he adds,

"Stop second-guessing yourself, and go be an artist. It's who your mom taught you to be."

Struck dumb by the truth of Aiden's words, Jake lets himself relax into his embrace for the rest of Hailey's kinetic light show. And in what seems like no time at all, she is snuffing out her fans and Oscar is beckoning him over. Aiden lightly squeezes his hand, and Jake leaves behind everything except the energy that has been bubbling inside him all day.

He flexes his fingers and rolls his wrists. *Breathe,* he reminds himself as he shakes out his shoulders and rolls his neck, striding over to Oscar. He accepts two poi from a rail-thin teenager Oscar introduces as Sean, and turns to Hailey to congratulate her on her performance.

"Thank you!" she says, bouncing on her toes and clapping her hands. She gestures to the small boom box sitting on a tree stump. "Did you bring music for your routine?"

Jake shakes his head. "I'm woefully underprepared."

"Oh, that's okay! Don't even worry about it, just come with me," she exclaims, her voice high-pitched and friendly and just oozing happiness. She grabs his wrist and leads him over to the dock, picks up her phone and starts scrolling. The screen lights up her face and casts shadows above her killer cheekbones. "What kind of stuff do you like?"

"Anything that has a good beat. Something that makes me feel."

She looks thoughtful, and then snaps her fingers. "I have a couple friends in Vancouver, and they sent me a demo EP for this band called Belle Sigma. I'm obsessed with this one song right now, it's called 'Touchstone.' Fantastic for spinning, especially the regular poi. You can do anything, and it just works."

"Sounds good to me," Jake says. He got used to improvising to whichever songs their group leader picked in college.

She waves him off with a grin, and he moves over to the makeshift performance area; as soon as he nods to her, she hits play. The song begins with almost dreamlike guitars; Hailey gives him a thumbs up as she passes by on her way to a seat, and Jake is suddenly aware of all the eyes on him. He shakes off his nerves as best he can and wraps the poi handles around his hands, lighting them with one swing into the campfire. Then he steps back and takes a deep breath.

"This is the new world, a world full of sin," the lyrics begin, and Jake spins the poi in a simple butterfly formation. "Links to my past keep on lingering. If you'll come with me I'll keep you safe; won't let this go to waste."

The sound of fire whips past him on each spin, and the familiar heat wraps around him; he picks up on the song's instrumental interlude—a plucking of strings as chaotic and treacherous as his own heart—and sweeps up into a four-beat weave, relaxing his body and letting himself move from side to side.

"You are the reason, the past is my rhyme. Take my hand and we'll be lost to time."

Corkscrew reels this time: Jake shortens the chains to spin in front of him and then up over his head. These are easy moves that he could never forget. He concentrates on feeling the music and anticipating the change in beat, which explodes into the chorus: "A step for you but five for me, take everything that I don't need. A touchstone in my shoe, my heart in your hands; we've lost too much but not this love unplanned."

Energy flows through Jake's arms and out into the poi as he leaps onto his toes and into one of his signature variations on a six-petal flower. He pushes the fire away and pulls it back, dancing with it until it feels like an extension of himself. Running the poi at vertical parallels for a transitional float, Jake feels his every nerve aflame; he's invincible, he's on the edge of the world, he's a superhero. The music is for him, just for him, and he's lightning leaping out of a glass jar as he spirals higher and higher into the stratosphere.

As he performs a simple modified alternating barrel roll, leaning back with one leg raised into the air, he catches sight of Aiden—no longer seated but standing at the end of the aisle between the benches. He's transfixed; the weight of his gaze would normally feel heavier than Jake can bear, but this time spurs him on. He dips back as far as he can and rights himself with a scissor kick.

"Darling, we were meant for this; I've been asleep in a different life."

Jake almost stops short but manages to cover with another float; the words catch him off guard and open his eyes all at once to the truth of—of everything. Every last word of encouragement spoken to him over the course of their road trip: Andrew telling him to make the mistakes first; the tour guide in Virginia and Aiden's stepmother thinking they were a couple; Nan leaving no room for argument when informing them that they belonged to one another in North Carolina; Charlie making clear on Thanksgiving what Jake still refused to see; even April's nudging and niggling and outright badgering throughout the first act of what he can no longer deny is a love story.

"A touchstone in my shoe, my heart in your hands; we've lost too much but not this love unplanned."

And then there's Aiden: telling him he had a teenage crush on him in Kentucky; pushing him to sing in Michigan; saving his life in Indiana; forgiving him in Minnesota; confessing his feelings in Wyoming; making love to him in Colorado; holding him together with a single Band-Aid in New Mexico. For all his faults, he's the best person Jake has ever known, and love will either tear them apart or give them a lifelong happiness.

He loses himself—in chasing the sun, in complex, layered butterfly and flower formations, in barrel rolls and windmills and threading the needle—until he's nothing but music and flame.

What lies just around the corner, or in six months from now, or in ten years... none of it matters when Jake is here and Aiden is—

Standing right in front of him, just out of reach of the poi as they flicker out with the song's final fade, watching Jake with a soft, awed smile, as if he's something sacred to behold. There is applause and cheering over the perpetual crackle of the campfire, but Jake's world narrows to Aiden, in the kind of silence that can only be found in the wake of a storm.

It's that small measure of peace he's needed. Some people fall quickly and easily into love, inhaling it like air. Jake has fumbled and tripped his way to the edge of a cliff. He doesn't know what waits at the bottom besides Aiden, but it doesn't matter.

He jumps.

"I love you," he breathes, the extinguished poi hanging limply from his hands.

Aiden freezes. His eyes widen and his lips part, a single puff of white the only sign he's breathing at all. Seconds seem bottomless, and Jake watches and waits for something—anything—to let him know that he hasn't just cast himself into oblivion.

And then Aiden steps forward and pulls Jake to him with crushing force. He rocks onto his toes, presses his forehead to Jake's temple and whispers, "I love you, too."

And Jake lands.

12,464 MILES

DAY EIGHTY-EIGHT: NEVADA

If Aiden's life were a movie, their time in Vegas would be the montage scene.

He can see it all as clear as crystal, so perfectly formed in his mind that he knows every shot, every transition and every angle. He even knows the kind of music he'd use—acoustic, starting with quiet strumming and heartfelt lyrics and building into something thumping and powerful. It would soundtrack the meeting of their lips by the campfire, as Jake drops his extinguished poi to the ground and links their fingers, neither of them heeding the wolf whistles and catcalls of their audience.

The first verse would accompany their hustle back to the RV, fires stoked and engines starting. Fade into smiles across the cab, Aiden's hand riding the air outside the window as they speed west along I-40, a panoramic shot of the hotel room he booked on a whim. Stock shots of the lights and sights of Vegas itself. Jake running down the Strip with Aiden's hand in his, looking for all the world as if this is the happiest he's ever been.

The song's quiet heart and perfect sentiment would help juxtapose shots of soul-deep kisses in dark corners of casinos with fast entrances and exits to each and every gaudy attraction they could find, and the cameras would capture them splitting their sides laughing as they took stupid photos of one another at Tussaud's, Jake complaining about the smell of elephant dung inside the Adventuredome at Circus Circus, them sitting in the mezzanine at Showgirls and loosely holding hands over the armrest and them getting tossed out of the Neon Museum for ditching the guided tour in favor of a heated makeout session behind the dead Stardust sign.

And as the song reached the hushed interlude, the scenes would be of a darkened hotel room and hands knotted in sheets, in hair, tangling before a tight squeeze of release; the gentle caress of Jake's fingers against Aiden's cheek, bringing him drifting downward, back to the earth.

One last series of shots would accompany the song's coda: Jake smiling softly at him from the bathtub through the open bathroom door; splitting a bottle of too-expensive champagne in the bar before returning to their room; fast kisses, laughing kisses, desperate kisses. Everything about the film in his head would be disgustingly cheesy, and Aiden would love every perfect second—because perfect is exactly what the last three days have been. It makes him miss filmmaking in a new way, one that has him scribbling stray thoughts and notes on scraps of paper, humming the riffs and hooks floating through his mind and wanting more than anything to fulfill his and Jake's dream of creating beautiful things together.

"We must be the only two people ever to come to Vegas and not gamble a cent," he muses to a sleepy Jake, who has only just awoken from the doze he fell into after they came back to the hotel room. They were almost drunk, rutting against one another before the door even closed behind them; somehow, they managed to make it to the bed, with a trail of clothes in their wake. Now they lie beneath soft sheets and blankets with all of the lights off but the drapes drawn back from the windows in the hope that they will see the Geminid meteors streaking by. Their hotel is on the outskirts, and the view from the room is nothing but highway and desert, so there's a chance.

"The house always wins," Jake replies. "And besides, I already gambled a lot the other night."

"Nah," Aiden says, scooting down and turning onto his side. "I was a sure thing."

"Exactly," Jake says, looking at him through one eye. "The house always wins."

The pause is comfortable, knowing, the kind that doesn't need to be filled with awkward glances or tentative touches—so much is out in the open, now. The walls have crumbled, leaving not rubble, but a foundation upon which they can build whatever they want. Even without the champagne, Aiden feels giddy.

"So," he says. "We've had two days in Vegas, done every tacky tourist thing we could think of, and you've fucked me every which way to Sunday—and it's only Thursday."

"That about sums it up, yeah," Jake replies. He traces Aiden's lips and kisses each one in turn.

"There isn't anything left that we haven't done?" Aiden asks.

"Not that I can think of."

"No fantasies about going to that drive-through chapel?"

Jake's bark of laughter is music. "Sure, Mr. Cliché, let's do it. I think I have a condom in my wallet from graduation that could be my something old."

"And we have blue M&Ms," Aiden supplies.

"Oh! Maybe you'll let me borrow that tie of yours that I'm never allowed to borrow."

"And I can wear the scarf you bought yesterday."

"Ah, Nevada." Jake sighs almost wistfully. "If only."

"If only," Aiden echoes.

Jake looks at him with a soft, tender smile. After a moment, he licks his lips and asks, "What, are we playing Relationship Chicken now?"

"Well, we both clean up," Aiden jokes, and scoots forward under the covers, sliding his thigh between Jake's.

"Mmm, you in that suit at the wedding," Jake trails off and shuffles up into the contact.

"Yeah?"

"You really have no idea how gorgeous you are, do you?"

Aiden turns his warming face into his pillow, but just as his air is starting to run out, something occurs to him. Grinning, he looks at Jake and says, "You said 'relationship.'"

"Shut up," Jake mutters, dropping his eyes, but his own smile betrays him.

"So... are we boyfriends now?" Aiden teases, ducking to look into his eyes again.

Jake surprises him with a firm kiss and even more with his answer. "That's completely the wrong word for what you are to me. But if we have to use conventional terms, yeah. You're absofuckinglutely my boyfriend."

"Because you love me, and I love you," Aiden murmurs, leaning forward and whispering against his lips, "and we're totally fucking screwed."

"That about sums it up, yeah," Jake repeats, and pulls Aiden in for another of those desperate kisses that have marked the passage of so many moments over the past two days. It's dizzying and disorienting, how Jake claims his mouth as if he never wants to stop, as if he's taking as much as he can because he doesn't know if he'll still have it the next day, week, month, year.

Aiden is breathless when he pulls back, shivering as the AC kicks in, and asks, "So you're sure there's nothing else you want to do while we're here?"

Jake looks thoughtful. He toys with the corner of his pillowcase and says, "There was this art show last year at The Cosmopolitan that I wish I could have seen. I read an article about it."

"Go on," Aiden prompts him.

Jake shifts, extricates his legs from Aiden's and turns around to settle his back against Aiden's chest. "Have you ever noticed that the longer you look up, the more stars you see?"

"We had this exact conversation in July at Thomas Point," Aiden reminds him, slipping one arm beneath his neck and the other around his waist. "What is it about this art show?"

At length, Jake answers, "It was called *Confessions*. The artist set up little booths where people could write their secrets on slips of paper. It was all done anonymously, like voting booths. She collected all of them and pinned them up on the walls. There were hundreds, maybe thousands."

"Sounds pretty cool," Aiden agrees, biding his time; Jake wouldn't bring it up without a reason.

"What would you confess?" Jake asks softly.

"That my life hasn't been the same since they stopped making Double Dip Crunch," he replies blithely, earning a sharp pinch on the thigh. He clears his throat and, as he looks out the window and catches the first meteor darting across the night sky, he hooks his chin over Jake's shoulder and answers honestly, "I realized that I was in love with my best friend while we were watching meteors together in Louisiana."

He expects Jake to tense in his arms, as he has done almost every other time Aiden has whispered the words; it feels almost too good to be true that instead, he simply relaxes further into Aiden's hold, hums happily and says, "That's a good one."

"What about you?"

"We might be here a while."

"I'm listening."

"Okay, well," Jake says, taking a deep breath as if to brace himself. With a small, self-deprecating laugh, he begins, "I once walked in on my best friend jerking off and used it as masturbation fodder for a month."

Prodding him in the ribs, Aiden says, "So I give you this deep confession—"

"Your first one was about *cereal*, so don't even."

"And you respond with, 'I used to jerk off to you.'"

"You were fucking hot, okay? I'm not sorry," Jake says.

"Come on, sweetheart," Aiden says, giving him a cajoling squeeze. "Tell me something real."

"That's my line," Jake jokes. "But okay, um..."

Heavy moments of silence pass, punctuated only by the steady sound of their breathing and the occasional set of footsteps passing by outside the door. When it seems like almost too much time has passed, Aiden says, "It doesn't have to be something monumental."

"I just can't think of anything that you don't already know about me," Jake finally says, his voice quietly surprised. "You were there for so much of it. And I've told you about last year, so..."

"Aiden, you—" Jake stops short to face him. His eyes are shrouded in darkness, but Aiden can feel the weight of them, as if his gaze is something tangible. "You know me better than anyone, better than I know myself, sometimes. And I think what took me so long was that I was terrified of losing you but also terrified of not losing you, of what all this would mean if I let it in."

"We were both scared," Aiden says. "Do you really think I would have let you off the hook in Delaware if I hadn't been?"

"I know, but... if you haven't noticed, I'm kind of obsessed with you." Jake's words come out stilted, almost clumsy, as if he's trying to make sense of them as he speaks. "And it... it made me feel so unsafe, because I've never been like this with anyone else. I've never felt like this, I never thought I was the kind of person who pins their everything on somebody."

"You don't—"

"Dan, can you... just let me try and get this out?"

"Of course."

Jake takes a deep breath and continues, "Some of the things I've put you through on this trip, and you were so patient with me... even the idea of getting to have this with you felt too good to be true, like everything would just go to shit if I let myself think it was a possibility, let alone have the reality. And I'm still kind of terrified, honestly, but it's always going to be you. I couldn't tell you all those years ago, but now? I can't *not* tell you. There's never going to be anybody else. I've been so stupid, and so blind, and I'm sorry it took me so long to get here."

Slowly, eyes fixed on Jake's, Aiden takes Jake's wrists and straddles his hips, pinning him to the bed. Jake is miles of body and skin beneath him, skin that makes Aiden suddenly wish they had factored in a stop at the beach in Goleta for when they get to the West Coast. He would love to drag Jake out swimming and then find his old hideaway cove along the cliff wall, where he could take his time licking the salt from Jake's freckles.

Instead, he entwines their fingers and leans down with parted lips: close, close, closer, and then he is consumed. The door between them is finally open, swinging on its hinges in the wake of a hurricane, and Aiden can feel the brave new world just beyond. Their lips barely brush, but Aiden's heart is racing and there's a tug in his stomach that feels like jolting awake to the sensation of falling. It's panic, pressure, realization; it's hitting the ground running, willingly tumbling headfirst into love.

He kisses Jake, and everything slows down. He can feel Jake's eyelashes against the apple of his cheek, Jake's lips soft and pliant under his own and a fanfare in his heart. He pours his every last drop of hope and fear and adoration and regret into Jake, silently apologizing for the wasted years.

"I love you," is his answer when he pulls back, his voice thick, and his eyes wetter than he can stand.

"I love you, too," Jake breathes, eyes wide and dark as he blinks up at him. "And my confession is that I realized I was in love with my best friend in an abandoned train station in Indiana. Right before he turned into a superhero."

The unexpected, lighthearted addition to the end of Jake's confession washes over Aiden and puts him back together where he briefly came apart—he laughs, and rolls off of Jake with no grace whatsoever as his body shakes.

When he catches his breath, he peeks at Jake through one eye and finds him looking back, tenderness crinkling the corners of his eyes as he reaches for Aiden's hand. His expression is full of warmth, contentment, awe. "This is going to be awesome, right? It's the start of something really, really great?"

Sobering, Aiden realizes where he's heard the words before—he said them to Jake over three months ago, sitting on Jake's back deck and counting the fireflies—and as Jake curls his fingers around Aiden's thumb, he replies, "I think maybe we're already in the middle of something really, really great."

"So what happens next?"

Drawing closer, just as Jake does every night even if they've fallen asleep with a gulf between them, he cups Jake's jaw and slides his hand back. His thumb fits into the groove behind Jake's ear like it's a space made just for him, just to be doing this. "You just have to be with me," he says. "We can figure the rest out later."

And as Jake meets his kiss, smiling into it with complete abandon, Aiden can practically hear the strains of a love theme picking up. They're only just getting started.

12,751 MILES

CHAPTER 10

DAY NINETY: CALIFORNIA

"I don't understand," Jake says as they draw closer to the neon-lit archway beckoning them onto Santa Monica Pier.

"What?"

"I don't understand. Why isn't it cold?"

"Sweetheart, this *is* cold," Aiden says, wrapping an arm around his waist and giving him an easy smile.

"We come from *Brunswick*," Jake counters. "It's *December*. This is *not* cold."

"Okay, you win," Aiden says. He chuckles and pulls Jake closer, away from the crowds milling on the sidewalk. He asks, "Isn't it kind of strange, suddenly being around this many people all at once?"

"Sort of," Jake says, casting his eyes around the pier and attempting to separate the snowbirds and tourists from the locals.

"Doesn't it feel great, though? Getting out of the RV for a few days, I mean."

They're staying at Matthew's ostentatious home on Georgia Avenue while he's in New York on business, scouting fresh talent for some new movie his company has optioned. While Jake is happy about the simple prospect of staying still, the rest of it leaves him a little ill at ease. Nothing is different—and yet everything is. They're happy, yet the ground still moves beneath them. Jake feels oversaturated, filled up and wrung out over and over. He can't seem to settle inside the love, not until things are certain, until "what happens on the road trip stays on the road trip" is but a distant, laughable memory.

And the crux of the matter: They're now doing all of this under the laser-focused gazes of everyone they know.

"Well, I don't intend on setting foot back inside until we have to," he finally answers; leaving the messy sheets and lived-in surroundings of the RV is a balm.

"Aw, you don't like my digs? I'm wounded," Aiden declares, palm to his heart, a comical look of shock and exaggerated hurt on his face.

Jake smiles but doesn't hold his gaze, focusing instead on the sea of faces and bodies around them as they turn into Pacific Park. Lights flash brightly under the dark sky and music plays from somewhere in the direction of the Ferris wheel.

"Hey," Aiden murmurs. "What's up?"

"Nothing, I just..." Jake shakes his head and shoves his hands in his pockets before finally meeting Aiden's eyes and saying, "We went public."

Aiden's tone is cautious as he replies, "We did. Should we not have?"

"No, I'm glad we did," he says. "It's just... you saw the texts."

"I did."

"*All* of the texts. There were a *lot* of texts. And April won't stop poking me on Facebook. I mean, who even pokes on Facebook anymore?"

"It's a lot of pressure," Aiden says, looking for the first time as if he's feeling it, too.

"Oh, thank *god*," Jake groans, unable to suppress the urge to turn and kiss Aiden; he barely cares that they're surrounded by people, because here they're wonderfully anonymous. Aiden's lips still taste of the lemon sorbet they shared after dinner, feeding each other with sundae spoons at the glossy walnut bar in Matthew's kitchen.

When he pulls away, Aiden asks, "Did you think you were the only one feeling it?"

"Yeah, actually."

"Why?"

Jake runs his fingers over the soft ridges of the thick cable knit cardigan Aiden is wearing, the one he nabbed from Jake's side of the closet this morning. "Do you understand why I fought against it all for so long?"

"Of course I do," Aiden says. "I was scared, too."

Shaking his head, eyebrows knitted together, Jake says, "But you always seemed so sure."

"Come with me," Aiden says quietly, taking his hand and pulling him over to an empty bench opposite the ticket booth; when Jake sits down, his hand clasped between both of Aiden's own, the wood is still warm from its last occupants. "I was sure of how I felt, that much is true. But sure of what you'd do? Honestly, I've never been less sure."

"So how did you... in Wyoming, you just—"

"I was sick of biting my tongue every time I wanted to say it. I was still terrified of ruining us and what we had, but I couldn't keep pretending," Aiden says. His thumb rubs Jake's knuckles, back and forth, back and forth. "And I don't think you could, either. Right?"

"Right. I mean, I've never been so scared in all my life. Still am, a little bit."

"Why?"

"It was always more than just putting us and our friendship in jeopardy. It was..." Jake pauses, averts his eyes and then forces himself to confront his instinct to run, and talks. "I was scared that you'd just leave again."

Aiden's thumb stops moving, and his grip on Jake's hand tightens. "Jake, I wouldn't—"

"Because I honestly think that I'd lose it if you did," Jake interrupts, words flowing irrepressibly now that he's started. "It took me this long to trust you again, Dan. And now there are all these people who want to know everything, and all *I* want to know is that... that I'll still have something to tell them when we get home."

Aiden stares at him for a moment as a muscle works in his jaw. "You've needed to say that to me for a while, haven't you?" At Jake's sheepish nod, he shifts closer and says, "Jake, I'm not going home—I *am* home. It's been right in front of me for nearly seventeen years. It just took me a while to figure it out."

Shaking his head in near disbelief, Jake's breath leaves his body in a shaky release he has been building up to ever since Aiden came back from London.

His eyes sting and he blinks rapidly, and even as he looks away, Aiden ducks right back into his line of sight.

"Sweetheart," he says, his tone solemn, "I've got you, remember?"

"You really do, don't you," Jake says, awed.

Aiden rolls his eyes and tucks two fingers beneath Jake's chin, gently guiding his gaze upward. Looking at him with an expression so painfully earnest and full of tenderness that Jake worries he might unravel, he says, "Always."

"I love you," Jake whispers, pitching forward to wrap his arms around Aiden's shoulders and pull him close. Aiden's fingers are still tucked under his chin, and his arm gets caught between them; his laugh is muffled against Jake's shoulder until they break apart.

"I love you, too," Aiden says, reaching for Jake's hand and linking their fingers. "Now, come on. We've got a first date to finish."

Jake wants to poke fun at the idea that this is a first date as they get in line for ride tickets, but as he considers the notion, he realizes that it's exactly how they've spent their day—albeit with a little more spice than most first dates, given that they made out in the back of Matthew's home movie theater for most of *Fight Club.*

Nevertheless, after they've bought enough tickets to get them on each ride at least once, he says, "I'm not sure this qualifies as a first date."

"Dinner and a movie. It totally qualifies," Aiden replies, swinging their joined hands as they set off toward the Ferris wheel.

"Ah, but we did it backward," Jake says.

"What haven't we done backward?" Aiden points out, and Jake smiles despite himself. "You know, I never realize how much I miss California until I come back."

"You finally got me here."

"And I can finally go on the Ferris wheel."

"What?" Jake asks. "You've visited Matt about a million times and you've never been here?"

"Of course I have. I was just saving the Ferris wheel for you."

They join the back of the short line beneath the giant wheel and Jake smiles to himself, thinking back to all the years they spent going to the annual bazaar at St John's. They would hold hands until they got to the top of the wheel, where they would each tell a secret. At twelve, it was, "Tommy didn't steal that cupcake from your lunchbox; it was me." At fifteen, it was, "I kinda have a crush on Drake." At twenty-one, Jake smiled and said, "I missed you," instead of, "Holding your hand feels strange and different and I can't figure out why."

Once they're seated and the guardrail is settled across their laps, Jake shifts close to Aiden and is reaching for his hand when Aiden's cell rings, blaring at top volume.

"I thought I'd set it to vibrate," Aiden says with an apologetic look as he pulls it out of his pocket. His brow furrows. "It's Matt. Do you mind if I..."

Jake waves him off with a smile, turning his attention to the view out over the bay as they rise into the air and the hundreds of lights sparkling over the water. He rests his head on Aiden's shoulder and sighs, tuning out everything save for his newfound sense of peace. It all seems to be falling into place—*finally, finally, I love you, finally*—and that torn seam of theirs is already resewn, the stitches doubled and trebled by the last three months.

"Yes, Matt, we got the video message. How did you even—never mind. I still don't get why you can't just text me like a normal person..."

He feels Aiden's fingers thread through his own as they inch slowly higher and considers what he'll say when they get to the top. He's already given away all of his secrets.

"No, that's—Matt, that's amazing! Okay, I'll... yeah. Yeah, I'll talk to Jake and let you know."

At the sound of his name, Jake sits upright in his seat. The gondola rocks back and forth and he looks at the neon colors playing across Aiden's face.

Aiden squeezes his hand and asks, "What's your secret?"

"I don't have any left."

"Looks like we need a new tradition, then."

"What did Matt say?" Jake prompts. Aiden glances down at the park from their vantage point at the top of the wheel.

"That movie he's just optioned, it..." Aiden pulls his hand from Jake's and scratches the back of his neck, looking at him sidelong. "He wants us both to come out here and work on it. Production assistants."

"I—what?" Jake splutters. "But we just graduated."

"I guess when he said fresh talent, he meant the crew as well as the cast," Aiden says, his tone full of disbelief. "He said he can't talk too much about it, but he'll give us more information if we're interested."

This is it, Jake thinks, his mind suddenly awash in a new kind of hope. He needs a plan, something concrete that doesn't ebb and flow like the never-ending stream of road lines disappearing beneath the RV. He needs certainty, to know that there is something more for them after they return to Maine on the same itchy feet with which they left. *This is what we've been waiting for.*

He looks at Aiden with wide eyes, reaching for his hand and finding a loose fist into which he burrows his fingers. He needs a grounding touch to keep from letting the heady drama of Matthew's announcement get to him.

Then, his stomach drops in a way that has nothing to do with the Ferris wheel's soft lurch downward. "But we're going to New York."

Aiden says nothing.

"I mean… what do you want to do?"

"Do *you* want to do it?" Aiden asks.

No more secrets. "Yes."

"What if…" Aiden shifts uncomfortably in his seat for a moment. "What if I told you that I don't know which one I want more?"

"I'd say that's okay."

"What if I told you that I'm scared I'll fail at whichever one I pick?"

"I'd say that's okay, too," Jake reassures him. "Look, we can't stop each other from failing, but we can pick each other up when we do. I've got you just as much as you've got me."

Aiden smiles at that. "I think I might want to, but it's big. Can you give me some time?"

"Of course, silly," Jake says, and leans over to press his forehead against Aiden's temple. For longer than he cares to remember, he's been picking the lock of his own joy, slowly feeling for the tumblers and gradually letting them click into place. Aiden is the only man who has ever given him joy without that bite of sorrow—he can have all the time he wants.

They're quiet for a while after that, Aiden obviously deep in thought about the choice before him. They don't speak again until after Jake has ducked out of the line for the West Coaster to look at a rack of key chains. He finds one so serendipitously perfect that he buys it immediately, not caring about the inflated price, and takes it back to Aiden.

Pressing it into his palm, Jake simply says, "Whatever you decide."

Aiden examines the keychain: heavy pewter in the shape of the United States, with one heart punched into New York and another into California, a dotted line connecting them.

Jake yelps as Aiden wraps an arm around his waist and dips him, crushing their lips together in a kiss that Jake can feel in his toes.

"I love you so much," he whispers, and as Aiden straightens, pulls them back upright and silently steps away with a beaming smile, all Jake can dazedly think is, *I am Jack's heart, grown three sizes bigger.*

13,045 MILES

DAY NINETY-FIVE: OREGON

"Seriously, whose idea was it to try and do this in a hundred days?" Aiden grumbles to his reflection as he struggles with his tie—he can usually do this in his sleep, but all of his attempts so far have been in vain.

"Let me," Jake says, moving in front of him and batting his hands away. He, of course, is impeccably turned out, his top two buttons open at his throat and his hair swept into an effortless mess of tufts and spikes that Aiden wants to tug. He quickly sets about his task, his long fingers deftly undoing Aiden's crooked handiwork. "You don't usually get worked up like this. We haven't even gone past fashionably late yet."

"You can't get an RV from Crater Lake to Portland in four hours," Aiden mutters, fists flexing uselessly at his sides. "We should have left earlier; fuck what Kathy Bates had to say."

"That's why you're annoyed, yes, but I'll bet that's not why you're nervous," Jake says, giving Aiden a knowing look. "So what's up?"

Aiden drops his head to look down at his feet, but Jake gently nudges his chin back up. "Why did he have to make me the guest of honor? I barely even did anything."

"You gave him the idea."

"What if he wants me to make a speech?"

"Aiden, come on. It's just Josh."

"He's not 'just Josh,' he's—"

"I know, I know, you've hero-worshipped him ever since our first AV club meeting," Jake says. "With his perfect hair and his perfect teeth and his perfect calves..."

"Bitter, much?" Aiden teases. Jake raises an eyebrow at him, and knots the tie just this side of too tight with a mischievous glint in his eye, but loosens it right away and tugs it this way and that. "Look, I know I'm being ridiculous. But he's one of the people who got me through high school, you know? He was always there for me, and sure, okay, maybe I looked up to him, but... it's *Josh*."

"He's always been talented, I'll give him that," Jake concedes. "But babe, you interned for a year under Dmitri Serafino and I never once saw you like this."

"'Babe,' huh? I like that," Aiden says. Jake smirks at him and pulls the knot taut, gives it one last pat and brushes off Aiden's shoulders. "I've just never been the guest of honor at anything before. And the wedding doesn't count; you were right next to me."

"And I'll be right next to you for this, dummy," Jake replies.

"I think I liked 'babe' better."

Jake moves behind him to tug the hem of his jacket straight, then looks at his reflection in the mirror and nudges his shoulder. "Wanna know a secret?"

"Sure," Aiden says, fiddling with his cuffs and casting an appraising glance down at himself.

"I'm nervous, too," Jake says. "I've never been the *arm candy* before."

Rolling his eyes, Aiden says, "It's not some big red carpet thing."

"Exactly," Jake says, quiet but triumphant, and Aiden smiles despite the butterflies in his stomach.

In truth, Aiden is nervous not just because they're about to attend the first and only public screening of Josh's documentary—the idea for which Aiden gave him, in a series of emails back and forth around spring break—but also because Josh has always taken on the role of big brother with Aiden, and has the uncanny ability to know when he's agonizing about something. Josh is going to read him like an open book, and Aiden isn't sure that he's ready to face the well-meaning interrogation that comes with it. The decision he now faces, between New York and Los Angeles, is consuming almost his every waking moment as he weighs pros and cons, envisions possible futures and tries not to think about what will happen if he decides on New York. When he told Jake back in Vegas that they would figure out the rest later, he didn't exactly count on "the rest" showing up to knock on a moving door.

"Come on," Jake murmurs, taking his hand and squeezing it. "We're about to be very *un*fashionably late."

After casting one final glance at himself in the mirror—with no dress code, they've decided to go all out and wear the same suits they wore to Toby's and Andrew's wedding—Aiden follows Jake out of the RV.

It's a chilly evening, and the breeze makes him grateful for the parking spot they've been able to claim just one block from the theater. The small sign above the door reads, *DECEMBER SHOWS: 20th — KIDS I USED TO KNOW,* and for a moment, a swell of pride quells Aiden's nerves. Then Jake is whispering, "I love you, I *love* you," before all but pushing him through a set of double doors bearing a poster for Josh's film.

Inside the Alberta Rose Theatre, two clusters of hanging white globes provide the only illumination save for the single spotlight trained on Josh, who stands center stage. Aiden blinks, surprised at how long his hair has gotten—he used to wear it close-cropped, and now it falls in tousled, coppery waves almost to his shoulders. He's dressed as Aiden remembers, in smart jeans and a plaid shirt, but he wears glasses now, with thick horn-rimmed frames that take up half his face.

"Speak of the devil!" Josh's voice rings out through the small theater—packed to capacity, Aiden sees, and pride surges in his chest. "Ladies and gentlemen, Mr. Aiden Calloway!"

The audience applauds, and Aiden's face grows hot as an usher appears at his side to direct them to the only two open seats, right in the front row. At the sudden attention, he has a wild urge to laugh or give a thumbs up or do a dance—the very reason he prefers being behind the camera—and the only thing that keeps him in check is Jake's unfaltering grip on his elbow.

Once they are seated and the applause has died down, Josh continues, "Now that we're all here, I'd like to officially introduce *Kids I Used To Know,* and to thank everyone who played a part in getting us here to the Alberta Rose.

"As I was saying, the idea for this film can be traced back to this guy right here," he says, pointing at Aiden with the same smile that used to make his knees weak. "We were emailing over spring break this year, commiserating about having to get jobs after graduation, and he said, 'At least we know what we wanna do. How many people do *you* know that have no idea? Because I know a lot of them.' So, Aiden, without you I'd probably still be roping high school drama clubs into shooting fan-written episodes of *Firefly*."

The audience laughs, a few people catcall from the back, and Aiden grins up at his friend, his nerves dissipating with Josh's easy, self-deprecating humor. Aiden has missed him.

"Well, now that I've test-driven my Oscar acceptance speech," Josh continues, pausing for more laughter, "thank you all for coming. The bar is open afterward and there'll be karaoke, so have fun. And now, I present to you all a labor of blood, sweat, tears and love: *Kids I Used To Know*."

With that, Josh nods to the back of the theater and jogs off to the side of the stage, out of the way of the giant screen. The lights dim and the film begins.

Josh has scored the opening with a soft, haunting piano piece that has a false brightness to it, and it flows perfectly beneath slow motion B-roll shots of students studying in libraries, sitting in lectures and walking around campus laden with textbooks. The introduction is short, as is Josh's style; he hasn't wasted any time grandstanding, simply provided enough footage to get his sparse opening credits out of the way.

"Do you know what you're doing after college?" Josh's voice asks; he's offscreen, holding out a mic to a willowy black girl who holds a stack of books that look as if they weigh more than she does.

"I'm majoring in philosophy, man, I've got no idea," she offers, and though there is laughter in her tone, the camera zooms in for a close-up of her troubled expression.

The first series of clips progresses in this way—Josh asks students about their post-college plans, and the majority of them are unable to give a firm answer. There's an interview with a professor who tells him, "So many kids go to college not knowing what they want to do, and even those who *do* figure it out while they're here, well… I see too many of them end up at Starbucks or in a McJob. We're not preparing them, giving them the tools they need to figure out what they really want to do, or to get the jobs they want. The system is broken."

Aiden grows increasingly uncomfortable as the documentary continues, with Josh revisiting a few of the same students at the beginning of the summer and then again in the fall to see how they're faring in the "real world."

"We all think that we're gonna do better than our parents did, you know?" one guy says as Josh interviews him in a café. He's wearing a Best Buy uniform; earlier in the film, he was shown graduating summa cum laude with a degree in business. "We tell ourselves that we're not gonna repeat the same mistakes and wind up in dead-end jobs, going nowhere. But when there are so few opportunities out there, what can you do except try to survive and hope that 'better' is somewhere around the corner?"

Right there is the heart of Aiden's dilemma: what he thinks he should do versus what he wants to do. The two are tangled around one another in such a mess that he can no longer find the end of either thread. What he thinks he should do—move to L.A. and work on the movie—means getting most of what he wants: a place to be with Jake; his lifelong passion, kickstarted into a career; a shitty first apartment and a Saturday trip to IKEA to spend too much money on a couch and bedroom set. But what he *wants* is the music, for it to flow out of him in more than just pockets of downtime. Jake ignited his inspiration in Vegas and has been unwittingly feeding it ever since, spurring Aiden to write a song that he hadn't known was inside him.

Faced with so many students who graduated only to be let down by the real world, or left with degrees they can't use, Aiden feels selfish for even considering it.

The documentary lasts just under an hour, but it's as if Aiden merely blinks and it's coming to an end in snatches of dialogue from disillusioned graduates playing over the music from the beginning. The final shot is a closing door that fades to black, ready for the credits.

As the lights come back up, Aiden swallows around the lump in his throat and joins in the applause, rising to his feet along with everyone else. He doesn't want to become a kid that Josh used to know, doesn't want to lay to waste all he's been working for in pursuit of a maybe. He doesn't want to diminish in the perpetual cycle of work, sleep, work, sleep to support a dream that perhaps he'll realize, but more than likely will keep on the backburner until he has decidedly missed his shot.

And then Jake turns to him, eyes shining with warmth and love before pulling him into a fierce hug, and Aiden is struck with a sudden clarity, seeing the future as if he's living it right now: the lights coming up at the end of the first movie they make together, their names rolling up the screen in white text, the audience cheering and clapping for *them*. It's what they've always wanted, what they've always talked about...

Why does it have to be right now? he thinks, the threads untangling with the simple embrace and the memory of flickering firelight. For so long, he convinced himself that all of this is transitory, their journey compounding his thoughts into days and miles and drive time rather than the lifetime at his feet. *Mom's on her third career; nothing's forever. We've got time. I've got time.*

"Josh!" Jake exclaims, cutting through Aiden's thoughts. He rises on tiptoe to hug their old friend. "You've definitely come a long way from the *Firefly* stuff."

"Well, we thought about featuring some aspiring space cowboys, but they've always got Comic Con," he jokes, and looks down at Aiden. He seems to tower even higher over him than usual. "What did you think?"

"It was incredible, Josh. Really," he says, holding Josh's damnably inquisitive gaze. "Honestly, I'd never have thought something like that could come out of an email whining about college."

"All you, my man," Josh says. He pulls Aiden in for his standard 'bro hug,' one hand clasping Aiden's and the other thumping the back of shoulder. Smiling slyly down at them with one eyebrow raised when he steps back, he adds, "And I hear congratulations are in order."

"Yes, thank you, we know it was a long time coming," Jake says. "When were you betting on it happening?"

"Actually, I was the last holdout," Josh says. "I figured you'd be at least twenty-five, you both had your heads so far up your asses."

"Thanks for the vote of confidence, man," Aiden says with a laugh, and punches his shoulder for good measure.

"I call 'em like I see 'em, you know that," Josh says, holding up his hands. He takes a long look at Aiden—too long and way too curious for his liking—and Aiden's stomach ties itself into a knot. "Since we're on the subject, what have you got planned for after the road trip?"

"Old habits die hard," Aiden says, stalling for time. He hesitates only briefly, but it's enough; he can see that shift in Josh's expression, the drawing back of his shoulders that means he's getting ready to hand out life advice like he's the Dalai Lama. Though the decision is new and he's barely had time to try it on for size, Aiden announces, "Matt's asked Jake and me to come out to L.A. and work on a movie his company is producing, so we're set."

Aiden feels Jake's posture go ramrod straight, and when he looks at him, a smile is spreading across his face like rays of sunlight breaking through heavy clouds.

"That's great, man," Josh says. "God, that's fantastic! I don't know many others who fell almost straight into a job, especially film students."

"I'd be stupid not to take it," Aiden says, "and L.A. is great, so why not?"

"Hey, man," Josh says. "That's the dream, am I right? I mean, sounds like you're both following your hearts or whatever."

Snaking his arm around Jake's waist, Aiden says, "We are."

"That's awesome. You guys deserve it," Josh tells them, as a voice Aiden doesn't recognize calls Josh's name from the other side of the theater—it looks like he might be off the hook. "Come on, there's a few people I want you to meet."

Over the course of the next hour, Josh introduces them to more people than Aiden can keep track of, including a group of five girls engaged in a heated debate over which versions of the *Lord of the Rings* movies were better, the theatrical or the extended. Unable to help getting sucked in when he hears one of the girls saying, "The theatrical versions are better because they're *shorter*," he loses Jake to the crowd, but looks for him every so often. He notices that Jake is standing straighter and smiling and gesturing more freely while he speaks to people whose names Aiden has already forgotten. He looks happy.

Eventually, when most of the girls have agreed to disagree and two have been whisked away by significant others, Aiden catches Jake's eye. He's sitting near the back, jacket removed, sleeves rolled up, and he's looking right at Aiden, smiling softly as his finger circles the rim of his glass. Aiden climbs the shallow incline without a second thought, gravitating toward Jake as if he's being physically reeled in.

Resting against the seat in front of Jake's, he asks, "What are you thinking about?"

"All of us in the AV club were pushing so hard to get out of Maine, and look at us now. You, me, Josh," Jake says, and sip at his drink. "We made it."

"Ah, Josh was always going to make it. He was gone before the ink on his diploma was dry."

"He had something to prove after how hard he had to fight for that full ride."

Aiden nods and glances back at the front row; Josh is surrounded by a group of men and women. The girlfriend Aiden recognizes from Facebook pictures is sitting in his lap.

"If New York is where you want to be, I'll go with you," Jake blurts, catching Aiden off guard as he always does.

He turns to look at Jake. "What did you just say?"

Jake sits up straighter in his seat, sets his drink on the floor and clears his throat. "I said that I'll go with you to New York. If you'll have me."

Aiden blinks and crosses his arms over his chest, as if it will stop his heart from beating right out of it. "Jake, of *course* I would, but... I mean, when you mentioned it in Santa Monica I didn't think..."

"You didn't think I was serious, I know," Jake says. "But I am."

It's too much to take in, too much to hold inside. It's everything he wants, but it's selfish, selfish, selfish. "No, Jakey. No, I want to work on this movie, and I want to be with you, wherever you are."

"I don't want you to do this for *me,* though." Jake's eyes shine brightly, his intent as pure and clear as sunrise. "I want it to be what's right for you."

"*You're* what's right for me. And you're one reason—not the whole reason," Aiden says, wrapping his fingers around Jake's arm. The gesture is as much an attempt to ground himself as it is to assure Jake. "I'm doing this for me. Honestly, I feel like L.A. is where I'm supposed to be right now. And I meant what I said to Josh; I'd be stupid to turn down an opportunity like that. Come on, Jakey. Even if it turns out to be a movie about killer shrimp from outer space, it's a dream gig."

"Oh god, I hope it's not killer shrimp," Jake says, scrunching his nose. He shakes his head. "You're *really* sure?"

"What, you need me to convince you?" Aiden teases, hoping his distraction gambit is working. *Anything, I'll do anything, as long as you believe me.* "Should I sing you that love song now?"

"Only if you let me sing it with you. We're a team, aren't we?" Jake looks as if he's expecting Aiden to roll his eyes and tell him of course they are, they always have been and always will be. And once again, Aiden can see that his tactics have worked, that Jake is diverted and the topic has been left in the dust. This time, relief makes him bend down to grab Jake's collar and pull him up for a crushing kiss. His lips tingle with the taste of Tequila Sunrise that lingers on Jake's tongue and at the corners of his mouth.

"Let's do it, then," Jake says breathlessly, looking up at him with a playful smirk.

"You wouldn't rather..." Aiden tugs at the fistful of collar in his hand. "Get out of here?"

Jake takes a step back, opening his eyes comically wide. "Aiden Calloway, are you trying to pass up the chance to be onstage? It's like you're a different person. Are you feeling okay?"

Aiden intercepts Jake's hand on its way to his forehead, threads their fingers together and gestures toward the stage. "After you."

It's a heady feeling, taking a step back to look at everything through a director's eyes once more as they hit the stage and take up their microphones. He can see exactly how everything would play out on a big screen—which angles would be used to capture the happiness in Jake's eyes; exactly which second the lights would catch on Josh's watch, drawing Aiden's attention so he catches Josh's suggestive wink; cuts to the knowing little glances he and Jake exchange as they sing to each other.

They're together now, and Aiden wants to laugh at how scared they've both been, how uncertain he has allowed himself to be even just tonight. If he'd known this was waiting for them all those years ago, he would have taken Jake to Dairy Frost when they were fourteen and reached for Jake's hand over the weathered Formica tabletop. He would have slow-danced with him at prom instead of quietly judging everyone else and nursing a cup of the cliché spiked punch. He would have recognized forever when it was standing right in front of him.

The song ends, Jake kisses the corner of Aiden's mouth and finally, standing on the stage of an old theater in Portland, Aiden comes home.

14,091 MILES

DAY NINETY-SEVEN: WASHINGTON

"Dan, I'm pretty sure I won't lose my mind in the few hours you're forcing us to spend apart so that you can go hang out with my ex-boyfriend," Jake deadpans, holding up the pair of rubber gloves he's about to put on and adding, "That is, unless you *want* to stay and help me clean. I still maintain that you cheated."

"You can't cheat at beer pong," Aiden says.

Jake snorts. "Getting naked isn't exactly regulation."

"It got warm," Aiden says, exaggeratedly earnest. "You were welcome to remove clothing as well."

"Still. Tipping the water bottle over yourself was a little much. This isn't *Flashdance.*"

"Well, you were winning. You know what that does to me."

"Ha! So you're admitting it!" Jake crows. Aiden has the decency to look shamefaced.

"It's not like *you're* totally innocent," he says, moving closer and backing Jake against the kitchen counter.

"Don't know what you mean," Jake says, squarely meeting Aiden's gaze, chin up and finger raised. "Choose your next words very carefully. Remember, I'm the one cleaning this place up so we can have her tidy for the drive home."

"Excited?" Aiden asks, leaning into him and setting his arms atop Jake's shoulders.

"Ready, I think," he says. "It's been kind of insane, to say the least. But I think I'm just ready to start everything. With you."

"See, now you're making me want to stay and take you back to bed," Aiden says.

"Always an option," Jake says wistfully, fingers dancing along Aiden's hip. "But no, go have fun with Brad the Great Deflowerer."

Aiden tips his head back and laughs, and the sound fills the kitchen. "And you're sure it's not weird?"

Jake nods. "I'm sure. Now go, I've got better things to do."

"Okay." Aiden grins and presses a kiss to Jake's mouth before casually tossing over his shoulder, "Love you!"

"Love you, too!" Jake calls after him, and once the door to the RV has closed with a soft click and he has watched Aiden walk away, his hair golden under the yellow lamps of the campground outside, Jake closes all of the blinds and gets to work.

It's a few hours before he finally takes a breather, and if he'd known there would be so much to do, he might not have bet the beer pong match on it. Both of them got into pretty good habits their first year at Bowdoin when they roomed together in the dorm, but by the time he finishes scrubbing the shower door, he's sweating and cursing Aiden for distracting him into losing.

He collapses onto the couch, then pulls off his gloves and sets them aside to dig his phone from between the couch cushions; he wants to see if he can finally beat level forty-eight of the game he's been stuck on for the past week and a half. But now that he's started to clean, all he can see around him is mess; he can't focus on the game with piles of papers haphazardly strewn across their small dining table and the plethora of empty food wrappers lying all over the kitchen counter. Sighing, he sets his phone back down and stands, stretching out his arms and cracking his back as he goes.

He takes a single step toward the dining table and promptly trips over the strap of his rucksack where it lies on the floor by his feet. Stumbling forward, he sends the papers on the table flying but manages to grab onto the back of the chair and keep himself upright. The papers fall to the floor with a *thunk,* which catches Jake's attention; as he rights himself, he drops into a crouch and moves the papers aside to uncover Aiden's black notebook, lying open and face up.

I'm going to miss the road, and all the incredible things Jake and I have seen together, he reads, eyes widening, *and I might have finally figured out that music and composing are what I want the most, but going to L.A. is the right thing to do—for both of us.*

Jake slams the journal closed with far more force than necessary and stands, looking down at its unassuming black cover. He presses his hands together in front of his face and starts pacing around the living room, his thoughts coming a mile a minute. Why did he have to see that journal entry *now?*

He's known about Aiden's journal since the early part of their trip and has never once given in to his intense curiosity, but now he needs to know more, needs to know everything. Jake picks up the journal along with the mess of papers on the floor, sits down at the table, flips open the journal to the most recent entry and works his way back from there.

The latest ones are happy and filled with Aiden's lighthearted humor; they have Jake smiling; tension drains from his limbs as he settles back into his chair. But all too soon he's on edge again. Reading their story not only in reverse, but also through Aiden's eyes, is discomfiting, as if he's watching houses being deconstructed into their component parts. The further back he reads, the more Aiden talks about movies—his dream of being 'the director' isn't who he is anymore. Somewhere along the way, Aiden has truly found himself.

Jake gets as far back as Florida and stops. His heart sinks heavily into his stomach.

"What happens now, Dan?" he murmurs, his fingers tracing patterns across the page. The territory is uncharted, and yet again Jake finds himself standing on shaky ground.

He fights off the familiar world-weariness threatening to settle over him and resolves to talk to Aiden about it whenever he returns—in the meantime, he can easily distract himself with tidying the bedroom and packing for their flight to Anchorage tomorrow. So he sets about putting things away and pulling out the warmest things he owns, folding them and placing them on the bed by his open suitcase. Within a matter of minutes he's humming, his troubles put away to be addressed later.

Upon finding one of Aiden's pens in the pocket of the cable knit sweater he'd borrowed in California, Jake smiles. The image of Aiden wrapped up against the almost nonexistent chill finally lets him shake off his lingering unease—that is, until he opens the drawer of Aiden's bedside cabinet to put the pen away.

Inside the drawer are dozens of scraps of paper covered in words and musical notes. Some of them only contain a line or two, while others hold entire verses. And then he finds a single, loose sheet of paper, the words painstakingly written in Aiden's neat, slanting script. A lump rises in Jake's throat, and he scans the page with stinging eyes.

Where am I from if home isn't home
And where am I running to
You've been by my side for the days, for the search
Does my future exist outside you?

I'm afraid of the taking and giving
But I know that safe isn't living

Am I ready to risk being happy?
Though I never grew into my shoes
Feels like I've been moving the mountains
Just to make it on home to the truth:
That you're where my journey began
And the only forever is you

Do you only see the crash and the burn
Or could you see us through my eyes
We've been on this ride for the weeks, for the months
Do you believe in the truth or the lies?

You're afraid of the taking and giving
But don't you know safe isn't living?

Are you ready to risk being happy?
Though you never grew into your shoes
Feels like I've been moving the mountains
Just to make you come home to the truth:
That you're where my journey began

And the only forever is you

We're afraid of the taking and giving
Now we know that safe isn't living

Now we're ready to risk being happy

Though we never grew into our shoes
Feels like we've been moving the mountains
Just to make it on home to the truth:
That I am the score to your movie
And my only forever is you

He reads the entire thing through three times, his grip on the page faltering until the paper falls and lands on the bed. The lyrics ricochet around his mind, and Jake swallows thickly. This is Aiden, the poetry of him finally in motion and so clearly what he is meant to do—Jake sees that now, and he's about to keep Aiden from it. If Matthew hadn't offered them the movie, they would go to New York without question. Instead, Aiden is following Jake to California and accepting a job that isn't his dream, isn't what he's meant to do.

Goddammit, Aiden. I knew you were doing this for me back in Portland, and I let you throw me off.

Jake takes a few deep breaths to stave off the nausea welling in his gut. He casts his eyes around the room, and suddenly it's as if he's back home, running his hands along the uneven mantel over the fireplace. One last look. One for the road.

He runs his fingers over the page and traces circles around the line, *We're afraid of the taking and giving.*

"But what have I given you?" he whispers. Aiden has given too much—and Jake has given nothing. He takes a deep breath, buries his face in his hands and considers. It feels too big, pressing in on him from all sides and leaching air from the room. He wonders again just when everything became so important, so weighted with responsibility.

He sits up, and his eyes land on his suitcase. Then it occurs to him: *This is what I can give you.*

With an eerie sense of calm, Jake retrieves his plane ticket from the folder in the glove compartment, calls a cab to the airport and scribbles a note that he leaves propped in front of the coffeemaker: *You deserve the chance to live your dream and you'll miss out on it if you follow me to California. Please don't do that, Aiden. Not for me. I love you, and I'm sorry.* He reads it over and over again, looking between it and the scraps of paper littered across the bed, the sheets pulled so tight it is as if he and Aiden were never here. Maybe that would have been best, if this is how it has to end... and hasn't that always been the great doubt? That this will end, that they can't possibly see it through without wrecking one another?

The cab arrives just as Jake is looking up SeaTac live departures on the laptop, checking for flights back to Maine. The earliest isn't until mid-afternoon, and now that he's made his decision he needs to be gone as soon as possible, so instead he brings up the details of an earlier flight to Anchorage—April and the band are heading straight back to Brunswick on Christmas Day, after all. Maybe he can hitch a ride with them.

Standing at the door to the RV with his suitcase in hand, Jake takes a long last look, whispers, "Goodbye," and leaves.

He's calm for the entire journey to the airport, even when he realizes that he left flight details open on the laptop and Aiden's papers strewn across the bed. He's calm all the way through the process of rebooking his flight and paying the transfer fee, even when his credit card is declined and he has to pay with most of the cash he has on him. He's calm for the ten minutes he waits to board with the other sleepy passengers on his 3:30 a.m. flight, even when April responds to his text by calling him and yelling at him until he tells her, "My flight gets in at six, so we'll talk about it then."

It isn't until he hands over his boarding pass and turns toward the concourse that it all catches up with him—he hasn't been calm; he's been *numb*—and all it takes is one word.

"Jake!"

He wheels around at the pained voice calling his name from across the gate lounge. Of course it's Aiden's. The expression on his face is pure torture—*I can't do this to you anymore*, Jake thinks—and it seems like one of those awful, clichéd movie moments, the ones in which the music has been building to a crescendo and suddenly dies the moment the two leads see one another again, as if everything can be solved in the quiet simplicity of eyes meeting across a crowded space.

The lyrics branded into Jake's mind, however, don't die. *Am I ready to risk being happy? Feels like I've been moving the mountains. Does my future exist outside you?* Eyes filling with unwelcome tears, Jake shakes his head—imperceptibly to begin with, but harder until the hope in Aiden's eyes darkens into something that makes Jake's gut solidify into a knot so heavy, it feels like setting down roots in the worn carpet of Gate Fourteen.

He ignores the screaming of his every cell, the muscle memory telling him to move toward Aiden and push him into a future that isn't Jake's to decide. Aiden takes one step forward, Jake one step back. Another—*I'm sorry*—and then another—*I'm sorry, I'm so sorry*—and then the fire in Aiden's expression is nothing but an image burning behind Jake's eyelids as he sprints down the concourse.

14,257 MILES

DAY NINETY-NINE: ALASKA
Aiden has had his notebook open for nearly an hour, writing and scribbling and writing and tearing out pages until finally he just writes, *Fuck everything.* After underlining it twice, he pushes the notebook away and rubs a hand over his eyes. It's nearly five a.m., and he's exhausted. But with the torrential downpour of rain battering the RV, not to mention the anger thrumming in his veins, there's no way he can sleep. In all his life he's never experienced such rage—not at Roberto Mancini, not at Jake in Chicago or Minneapolis, not even at his own father. The only thing keeping him from going postal and trashing the RV is the memory of his grandfather that lingers in every square inch of the place.

Now that Jake is gone, there is too much silence. The air is too static. Some of his things still hang in the closet, and he has left behind his toothbrush, and there is some leftover lasagna in the refrigerator; but these are all traces of a love now lost. For the first time, Aiden imagines, really imagines, what his life will be like without Jake, because Jake was right; they won't recover from this. But that isn't what makes Aiden angriest—no, it's the fact that when he imagines his life without Jake, he sees nothing.

Aiden's phone, vibrating on the table, pulls him from his thoughts. When he picks it up, he sees April smiling up at him from the screen.

After a moment's hesitation he answers, "Hey, Flower."

"Hey," she says quietly. "Um... are you okay?"

Aiden snorts. "Who the hell does he think he is?" he spits out, under no illusions that April is in the dark. "He keeps me hanging for months, fucks somebody else to try and get me out of his system or *whatever* the hell that was, and then when he finally gives in like it's some big chore, he up and fucking leaves the day before my birthday."

"Jesus, Aiden," April whispers, and in the background Aiden can hear the sound of a door closing. "What happened?"

"The movies and TV shows lie."

"Okay..."

"They make chasing someone through an airport look a shit-ton easier than it really is," Aiden says, his words trailing into an almost hysterical laugh as he begins to pace the length of the RV. The anger surges up in him anew and he can't dam it up anymore; he has nowhere left to redirect it, so he lets loose. "They wouldn't let me check in using my ticket to Anchorage, so I had to buy a goddamn ticket to Nebraska just to get through security, and then getting through security took forever, and for what?

"For nothing; it was all for fucking *nothing,* because I caught up to him and he *still* left!" Aiden exclaims, voice rising. "And do you want to know the worst part? I don't get it. Nothing happened! I went to hang out with some friends. He was happy when I left, and now he's just gone. So I guess that's it. It's over. What happened on the road trip will stay on the fucking road trip after all."

"Aiden, what the *fuck* is going on?" April asks.

"I was hoping you'd tell me," he says, waving his free hand and letting it drop to hang limp at his side. He stares through into the bedroom, just able to see scraps of paper strewn across the end of the bed. "I guess Jake found the lyrics for a song I've been working on and he just took off, says I shouldn't let him hold me back from my dream—which apparently he knows *so* much better than I do. He says he doesn't want to get in the way of me making music."

"Motherfucker," April says. "That fucking *idiot;* I can't even believe him sometimes."

"Pretty much, yeah. And—actually, no, this is the worst part: it's just like him to take off right before a storm hits. Everything out of SeaTac is delayed and I can't do anything, so I'm just sitting here like a fucking loser," Aiden says. "Is he with you?"

"His flight gets in at six," she says, "and I'm the asshole who said I'd go pick him up. To be honest, I'm tempted to fucking leave him there."

"Don't do that," Aiden says automatically—even with his blood boiling. Sighing again, he says, "You're his best friend. He's gonna need you."

After a pause, she asks, "And what about you?"

"What do you mean, what about me? Game's over, I might as well go home," Aiden says.

"Excuse you, but no. That's not what's going to happen," April says. "No, that is not the Aiden Calloway I know—"

"April."

"You two fucking love each other, okay? And it's more than that; this has been going on for years and I've seen it, fucking everyone has—"

"April."

"And you and Jake are the only ones who have this habit of not seeing what's right in front of your dumb-ass faces."

Aiden drops heavily onto the couch, his exhaustion finally getting the better of him. Pinching the bridge of his nose, he says, "April, I'm so fucking tired. I'm tired, okay? I'm tired of putting myself out there, I'm tired of waiting and being patient, and I'm tired of chasing after him when he's given me no reason to. I mean, honestly, what am I even still doing here? I should have just cut my losses and turned the fucking RV around as soon as I got back."

"Was it worth it?" she asks. "All the putting yourself out there, all the chasing. Did it make you happy?"

Aiden bites down on the inside of his cheek, exhales slowly and wishes he hadn't picked up the phone.

Without waiting for an answer, she continues, "You love him. That's what you're still doing there."

"I wish I didn't. I wish that none of this ever happened."

She scoffs, and he pictures her tossing her hair over her shoulder and tilting her head to look at him from under her eyelashes, one eyebrow raised knowingly. "No, honey, you don't. So what are you going to do now?"

Aiden casts his gaze around the inside of the RV, at the inescapable traces of Jake everywhere, and then closes his eyes against it all. "Maybe I should go back to Brunswick. See if we can talk this all out when he gets back."

"Talking about your *feelings*? What a world," she deadpans.

"Well, what would you suggest?"

"You've still got that ticket to Anchorage, right?"

"*No,*" Aiden says. "I mean—yes, I do. But I'm not chasing after him anymore. If he wants me, he can come fucking apologize."

"Oh my god, you're both as bad as each other!" she exclaims, exasperation so clear in her voice that he feels as if she's just taken him by the ear. "Maybe if both of you had just stopped being such guys about this whole thing and actually, you know, *talked* to each other from the start, we wouldn't even be having this conversation right now."

"Yes, April, I get it. Okay? We've both been dumb as shit," Aiden says, and then takes a deep breath and lets his indignation roll off of him. "So... you're telling me to come to Anchorage."

"I'm not telling you anything." Her tone is far gentler this time, and he pictures her taking the seat next to his and squeezing his shoulder in that comforting way of hers. "I'm just saying that you already have the ticket, and I don't think this is over until it's over. And..."

"And what?"

"And maybe you should go play your song. The one you've been writing. And then... then do whatever you need to do," April says. "I'll be here for you whatever happens, you know that."

"I know," Aiden says. With a faint smile, he adds, "Thanks, Flower."

After they hang up, Aiden trudges into the bedroom, fighting off a yawn and blinking to keep himself awake. Way too much has happened over the past few hours for him to process, too much to even leave space to care that Jake found his song. He brushes most of the scraps of paper off the sheets and watches them flutter to the floor, hating the fact that his anger is slowly dissipating and leaving behind a terrible, scarring ache—Aiden *misses* him, and what he hates the most is, if he'd known their last kiss would be their last, he wouldn't ever have stopped.

He collapses onto the bed and stares up at the ceiling until it blurs. He sees himself in Philadelphia, shell-shocked, Jake curling into him and falling asleep; in West Virginia, frantic, Jake's fingers twisting inside him. The rain hammers dully on the roof and the windows, and the taste of his single cocktail has long since turned stale in his mouth. He recalls Portland, disbelief, Jake promising him the world, and Bowdoin, comfort, Jake's double-spritz of morning cologne never changing from one day to the next.

The sheets grow warm beneath his cheek, and he turns his head to look at the clock on the nightstand. *Jake, Jake, Jake.*

He gropes around until he finds the lyrics he copied onto a clean sheet of paper in his neatest hand. He opens his mouth, but no sound comes out. *You win, Jakey,* he thinks bitterly. *I've officially got nothing left.*

He folds the paper and holds it against his chest, his eyes close, and as he finally drifts into sleep's lonely embrace, he thinks of Jake and wonders if, somewhere up in the sky, he's doing the same.

I swear to god, when I get a hold of him, Aiden thinks as he pushes his way outside and a blast of frigid night air assaults him. *First, he leaves. Then April reads me the Riot Act. As if that wasn't bad enough, I'm so dumb that I decide to follow him. And then I get to spend the entire flight sitting next to a crying baby. On Christmas fucking Eve.*

These are all trials for which he can shift at least a little of the blame to the storm over Seattle that delayed all outbound flights until late evening. He'd awoken to it around noon, the rain shot with sleet and hailstones that pelted the RV until he wanted nothing more than to bury his head beneath his pillow and go back to sleep. Instead, Aiden had given in to the tugging in his gut.

The one thing for which he can't shift the blame, however, is his utter failure to pack anything appropriate for Alaska. Fissures in his self-trust had distracted him, and somehow he had made it all the way to the departure lounge before realizing that he'd packed only for warm weather. Which is why he is standing outside Ted Stevens International Airport dressed only in jeans and a button-down, freezing his ass off and cursing under his breath.

He yields three cabs to other harried-looking passengers before deciding that, in this particular instance, manners are for squares; he jumps into the next one that comes along.

"The Tap Root on Spenard Road, please," he tells the driver, raising his voice over the country music crackling on the radio. The driver only grunts, and Aiden can't exactly blame him for not launching into conversation. It's Christmas Eve, after all; he probably has a family to get home to.

The ten-minute journey passes at a crawl, but finally they pull up outside an unassuming one-story building with red siding and the name of the bar in contemporary, swooping text to the right of the door. Aiden pays the fare, hands the driver a generous tip and retrieves his suitcase from the trunk.

The second Aiden sets foot inside, he sees Jake sitting at a small round table by the artfully weathered bar, watching April and the rest of the band onstage. His shoulders slump and, despite his immaculate outfit, his hair is standing almost on end, going in fifty different directions. Jake's posture stuns Aiden; this is how Jake used to hold himself. It's been less than twenty-four hours, and it's as if he's looking at an entirely different person.

A soft guitar intro fills the bar, and Jake shifts uncomfortably, his body language matching Aiden's inner turmoil. As Aiden approaches Jake's table, April's haunting voice floats through the speakers and makes him catch his breath.

Bending down to speak into Jake's ear, his heart louder than his words, Aiden asks, "Is she on her own tonight?"

Jake starts and looks up at Aiden through wide, panicked eyes. He visibly swallows, flicks his gaze toward the stage and answers in a thin, rasping voice, "Mostly."

Aiden gestures to the empty chair next to him and Jake nods. "How's she doing?"

"Some upbeat stuff, but mostly ballads. Seems like that kind of crowd," he comments, glancing around as if to ensure he looks anywhere but at Aiden. "I requested 'My Love' by Sia about an hour ago. She was flawless, as usual."

"The *Twilight* soundtrack, really?" Aiden asks, attempting to overcome the awkwardness with their usual good-natured ribbing.

Jake looks at him sharply and then gives in to a wry smile. "Just because they're bad movies, doesn't mean the song is any less beautiful."

"It *is* beautiful," Aiden concedes, "and at least *Eclipse* was the best one of the series."

"Probably had something to do with David Slade."

"Probably."

They fall silent. Jake picks at the label on his almost empty beer bottle and Aiden fiddles with his suitcase handle, trying not to watch him. He doesn't want to be the first one to break, not this time. Not when, after getting over the initial shock, Jake looks utterly unsurprised to see him.

When Aiden looks up at the stage, he sees April watching him with kind eyes. She seems to be singing for them, and all that is broken between them.

At length, the better part of the label shredded, Jake stills his hands and turns toward Aiden. Without meeting his eyes, he asks, "Why are you here?"

Aiden's anger flares back to life, and he crosses his arms over his chest to keep from reaching out and shaking him. "You know exactly why I'm here, Jake. I'm here because this isn't finished, not by a long shot."

Jake shakes his head, blinking rapidly. "I wanted to..."

"Wanted to what, Jake? Wanted to see me free so that I could go off and 'live my dreams' without you?" Aiden hisses, voice low so as not to cause a scene. He still has *some* manners. "Newsflash: I don't need you to rescue me, and I'm not your fucking holiday pet. I'm not someone you can keep around while I'm fun and then kick to the curb whenever it's fucking convenient."

"That is *not* what this is," Jake says. The anger in his tone gives Aiden a perverse sense of satisfaction.

"That's *exactly* what this is," he counters, leaning forward over the table. "This is you suddenly having to stay the course with another person, and that *terrifies* you. But why wouldn't it? Especially after *all* you went through with Max, and *all* those boys that turned out not to measure up after you sort of fell for them, and let's not forget how my leaving for a year was *all* about you."

"Don't—"

"You owe me a fucking explanation, Jake Valentine."

"I know. I..." Jake trails off, shaking his head. His eyes are trained on the bottle in front of him and he pulls his Saint Christopher from beneath his shirt, running his fingers along the chain and capturing the silver disc between his thumb and forefinger. "All of this, it's... it's too much all at once. You, and this trip, and L.A.—something has to give sooner or later, right? Because I can't possibly have all of it."

"Why not?"

"Because no one gets *everything* they want," Jake says, and finally looks up. His eyes are close to brimming over, and the sight of it stings. "Who the hell am I that I get to be with you *and* take you with me to do something that's my dream?"

"Jake—"

"But that's exactly it, Aiden—*my* dream. Your dream is up on that stage," he barrels on, gesturing to the band. "And I can't take that away from you. I won't."

"So why didn't you even *think* about New York again?" Aiden asks. "Better yet, why didn't you even give me a chance and *talk* to me about it before making me chase you all the way to fucking *Alaska?*"

"I'm sorry—"

"And how *dare* you ever say that you're afraid *I'd* leave *you*. You remember that, on Santa Monica Pier? How you said that *you* didn't trust *me?*"

"Of course I do—"

"I mean, you do get that, by trying to make this about me, you've actually made it all about you, right?"

"Aiden, I'm *sorry!*" Jake exclaims, earning them a few dirty looks from nearby patrons. In a lower, yet somehow even less controlled voice, he says, "I'm sorry, I *am*. I told you not to follow me; I never wanted this."

"Of course I followed you, you fucking idiot. You took what we were finally starting to build together, and you threw it away just to prove yourself right. And I need you to know exactly how much you fucked up. 'Sorry' isn't going to cut it this time, Jake, because you know something?" Aiden's hands shake and his voice becomes less and less steady. "You read the lyrics. You saw what they said. I wanted to be the score to your movie. That's kind of how I started to think of us lately—me the music, and you the pictures. But maybe I should just be a deleted scene. Maybe that's all I was ever going to be. And if you want to leave me on the cutting room floor, then *leave* me there. I don't want to chase you anymore."

Jake's hand shoots out to grab Aiden's wrist. "I wanted to come back to you as soon as the plane took off," he says in a rapid near-whisper, looking at Aiden with wild, desperate eyes and tears slowly rolling down his face. "Please, Dan. *Please* tell me how to fix this, how to fix us."

Gently, Aiden pulls out of Jake's grip. He isn't angry anymore—he's sad, resigned and exhausted by the last three and a half months. He sighs and gets to his feet as April's song finishes; the crowd loudly applauds her, and after thanking them, she looks at Aiden with a tentative smile.

And then she starts to play a completely stripped-down, acoustic version of "Anything Could Happen." Aiden barely stops to wonder how she knows

about the song, though he could make an educated guess, given that Jake
has been with her for nearly eighteen hours and she pulls no punches when
she's after information. She probably thinks she's helping rather than playing
out the tearing asunder of something that could have defined the rest of
their lives.

Jake gazes up at him with the look of a heartbroken man—Aiden knows
it from this afternoon, when he caught sight of himself in the bathroom
mirror. But even with their song playing, a hushed affirmation to which
they should be listening with soft smiles and even softer words, Aiden hasn't
the wherewithal to tell Jake that all of this can be mended, not with jagged
edges pressing between his ribs and a desolate future wrapped tightly around
his chest.

Standing up straight, he blinks back tears and takes a deep, shuddering
breath. "It shouldn't be this difficult, Jake. Maybe we're too broken to fix.
I might be here, I might have come after you, but I—I... I'm worth more
than this."

"Aiden, please," Jake begs, hiccoughing over a sob, "please stay with me."

He bends down, cups Jake's face with both hands, and kisses his cheek. He
lingers there a moment, presses his forehead to Jake's temple and wills himself
not to cry even as a tear slips free and disappears into Jake's skin. "I can't."

Screwing his eyes tightly shut, he lets Jake go. He turns his back on the
interior of the Tap Root and starts walking, pulling his suitcase along behind
him as he winds through tables of patrons who pay him no mind; and even
when he hears Jake calling his name in a strangled voice, he keeps moving.

It's freezing outside, the empty streets silent as snow begins to fall, and his
ragged breaths come out in thick plumes of white that he walks through as if
beginning to traverse the foggy future he sees before him. He had everything,
and now he's leaving behind only footprints that will soon disappear.

The more Aiden tries to blink back his sorrow, the stronger it hits him.
He makes it as far as the gas station across the parking lot and stops, hanging
onto one of the roof pillars as he doubles over and swallows convulsively.
It *hurts*, cold and deep in his gut, radiating outward until he's freezing
with it, his hands shaking against the concrete. His head is swimming with
flashbulb memories of sun-chapped smiles and snow-bitten touches, and
he's shattering.

How can it end like this? How can it end at all?

His instincts tell him to go back, grab Jake's hand and never let go, but where would he be taken if he did that? What would—

"You're not a deleted scene."

Aiden jumps so quickly that he hits his head on the pillar. Pain explodes behind his eyes and he sways on his feet, and strong hands grip his arms to keep him upright. He raises a hand to cradle his head and squints at Jake, who, impossibly, looks even more wrecked than Aiden feels.

"Are you okay?" Jake asks in a small voice full of contrition, his deep green eyes looking at Aiden with concern.

"Peachy," Aiden manages, his heart pounding double time. "Today really can't get any worse, can it?"

"Never say never," Jake murmurs, then slowly pulls Aiden's hand away and examines his head in the dim light of the streetlamps. His fingers gently comb through Aiden's hair and it takes everything Aiden has not to close his eyes and give himself over to it.

"You came after me," he says.

"And I'm glad I did," Jake replies, "seeing as you're going around giving yourself concussions now."

"Well, if you hadn't come out of nowhere to tell me—" Aiden pauses. "What did you say before?"

Jake's hands fall away. "I said that you're not a deleted scene, Aiden."

Aiden shakes his head and winces at the dull throb. "I can't trust that. How am I supposed to trust that?"

Jake looks up, blinking and inhaling deeply. "You don't have to," he says. "I'm not asking you to, and I don't deserve your trust. I don't deserve *you.* But I had to come after you, I had to try."

"Jake..."

"I don't want it to end this way, Aiden. I don't want it to end at all."

"You haven't exactly..." Aiden trails off, gesturing around them.

"I know," Jake says. "That's why... here—"

Aiden watches as he produces a Band-Aid from his chest pocket. Quickly pulling off the backing, Jake sticks it onto the front of Aiden's shirt, right over his heart. He leaves his hand there and, with his eyes fixed on it, says, "I'm not crossing my heart. That's pretty worthless at this point, and if you swear, you have to swear on something you believe in." He looks up, eyes shining in the dim light. "You're the only thing I believe in anymore."

"What are you promising?" Aiden asks slowly.

"Back in Vegas, you said that I just have to be with you. That we'd figure out the rest later," Jake says. "But I'm not promising that, because promises have to be specific. So I'm promising to be with you, to follow you wherever you want to go, to never judge you when you eat an entire loaf of sourdough in one sitting and to love you with everything I have."

Aiden wants to smile, wants to breathe out the relief that floods his system; the sensation of being wanted, feeling special, and knowing that he needs no more than this is dizzying. Stalling, he asks, "Where the hell did you get a Band-Aid?"

"There was a first aid kit at the bar," Jake says. "I had to give them my last twenty dollars for it, so if you don't take me back I'm pretty screwed, because I don't have cash for an airport cab."

"You paid twenty dollars for a Band-Aid."

"I guess I sort of... volunteered the money? But I was desperate! It was either that or cut myself, and you know how I feel about blood. Plus, then I would have *needed* the Band-Aid..."

"Some cabs take credit cards these days."

"My card's not working, and I can't believe you're bringing in *logic* to ruin my perfect scene!" Jake exclaims, throwing up his hands with an almost hysterical laugh. Humor gradually fading from his expression, he swallows and says quietly, "This is our movie moment."

Aiden shakes his head. "Movies end."

"I don't want ours to," Jake says quickly, his fingertips curling into Aiden's shirt.

"Couldn't you have realized that, I don't know, yesterday?" Aiden asks, trying not to let his lingering frustration creep into his tone, not when Jake is finally, *finally* being honest.

Jake gives him a lopsided, slightly pained smile. "April kinda... beat it out of me. Literally."

It's not funny, not really, but Aiden can't help a dry chuckle. "You know," he says, momentarily breaking their glance and looking down at Jake's hands, where his skin is paler than usual and his knuckles paler still. "You call me the nomad, but you're the one who runs."

Nodding slowly, Jake takes half a step back, as if out of shame. "Maybe I just had some running to get out of my system."

"But you're done now?" Aiden asks, looking at him and silently imploring him to say yes.

"No," Jake says, and Aiden's heart falls until he adds, "it's who I am. Remember what I said back in Providence about not settling? The difference now is that... that I found someone I'd like to run *with*. And he makes me not care about where I'm running to."

"Why not?" Aiden asks.

"Because," Jake says, stepping closer and reaching up to Aiden's cheek; Aiden leans into the touch and meets Jake's eyes. "Because he makes everything else go away. I've loved him for nearly seventeen years, and one day I'd like to be able to say that I've loved him my whole life."

Aiden studies him for a moment—the dark circles underneath his eyes, the wrinkled front of his shirt, the slump in his shoulders under the weight of his penance—and out of the corner of his eye, he sees snowflakes falling. Falling with them—slowly, gradually, steadily—is easy, because it's right. He steps forward and crushes his lips against Jake's, swallowing Jake's surprised squeak and humming against his tongue. Jake tenses, but then seems to melt back into his former self, standing straight and winding his arms around Aiden's neck as a gust of icy wind sweeps past.

A clock strikes midnight somewhere in the distance and, breathing heavily as he pulls back, Jake kisses just to the left of Aiden's mouth. "Happy birthday, Dan," he whispers breathlessly.

"Merry Christmas, Jake," Aiden replies, wrapping his arms around Jake's waist.

"Tell me something you want," Jake says.

"What, you didn't get me anything?" Aiden asks, and finally, Jake smiles. "There *is* something, actually."

"Hit me."

"I want you to *never* do that to me again."

"I promise," Jake says quickly, nodding wide-eyed. "What else? What else do you want?"

Considering for a moment not only the question, but also the choice before him, Aiden realizes that it isn't a matter of caving or going with the flow anymore. With the exception of Wyoming, he's been choosing to sit back and let things happen for far too long.

"Just you," he says with utter conviction. "I just want you to stay with me. For good."

Jake closes his eyes and smiles, letting his head fall back. The world is lit as if from below by the white carpeting the ground; it covers the black and gray and makes everything seem brand new. They aren't so far from the bar that Aiden can't hear the music; as Jake takes his hand to pull him away from the pillar, he can just hear April winding up the song that brought their love story to life.

"Come on," Jake says, reaching for Aiden's suitcase. "You're shivering; let's get inside."

"I'm not cold," Aiden protests, and tugs on his hand. "There's one other thing."

"What is it?" Jake asks.

"What happens on the road trip stays on the road trip," Aiden says. "When we get to L.A., we both get a fresh start."

"You're sure? About all of it?" Jake asks.

"Who says any of it has to be permanent? So we go to L.A. and make a movie about killer shrimp," Aiden says. Jake chuckles and bites his lip. "Then maybe we end up in New York for the next thing, or Europe, or Australia. Maybe even the Steve side of Montana if we're really lucky."

"My own personal lumberjack? Ugh, L.A., what was I *thinking?*"

"My point is—"

"We'll be together," Jake softly cuts in, "so who cares where the road goes?"

"Exactly," Aiden says.

For the moment, they don't need any more words—that much is clear in the way Jake simply takes Aiden's suitcase and interlaces their fingers. They walk back to the bar in silence, save for returning the Christmas wishes of the two punky girls smoking outside.

"I'm so sorry, Aiden," Jake says outside the door. "I'm sorry I did that to you."

"For now, just... just be with me, okay?" Aiden says, his fingers curled around the door handle.

"Okay," Jake says. His mouth twitches into a smile, and after one last quick kiss, Aiden follows him inside.

15,703 MILES

DAY ONE HUNDRED: HAWAII

The moment he stepped off the plane at Kahului Airport, the island's warm air wrapped him in a welcoming embrace, and Jake finally began to breathe freely again. Here in Hawaii, the oxygen is somehow far more plentiful than on the "mainland," as he keeps hearing locals refer to it, and when he steps out of the Beachy Keen gift shop, he takes in a deep lungful of the fresh night air.

He drives their rental car back to the hotel at a leisurely speed; his stomach is still full almost to bursting from dinner at Mama's Fish House, a casual yet high-end restaurant in Paia where it seemed that everything on the menu had been caught by a local that same day. Now that he has a little time and space to himself, he feels ready to begin processing everything that has passed between him and Aiden over the last twenty-four hours.

All that he can really remember, however, are flashes: the warm squeeze of Aiden's palm, at odds with his cold fingertips as they walked back inside the Tap Root; the strangely unfamiliar sound of his own laugh when Aiden made a joke about The Cannery back home in Brunswick; the burn in his cheeks when, in their hastily procured hotel room, he studied the expressions playing on Aiden's face as Jake showed him all his video diaries.

And the talk, that long overdue talk; hours and hours of speaking until their throats were hoarse and their mouths parched, touching and kissing for bottomless minutes in between just to let their voices rest. Spurts of sharp anger that leapt into the air and yet fizzled faster than they erupted, like fireworks that still linger in the recesses of Jake's mind. Long ribbons of apologies and explanations unfurling, honesty pulled from them both until at long last everything was laid bare—their secrets, their lies and their deepest fears.

Then, this morning, his heart safely in Aiden's hands and Aiden's hand in his, they said goodbye to their friends and started walking. The first step felt to Jake as if it encompassed all fifteen thousand miles they'd traveled together, and so many more besides.

When he arrives at the beach where he asked Aiden to meet him, Jake takes a moment to slip off his shoes and look out at the shoreline. He can see Aiden sitting with his knees drawn up to his chest, silhouetted against the water, the breeze rippling the back of his red T-shirt. Even from the back he looks peaceful, and Jake approaches slowly, the soft white sand muffling his steps.

Not wanting to startle Aiden, Jake quietly says, "Hey," and drops onto the sand next to him. He sets down his shoes and the paper bag he's carrying in favor of wrapping his arms around Aiden's waist, and smiles when Aiden shifts to loop an arm around his shoulders. "What are you thinking about?"

"Fifty states in a hundred days," Aiden replies, his tone conveying a certain amount of disbelief. "We really did it."

"Did you think we wouldn't?" Jake asks.

"Well, the buzzword was 'ambitious,' wasn't it?" Aiden says. "But we made it."

"Look how far we've come," Jake says, his exhalation caught by the evening breeze rolling in off the ocean. "You patched things up with your dad; I finally managed to come to terms with mine; we're going to work on a movie together... everything's different now."

"It is," Aiden agrees. "Especially us. Do you..."

"Do I what?"

"Do you think any of it would have happened if we hadn't come on this trip?"

Jake mulls it over for a few moments, casting his mind back to the day that Aiden came back to Brunswick, taller and broader and worldlier. Though it took next to no time for them to find their groove again, Jake now knows that there was a marked difference in their relationship, even though he'd denied it for so long.

"Yes," he finally answers, looking out at the waves lapping gently at the shore. "There might have been less drama, or... maybe there would have been even more, I don't know. But it would have happened. It was bound to, one way or another."

"I think you're right," Aiden whispers, inclining his head toward Jake's and kissing his hair.

"Do you think you would have figured out your dream if we'd stayed in Brunswick?"

"The only reason I *have* that dream is because of you," Aiden says. "But like you said, it would have happened, one way or another. Don't get me wrong; I still love film, and I still want to make beautiful things with you like we always talked about, but now it's..."

"You're the music, and I'm the pictures," Jake finishes quietly. "I guess it just never really occurred to me that I was worthy of that."

"There's a reason I didn't just turn around and head for Maine, idiot," Aiden says fondly. "Do you really think I would have gotten on a plane for anyone else?"

"I'm sorry for what I put you through," Jake says quickly—he feels as if his need to apologize will never wane. After the sixth or seventh time, Aiden had begun absolving him with kisses and he does so now, craning his neck and kissing each of Jake's lips. The warm pressure of his mouth is an intoxicating catch and release.

"I got something for you," he blurts when they pull apart.

He's been waiting, biding his time for the right moment, and there is no better moment than this. He inches away, sits up straight and reaches for the paper bag emblazoned with the Beachy Keen logo. Biting his lip, he pulls out the floating lantern he bought, along with a novelty lighter decorated with glazed seashells, and presents both items to Aiden. "What are these?"

"Your birthday and Christmas presents," Jake says. "What I actually got you is still back in the RV, so these are just placeholders, I promise."

"You got me a floating lantern?" Aiden asks, looking at Jake with so much warmth and fondness in his eyes that Jake can't quite hold his gaze, else he'll never be able to get out the speech he's been preparing all day.

Gently, he takes the lantern back and sets about unfolding it. "I heard they do this on Magic Island every year," he begins. "Thousands of people show up and light these lanterns. Some people do it to remember people who've passed on and some pray for their future, and then they float them out on the water. It's—it's silly, but..."

Jake fixates on the lantern's waxed paper folds, as if he's constructing something far more substantial. And then Aiden's hand finds his knee; it's a simple touch, but a tether nonetheless.

"Last night, there was one thing I didn't tell you about," Jake says, hands faltering on the lantern. "I actually thought about it just before I fell asleep, and it's been on my mind ever since."

"Okay..."

"You never asked about what happened in South Carolina, and I was grateful for that, because even after my big drama moment in Santa Fe, I didn't want to talk about it," Jake admits. "I was sitting by the fountain thinking about Mom, and this professor came over to me. He looked like every stereotypical movie professor, you know? Tweed jacket, mustache, briefcase, the whole nine yards. Anyway, we got to talking, and... and he asked me to toss a coin into the fountain and make a wish. I know you're not supposed to tell people your wishes because then they won't come true, but I'm swearing to you right now that I will *make* this wish come true."

"What did you wish for?" Aiden asks.

"I wished to be what you need me to be," Jake says, twining their fingers together and looking deep into Aiden's eyes, willing him to believe. "Aiden, what we have—what I have with you, it's..." he trails off. "It's beyond *anything*. I've never believed in not having control over what happens to me, but *you* happened, and I didn't have any control over that at all. You were the best thing that ever happened to me, and you still are, and I knew as soon as that plane took off that I was doomed because you're *it*. You're the end of the movie."

Aiden blinks at him for a moment before looking up and sighing gruffly. He clears his throat and wipes his eyes, pauses for a moment, and then turns to kiss Jake.

It's one of those kisses that makes Jake feel as if he's drowning in Aiden, seventeen years old all over again, with his hands shaking almost uncontrollably as they tangle themselves in Aiden's hair and hold on for dear life. *How could I have ever even tried to walk away from this?*

Breathing heavily as he pulls away, Aiden says, "Jake, you're exactly who I need you to be. Because you're it for me, too, you know. Ever since we met."

Though Jake's eyes still feel raw from all the emotional purging he's done over the past forty-eight hours, they fill with tears once more and he pitches forward to bury his face in the hollow of Aiden's neck, fingers twisting into his shirt and clutching tightly. The sound of paper crumpling makes him pull back, sniffing harshly and laughing at Aiden's amused smile. "Shut up," Jake chides him, picking up the lantern and straightening a crease. As he passes it to Aiden and hands him the lighter, he says, "Make a wish."

Aiden turns the lighter over and over between his fingers, watching Jake with a small smile, then gets to his feet, holding the lantern aloft. In the next instant it bursts into life and the faint lines etched into the paper are suddenly fully distinguishable; all around the outside of the lantern are drawings of birds and fish, musical notes and swirls, flowers and flames.

"Get up here," Aiden says, and Jake stands to take the other side of the lantern. They hold it between them, taking the time to study the drawings in all their intricacy.

"What are you wishing for?" Jake asks, quickly adding, "Don't tell me if it won't come true."

Sighing a little, Aiden answers, "I wish this trip didn't have to end. I wish we could just stay here."

"Well, we've got three days," Jake points out. "And maybe one day we can come back."

"One day," Aiden says wistfully. "What about you? What's your wish?"

"I've wished for enough. Besides, it's *your* birthday."

"It's also Christmas," Aiden says, stepping closer so that they have to raise the lantern over their heads. It's beginning to tug at their hands as it fills with heat, and Jake briefly wonders what it would be like to just float away into the atmosphere, Aiden by his side and the trappings of the world left far behind. "Come on. There must be something."

Jake looks up at the drawing nearest his fingers: a couple in a close embrace. "I wish you could've been my first," he says, the words tumbling out of his mouth almost before he has time to realize that they are unequivocally true. "We should have been each other's firsts."

Smiling at him, Aiden raises his eyebrows and pushes the lantern out of Jake's grip and into the air. They watch it rise, swaying this way and that, following the breeze on its journey skyward. Aiden's hand finds Jake's, and he nudges his leg. "Don't you think it's more important that we're each other's lasts?"

"You're way too smooth for your own good, Calloway."

Aiden hums as his knuckles drift back and forth over Jake's leg, and even though there are thousands of miles between them and Brunswick, the distance doesn't matter; it's another one of those moments from Jake's back deck, the kind that makes Jake wish life had a pause button. But the wish is fleeting. This time he's looking ahead, seeing a life laid out before them filled to brimming with the promise of breakfasts spent kissing crumbs from fingertips, long nights devoted to burying themselves between heated skin and soft sheets and a movie library they'll look upon fondly because it will contain every single movie they've watched this trip. They'll sift through screenplays until Aiden finds the right story to tell through his music, and hop on and off planes holding hands until Jake finds the right location in which to tell it.

"Well, I'm not *that* smooth..." Aiden says, interrupting his thoughts. At Jake's raised eyebrow, he shifts from one foot to the other and says, "I'm sort of desperate to know what this other birthday present is..."

"Oh, it's... it's nothing," Jake says. "It's just a DVD."

"What DVD?" Aiden presses.

"Our movie," Jake answers quietly. "I got you *The Lion King*."

"Jake..."

"Because that's what started it all, right? That's where we began; that's where you changed my life, so I thought..."

"No such thing as history," Aiden murmurs. "Who's the smooth one now?"

Jake doesn't have space to reply; Aiden twists his hand into the collar of Jake's shirt and gently pulls himself closer. They meet in the middle and Jake sighs into the kiss, letting his hand move along the roughness of Aiden's stubble. Aiden tries to tug him down onto the sand but Jake stops him. He wants to give him one last placeholder gift, the one inspired by a story he's been thinking about ever since Santa Fe.

Pulling his phone from his pocket, he says, "Dad once told me about the night he and Mom got engaged. After he asked her, she blindfolded him and walked him over to their tape deck and told him to pick out a tape. The first song that came on was going to be their song."

"And what was it?" Aiden asks, looking down at the phone.

"Car Wash," Jake says with a chuckle. "He said they did the jitterbug until they fell over laughing."

"Is this going where I think it is?"

"I was just thinking, even with all the songs we've listened to and sung along to and danced to, and even with the one that you wrote... there isn't really one that's *ours*."

"Are you forgetting about "Anything Could Happen?" It was playing the first time you kissed me," Aiden reminds him. Jake closes his eyes; that song is now forever tainted by harsh but deserved words and bitterest shame.

"It was also playing last night," he says—the thought is surely still as fresh in Aiden's mind as it is in his own, and this is one moment he knows will be perfect, however it turns out. "I want us to have one that we can dance like idiots to if we have to."

Silently, he unwinds the earbuds he keeps wrapped around his phone, puts one into his own ear and gives the other to Aiden. The trembling is back again, everything feeling a little too full, as if he might burst out of his own skin if he doesn't let Aiden hold not just his hand but all of him. So he wraps one arm around Aiden's waist, closes his eyes and hits shuffle.

Whatever the song is, it begins almost too quietly for Jake to hear, a gradual building of strumming guitars that he barely recognizes. Aiden takes his hand, sandwiching the phone between their palms, and starts swaying. As he pulls back to look into Aiden's eyes, Jake realizes that it couldn't have been anywhere but here. It couldn't have been one of many teenage runaway nights, riding bikes up to Coffin Pond or down to Thomas Point. It couldn't have been spring break at Hampton Beach, playing cards on the floor of the pavilion until after sunset. It couldn't even have been being squeezed into April's lounger on July fourth, watching the fireworks with Aiden's breath tickling the back of his neck.

Everything up until now—the flames and heat of Providence; Jake's misstep in Philadelphia; their first kiss at land's end in Key West; ceilings crumbling and falling before them in Gary; a music box containing a train ticket that concealed the worst intentions and fears; the moment he saw the "I love you" in Aiden's eyes, one starry night in New Orleans; resisting Aiden with everything, with words and snow and fire until nothing else remained but to leap and hope to be caught—has been leading to this otherworldly island.

No Z without Y, no Y without X, back and back and back. All of it has led to this moment in which the score dies out and leaves two people looking at each other in simple silence, everything suspended save for their racing hearts.

The singing begins, a story of believing in dreams and going after them, of life being on the right track, of hearts alive with the promise of tomorrow— of driving on.

Aiden sings along with a smile in his voice. His lips brush Jake's ear as they sway on the sand. "How does that sound?" he asks.

Jake smiles into his shoulder. "Like the end of the beginning."

18,500 MILES

CLOSING CREDITS

SATURDAY, 14 MAY 2022

"Do you think that's it? Because I think that's it," Brian says, pushing his shaggy brown hair off his face and leaning forward in his well-worn swivel chair. His finger pushes a button and just like that, he's holding a hard drive in his hand—a hard drive that contains the first raw copy of *Chasing The Sky*. He holds it up, dangling it between his thumb and forefinger, and says, "Yep. That's it, right there."

Aiden leans on the arm of his chair and smiles, blinking at the drive and suppressing yet another yawn. It's been over twelve hours in the cutting room; his neck aches, his contacts irritate him, and he's about ready to get the hell out of here—but there it is. There's his story, *his and Jake's story,* ready to be seen. He woke up this morning to the knowledge that today would be the last day before editing wrapped for good, but now that it's here, he can hardly believe it.

It's been four years since Jake and Elsie, a collaborator they found through Matt's company, finished writing the screenplay, and two years since Accent Features picked it up. It's been months of shooting and weeks of editing, making what has seemed like millions of minuscule tweaks and changes, until Aiden thought he might scream. But it's finished. They're finished.

The film is complete. They've done all they can; the rest is up to the critics and the box office.

"We're done," he breathes, torn between bolting with the drive and sitting in his chair until he's sure his feet can carry him. "That's absolutely it."

"Hell yeah, it is," Brian exclaims, swiveling in his chair and high-fiving Aiden so forcefully it stings his palm. At Aiden's visible wince, Brian claps a hand on his shoulder and gives him an apologetic smile. "Sorry, man. I'm just happy we've finally got it in the bag, you know? It's the first time I'll get to put my girls to bed in over a month."

"I know how you feel," Aiden says, feeling lighter than he has in weeks. "Jake and I have barely seen each other lately."

"Oh yeah?"

"Yeah, he's been out in Cali this week visiting his sister and her husband. But he gets back today, so..." He gets back today, and Aiden can't wait to show him the movie. *Their* movie.

"It's rough," Brian says, clearly oblivious to the worlds shifting inside Aiden's head, the call of the past ringing out in time with the sound of his present. "But I've gotta say, you're one hell of a music supervisor. That song you found for the scene on top of the RV, what was it..."

"'This Is The New Year,' A Great Big World," Aiden says.

"Right. Genius! And I'm still not over that first montage with 'Green Onions,'" Brian says, and collapses into laughter, pounding his fist on the bench. Aiden can't help joining in.

"Just this side of cheesy, right?" he says between laughs. "I couldn't resist."

"Nor should you, sir!" Brian tells him in a ridiculously exaggerated British accent, complete with knee slap and the checking of an imaginary pocket watch. Over the years, Aiden has come to appreciate that editors tend not to be the most together of people, but these days it just washes off him. "So what are you working on next? Anything lined up?"

Aiden shakes his head. "Nothing definite yet, but my brother mentioned something about a gig on his next big-budget, so I've gotta head out west next month. What about you?"

"Moving into small screen. They're gonna be shooting the next Marvel spin-off right here in the city, so I'm sticking around for that," Brian says. He passes the drive back and forth between his hands before he finally hands it over. "But you, you get out of here. Get this back first thing tomorrow or they'll have my head, but go on. Get out."

"Understood," Aiden says. He slips the drive into his messenger bag, shrugs his jacket on and pulls his sunglasses from his pocket. Standing, he shakes the hand that Brian holds out to him and says sincerely, "Great working with you, man."

"You too, Calloway. Don't be a stranger."

"'Course not. Say hi to the girls for me."

"Will do," Brian says. Halfway through swiveling to face the screens again, he stops and looks at Aiden. "Did all of that really happen? I mean, it must have been a pretty insane trip."

Aiden smiles, his hand on the door to the editing suite. "Ask Jake. He wrote it."

He leaves the studio with a spring in his step and excitement bubbling in his stomach. He gets on the subway at West Twenty-eighth and taps his foot all the way home to Cobble Hill, where he picks up a bunch of gerbera daisies from the vendor on the corner.

He climbs the steps to their brownstone and lets himself inside, thrilling at the sight of Jake's suitcase standing by the end table. He drops his keys on top of the messy pile of mail he's had neither the time nor the inclination to read while Jake has been out of town. Music is playing in the living room, something happy and bouncy that sounds like the band Jake has been obsessed with for the past month. Aiden closes the door and hangs up his jacket, then retrieves the drive from his bag and hides it behind his back along with the daisies.

Jake sits on the couch, facing away from him, and Aiden watches him for a few moments, appreciating the sight of him back here at home after what has felt like an endless week. His blond hair is lighter than usual, shot through with California sun, and the freckles on the back of his neck are barely distinguishable from his tan.

"California always did agree with you," he says.

Jake almost jumps out of his skin but recovers quickly, dropping the shot list he's been studying and pulling off his reading glasses. He scrambles over the back of the couch and launches himself at Aiden, throwing his arms around his neck and kissing him with all the hunger of a starving man.

"Are you—here again?" he asks between kisses.

Chuckling into his mouth, Aiden pulls away and says, "I missed you, too. How's the fam?"

"Good, great, everyone's fantastic," Jake says breathlessly, his eyes sparkling. Aiden is almost taken aback; Jake wasn't this excited when he got back from spending a month on location in Nova Scotia while Aiden composed a score with the California Philharmonic. Jake bounces on his toes and repeats his question, "Are you here again?"

By way of an answer, Aiden produces the flowers and the drive from behind his back, holding them out with a smirk. "It's finished."

Jake looks between both items as if unsure which to take first, but after a moment he accepts the flowers and looks at Aiden. "It's really done?"

"It's really done," Aiden says, "and I've only got this copy until tomorrow, so we have to watch it tonight."

"Okay, then," Jake says, all business, "you get it set up while I put these in water—by the way, thank you, I love you, you're the best—I'll order in, and we'll watch it right now."

With that, Jake sweeps out of the room, leaving Aiden to stare after him. Something is definitely weird. Whatever it is, Aiden knows he'll find out sooner or later, so he makes short work of getting everything connected and by the time he pauses their movie on the first frame, Jake is curling up next to him on their black and beige couch, looking deep into his eyes and smiling in that way he does when he's got a secret he's bursting to share.

Before Aiden can ask, however, Jake says, "I'm so proud of you. I'm proud of *us.*"

Aiden smiles and kisses his cheek, says, "Me too," and hits play.

He was expecting that they would remain utterly silent, since they're watching this all the way through for the first time; on the contrary, they talk constantly, pointing out shots they love, Aiden praising Jake's script, Jake gushing over the two songs that Aiden wrote specifically for the soundtrack. "The Only Forever" remains theirs and theirs alone, for the rare nights when Aiden brings his guitar into the bedroom and quietly picks out the tune while Jake lies under the covers with his hair sticking up as he sings along.

Three and a half months summed up in two hours of screen time, yet the way Aiden gets lost in it, it feels like twenty minutes. And as the screen fades to black on the closing scene, Jake's hand finds his in the dark.

And then two lines of text appear on the screen:

Screenplay by
Elsie Brett and Jake Calloway

Seeing Jake's name on the end credits of a film is something that never fails to make Aiden grin, so at first it doesn't occur to him that the film shouldn't have credits, yet. Nor does it occur to him that the names of the screenwriters would not appear first, ahead of the directors and producers. It isn't until Jake squeezes his hand and Aiden turns to him, still grinning, that he realizes what is fundamentally wrong.

Jake's last name is Valentine.

Jaw dropping, Aiden looks at the screen and then back at Jake, who is watching him, waiting. And all at once, the pieces slot together: Brian forcing him to take a fifteen-minute break right before they got to the final scene; the way Jake has been acting since Aiden got home; the strange, collar-creeping feeling he's had all day that some prophecy from the past is about to be fulfilled.

"If the time was right, if he was the right guy... yeah, I think I'd like to get married."

"Proposal?"

"Something simple. Quiet and intimate, just the two of us. Not on an anniversary or a birthday or Christmas. Definitely not on Valentine's."

"You did this?" Aiden breathes, feeling as if he's about to vibrate out of his skin.

"I called in a favor," Jake says. His voice sounds as if he's on the other side of a wall for all the static screaming in Aiden's ears. Jake reaches into the pocket of the threadbare Bowdoin hoodie he's wearing and pulls out a tiny box wrapped in deep red. He turns it over in his hands, looks at Aiden with nearly three decades of love in his eyes and asks, "I think it's about time, don't you? Stoke the fires?"

Aiden opens and closes his mouth a few times. That little red box has been so far from his mind for years. So many times they talked about it and agreed it wasn't the right time, and neither of them have ever felt the need for rings or pieces of paper, and even now it probably isn't the right time, but—

"Dan?"

His eyes meet Jake's, and it *is* about time.

Aiden smiles. He laughs. And, his voice a trembling wreck, he answers, "Start the engines."

THE END

ACKNOWLEDGMENTS

To Annie Fleck, CL Miller, Lex Huffman and R.J. Shepherd at Interlude Press: You're the truest rock stars I know, and it all began on a weathered, sun-drenched porch in New York. Who'd have thought?

To Carrie Pack, my soul-sister, for keeping me in check, pushing me to think outside the box and talking me off the proverbial ledge more times than I can count.

To Lissa Reed, for her epic hand-holding abilities, her endless patience in being my Fort First Draft and for truly understanding what I mean when I say, "I'm *such* a writer."

To Killian B. Brewer, for being a beautiful human and an invaluable resource—he knows why.

To Jennifer Dumin, for helping me make music and for her Philadelphia heart.

To Rachel Sharpe, my Alpha Beta, who was there at this story's birth and held my hand through much of it.

To Carl Skelton-Baker, my brother from another mother, who also has universes in his head and doesn't mind helping me explore my own.

To my fellow Interlude authors, my pals and gals on Tumblr, and my friends and readers across the Internets: Thank you for all the handy information, not to mention the endless support and encouragement.

To Mrs Wheeler, my first teacher, who got me reading and always encouraged my creativity. *Dilly the Dinosaur* forever! 🎸

About the Author

MIMSY HALE lives in Suffolk, England, with her roommate and four cats. Having dropped out of school at the age of seventeen, she's a long-term office drone with paperback dreams and universes in her head.

Mimsy is a Brit gal with an American heart, and can often be found staring off into space and having conversations with her characters—or finding new ways to slip quotes from really bad movies into everyday conversation.

She came back to writing in 2012 after a long absence, the spark of creativity inside her that she discovered at a young age finally fanned into an all-consuming flame... And she's been suffering the side effects ever since.

Already a bestselling ghostwriter, she has learned that novels are where her heart truly lies.

100 Days is her debut novel. 🐾

interlude press

A Reader's Guide to *100 Days*

Questions for Discussion

1. In the book, Jake and Aiden agree to a "no strings" sexual relationship for the duration of their road trip. How does this alter their existing friendship?

2. How does their approach to traveling change over the course of the road trip?

3. Both Jake and Aiden face issues with their fathers on this trip. How are their experiences different? How are they the same?

4. How does making peace with the past influence Jake and Aiden's futures?

5. How do the music and movies Jake and Aiden carry with them on the trip serve as touchstones?

6. Jake and Aiden have different sexual histories and approaches to romantic relationships. How does this affect the progression of their relationship?

7. Jake and Aiden's friendship is partly built around a mutual love of filmmaking and common goals they set for themselves as teenagers. How do their goals change, and how does this influence their story?

8. The supporting characters seem to recognize Jake and Aiden's true feelings for each other before they do. Why does it take the boys so long to wake up to how they feel?

9. How would the story have change had they veered off course, or ended the trip early?

Also from
interlude  press ™

Now available from

interlude  press™

interlude press.

One Story Can Change Everything.

interludepress.com

Twitter: @interludepress * * * Facebook: Interlude Press
Google+: +interludepress * * * Pinterest: interludepress
Instagram: InterludePress

CPSIA information can be obtained at www.ICGtesting.com
Printed in the USA
LVOW11s1447190415

435212LV00012B/736/P